Mission

On

Soleil

Book One
Keepers of the Universe Trilogy

Alexandria Chiaro

Hardcover ISBN: 979-8-9873179-0-7
Paperback ISBN: 979-8-9873179-1-4
EBook ASIN: B0C39HWMWP

Cover Design and Illustrations by Gretchen Caughey

Dedication

*I thank God for blessing me with life and ideas.
I thank my wonderful parents, my awesome
sibling, my loving sons, my family,
and my outstanding, genuine friends
who have been with me along life's journey
encouraging me each step.*

Mission on Soleil

Book one
Keepers of the Universe Trilogy

Welcome to my trilogy story of Keepers of the Universe. This story takes place on the planet Soleil (So-lay-El) in the Estellas Galaxy.

The other planets so far discovered in this galaxy are:

Tertammi (Ter-tam-mi)
Acheeas (Ah-shae-us)
Chiaras (Key-r-us)
VeNoma (Ve-No-ma)
Kareenia (Ka-ree-knee-ah)

You will meet the Chiawaukas (Key-a-wau-kas). Supreme Guardian Beings. Their home planet...well, that will be uncovered as you journey through this story.

The title for this trilogy came to me while at church with my mother. I sat on the title for about three years. I wrote book one, book two and stopped on chapter 20 in book three so I could go back and rewrite books one and two.

I hope you enjoy each book of this tender, adventure trilogy – Keepers of the Universe

Enjoy the Night Sky

Sincerely,
Alexandria Chiaro

Chapter 1

CORRECT COORDINATES

Victor and Viana feel an intense vibration from beneath the boulder they are sitting on. Viana clasps her hands onto the boulder as if that will help.

Victor leaps down yelling, "Come on, Viana!"

Viana jumps down. The ground under their feet ferociously trembles and they can hear a reverberation deep within Soleil.

"Victor, we have never experienced an earthquake here on Soleil!" Viana asserts as she tries to balance her three-foot-seven-inch-tall body.

"I don't believe it is an earthquake, Viana," Victor insists. "The vibration of the planet surface and what we felt on the boulder would certainly indicate such, however, my intuition tells me we truly are at the correct coordinates the Ancient Writings foretold."

"Oh, Victor," Viana trails off with a heaviness weighing on her.

"Make the call." Victor solemnly instructs.

Placing her index and middle finger on her left temple she contacts their headquarters. "We need to speak to the High Priests." Viana conveys.

Viana nods. Squeezing her hand tightly, she then opens it. A round, snow globe shaped object appears, levitating into the air above her hand. Two Chiawaukas appear adorned in beautiful, priestly robes.

"How may we guide you?" enlists High Priest Akshai.

Victor summarizes as the seismic quivering subsides, "As you know, you stationed us here twelve, may I say, long months ago. For the most part, Viana, and myself especially, have nearly given up hope that we are even at the correct location where we will discover the two families that possess the Chords of Chiawaukas, the auras, or the evil that was contained here centuries ago. Today however, we experienced a vibration on the planet's surface which would certainly signify an earthquake. I humbly request you verify the coordinates The Ancient Writings speak of, your highness."

High Priestess Ammerie opens the Ancient Writings, turning to the pages that describe the location of their mission. She raises her head, making eye contact with each, clearly assuring them, "Victor, Viana, you are at the correct coordinates that we discern the Ancient Writings speak of. We are sorry you feel your time there has been long. But indeed, we trust you will be successful on your mission, no matter the length it takes."

"When will you be at the mine again?" inquires High Priest Akshai.

"Tomorrow," Victor communicates.

"You both have done well. Keep us apprised," instructs High Priest Akshai.

Victor and Viana bow as the high priests and the snow globe object vanish before their eyes.

"Victor, what is it you believe?" interrogates Viana in her crisp voice. "Did you think we were not at the correct coordinates?"

"Honestly, Viana, I was beginning to have my doubts. I believe we have been stationed on Soleil twelve long months. The mountain ranges are breathtaking. The rivers are full of energy. Most of the humans we observe seem noble. Yet, we have seen no auras nearby, which would reveal the two Chords of Chiawaukas families. Now that we have confirmation of our location, I believe what we experienced today is a premonition of what is to come, and discovering the location where the evil beings were imprisoned centuries ago is close at hand.

"Hearing your words just sent chills through me," utters Viana. "We've been waiting a long time to find some clue the Ancient Writings speak of and the auras of the Keepers." Viana envisions, *the two families that possess the Chords of Chiawaukas, once joined by marriage, will be ordained the Keepers of the Universe.*

"We may discover more clues tomorrow at the mine," Victor states.

"Yes," nods Viana. "We have been really spoiled this past year, staging ourselves in a treehouse on a spectacular, mountain-valley ranch, enjoying the peacefulness of Chamberlain Kingdom, and just lounging on these boulders," Viana points.

"Well, our mission is clear: Find the families with the auras. Protect and train them. Keep the evil imprisoned. Sounds easy," professes Victor.

"We are Chiawaukas. Supreme Guardian Beings. Everything should be easy, one would think," alleges Viana.

Chapter 2

ANOTHER MYSTERIOUS NIGHTMARE

Night has fallen across the land. Victor and Viana are at rest in the treehouse they have called home the last twelve months.

"Oh, look! It appears the family in the ranch house is going to bed. Let's listen in," Viana suggests making an arc so they can view into the master bedroom.

"You're hopeless," Victor grumbles scooting a bit closer so he, too, can see and hear.

Antonio begins speaking, "I'm going to the mine tomorrow to check on supplies and a few things. Plus, I want to make sure Marco has a good start. He's a hard worker with a good work ethic, I think he will do well."

Snuggling closer to Antonio, Francesca rests, "Yes, it will be fine. Our oldest is seventeen now. He has been begging us to let him work. We have taught him well. I feel at peace knowing you'll be there on his first day."

With his arm wrapped around the love of his life, Antonio kisses the top of Francesca's thick head of curls, while twirling some locks with his fingers, "Soon both our sons will be grown, and out on their own. Time has flown."

"Yes, it has, my husband," Francesca nestles into the warmth of Antonio's arm and chest.

Viana closes the arc. "It warms my heart to see the tenderness of this couple."

Victor nods.

Victor and Viana both get comfortable, gazing at the night sky and enjoying the nocturnal wildlife.

Two and a half hours later a startling, shrill scream breaks the night's silence. Instinctively, Victor and Viana's eyes met. Viana reacts, faces the ranch home, and waves her arm in an arc. Instantly the exterior walls of the ranch home are transparent and they are once again viewing the events within.

Francesca is sitting in the middle of the bed frantically scanning around. Antonio sits up as well, taking her hand in his.

"Another bad dream?" he asks.

She continues to sweep the room with her eyes, then looks at Antonio.

"It is the same nightmare. Terrifying, black clouds of hideous beings, hovering, swirling above someone's head. I can't determine who it is. I sense it's family. Petrifying." Francesca sternly divulges.

"It's a frightening dream. It's haunting that you have been experiencing the same nightmare repeatedly. Do you want me to turn the light on?" Antonio communicates.

"No," Francesca lies back onto her pillow. "I will figure this out."

Antonio leans over Francesca giving her a loving kiss. She closes her eyes.

Viana moves her arm in an arc, closing their view to the Mancini home.

"Okay…now *that*, along with the vibrations we felt earlier today has renewed my hope that this assignment isn't completely boring," Victor ascertains in his clear, deliberate, medium-bass voice, while motioning his hand with a pointing finger.

"Now *you're* hopeless," mutters Viana.

"We have some time before we station ourselves outside of the mine for tomorrow's assignment. Let's surveil the town to see if there is any other excitement we may be missing," Victor motions.

Chapter 3

MARCO'S FIRST DAY AT THE MINE
MAYELLA 25TH 1537

Antonio and Marco arrive at the mine. As they step down off the wagon, dust stirs from the boots of the mine foreman Pearce who is approaching the two Mancinis. "Well, welcome to our team, Marco," Pearce extends his hand to shake Marco's hand.

Looking Pearce in the eyes, Marco firmly grips his hand, "Thank you. I'm certainly looking forward to being a part of the team," Marco conveys.

"Pearce, will you please escort Marco to Curtis? I'll unload supplies I brought," instructs Antonio.

"Yes, Sir," Pearce replies. "Come on Marco, Curtis won't want us to delay."

"I'll see you at lunch break, Marco," Antonio winks at his oldest son.

"See you then, Pop," Marco responds.

"Oh, and Marco, be safe. Make it a great day," Antonio emphasizes with his deep, rugged voice.

Pearce leads Marco into the office building where Curtis is going over his daily planning. Pearce knocks on the open door of Curtis's office, "Curtis, I have our new hire here."

Curtis, not even looking up from his desk, motions for them to enter.

Marco and Pearce stand in silence, awaiting acknowledgment of their presence from Curtis.

After shuffling through some papers and folders on his desk, setting them in their designated locations, Curtis peers up seeing the two standing there. Curtis scoots his chair back to stand. "Look who we have here. Marco Mancini. Wow! Old enough to join our team," Curtis confirms outstretching his hand to shake Marco's. "Welcome aboard."

Curtis O'Brien possesses extensive knowledge about the mine. He has worked at the mine under his father's guidance since his graduation from high school and celebrated his father's retirement last year. Curtis's father was trained by Antonio's father, Don, enjoying a lifelong service to the mine. When common sense mining is called for, they now consult Curtis first.

Curtis picks up his personal tool pack and motions for Marco to follow. Curtis explains their task in clear, decisive language. Marco understands immediately this man puts up with no nonsense. That suits Marco. Nearing the mine, they stop where tools are kept. Curtis hands Marco the tools he will be using.

The wedge and sledge hammer work they perform as a team. Swinging the pick effectively has more technique than Marco anticipates. Curtis demonstrates he shouldn't aim in the middle of the Krystyleen, but to use the pick's point to dislodge a loosened piece; and when to recognize the wedge is the most effective tool. Marco requires no instruction using a shovel and wheelbarrow. Mucking out horse stalls through his youth provided plenty of practical experience. Curtis observes as Marco methodically aims his pick at the seam of Krystyleen running through the wonderous rock.

"You're doing good. Always remember to try and break the Krystyleen on the veins you see running through it without disrupting or breaking any of the colors." Curtis shines his lantern toward the walls, ceiling and even the floor of the mine. It enables Marco to see the brilliant array of colors throughout the Krystyleen. "Each of these colors represent a different level of energy source. That's how everything is powered, Marco. But I'm sure you know this since your family has owned this mine for generations. I guess I'm used to telling new hires about the Krystyleen," conveys Curtis.

"It's okay. It's kind of nice hearing your tutorial," Marco offers.

"The only death we have had the misfortune of, is the one you probably remember. You were just a little boy. I remember your mother taking you and Gino with her to help the wife. Krystyleen is actually not too heavy nor too sharp to hold and work with. However, a piece broke from the ceiling spiraling down with some force hitting the miner's head, knocking him to the ground. Just a freak accident. That's why we now wear this modified protective gear. The energy source from the Krystyleen is unexplainable. But centuries ago, they discovered once the sunlight hits it, the Krystyleen becomes a power source. The variety of the speckles of colors distributed throughout the Krystyleen represent different energy levels. This mine provides Krystyleen to our kingdom as well as neighboring kingdoms. Word of it over ten decades ago even reached the coastal regions resulting in a demand throughout the continent. This is the only known Krystyleen mine on Soleil. It has been able to provide Krystyleen for centuries."

Marco humbly smiles, knowing this mine is a part of his heritage.

After a few minutes, Curtis picks up his tools relocating himself to work a few feet to the left.

Marco quickly adjusts to the exertion of swinging a pick and loading Krystyleen onto a wheelbarrow. He welcomes the challenge of strenuous, difficult work.

After an hour, Marco Mancini pulls off his leather gloves and wipes a handkerchief across his sweaty forehead, squaring his shoulders. *Mother and Pop will be proud of my hard work. They will see I am a man.* Pop felt it necessary, yet again, to drill safety rules at me on our way to the mine. *Doesn't he realize he has been telling me the same precautions for years? Doesn't he trust my common sense? Or perhaps, I displayed disinterest, causing him to think I was not absorbing what he was teaching.*

The tasks become routine. Marco's mind wanders while his body performs the repetitive movements. *I wonder what is the deal with Mother and Pop. Sometimes they speak to me like a man, then in a flip they behave like I am five years old telling me how to do things! Like telling me to put my jacket on.* Marco swings hard dislodging a large chunk of Krystyleen.

From the moment Marco announced his intention to accept a job at the mine, his mother presented numerous reasons why she believed he should not, her main argument stressing the dangers. His entire life, Marco heard his mother telling Pop to be careful whether he was working at the mine or on the ranch with the cattle and horses, so he expected that. He also knew his mother had helped wives care for their injured husbands after a few rare accidents, towing him and Gino along so they could all help with daily chores of the family. And once, Marco recalls what Curtis reminded him of, a miner died. Marco knew his mother truly understood the pain and heartache associated with the dangers of the mine.

I am always careful. Accidents happen due to carelessness. Marco thinks to himself.

Marco wants his parents to be proud of him. His pop not only stands tall with a strong body frame, he is a revered leader in their kingdom. Marco wants to follow in his parents' footsteps.

Marco adjusts his stance, taking another hard swing. *My mother can sure be stubborn. First, she brags about how mature I am to her friends, then I announce my plans to work at the mine, then SHE suggests other jobs instead. I guess I can see her point, or try to. I am her oldest. How can I be like her and Pop if I'm not allowed to work hard and prove myself?*

"What's the pouty face about?" Curtis quizzes.

"Just my parents. My mind is wandering and I'm thinking of their reservations they have of me working here." Marco shrugs.

"Ah, that," Curtis gestures. "That, Marco, is a parents' love. A normal response as their children grow.

"I suppose you're right." Marco relays.

"And, Marco, I know for a fact your parents are extremely proud of you. I have heard them both brag about how you can handle any job you choose." confides Curtis.

Marco smiles.

"Let's break for water." Curtis suggests.

"I guess to my parents I will always be their little boy even though I *AM* the oldest." Marco leans his pick against the mine wall. "It seems they will always try to protect me. They taught me all good things involve some risk. It makes no sense."

Curtis pours the last of the water into Marco's cup. "I'll refill this jug at the well by the entrance," announces Curtis. "Take a break until I return in a few minutes. As for your parents, Marco, it will probably make no sense to you until you are a parent yourself."

"You are possibly right," Marco admits.

Marco appreciated Pop's morning advice to pace himself. It was already close to lunch. He didn't feel worn out at all. Marco felt he didn't need to stop longer than drinking his cup of water took. He decides to resume swinging away at the Krystyleen on the wall to his left.

A massive amount of the wall ruptures, crumbling to the floor leaving a huge black chasm. Immediately a hissing erupts. Cold air blasts Marco propelling him backward. He stumbles on loose rocks. Marco experiences a chilling, evil presence swirling around him as he lies defenseless. A strange, frigid vortex sucks energy from his being, growing in size and intensity as each breath is removed from Marco.

······⟋⟍⟍⟍······

Curtis shivers as a burst of artic wind rushes him, snuffing out the lantern when he enters the tunnel where he left Marco. The hairs on the back of Curtis's neck stand up. When the wind subsides, he relights the lantern inching forward until he finds Marco lying on the floor. Curtis instantly blows three blasts on the whistle all miners wear around their necks to alert others of emergencies. Each vein has a designated number, so rescue teams will not lose precious time locating accidents. After a pause, he puffs three times into his whistle again. Fear creeps over him as he examines Marco. No sign of body movement. No breath. "Marco. Marco. It's Curtis. Marco." No response.

Curtis lifts Marco's hand checking for a pulse. It's icy as if he had pulled it from a bank of snow. "Help! Someone, help!" Curtis gasps for air.

Antonio enters the vein. "Marco! Curtis! What's going on?" Antonio shouts running toward the two.

"I don't know. I returned from filling the water jug to find Marco lying here," Curtis exclaims as he glances from Marco's body to Antonio. "He has no pulse, Sir, and his body is lifeless."

Antonio drops to his knees beside Marco touching his face. Terror sweeps through Antonio's inner fiber seeing the face of his son with a greyish, pale-white color, instead of his youthful, healthy, skin tone as if there is no blood in him. "Quick! Get a stretcher. Summon Doctor Gerard. Marco needs the warmth of the outside air-out of this biting cold. Send someone to ring the church bell, notifying Francesca to come."

Chapter 4

THE ESCAPE

Victor and Viana are reclining in the centuries-old oak trees west of the Mancini Mine entrance. The area's scenery could blissfully whisk them into daydreaming; however, they are on high alert.

Viana bolts to her feet. "Victor, did you sense that? Something's happening. Look! A filmy, dark cloud is shooting out of the mine entrance. No, wait." Viana places her hand on Victor's arm, "That's not a cloud. If I remember the pictures in the history books correctly, it's Cryptolores! Look at the one who's leading them out! It must be their commander! I wonder if it is Scaleon. He's coiling above the entrance. Look at him darting high above the trees with his myrmidons following. Do you believe any humans can see them?"

Victor, after glancing around, surmises, "No. The only thing the humans sense is the drop in temperature. I agree. It must be their commander. I believe it to be Scaleon. The bulging eyes and fangs in that legion is an arresting, frightening sight! Hundreds of ghouls swirl around him!"

"How can the humans not hear those shrill shrieks? It's like a high-pitched ringing in the ears, yet much worse." Viana stands transfixed. With her hands covering her ears, she shakes herself to regain focus. "We must enter the mine at once to protect the humans inside."

"The Cryptolores outnumber us." Victor warns. "Their horrendous howls are unnerving. This must have been the location of their imprisonment centuries ago. How did they escape? Contact headquarters. This predicament could become mortiferous."

Viana places two fingers on her left temple as Victor stealthily watches the mine entrance.

Viana announces, "After further analysis of the Ancient Writings, headquarters validated the Cryptolores were imprisoned at this location. I confirmed we just witnessed Scaleon and a mass of evil beings which are Cryptolore troops, escaping from the mine. Reinforcements are on the way. Zeek and Razel are transporting to our coordinates. After they arrive, you and I are to investigate inside the tunnel. Wait a minute. I'm receiving further instructions," Viana places two fingers on her left temple as she listens. She nods her head turning toward Victor. "Pixel and Piper will also be deploying to assist us."

Zeek and Razel materialize beside Victor.

"Teleporting takes my breath away," Zeek puffs as he places his hands on his knees struggling for air.

"Wimp," teases Razel as she gently bumps into the side of Zeek. "You know I am just kidding. Are you, okay? Do you need your inhaler?"

"No. I am good, thank you." Zeek takes in a deep breath and stands a proud four-foot-tall with his shoulders back sporting his slender, muscular frame.

Piper appears. Pixel arrives a second later, her body changing through an array of colors.

"I'm so excited!" proclaims Pixel. "An assignment on Soleil at the location The Ancient Writings speak of!"

"This situation is critical. Get control of your emotions. You'll be of no use to us flashing a rainbow of colors. It interferes with our invisibility on this planet," urges Victor.

"Roger that!" acknowledges Pixel, closing her eyes while breathing deeply. Gradually her natural color of blue settles to a red chameleon appearance.

"Somehow Scaleon and the Cryptolores escaped their captivity," Victor peers from face to face of each Chiawauka, making sure they understand the gravity of their assignment. "Viana will brief you on instructions from headquarters."

"As in any perilous circumstance, remain vigilant," Viana instructs. "Victor and I will investigate the tunnels. Headquarters ordered us to discover where these beings originated in the mine. I sense someone inside the mine is injured. We're to ensure the humans escape without coming under attack from unseen demons. You four, track the Cryptolores that emerged moments ago.

There appears to be a filmy, black cloud looming above the town's edge!" Viana declares pointing north.

"Such a massive swarm! We'll need reinforcements if a confrontation develops," exclaims Zeek.

Victor informs, "The overall mission is to remain undetected. Observe. Report. Monitor the activities of the Cryptolores. If the group breaks up, divide and follow them. Do not interfere with anything they do. They must not perceive we are shadowing them."

Victor is shaking his head as he and Viana tread to the mine entrance.

"What gives, Victor? I see you shaking your head pretty intensely," Viana pries.

Still shaking his head, Victor abruptly stops, looking directly at Viana.

"Viana, it isn't just Scaleon and the demons, I infer it is the warlord Alchodor and his knaves."

A shiver rushes through every part of Viana, "Oh, Victor, in all the commotion I had forgotten about the warlord Alchodor." After a pause, Viana continues, "It's okay. Our ancestors were able to imprison them before. We will be able to. When we find the Chords of Chiawaukas families, well, once they become the Keepers of the

Universe, the Cryptolores are no match for us Chiawaukas, or the Keepers!"

"You speak truth, Viana. I am very confident of the powers bestowed on us. My concern is all the havoc that will be unleashed until they're in captivity once again," reflects Victor.

They turn, continuing on the way to the mine entrance.

Viana grabs Victor's arm as they enter the mine.

"Stay near the walls. We will not be visible or detected by the humans or the evil beings. We must find the humans," Victors deliberate voice directs as his eyes search the depths of the tunnels.

"Learning about the Cryptolores frightened me in our training! They possess an inherent capacity for tremendous evil," Viana reveals.

Once they reach the first tunnel bend, Victor signals for Viana to plaster herself against the wall. Another filmy, black cloud rushes past emoting hideous laughs. A double-horned Cryptolore rotates, propelling the demons toward the mine entrance. The temperature once again, plummets.

"That has to be Alchodor. Seeing them sends shivers up my back even without the significant temperature drop," whispers Victor. "We must be observant for straggling demons. An overwhelming existence of evil is heightening my senses!"

Viana and Victor proceed with caution to the next bend in the tunnel.

Curtis runs past them toward the entrance as the two Chiawauka guardians enter the area where a victim lies on the tunnel floor.

"It appears no evil beings remain in this area, though the temperature drop caused by their presence remains. Set up a security screen at these supporting beams to prevent Cryptolores from re-entering this tunnel. Use the screen designed for humans to pass through unimpeded. I'll see if I recognize the person on the ground while evaluating his condition," Victor directs, assessing the situation.

As Victor approaches, about ten feet away, he recognizes Antonio Mancini who is kneeling by the victim's side examining him for injuries. Stepping closer, Victor gasps. He can see a faint, blue and purple aura around the victim's head. Victor launches into the air and circles above to see the face. It is Marco Mancini, Antonio's oldest son.

Victor's mind races. *This must be the sign foretold in The Ancient Writings- the sign of the aura which marks those who belong to the Chords of Chiawauka families. We must place a protective shield around Marco to prevent deterioration.*

Victor lands and turns to Viana, "Do you see it- the aura halo?"

"I do. It is faint, but definitely visible to us," Viana quietly says, then reaches for Victor's arm and exclaims, "Victor, look! There is a pale, green aura around Antonio's head. The outside light must have prevented us from detecting the auras. I believe we have discovered one family that possess the Chords of Chiawaukas."

They inch forward.

Victor reaches for Viana's arm, "Their auras are very faint, with the dim light of one lantern, the essence of the aura is refracted. They must not be aware of their powers, nor implementing them," concludes Victor now standing at Marco's feet.

"Marco, oh, Marco. Hold onto life," Antonio pleads, caressing his son's face. Antonio's head drops, "I arrived too late." With that admission, Antonio rests back on his calves hugging himself as tears of loss stream down his face.

"Hurry! We must install a protective shield over Marco's body while Antonio isn't in physical contact with him," urges Victor.

Viana and Victor spring into action, creating a shield that promptly molds to Marco's shape.

"That will protect his body," Viana softly says.

"Now, for the Flower of Virtue. Hold out your hands, palms up," Victor reaches toward Viana, touching his fingertips to hers.

Together they chant:

"Ancient Ones, the time has come-
Chords of Chiawaukas are being spun.
The sign of the aura
Reveals a virtuous soul.

Guard this Keeper of the Universe-

As you have foretold."

The Flower of Virtue manifests in their palms. They reverently set the sacred, pearl white flower on Marco's chest as the echo of boots running on the mine floor bounces off the walls.

"Hurry! Marco's a few feet down the tunnel," Curtis shouts as he bursts into the passageway.

Antonio leans over, "Son, help has arrived. Hold onto whatever life is left in you."

Two miners carrying a stretcher arrive shortly after Curtis.

Looking up to the men, Antonio instructs, "Be careful. He may have internal injuries."

The men gently transfer Marco's body to the stretcher proceeding to the mine's entrance.

"Viana, look at that hole. I can't see a back wall. It's enormous. No telling how many heinous beings were contained in there. It has to be the prison for the wicked Cryptolores. It is recorded they were cast into a dark underground chamber when the Estellas Galaxy purification took place. They were to be enclosed in the cavern for all eternity," remembers Victor. "It appears Marco broke through the seal which confined the Cryptolores. Nothing is left inside." Victor peers into the immense, yawning black hole.

"Scary. Let's report all we have witnessed to headquarters," recommends Viana. "They'll assess this intelligence and instruct us how to proceed."

The Chiawaukas follow the humans out of the mine, removing the invisible, security barrier as they exit.

Chapter 5

WHAT'S HAPPENED

Gino bounds in the kitchen door. "I smell apple pie!" he pronounces as he eyes the pies cooling on the counter. "No one makes pies as good as yours! Are they for dinner, or may I eat a piece while it's still warm?" he asks his mother.

"You have certainly learned flattery from your older brother and your pop. I can use a break, I'll cut a slice for us both," Francesca smiles at her youngest son patting her hands on her flour smeared apron. "Since this is Marco's first day at the mine, I decided to make two of his favorite pies, Apple."

"Yum, mine too," Gino expresses.

Francesca winks at her son Gino. "Mine is chocolate meringue, or cherry. Pies are so delicious. Wash your hands, then pour us some water, please."

Gino makes an exaggerated gesture examining his hands before reaching for the soap. Francesca laughs out loud while setting the plates of pie on the table.

Gino set the glasses of water on the table noticing his mother dab at a trickling tear rolling down her cheek. "Is there something wrong, Mother?"

"No, dear," Francesca replies followed by her little laugh. "Well, it just hit me, watching you pour our water. My babies have grown up too fast. Marco is now working at the mine, and look at you, so grown-up," Francesca smiles at her youngest son, Gino.

Gino reaches to his mother, "It'll be okay. I remember you always told Marco and me to be strong, brave men like Pop."

"I just thought it would take a little longer. In a blink, it seems you're both grown. Tell me about the rest of your day," Francesca reaches to Gino's hand.

Gino points to his mouth full of pie and expresses a gesture of "wait."

"So delicious, Mom," Gino begins to place a second forkful of pie in his mouth when he abruptly sets it back on his plate, "Did you hear that?" Gino exchanges a concerned look with his mother. "The church bell is ringing nonstop. There must be an accident at the mine."

Francesca freezes. Pausing, ... "Something has happened to Marco. Is Jolly still saddled?"

"Yes," Gino answers.

"You ride Jolly, I'll saddle Lady and follow," Francesca orders as she pulls off her apron following her youngest son out the back door.

Gino rides Jolly full gallop. As he approaches the mine, he experiences a drastic temperature drop along with high winds. Glancing at the sky, he sees no clouds. Some towns people are streaming toward the mine after they heard the church bell ringing. Gino then sees his father walking beside two men carrying a stretcher. Gino slides off Jolly, leaving her untethered, running toward them.

"Set Marco in the sun," Antonio commands. "Where is Doctor Gerard?"

"Can I help?" Gino anxiously asks, as he stops at his pop's side looking at the victim. "Marco? No! It can't be Marco!" bemoans Gino, dropping to his knees next to his older brother, running his hands over Marco's lifeless arms. Gino uses his forearm to wipe away his tears.

"Where's your mother?" questions Antonio.

Gino searches the crowd. "I do not see her yet, Pop." Gino continues to scan the countryside, catching sight of his mother approaching.

Francesca is on the outskirts of town slowing Lady's gallop to a trot when she feels the dramatic temperature change chilling her. She hunches down close to Lady sensing an immediate need to veer Lady to the left. Then bringing Lady to a halt, Francesca turns, viewing a black, hazy, filmy cloud forming over the Kingdom of Chamberlain. She then focuses directly above her, witnessing what appears to be a formation in the shape of a neck rising into the clouds. A surge of negative energy rushes throughout Francesca. Tingles that feel like electrical currents race through her body as she senses a dark, malevolent presence, filling her with a sensation of fear and anxiety. A moment of déjà vu strikes Francesca, as if her repeated nightmares are manifesting.

Gino is observing his mother's movements. She turns toward him; her face is ashen.

Gino signals to his mother waving his arms, "Mother, over here! Quick!"

Antonio looks and sees Francesca dismount Lady and run toward them.

Within a foot, she stops, collapsing to her knees at Marco's side. Gino feels helpless.

"I'm here, sweetie. I'll take care of you," Francesca assures gently stroking Marco's cold cheeks. Her eyes begin to water. "No. What happened to our son?" she utters, slowly turning to Antonio.

Antonio grabs a blanket from one of the horses, wrapping it around Francesca, embracing her in his arms. "This is how I found him after the whistle alarm sounded. He couldn't have been down for more than a few minutes. I had the men set him in the sun due to this unusually cold temperature. I don't understand what's happened. Our son is gone."

Francesca gazes toward town staring at the odd shaped cloud formations then turns backs to Antonio. "Who placed this flower on his chest?"

"No one I saw. It was there when we moved Marco to the stretcher. The entire affair is bizarre. Curtis was refilling their water jugs at the well when Marco penetrated the mine wall accessing an underground cavern. The escaping air lowered the temperature in the area. He possibly inhaled poisonous gas. I found no obvious injuries. Nothing makes sense. This is a suspicious accident."

Listening to his parents' conversation, Gino stands in horror. He pulls up his collar, shivering in the unseasonably cold air for Mayella.

Francesca once again glances toward the haze that hangs over the kingdom. "My nightmare," she murmurs.

Gino overhears her words and wonders what she means.

"What happened?" inquires Doctor Gerard approaching the Mancinis at a brisk walk.

Gino steps out of the way hoping the doctor can revive his older brother.

"Curtis was gone for only a few minutes. This is how he found Marco upon his return," Antonio informs.

Doctor Gerard kneels down placing his stethoscope on Marco's chest. Gino probes Doctor Gerard's facial expressions. He watches Doctor Gerard compose himself before turning to Antonio and Francesca.

"I'm so sorry. After Father Romano arrives, I'll instruct the men to transport Marco's body to your home so you can prepare him for burial," Doctor Gerard delivers.

Father Romano is drawing near. Antonio steps toward him, and reaches to shake his hand. With feelings of desperateness and anxiousness surging through his body, Antonio cries out, "Father! Please, come quickly! Pray the Anointing of the Sick over him."

Father Romano glances to Doctor Gerard. The doctor lowers his head, shaking it. Father then reaches his hands out placing one hand on Francesca's arm, his other hand on Antonio's arm, "Marco was a fine young man. Please accept my deepest sympathy. I'm sorry, son, I can only administer the Anointing of the Sick on the living." Father Romano kneels at the head of Marco and prays. People quietly gather around, feeling the sting of the death of Marco Mancini, the oldest son of a prominent family in Chamberlain kingdom. When Father finishes the prayer, he stands, "Do you want me to see if Bill Oliver has an appropriate casket available?"

Antonio gives Father a barely noticeable nod.

Gino's observing his mother kneeling beside his brother. "What a beautiful flower, same as my Marco. I'll take it with me." Francesca gingerly picks up the unique, mysterious flower, cradling it as Gino escorts her to Lady.

"Mother, let me hold the flower while you mount Lady," Gino suggests.

The temperature remains chilling with biting gusts of wind. Gino returns the flower to his mother once she settles in the saddle. "Let me help wrap that blanket around you," Gino insists reaching to assist.

Gino gets on Jolly, with Lady's reigns in his hands, he leads them home. Shivering, he searches the sky for signs of a storm.

As they near their ranch, the winds are calm, and the temperature is as pleasant as when they left.

Chapter 6

PROCESSING

An hour later, Gino joins his mother on the front deck. She is rocking in the handcrafted rocker Antonio built for her. She had held each of her sons during their early years in this rocker. Francesca clutches a beautiful crystal dish containing the unique flower she had found on Marco's chest.

"Is your pop done with the preparation of Marco? I set out his best clothes," Francesca softly inquires.

"Yes. Pop wanted to spend time alone with Marco, so I came out here," Gino leans against the deck rail a few minutes, then turns, facing his mother. "How did you know something happened to Marco?"

"Call it a mother's intuition. But it *was* stronger than that. I just knew," Francesca fingers the flower petals. "Then, approaching the mine...the wind gusts, the unusual cold air. It felt wrong. It felt...evil."

"It freaked me out!" confesses Gino. "I can't describe it, but it felt weird. I've never experienced a weather change like what occurred near the mine today. It was eerie."

Francesca concurs, "It was."

"Look at it here on the ranch. It's a beautiful spring day," Gino flings his arms wide and toward the sky. "But the wind and freezing temperature near the mine... it's very odd, Mother."

The crunch of the gravel drew Gino's attention. "Mr. Oliver is coming up the drive. He'll need help unloading the coffin. I'll tell Pop he's here."

Bill Oliver walks toward the front deck, removing his hat. "Antonio, Francesca, Gino, please accept my condolences," Bill turns to look at Francesca, "your parents asked me to tell you they'll be out shortly. They're locking up the store."

Francesca secures the door as the men carry the box into the living room. She supervises its placement. After arranging a pillow and Marco's favorite quilt, Antonio and Gino gently place Marco's body in the exquisitely finished oak casket.

"I'll be going. Is there anything you need or messages you need me to deliver in town?" Bill rolls his hat in his rough hands.

"No. Thank you for arriving so quickly," Antonio pats Bill on the back while gazing at his son.

Francesca takes a comb to Marco's thick, wavy hair, then places the beautiful, mysterious flower on his chest for the finishing touch.

Leonardo and Sophia Montanelli burst into the living room shortly after Bill leaves, rushing to their daughter Francesca, and Antonio.

Tears flow as they cling to each other.

Sullivan and Katherine Carlisle arrive next. They grieve with the family as only best friends can. Then they take charge of preparations for visitation from the community.

Sully enlists Gino's brawn to arrange chairs in the living room and family room, which will accommodate the large number of mourners who will be paying their respects. They place chairs for the grandparents and parents together. Gino sets a chair for himself between his parents. Sully positions himself at the front door to greet guests. Katherine assumes control of the kitchen.

Neighbors bring food. Some friends assist Katherine as she makes necessary preparations to serve refreshments to a steady stream of towns people who are arriving throughout the afternoon.

Antonio and Francesca greet each person, listening to those who share how Marco made an impact in their lives.

Curtis approaches Antonio with his head bowed, "I'm so sorry. I should not have left Marco, even for a few minutes. He was so young and inexperienced. If I had only stayed with him, or sent him for water. I've never lost a man on my team. I'm sorry," Curtis's efforts to refrain his tears ends.

Antonio reaches his arms around Curtis. "It isn't your fault. You did all that you could." The two muscular men cling to each other for several seconds.

Gino puts a tough face on to cover his turmoil. Feeling smothered by the mourners, he can't decide if he wants to hit something or run away from it all. More than anything, he wants Marco back. Gino would just like to be alone with his parents. It is awkward with all these people around.

When his best friend Luke Carlisle enters the room, Gino could no longer control his emotions. They hug and cry.

Antonio sees the two, and wraps his arms around both boys, "Why don't you guys go out back? Get some fresh air."

They nod their hanging heads.

A few minutes after Gino and Luke retreat to the backyard, Ben Carlisle joins them. Even though Ben is three years older than Marco, the four enjoyed a tight friendship. He embraces Gino in a hug. "You know, I love you and Marco like brothers. Man, it will be tough without him. Remember, I'm here for you, Gino. As your friend, and big brother."

Gino manages a melancholy smile.

One of the high school girls, Camille Thomas, is helping the ladies working in the kitchen to set up refreshments on the picnic table for the large group of school friends gathering in the backyard. When Camille has time throughout the day, she stands by Luke.

As the sun lowers, people begin to go home.

........⟨⟨⟩⟩........

Sully Carlisle joins his sons and Gino at the picnic table after the other teens leave. "Boys, it's time to head out. Ben, I need you to drive the wagon home with your mother. I'm standing vigil tonight over Marco's body. Sad deal. I love that boy," reaching for Gino, he firmly hugs him.

Katherine Carlisle unties her apron when the guys enter the kitchen. "I'm ready to go as soon as I say goodbye to Francesca. Gino, your parents will want to see you."

Dutifully, Gino follows her into the family room.

"The kitchen is in order. Breakfast is ready to warm. I'll manage the luncheon tomorrow. Ladies from the kingdom have volunteered to serve food after the service. Dear Francesca, try to get some rest," Katherine hugs Francesca.

Sully shakes Antonio's hand. "John, Peter, and I are standing vigil tonight."

"I appreciate that," Antonio offers. "You're a good friend."

Francesca stretches, "I'm spent. I doubt if I'll sleep tonight. I'm going out back."

Antonio and Gino follow her onto the back deck where she plops into a rocker. "Everyone has been so thoughtful, but I'm glad to see them go. We all need some time to process what has happened today." Reaching toward her youngest son as he sits in a chair beside her, "How are you, sweet Gino?"

"I don't know," he pauses. "I have terrific friends. They told great stories about their experiences with Marco.... especially Luke and Ben. Camille said sweet things. She kept the picnic table stocked with food. It helped a little bit. But the idea of life without Marco.... honestly, I'm in a fog."

"As we all are," confesses Antonio.

"What a breathtaking sunset...as if heaven is celebrating Marco entering. I'll sit here on the deck for a while," Francesca decides.

Gino scoots his chair closer to his mother's rocker. Antonio walks over standing behind them both, placing his left hand on his wife's shoulder, and his right hand on his son's.

Silence fills the minutes, each processing their own emotions.

"The mountain air is chilly. I'll fetch your sweater," Antonio disappears through the door.

Returning, he helps Francesca as she reaches one arm into a sleeve, then the other.

"Thank you." Then, Francesca asserts, "I want to hike to the river."

"Dear, the sun just went down behind the mountains." Antonio responds.

"There's a crescent moon tonight. It'll provide some light. Plus, I know the path," Francesca adds.

"I'll go with Mother, Pop." Gino chimes in.

"Take your gun," Antonio advises.

Gino smiles at his Pop, patting the slight bulge at his right hip.

"I'll talk with Sully and the guys inside. Their stories will distract my mind for a time being. Please, don't be gone long," Antonio submits.

Chapter 7

TIME AT THE RIVER

Francesca and Gino walk across the yard to the trailhead, a gap in the tall pine trees west of the back deck. Francesca places her feet assuredly to avoid stumbling over occasional rocks. The trail curves easing to a gentle slope leading to the river.

The mountain river spreads before them. Low bushes blanket the river's edge. The water ripples, and large rocks protrude in the current to form rock islands. Such beauty. They pause to enjoy the spectacular scene. Constellations are emerging while they gaze.

Francesca sits on one of her favorite boulders nestled into the bank at the water's edge, as if God perfectly placed it there Himself. Gino positions himself next to his mother.

Francesca exhales, "I do believe this is the most soothing place on Soleil. What a blessing it's on our property! Being outside in nature's beauty, a mountain river, refreshes me, inspires me, energizes and calms my soul all at the same time." Francesca smiles searching the night sky, "Do you see Star Points? I find observing the night sky revealing the constellations in our galaxy, fascinating." Francesca maintains with a renewed energy in her voice, smelling the scent of the pines that surrounds them.

"I can hear the energy in your voice, Mother," Gino conveys. "I'm glad I came with you."

Francesca gleams, "Me too, Son," closing her eyes, taking another deep breath through her nose smelling the scent of the pines. Francesca lets out her breath, opens her eyes, looks around, then directly at Gino. "Ever since your Pop and I began dating and were married, I have hiked here often. The past year though, and maybe from time to time throughout the years, I sometimes get the feeling something or someone is watching me. I could never see any tangible evidence to confirm that feeling, however, I sense that same invisible presence tonight."

"Are we in danger?" Gino stands.

Francesca replies with her little laugh, "No, sweetie. Sit back down."

Gino keeps his hand on his gun as he cautiously sits back down.

"It's always left me with a feeling of peace and inner strength," Francesca asserts.

The two Mancinis resume sitting in silence, watching the moonlight dance on the ripples of the water. A few minutes pass, Francesca breaks silence softly singing,

Everywhere I go, I take you with me-
Everything I do, I want to share with you-
Not a day goes by-
When you don't cross my mind-
Forever in my heart-
I love you.

"Mother, how beautiful!" exclaims Gino. "I haven't heard you sing that before."

"Thank you. It just came to me. That's how I feel about your father, Marco and you. Even though Marco is gone, he will forever be in our hearts." Francesca stares over the river. With a boost of energy Francesca requests, "Sing it with me, Gino."

Gino is a bit shy at first. But as they sing, his baritone voice becomes confident, matching his mother's clear soprano in its earnestness.

Looking at his mother with pride, Gino attests, "That was cool! I don't know that I sense an invisible presence, but I am pretty sure we just nailed our vocals!"

Francesca and Gino both smile with a peace in their spirits and a song in their hearts.

"I can't explain it, but I sense the life of an invisible being. I recall a non-threatening tingling sensation. I'm sure it existed quite some time before I recognized it as special...something extraordinary. On a few occasions I purposely sought out the presence I had encountered, unsuccessfully though. But my awareness to its existence grew. Today near the mine though, I felt an eerie, dark presence all around. Only your father knows about the recurring nightmares I have," Francesca recollects.

"I thought I heard you murmur something earlier today," Gino shares.

"I did, sweetie. It was as if my recent, repeating nightmares were manifesting before my eyes. It was quite disturbing." Francesca establishes.

"So... your nightmare came to life today?" Gino questions.

"I believe it did," admits Francesca.

"That's just scary. Looking back, you have always seemed to have an upper hand in situations, like you know the outcome, or...I don't know, I can't place it. You just seem to have a special gift the rest of us do not possess." Gino comprehends.

"I don't know about a special gift; I just try to be attuned to my surroundings and the people I'm nearby." Francesca stands, "We better get back before your Pop comes looking for us."

"Does Pop know about the invisible beings you sense?" Gino wonders.

"No, dear, you are the first person, and only person I am sharing that information with at this time. Can you imagine if people thought there were beings on our property?" Francesca proposes.

"Yeah, I didn't think of that. You're right, Mother. I, too, will keep it a private matter. But what about Pop?" Gino asks.

"I know. I have contemplated telling him, but I fear him feeling his duty of protection, would try to prohibit our hikes to the river. And I need that, Gino, for my wellbeing. With Marco's accident today, in addition to my nightmares, Pop has enough to worry about. No reason to add to it, at this point anyway," Francesca surmises.

"I agree. Wow, you sure have a lot of thought process going on, Mom. No wonder you need hikes to the river," laughs Gino.

Francesca joins Gino in laughter.

Then, there is a pause.

"I'm going to miss Marco so much." Gino reflects.

"I know, sweetie," Francesca empathizes, running her fingers through Gino's thick, wavy hair.

Gino takes his mother's arm wrapping elbows with his, leading them safely up the moonlit trail to their ranch home.

Chapter 8

VICTOR AND VIANA

Once the Mancini family returns to their ranch home after the accident, Viana and Victor post themselves in the treehouse Antonio Mancini built for his sons when they were young. The Chiawauka Guardian Beings have spent much time here over the last several months.

Victor positions himself, "What a perfect observation site. We've stationed ourselves in it this entire year, not even thinking about it strategically. We will be able to watch the mourners come and go, possibly see auras, and most importantly, we will sight Cryptolores before they attempt to enter the vicinity."

Viana settles herself so she can spy the backyard, "I see no activity in the back, do you notice anything in the front?"

"No, to my relief, I see no signs signaling the Cryptolores are present," Victor shoots a glance toward Viana, "How could we miss catching sight of any auras for a year? Since we witnessed two Mancinis with auras, the rest will have them. If the female has the red and white aura, we have successfully identified one family of the Chords of Chiawaukas."

"Don't beat yourself up too much, Victor. I assess the auras on the two Mancini males are faint due to them being oblivious that they even have powers, let alone using them," Viana states quite frankly.

Victor, shaking his head with frustration. "If this is one of the families the Ancient Writings speak of, they completely have no clue of any magical powers they hold. They are caught up in their daily lives, chores, loving and providing for their families, which is good, but, Viana, their possibilities are limitless. And they have no clue," Victor throws his arms about.

As Victor paces the treehouse keeping eye on the front, he places his arms behind his back and stops. "Viana, reflecting back, there were several instances that we witnessed the Mancinis behaving with strength and calm. We failed to recognize it as anything other than noble human behavior. There was the incident of Marco and Gino stopping a fight last Augusteil at the Summer Fling between two groups of teens."

"Ah, yes," Viana recollects, "and the time Antonio calmed the frightened horses when a child fell from the wagon seat. Marco pulled the child to safety. We detected nothing during those potentially dangerous situations. We were focused on finding the auras, unable to see anything other than their humility and recognize acts of unique, calm strength."

"I wonder if headquarters will change our orders from merely observing to protect and train if this family is indeed a Chord of Chiawauka," Viana surmises.

"My guess, is yes," Victor states.

Mourners are coming and going under the scrutiny of Victor and Viana.

"You're going to wear your neck out Victor, what is it?" Viana inquires.

"Just the upstanding character Antonio and Francesca display. It appears they are comforting the people who want to console them. No wonder they are an influential family in the kingdom, amazing humans," Victor evaluates.

Viana nods, "Katherine Carlisle and her two sons just left. Sully and two men intend to stand vigil tonight. The Carlisles are another outstanding family. Katherine took charge of refreshments and the kitchen, where the women found refuge to express their emotions," Viana recalls.

Viana and Victor observe Francesca sitting on the back deck as the sun disappears behind the mountains.

"Francesca may have a dim aura. I can't tell for sure yet," Viana debates. Scanning the area for Cryptolores, she glances back to Francesca catching her breath. "Look, Victor! Her aura *is* red and white; verifying we have found the primary source of the Chords of Chiawaukas in this family."

"It's very clear. Not as strong as I would hope," Victor concludes. "However, we have now confirmed one family. My guess is by the strength of her aura, or lack thereof," Victor clears his throat, "she is aware, to some degree, she possesses something supernatural."

"Francesca and Gino are walking into the trees. I'm going to stay close to keep watch, protecting them if needed," Viana declares.

"I'll communicate with the other teams, and contact headquarters before I join you," Victor formulates.

Victor places his index and middle fingers to his left temple communicating to the other teams and headquarters. He then whisks himself to Viana.

"When I informed headquarters with details confirming we have found a Chords of Chiawaukas family, they repeated we are to vigilantly guard Francesca, the primary source," relays Victor.

Victor also reports, "Our comrades witnessed the Cryptolores encircling over Francesca when she approached the mine earlier today while we were in the mine. A black, filmy cloud formation in the shape of a long neck supporting a grotesque head lowered from the hovering cloud, brushing over her as she neared the entrance. Winds whirled, circling her. Then, the grim looking anomaly retreated, entering back into the bizarre cloud. Piper suggested the Cryptolores recognized something unique about Francesca and were aghast. The mass of spirits appeared disorganized for several minutes. While Gino and Francesca were returning to their ranch, the horde billowed and the monstrous head swooped to loom within a few feet of them, resulting in another burst of artic air, in which Gino and Francesca pulled their collars up in the turbulent winds. It appears that when the hideous face spotted the Flower of Virtue Francesca was protecting, it screeched ear-piercing howls launching itself, ascending thousands of feet forming an undulating mass emitting terrorizing shrieks as if repulsed by the presence of the flower."

"No wonder headquarters repeatedly commanded us to vigilantly protect Francesca. After receiving our reports, along with the data from the other Chiawauka teams, I'm sure our High Council is developing a plan," presumes Viana.

"Francesca definitely had an impact on the Cryptolores. Piper also relayed once the Cryptolores soared into the sky, the formation divided into two groups maneuvering, diving, whooshing, twisting, what appeared as an attempt overtake each other. They recoiled together, now hovering above Chamberlain Kingdom," Victor finishes.

"Hearing what occurred wears me out, and we didn't even witness it," Viana exhales. Let's pay attention to what Francesca is saying," Viana recommends.

"Did you hear her say she felt our presence, Viana?" Victor astonishes.

"I'm going to send her the ancient Keepers of the Universe Song. Let's see if she receives it, Viana decides.

Everywhere I go, I take you with me-
Everything I do, I want to share with you-
Not a day goes by-
When you don't cross my mind-
Forever in my heart-
I love you.

Viana grabs Victor's arm with her hand shaking it, "Wow! Listen to that, Victor! She is singing it! I'm impressed! We need to report this to headquarters. I'm sure they will tell us to commence training," Viana supposes.

Victor puts his finger to his lips signaling Viana to be still. They hear Gino begin singing with his mother. As he did, a faint, blue and purple aura adorned his head. Victor and Viana are mesmerized as they listen to Francesca and Gino sing the ancient sacred song. Leaves rustle, startling them. Victor and Viana scan the shadows searching for danger. It is an otter slipping into a pool of crystal water.

"Gino's aura has manifested," whispers Viana, "did you hear Francesca say how she has sensed our presence in the description of invisible beings?"

"Yes. Simply amazing. Well, these discoveries today change everything. Clearly, I mistook this for a boring assignment! That is no longer the case!" Victor declares.

"I wonder how long Francesca has been realizing her powers. As she uses them, they will increase in strength. She'll need our assistance to expand them, in addition to keeping a reign on them. I'll contact headquarters with our updates," Victor places two fingers on his left temple.

While Victor communicates with headquarters, Viana surveys their surroundings, hearing some of his conversation.

"Yes, Gino has an aura as well. The entire Mancini family. Affirmative, I agree. We need another pair of Chiawauka guardians on stand-by. We believe the second Chords of Chiawaukas family will be in this area," Victor ascertains.

Victor lowers his arm while he and Viana stare at each other, then back to Francesca and Gino.

Chapter 9

Francesca moves in a daze methodically performing her morning routine. Walking into her closet she casts her eyes upon her dresses searching for the perfect one for her oldest son's funeral. She shuffles through her dresses quickly, seeing her black dresses, *"Ugh,"* she feels. *"Depressing."* Then she sees it! Her eye-catching nautical dress! White, with an empire bodice that features navy blue and white horizontal stripes. The piping sports red with tiny white polka dots around the sailor style collar and empire waist, with a perfect size bow in the center of the waistline, separating the white skirt from the striped bodice.

Beautiful! That's it! Marco commented on how pretty I looked in this dress. When was that? A week or two? It doesn't matter. He loved it. That's what matters. Francesca thinks to herself.

Francesca slips the dress on over her head wondering, what accessories?

As she reaches to the side zipper, she feels the warmth of Antonio's large hands. One hand holding her dress while the other hand zips her dress up. He then wraps his muscular arms around her, enwrapping her in an embracing hug.

"Your beauty casts a spell on me even in sadness," Antonio professes.

Gazing into his eyes Francesca surrenders, "You don't think it is too..." She stops to hear Antonio's words interrupt.

"No. My dear, it is perfect. Marco loved seeing you in this dress, and I completely trust your judgement. That is how your strength shines, you go with your gut, not what others think," Antonio proclaims.

A smile overtakes Francesca's face reaching for the pearls her grandmother Anneliese gifted her on their wedding day. Handing the stunning necklace to Antonio, he places it around her neck, clasping it. Gentle smiles exchange. Antonio sits on their bed admiring his wife as she reaches for her red hat and red shoes completing the nautical outfit.

"Breakfast is ready if you're hungry," Antonio informs.

"I'm not. I just do not have an appetite," Francesca admits.

"Me either," voices Antonio.

Antonio stands facing Francesca, "You're gorgeous, sweetie. Marco would approve of your style." Placing his strong hands on her athletic arms Antonio gently blows away the few tears trickling down her cheeks sealing her lips with his.

"I'm thankful you were at the mine yesterday," Francesca divulges.

"Me too," agrees Antonio as he takes her hand and they walk into the living room.

Gino looks to his parents when they enter, "I told Sully and the guys I wanted some alone time with Marco. They went to the kitchen." Gino returns his sight to his brother, "He looks so peaceful."

"He does," Antonio reassures standing behind his son, placing his hands on Gino's shoulders. "Remember though, we believe his spirit is alive and has moved on," reminds Antonio.

Gino reaches his hand up placing it on his father's, "Yes Pop."

......⌒ℓ⌒......

Francesca decides, "I'll take the flower with me today, and then keep it on our mantel. You may close the casket whenever you are ready."

Antonio and Gino gingerly close the casket lid securing the lock. Sully, Peter, and John enter through the kitchen doorway. Gino holds the front door as Antonio and the three men transfer the casket to the wagon. Once the Mancini family seat themselves in the carriage, Sully takes the reigns.

Antonio makes eye contact with Sully, "Thank you for hitching the horses to the wagon and the carriage. You are a good friend and neighbor. And Katherine, taking charge of our kitchen and the refreshments, well, we are just very thankful to call you both, our friends."

"Antonio, Katherine and I feel the same for you and Francesca. Your sons, are like our own sons. All those camping trips we went on as they were growing up. Game nights, cookouts...we're family." Sully shares. "Katherine will serve food she brought a while ago for lunch after the ceremony," adds Sully.

The crowd of people part making room for Sully to drive the carriage close to the Mancini mausoleum where Antonio's parents and grandparents are interred. The subdued conversations cease. Antonio, Francesca, and Gino follow the pallbearers as they carry the hand-crafted casket to the stand where it will rest during the memorial service.

King Theodore and Queen Eloise proudly occupy chairs in the row behind the Mancini family. As soon as the family is in place, Father Romano addresses the gathering.

Francesca hears the words spoken by Father Romano, but his words do not resonate. The sun is shining brightly. The people are quietly gathered. The birds are chirping. But everything seems unreal.

When Father Romano refers to Marco being a fine young man, Francesca holds her head high. But during the prayers and ceremonial part of the service, her mind wanders, casting her eyes solely on the unique, beautiful flower she holds in her lap. When Father Romano pronounces the last "Amen," she whispers,

"Everywhere I go, I take you with me. Everything I do, I want to share with you. Not a day goes by, when you don't cross my mind..."

Gino joins his mother, reciting the last line in the song, "Forever in my heart, I love you." Instinctively, Gino places his right hand on the casket making no effort to wipe tears from his face. "I love you, Marco."

Antonio leans toward Francesca quietly suggesting, "Let me help you." She squeezes his hand as she rises. Antonio reaches his arm around her shoulder. Together they stand tall. Their sorrow is apparent. Antonio turns to Father Romano, "Thank you, for the lovely service," supporting his wife's elbow, Antonio gently escorts her to the carriage.

Chapter 10

Viana and Victor's instructions after the mine incident are very clear. Track the Cryptolores. Zeek, Razel, Piper, and Pixel follow a safe distance behind the filmy, dark cloud of Cryptolores to avoid being discovered.

"We don't need to worry about them detecting us," assesses Piper, "they're swarming and howling, completely self-absorbed."

"Revolting! They sicken me," announces Pixel as her hue changes from blue to red while she struts around.

"Get ahold of yourself, Pixel. You cannot let your emotions dictate your color. Remember, we're on a mission and must follow orders precisely without displaying excitability. It's tough. I struggled when I was your age," Razel extends her arm around Pixel to calm her, admitting, "Only, I turned green."

"Be alert. Upheaval among the Cryptolores," Zeek warns, pointing.

The four Chiawaukas focus attention on the surging cloud. At first, it spirals high into the sky, immediately doubling back, then dives to the terrain at breakneck speed. The cackles develop into a deep, consistent rumble intensifying as they plunge.

"What in this world are the Cryptolores doing? Trying to kill themselves?" Pixel exclaims as she turns a lighter shade of red.

"No, it's one of their rituals. Cryptolores perform specific patterns when making decisions, or preparing to carry out their plans," Razel reassures as she reaches her arm around Pixel, again. "It's okay to watch. We're hidden."

The four Chiawauka guardians study the unnerving phenomenon.

A tremendous blast erupts, breaking the barrier of sound with unusual, livid, lighting flashes. Thunder rolls across the sky: frightening, and formidable at the same time. The Chiawaukas are able to distinguish Alchodor and Scaleon streaming in what appears to be choreographed formations throughout the swarm leaving entwined trails. The stench of a trash dump permeates the air.

"Yech! Just vile!" declares Pixel tossing her head, changing colors from red to black, back to red.

An instant before the crazed, flashing cloud plummets into Soliel, it splits. The smaller group spins off to the southwest. The larger cluster gains velocity soaring north. Static electricity charges the air. The Chiawauka guardians stand perfectly still until the atmosphere settles. They simultaneously exhale.

Zeek recovers first. "Razel and I have experience with stealth tracking. We'll monitor the group traveling southwest toward the wilderness. Piper and Pixel, you two follow the cluster heading north. Remain undetected, and stay in communication with us."

⁙⁙⁙⁙⁙⁙

Upon receiving their updated instructions based on their discoveries and the events that have taken place, Victor and Viana reattach themselves to the Mancini family, while their comrades surveil the Cryptolores.

"I ache for this family, I wish I could communicate a few comforting words," confides Viana.

Victor sternly directs, "Don't you dare even try, Viana. It's too early for us to reveal ourselves to Francesca, even if she suspects awareness of our presence. Her emotions are fragile, we need to be mindful of that. Who knows how she would respond."

After the funeral, Victor and Viana hover above the Mancini carriage on the return trip to the ranch. Victor scans the grounds searching for signs of trouble from the Cryptolores.

A long procession of wagons follows the Mancini carriage to the ranch. Sully parks near the front door. He assists Francesca to the ground. Antonio and Gino silently pace themselves behind.

Viana positions herself on the open stairway to observe activities in the home. Victor monitors the grounds.

Francesca heads directly to the kitchen pantry reaching for a small, glass-dome cake plate stored near the back on one of the shelves. She wipes a thin layer of dust off placing the flower inside. Antonio stays close to his wife as she prepares a special location on the mantel above the fireplace for the unique flower found on Marco. Antonio draws his arm around her while she stands staring at the mesmerizing bloom. *"Mother, you look beautiful. You rebel."*

"Honey, lunch is ready," Antonio's urges in his low voice, giving her upper arms a gentle squeeze. "We should try to eat something."

Staring at the flower as if in a trance, "Did you just hear that?" Francesca insists slightly tilting her head.

"Hear what, honey?" Antonio asks.

Francesca slightly shakes her head and shrugs. "I guess nothing. But earlier I could have sworn I heard thunder. I scanned the sky, not a cloud in sight. Did you hear roars of thunder a bit ago?"

"No. You have a keen sense, maybe there was thunder passing in a neighboring kingdom, and the atmospheric conditions allowed you to hear it," Antonio hypothesizes.

Francesca's blue eyes look worn, "Perplexing."

Antonio manages to down a few bites. Francesca uses her fork only to push her food around on the plate. Gino eats about half of the serving he was given. As soon as he can, Gino excuses himself, retreating to the barn with Luke, Camille, and Ben.

Quiet chatting between family and friends accompanies the meal. Different guests attempt to draw Francesca or Antonio into conversation. Antonio offers polite, lackluster responses. Francesca relocates to the rocking chair on the deck. She has no interest in visiting with any guests. She gathers her strength being alone.

Sophia and Leonardo join their daughter on the deck. The three sit in silence.

Francesca relocates to sit between her parents on the comfortable, glider bench. Sophia and Leonardo place their arms around their daughter. They gather strength from holding each other. After some time passes, Leonard and Sophia stand.

"Honey, we are going to go. Or, if you want, we can stay in the guest room for tonight." Sophia offers.

"I like that idea." Leonardo concours.

Francesca smiles as she gazes into the eyes of her loving, supportive parents.

"We'll let you be. We're going inside." Leonardo squeezes his daughters' hand. Sophia and Leonardo retreat to the inside.

Viana perches herself only a few feet away from Francesca on the corner of the deck rail.

As the afternoon progresses, friends drift outside in efforts to engage with Francesca, expressing their condolences, squeezing her shoulder or patting her hand, they return to their homes resuming their normal lives.

"The Carlisles are the only ones remaining. I wonder how the Mancinis will process the loss of Marco?" Victor shakes his head as he sits beside Viana.

Sensing movement, Francesca sharply turns her neck in the direction of Victor and Viana. She just stares, investigating the area.

Katherine grasps Francesca's hand and kneels before her. "Francesca, Francesca." Katherine gently delivers.

Francesca turns her head from inspecting the deck rail, meeting Katherine's eyes.

"Dear, the kitchen is in order. Food for tomorrow is in the refrigerator. I'll check on you in a day or two. If you need me, please don't hesitate." Katherine consoles reaching her arms around her friend, hugging with love friends share.

"Why don't you come in now, babe?" Antonio's deep voice breaks the abysmal state Francesca is in.

She stands, taking his hand.

Viana declares, "Victor, did you notice Francesca examining where we are sitting? Francesca senses our presence, again. In addition, she alluded to hearing the thunder the Cryptolores were creating. She didn't see them, but she heard the sound filling the sky."

"Yes, we are really going to have to be careful," Victor kvetches. "Maybe, at some point, we will employ the magical properties of the flower as part of Francesca's training."

Viana glances around the ranch, "With the funeral day over, surveillance should be routine. What's the latest from the other Chiawaukas?"

"There is not going to be anything routine in our future with the escaped Cryptolores roaming around," Victor theorizes. "The Cryptolore legion split. Zeek and Razel are shadowing the group speeding southwest into the mountain wilderness." Victor cocks his head in thought, "Piper and Pixel are an entirely different story. They're observing a large assembly of Cryptolores looming over the north side of Chamberlain. I haven't received any further intelligence from Piper since early this morning."

Viana leans her head forward, "I'm worried about Pixel's inexperience. I sure hope she's resilient enough to handle tough, unpredictable situations."

Chapter 11

THE POSSESSION

"Stay alert! They're on the move," Piper barks orders at Pixel. They track the Cryptolore assembly speeding north led by Alchodor. The swarm impetuously halts above Chamberlain Castle. It hovers in an undulating mass until dawn.

"Those demons give me the willies. I wish I would have paid more attention in the academy class covering the Cryptolores," confesses Pixel as she watches the ominous dark cloud.

Piper assumes the pose of a lecturing professor. "Let me refresh your memory. The Estellas Galaxy High Court sentenced the evil Cryptolores to eternal banishment. A cavern here on the planet Soliel was selected for their imprisonment. The High Council appointed the Chiawaukas to fill the cavern with an anesthetizing gas to keep the Cryptolores indefinitely in a comatose state. As a safeguard in the unlikely event they escaped, two Soliel human females in two unrelated families were infused with life energy from the High Priest and Priestess, hence the Chords of Chiawaukas which can be activated if needed. Otherwise, the females pass this trait to their oldest daughters. According to the Ancient Writings, it states that these two families, at some point, will have one of their generations joined by a marriage. At that moment, their powers will fully ignite. It is then, we can completely step in, train them, and commission them Keepers of the Universe. That's the simplistic synopsis of our class." With a flourish, Piper bows. "That is, if we find the second family that possess the Chords of Chiawaukas."

Pixel giggles, "Thanks for the review," turning pink.

The mild rumble emitted by the dark cloud quickly escalates into ear-piercing screeches. The Cryptolore throng billows. Two gigantic gyrating columns form. Irregular bolts of lightning flash across the sky. Spiraling pillars periodically jab discharging deafening, thunderous roars. Ozone temporarily compromises the air.

Pixel slaps her hands over her ears as she becomes a dark shade of blue. "They're battling. Let's leave. I can't stand it."

"Control yourself, Pixel. As a trained Chiawauka guardian, you can endure this sight. Remember your training at the academy. Please, get ahold of yourself. Flashing colors expose you. Blend with your surroundings. Be observant," encourages Piper.

"I'll do my best." Pixel takes in a deep breath and exhales, focusing on the enemy. She freezes. After a pause she grabs Piper's arm as they witness the black, filmy cloud of Cryptolores bombard the castle entering through chimneys, open windows, and keyholes.

Piper moves his arm in an arc, making the western wall of the castle transparent. "Look at Alchodor and his followers slithering through hallways and rooms searching for the selected target to host. He'll possess his victim like a parasite. His demon followers can temporarily inhabit a victim at Alchodors bidding. The rest of the time they linger nearby to influence other beings, human or animal, into wickedness. Be vigilant."

Pixel fans her hand in front of her face, "To be able to smell the stench at this distance! Appalling!"

Piper signals Pixel to be still.

"I hear what sounds like a young child crying." Pixel conveys as she changes to light brown. "Hush, little one. You'll attract those monstrous villains." Pixel faces Piper, "Is the baby in danger?"

"The cry will make no difference. Alchodor chose his victim when they were sweeping over the castle. Now they are searching for the room his victim is in," Piper maintains.

"I'm going to where I heard the crying." Pixel flies off.

Piper follows.

Pixel lands just outside the nursery, then sharply draws in her breath.

Piper settles beside her on the nursery balcony. "What is it?" he questions.

All Pixel can do is point. The invading legion is entering under the door.

Pixel cowers behind Piper. "Please, can't we do something to protect this innocent life? Shouldn't we use our powers and stop the Cryptolores from whatever malice they intend?" Pixel pleads.

Piper's experience and confidence stand out. "A moment ago, I contacted headquarters requesting they allow us to prevent the Cryptolores from possessing the royal family. They denied my petition. We are to observe only, and not be detected. We have orders not to intervene until our Chiawauka teams discover and train the two females that have the red and white auras, along with their families."

"I can't bear this," moans Pixels. "Poor baby."

Instantly, the Cryptolores circle the crib holding the prince. The hideous, petrifying head of Alchodor emerges. Elongating his neck, he rises almost to the ceiling peering down on the defenseless toddler. In a split second the demonic warlord Alchodor swoops down invading the prince's body through his eyes, his ears, his mouth, and his nose. The toddlers cry ceases abruptly. Then out of the princes' mouth is a wail. Not the bawl of a baby, but a maniacal caterwaul. He is possessed.

Suddenly, the prince stands quiet in his crib, watching the lethal Cryptolores enter his nanny. She collapses onto the nursery floor before his eyes. He then looks around as if seeing his room for the first time.

Piper and Pixel remain on the balcony undetected. They retreat to a tree near the west edge of the castle grounds.

"Calm down!" Piper insists placing his hands on each of Pixel's arms. "You're exhibiting a rainbow of colors. Get control of yourself or the Cryptolores will detect you. Truth be told, I'm struggling to keep myself invisible. But you have the strength, Pixel. Set your mind to it," Piper encourages.

Pixel declares, "Even though you gave me a re-cap, watching a Cryptolore possession unfold before my eyes sends spine-chilling, heebie-jeebies throughout my whole body. We were right there, Piper, and we stood by. How can our High Council be okay with this?"

"Many people will be affected catastrophically. Our hands were tied by orders from headquarters, who base our mission on the Ancient Writings. According to the transcripts, a predetermined time will arrive to apprehend and incarcerate the Cryptolores, or destroy them," Piper illuminates.

"That time can't come soon enough! I vote to destroy them, Piper!" Pixel expresses, rapidly flashing every hue of the color wheel then settling to a red. But then, white polka dots begin popping up one by one by two by three, until Pixel's entire red body is covered in white dots.

"Be patient, my friend. We have to trust headquarters has intelligence we do not," Piper imparts. Out of the corner of Piper's eye he thinks he sees spots appearing on Pixel. He takes a second hard look. "Pixel, are you aware you are covered in white dots? That's just peculiar."

"I am? Oh, boy. Now, I think I'll like that. I will look in a mirror so I can see them myself." Pixel giggles. "Piper, do I look like a strawberry?"

"Do you want to look like a strawberry?" Piper raises an eyebrow inquisitively questioning Pixel with a cracking of his voice.

"Yeah. I'd be fine with that. Maybe red with white dots will be the color I settle into." Pixel stands looking at her arms and legs, relishing in the colors.

Chapter 12

DARKNESS FALLS ON THE CASTLE

King Theodore and Queen Eloise collaborate in the spacious royal office. The day is moving along splendidly. Weekly reports produce no surprises. They run a peaceful, productive kingdom.

Sullivan Carlisle, the royal ranch's agricultural supervisor provides a satisfying update. Due to Sully's skill in farm management and animal husbandry, the royal agrarian investments thrive.

The grounds keeper, Wilson, approaches the king and queen with a design to update the flower beds at the driveway entrance. A new walking path through the wooded area, around the edge of town, loops past the castle drive. Eloise especially likes his idea for building a gazebo surrounded by flowers and bushes. Walkers would have a beautiful location to rest at the ground's entrance.

Chef Pierre presents menus for the upcoming week and smiles when the royals compliment the skills of the kitchen staff.

Andrew, the royal butler, highlights the appointment schedule for the next seven days. The king praises his organizational expertise.

"We thank each of you for doing your jobs so well. The queen and I believe we have a remarkable staff and team. Thank you, all."

Andrew escorts Sully and Wilson to the door and returns to his daily business. Chef Pierre returns to the kitchen.

The king and queen clink their tea cups in a toast to all their good fortune.

Their smiles rapidly turn to dread as they hear their son, Prince Rupert, scream dreadfully, then wail. The frightening cry easily carries from the second story nursery to the main level office. The king and queen eye each other in astonishment. Rupert almost never cries. He laughs, giggles, babbles. Wail? Never.

King Theodore dashes through the office door, followed by the queen.

The king takes two stairs at a time to reach the second story. All is silent. The staff stands frozen in shock.

The king pauses in the hallway outside the nursery catching his breath. Eloise catches up with him.

"I no longer hear Rupert's cries. No need to unsettle him. Let's collect ourselves before we enter. Mary must have the situation under control," derives Theodore. He takes a deep breath opening the door for his wife and himself.

"Hi there, sweetie," offers Eloise.

Rupert does not acknowledge his mother's presence with his normal smile as she takes another step closer to his crib. Nothing. No reaction.

"What's happened?" Eloise asks as she dashes to where her son sits. He is unresponsive in the corner of his crib staring at something, but yet not staring at any particular thing: just an unblinking gaze.

Eloise reaches to pick up her son, but Theodore restrains her.

"Look at the room," The king insists.

Eloise struggles, "Let me go. Rupert needs me," exasperates Eloise as she tries to pull away.

Gently, but firmly holding the queen, the king orders, "Look around the room before you touch him."

The spell of a mother seeking to protect her child is now broken. She quickly scans the room and glances at the king. Eloise then slowly reinspects the room with a keen eye.

The toys and books are in their proper places. No signs of struggle. The queen's eyes befall what the king has been wanting her to notice. Mary, their nanny, is lying on the floor near the window with Rupert's teddy bear clutched in her hand. Strangely, wind is blowing out of the room instead of flowing in. A faint stench fills the air. Eloise shivers looking at her motionless son. She grabs the side of the crib to steady herself as her head races trying to make sense of the scene.

Reaching to wipe her nose and eyes, Eloise yields to her husband, "I'm okay. Please, go check on Mary. You can let go of me now. I'm okay, dear."

Theodore drops his hands from Eloise's arms and sprints to Mary. He kneels beside her, carefully taking her wrist in his hand checking for a pulse. "She's gone," he announces focusing toward Eloise.

The king snaps into action. Racing to the hall just outside the nursery door, the staff have been waiting. "Andrew, alert the guards. Have one team summon Doctor Gerard, and another team bring Sheriff Ryan Patrick. Also, Andrew, please assign someone as temporary nanny. Set up an interim nursery across the hall from our chambers. The rest of you, don't disturb anything. I want the sheriff to investigate. Something despicable took place here, and my son witnessed it," instructs the king.

"I want to take Rupert out of here," Eloise picks up her toddler. She tries to snuggle him into her shoulder and let him mold to her body, as he normally does, but he is rigid. She glances at Theodore, dismay in her eyes. "I'll take him to our bedroom," her voice trembles.

King Theodore instructs, "Andrew, I'll be in my room with my wife and Rupert. Please escort Doctor Gerard to the nursery so he can examine Nanny Mary, then afterwards to my quarters to check Rupert. Also, notify me when Sheriff Patrick shows up."

"Yes, sir. I'm on in it," reacts Andrew darting down the stairs.

The king follows behind, heading to his bedroom. Upon entering he sees his son stiffly sitting on their bed; Eloise is at his side with tears streaming down her cheeks.

"I can't imagine what happened, and my baby seems to want no part of snuggling," anguishes Eloise. "Rupert gets inflexible when I touch him. He seems to prefer sitting on the bed by himself. Where did my loving, little boy go?" Eloise dabs more tears.

"I'm wondering what happened to Nanny Mary. It seems like it's taking so long for the sheriff and Doctor Gerard to arrive." The king paces. Turning toward his wife, he stops. "I feel helpless."

Just then they hear a soft knock at their door.

"Doctor Gerard has arrived sir," Andrew announces.

The king immediately extends his hand to shake Doctor George Gerard's hand. "Welcome. We've been awaiting your arrival." The king expeditiously escorts the doctor to the nursery to examine Nanny Mary.

Andrew is now escorting the sheriff down the hall to the stairs.

"Well, that's perfect timing, Sheriff Patrick," remarks the king. "The doctor just arrived. Let's go see about the nanny's fate."

With that, the four men trek up the stairs to the nursery. The sheriff takes the lead. "I'll enter the room first if you don't mind. I deem it as a crime scene unless my investigation discloses otherwise," commands Sheriff Patrick.

The sheriff methodically examines the room, inspecting every inch of the room, from the door to the crib to the open window. Kneeling down at the side of Nanny Mary, examining her body, and her eyes, he notices something very chilling, creepy even. He pulls out a note pad from his pocket and records his findings. "Doctor Gerard, will you come over here a minute please," the sheriff requests.

"Certainly," responds Doctor Gerard approaching the sheriff.

"You have not examined her yet, correct?" questions Sheriff Patrick.

"No, I arrived moments before you," the doctor relays.

"Kneel down and examine her now, please," requests the sheriff.

Doctor Gerard kneels down next to the sheriff, by the side of the nanny. He proceeds to do an investigative examination. The last thing to view is her eyes. The doctor also opens her lids. He rapidly sits back as if he has seen a ghost. He and Sheriff Patrick stare speechless at each other in disbelief.

Sheriff Patrick broke the abnormal silence, "Does anyone know what color Mary's eyes are?"

"Yes, I do," Andrew proudly informs. "Her eyes are...were a beautiful sky blue."

The three men look at Andrew inquisitively.

"I know this because, frankly, I so enjoyed her company. Just peering into her eyes as she would speak filled me with a sense of happiness. She was full of life." Andrew confides.

"What is it?" the king questions.

Sheriff Patrick and Doctor Gerard peer at each other, both making entries on their notepads.

"It's nothing," Doctor Gerard answers. "I just wanted confirmation. Thank you for assisting."

The king gestures, "Excuse me that I won't be seeing you out. I'm going to my wife and son. Andrew will escort you out when you have finished Sheriff Patrick, and doctor if you would please examine Rupert when you are done here."

"I have a few questions for you," expresses Sheriff Patrick, I'll walk you out.

After a few questions from the sheriff, King Theodore feels an urgency to return to his bedroom where his family is. He runs down the flight of stairs and into his bedroom chambers. There, he is greeted by his son glaring at him with a sinister, lop-sided grin. A chill engulfs Theodore's inner being. The king shudders.

Queen Eloise is sitting with her feet in a chair, her knees bent, arms wrapped around them, rocking herself, quietly crying. "Where has our adorable little boy gone?" reaching out with one hand toward her husband.

The king stands next to his wife holding her hand. Minutes later they hear a quiet knock at their door.

The king walks over and invites Doctor Gerard in.

"May I examine the little guy?" Doctor Gerard requests.

"Yes, please," the king quickly answers.

"Yes. Please return my little boy to me," the queen anxiously pleads.

Doctor Gerard sets his medical bag down, and reaches for his stethoscope. As he places it on Rupert's chest and back, the doctor visibly notes the prince's behavior.

"He likes to play with this stuffed bear, if you'd like to try it," Eloise suggests reaching her arm out with the stuffed bear in her hand.

Doctor Gerard takes the bear, places it in front of Rupert, "I hear this little bear is your buddy," making the bear dance around Rupert, hoping to solicit a response.

Nothing the three adults did could disrupt the blank stare.

"His heart rate is a bit fast. His breathing is shallower than normal," informs Doctor Gerard. He checks Rupert's temperature. Then, pulling his otoscope out, he examines Rupert's ears. Returning it to his bag, he then reaches for his ophthalmoscope and looks into the prince's eyes. He frowns, and places it back in his bag, also.

"I see nothing of real concern so far. He's pale. His breath feels a bit too cool; however, his temperature is in normal range. It's strange. I'm journaling this in his file. I believe he is experiencing some type of shock. His eyes appear unusually dark. Have you noticed that?" the doctor questions the king and queen.

"I'm sure it's just the lighting," Queen Eloise defends.

"Tell us something we don't know! Of course, he's in shock! He saw his nanny's death!" lashes out the king.

Eloise places a restraining hand on her husbands' arm, "Let's hear what the good doctor has to say."

Doctor Gerard rubs his chin with his left hand, then turns his hand outward, "I see no physical signs of injury. Children his age are resilient. My advice is to be patient. Keep his normal schedule. Watch his reaction to everything. Gradually increase touching him as he tolerates it. Bring him to my office in a week for a follow-up. If you need me before, or if he exhibits any unusual symptoms, don't hesitate to contact me."

Queen Eloise has her arms crossed over her chest with a hand gripped to each arm, nodding to Doctor Gerard, "Thank you."

"Thank you, Doctor," Theodore walks him out of the bedroom.

Chapter 13

Pixel and Piper sit in the large branches of a tree near the nursery balcony. Witnessing the Cryptolore possession of a toddler and the destruction of life appalls them. Piper waves his arm in an arc making visible the activities in the castle.

They see Queen Eloise carry her stiff child from the nursery.

"Discovering the Mancini's auras confirms they are one of the two families of the Chords of Chiawaukas. The words of the Ancient Writings are manifesting before our eyes. Our mission, for now, is to be watchful of Alchodor and his followers." Piper reiterates.

"It is so much worse witnessing evil, than hearing about it from a teacher. I can't bear to watch what happens next." Pixel crosses her arms turning shades of red.

"Take a deep breath. Exhale slowly." Piper demonstrates. "Do it again."

Pixel says, "Thank you, Piper. I'm already dreading what we will be encountering during our assignment here on Soleil."

Piper laughs, "Wasn't it just two days ago you were so excited being assigned to Soleil?"

Pixel almost begins changing her color from red to pink, but catches herself, "Okay, you got me there, Piper. I guess I have heard Soleil's beauty resembles Earth. Just in a different galaxy in a neighboring universe. As a young Chiawauka, I always dreamed about being stationed on Soleil. And now, to be an active part of the Ancient Writings as they unfold, well..." Pixel pauses, her color rapidly flashes red to pink to yellow, to green to aqua, like a box of crayons displaying each color. "Well, Piper, it's like a dream of a lifetime to be here on Soleil, and to be part of the Ancient Writings."

Piper scratches his head, "Pixel, I have never thought of it like that. Very insightful. And, you speak truth. We will be instrumental in caging or destroying the demons, thus protecting our galaxy from their destructive evil. We indeed are part of the Ancient Writings," ponders Piper.

Piper waves his arm closing the arc. Reaching for Pixel's hand, he invites, "Let's go back to the nursery. I want to investigate."

Pixel and Piper transport over to the balcony. Piper looks right at Pixel, "That was good timing, the humans are just now entering the nursery. Remember, be quiet, and do your best to refrain from changing colors. Let's watch the humans."

Andrew opens the door for Sheriff Ryan Patrick, Doctor Gerard, and the king. The sheriff explores the room, examining everything with a trained analytical eye. "Has anyone touched or removed anything in the room?" Sheriff Patrick questions.

"Everything is as it was. Except for the boy. The queen took the prince to their chambers," Andrew explains.

Sheriff Patrick makes a thorough, investigative sweep through the nursery. He makes his way to the window by the balcony, then peers out of the window in all directions. He turns, stepping beside where Nanny Mary lies. He kneels down beside her, inspecting her body, then summons the doctor to join him.

The Chiawauka team plasters themselves against the balcony wall when the sheriff inspects the window and balcony area. "That was close. He certainly startled me when he stuck his head out here on the balcony." Pixel exhales.

"Remember, we are invisible to normal humans," Piper affirms.

"Is my color fine?" Pixel questions.

"Pixel, yes, your color is fine," Piper determines with a grin, "Now, let's listen. The sheriff is about to examine the nanny." Piper motions with a finger against his lips.

"There's no evidence of violence. Did anyone hear anything?" Sheriff Patrick quizzes.

Andrew shakes his head, "The only thing all of us heard was a peculiar scream from the prince. A blood curdling scream, if I may, sir," looking for approval from the king.

"A scream?" the sheriff looks inquisitively at the king and Andrew.

"Yes, more of a shriek. The royal couple were enjoying their tea after a morning report meeting. They darted upstairs, as we all did. The prince was sitting as if he was comatose in the corner of his crib. The king checked for signs of life on Mary. She was already cold. Then the king ordered me to have the guards notify you and Doctor Gerard," recounts Andrew.

The sheriff inspects Mary's body for signs of foul play, then lifts her eyelids.

"Piper, why is he lifting the lids of her eyes?" Pixel places her hand on his arm.

"Wait here." Piper immediately zooms over and positions himself behind the sheriff's shoulders.

"Doctor Gerard, have you examined Mary yet?" asks the sheriff.

"No. I arrived just moments before you. Also, I was waiting for you to administer your investigation," Doctor Gerard answers.

"Kneel down and examine her now," summons the sheriff.

Doctor Gerard walks over to the victim, kneels beside her to examine her body, ruling out a heart attack and finishes by pulling back her eye lids. A ghastly expression comes over the doctor like he has seen a ghost.

"Does anyone know what color Mary's eyes are?"

"Yes, sky blue," answers Andrew.

The doctor and sheriff stare at each other. The sheriff stands, tapping his pen to his notepad. "Very unusual."

"I have a few questions for the king, if I may speak to you alone, sir."

The king complies accompanying the sheriff out of the nursery. Pixel decides to ease herself over Doctor Gerard in a suitable observation position peering over his shoulder.

"Be careful, Pixel," commands Piper.

"He's lying! The doctor is journaling Mary's eyes as normal but unresponsive. He wrote Mary died of an apparent massive brain aneurysm. Her eyes were solid black! No whites were evident." Pixel begins turning an array of colors.

Piper motions Pixel to get out of the room, "You're changing too many colors, leave the area," waving his arms.

Pixel relocates to the window ledge.

"Relax Pixel, Doctor Gerard is inventing a report that will not frighten the community when they learn of Mary's death in the castle. It's highly unlikely Chamberlain experiences two deaths from unnatural causes in six months. Now there are two deaths in two days. I agree his dishonestly is ugly. But he deems it necessary." Piper reaches his arm around Pixel, comforting her.

Pixel takes several deep breaths. Closing her eyes, she thinks of her mother's love. "For the sake of the little one, I will be assiduous."

Doctor Gerard finishes, addressing Andrew, "Mary's body is ready to be transported to my office for funeral preparations."

Within minutes, John and one of his reliable stable hands appear with a blanket and stretcher. They roll Mary's body onto it, gently folding the sides over her, carefully lifting her. As they carry her out of the room, Piper and Pixel notice a black haze oozing out from the blanket as the demonic Cryptolores vacate the body of their victim. The filmy form momentarily lingers over the area where Mary's body laid, as if they're gloating at their deed. Then in a flash, streak out the window.

"Should we follow them?" Pixel hesitantly asks.

"No reason to. They won't veer far from their Warlord. Let's leave and regroup." Piper directs.

Piper and Pixel transport to a cluster of trees west of the castle.

"I'll contact headquarters...you contact the other teams." Piper's index and middle fingers were already on his left temple before he had finished communicating his orders to Pixel.

Pixel gazes at the castle after her connection to the other teams.

"What did you learn?" quizzes Piper.

"Thankfully, Zeek and Razel witnessed no possessions of humans or animals, yet. It appears a wolf pack is being targeted though. Headquarters updated Victor and Viana's orders to train, in addition to observing and protecting the Mancinis," Pixel reports.

"Our orders have been updated as well. We are not only to observe, but protect the king and queen," instructs Piper, "Any powers we employ must appear to be luck. Talk about difficult," kvetches Piper.

"Is that all?" Pixel inquires.

"Headquarters requests we coordinate with Victor and Viana. That perplexes me. How can Victor and Viana assist? Is there a connection between the Mancinis and Chamberlains?" Piper bends his head from left to right.

Pixel brightens, literally changing to a bright pink, "I wonder if the Mancini lady and the queen are friends. Maybe the king and the Mancini man were childhood friends. So many possibilities. Viana said the Mancini ranch is about three miles west of the castle."

"Perhaps," contemplates Piper. "Victor communicated yesterday the Mancini lady is an impressive woman." Piper taps his chin. "What do you think about using her to encourage Queen Eloise? The queen is feeling very helpless. You did say Victor told you they are to train now as well. Sounds like a perfect teaching scenario."

"Brilliant idea, Piper! I'll contact Viana," Pixel smiles enthusiastically.

Chapter 14

RUPERT'S BEHAVIOR

Over the course of the following week, Eloise often repeats, "Where has my adorable, fun-loving baby gone?"
The king is full of sorrow and concern. No one has any answers.

"I hired a new nanny yesterday. Remember Carol Mitchell? We honored her last year when she retired from Chamberlain Children's School. She's a widow and more than willing to live in the castle. Hopefully, she will be able to handle whatever ails our son. She's moving in today," informs the King.

"Thank you for taking care of the interviews, Theo. Rupert's behavior has consumed all of us this week...well, with him throwing things, kicking at our staff, trying to pinch and hurt you and I... I am just thankful you were able to remain focused and carry out responsibilities." Eloise lovingly smiles at her husband. "Yes, I do know Carol. You made a wise choice."

Theodore takes the hand of his wife in his and they exchange a tender moment.

That evening, Carol brings Rupert to the dining room dressed in fresh clothing. When she attempts to place him in his highchair, he gyrates so violently she cannot keep him in her grasp. Theodore grabs his son the instant he twists free. Rupert flashes a triumphant grin at Carol.

"Thank you, sire. I do apologize my lady," Carol graciously bows to the queen.

"No harm done this time. He's become quite rebellious since the incident." Eloise sits back down. "I apologize to you, Carol. I do hope you'll stay and accept this challenge."

Rupert allows his father to set him in his highchair. When his food arrives, with one quick sweep of his arm, it's all on the floor. Servants scurry to clean up the mess. Eloise's hand covers her mouth.

Carol takes control when the new plate of food is brought. She situates it on the table just out of the toddler's reach. When she attempts to feed him a spoonful of Chef Pierre's delicious macaroni, Rupert clamps his mouth together and turns his head.

"Maybe he wants to serve himself. Place the spoon in front of him," a helpless Queen Eloise suggests.

Rupert seizes the spoon and slings it across the room.

The king is doing everything he can to contain himself.

"Carol, try placing a few bites of chicken near him, please. He likes chicken," Eloise encourages.

Carol cuts a few bites of chicken placing it within Rupert's reach. The prince picks up one bite at a time, purposely dropping each piece on the floor with a gleeful grin.

"My son was never a finicky eater before the incident. He has to be hungry." Eloise assumes.

The king pushes his chair back from the table.

As if on cue, the chef parades a tray of dessert choices into the dining room. Rupert squeals, reaching with both hands toward the dessert tray in an attempt to grab some.

The standing king eyes Eloise, "If you want to allow him to have dessert after this outrageous spectacle, I understand. I know you want him to eat something. I would let him go hungry and see if his attitude is better in the morning." The king asseverates.

"Let Rupert have a small slice of the chocolate fudge dessert," decides Eloise.

Chef Pierre hesitantly places a piece in front of Rupert.

Rupert snatches the dessert as quickly as he can, smacking his lips and grinning after the first bite of the rich dessert. Carol relaxes a little when she sees him smile. Then Rupert seizes the remainder of the dessert smearing it all over his face and bib in a joyous outburst.

A stern look overtakes Carol's face. She takes a deep breath, then gently, but firmly, picks up the mischievous prince while he's still licking dessert off of his hands. "This calls for a bath. Then I will read you a bedtime story." Carol confidently delivers. Thinking to herself, *which story talks about eating the children...or maybe the one where the witch bakes them....Carol, just stop. Ugh, what a naughty little boy. I can't believe the royals are putting up with this nonsense. They must be scared of him. Should I be scared of him? How did Nanny Mary die?*

"Let us know if you need anything. We will be in the reading room. Report to us when he falls asleep," Eloise instructs, tucking her hand under the elbow of Theodore.

"Doctor Gerard may have said to be patient. But our sons' behavior at dinner tonight is unacceptable, Eloise. I'll not have it. We cannot coddle him and reward him when such malicious behavior occurs. He throws things. Hits people. Breaks stuff. If this is the type of boy he is going to be, let alone when he becomes a man, how can I ever leave my throne to him!" the King rages. "I just wanted to spank his naughty, little rear, Eloise," admits King Theodore.

Eloise is taken back by the anger her husband displays. She composes herself, "Dear, he is a toddler, maybe his behavior is just a coincidence of the incident. Maybe, his testing us is a normal phase of childhood development at this age."

The king paces, "Perhaps, you are correct, my dear. I'm sorry. His bad behavior stirs such anger in me. It's embarrassing that a part of my loin can behave so atrociously!" The king approaches Eloise, kneeling in front of her. "God help us."

Eloise reaches for her husband and rubs his neck and shoulders with her petite hands. Dropping her head, resting her cheek against his, they sit in silence.

⁓⁓⁓

About forty-five minutes later, Carol reports to the reading room. She curtsies to the royals.

Eloise gives Carol a half smile, "I apologize for our son's behavior. It is inexcusable."

"You warned me the prince has become a bit of a challenge. You are right," yields Carol. "Excuse my boldness, but granting him whatever he wants is not going to improve his behavior."

"We agree. But we're stumped at knowing what to do," responds Eloise.

"I recommend he not be allowed to take his meals in the dining room where he has an audience until he can behave civilly at the dining table," suggests Carol.

"But meals are a bonding time," insists Eloise.

"The arrangement would only be temporary until he begins eating what he is served without throwing tantrums," informs Carol.

"It can't hurt to try," agrees Eloise, looking to the king for his reaction.

The king simply nods his head and turns away.

Chapter 15

SEEKING PROFESSIONAL HELP

Eloise inconspicuously observes the new nanny.

Under Carol's recommendations, the prince's eating behavior gradually improves. Eloise's hope bolsters.

But Eloise is still concerned because Rupert's laughs are usually the result of mischief. The prince delights in inventing new ways to shock the adult world he lives in.

Rupert demands every bit of everyone's attention. Naptime also does not come without some sort of battle. He incessantly cries and throws things from his crib, which results in no toys being kept in or near the crib. The king, queen and nanny relentlessly try different methods, from walking him in their arms, in the stroller, and singing to him. Nothing is successful. Rupert often cries until he grows so physically exhausted, sleep overcomes him.

In some aspects, Rupert displays minuscule improvement. Carol remains consistent, gentle, playful, yet firm with the prince. Eloise notices Carol has managed to gain her son's trust. Rupert often seeks Carol's affirmation. If anyone other than Carol or the king and queen try to hold Rupert, he twists and squirms until they put him down. Then he runs nilly-willy around the room defiantly giggling.

The baffled royal parents seek Doctor Gerard's advice once again.

......⚬⧽⬡⧼⚬......

Doctor Gerard shakes his head in frustration. "I'm sorry, but I find nothing physically wrong with Rupert. He is too old for colic. Maybe he has a food sensitivity," suggests Doctor Gerard.

"We are feeding him a limited range of food! Sweets and mashed potatoes! We are also feeding him away from the rest of us, hoping without adults nearby, he will eat," Eloise voices impatience. "I don't know what else to do!"

"I believe, without a doubt, it is the result of the trauma from Mary's death. Have you been able to figure that out yet?" asks Doctor Gerard.

"Well, if we had determined what happened, don't you think we would have remedied the problem instead of adjusting our every move around Rupert's behavior," rebuts the king. Thinking to himself *obnoxious behavior.*

Doctor Gerard softens his approach seeing the level of annoyance the king is expressing. "Sometimes, things have a tendency of correcting themselves. If your son develops a fever, vomiting, or any other symptoms, contact me at once. Just seeing his nanny collapse is enough for shock regardless of what occurred before."

......⚬⧽⬡⧼⚬......

Another wearisome week goes by. Eloise frets as her son's distress does not lessen. Misbehaviors prevail. Temper tantrums grow more intense. At times his crying is unceasing.

The king and queen summon for Doctor Gerard for a third time. Doctor Gerard still finds nothing physically wrong with the prince. Queen Eloise cries in exasperation. King Theodore demands Doctor Gerard recommend a physician who possesses skills to diagnose his son's problem and prescribe immediate treatment.

Doctor Gerard refers them to expert pediatricians in neighboring kingdoms.

Over the course of the next month, the king and queen take their son to neighboring kingdoms, seeking medical expertise to identify his ailment. The doctors they consult do not know of a cure. The recommendations are nothing new or that they hadn't already heard. One physician suggests they seek psychological counseling. Theodore and Eloise feel insulted.

With a blood-curdling scream, their sweet two-and-a-half-year-old transformed from an enjoyable child into a miscreant brat.

The king and queen decide to make the best of their situation, hoping their precious child will outgrow the baleful stage. The royal couple discuss at great length, contemplating if they should have another child.

Chapter 16

JULIAH 19TH

Francesca wipes her hands on her apron when Gino bursts into the kitchen. She greets her son with a big hug.

"I'm starving. How soon until dinner?" Gino inquires.

"We're waiting for your grandparents to celebrate your mother's birthday," Antonio informs.

"Oh yeah, Mother. Your birthday. How old today? Sixty-seven?" Gino laughs.

Francesca laughs, and says, "I see your wit never rests."

"I'm just kidding, Mother. You're the bomb," Gino asserts.

"Francesca, your parents just arrived," Antonio alerts.

"Help me set the table please, Gino," requests Francesca.

"Anything for a senior citizen," Gino laughs.

Francesca can't stop smiling from ear to ear at her son's sense of humor.

Antonio escorts Sophia and Leonardo to the dining room table.

Sophia is carrying a sack with pink and lime green stripes and a bright, happy flower in the middle. She reaches to her daughter Francesca. "For you, my beautiful daughter. We love you. Happy birthday, sweetie." Sophia hugs Francesca and hands her the gift sack.

Leonardo also greets Francesca with a hug, "Happy birthday, honey."

The five sit at the inviting table with settings perfectly placed: cloth napkins folded in triangles, crystal glasses at the upper left corner of each plate.

"Sweetie, you decorate impeccably," Sophia proudly notices.

"Gino helped me today, Mother," Francesca admits.

"Your skills impress me, Gino," declares his grandmother, Sophia.

"Here, here," Leonardo raises his glass. "I'd like to toast my beautiful daughter. Wishing you a wonderful birthday. And may I say, you are a remarkable woman, Francesca, honey."

Antonio follows Leonardo's lead, "To the love of my life, happy birthday. You are as beautiful, if not more so, than when I met you. I'm certainly glad I walked into your parents' store one day many years ago."

Gino raises his glass, "To a pretty great mom, how old are you?"

Everyone laughs.

"It's not polite to ask a lady her age, Gino," instructs his grandfather Leonardo.

Francesca laughs, "It's okay, Dad." Francesca pauses, as if something just inspired her. "Gino, I am thirty-seven today." Francesca proudly announces. "And from this day forward, I will be thirty-seven. Every day, every year. I am thankful for each of you. And I am thankful God allowed us to know Marco for seventeen years. Amen. Enjoy the meal."

Each family member exchanges a significant look at each other before feasting on the delicious birthday meal.

Gino breaks the sound of eating, "Bill Oliver needs some help tomorrow. I stopped in his shop when I was in town with Mother. May I work with him tomorrow, Pop?"

"Yes, Bill is a good man and a talented carpenter. Do you know what you will be working on?" Antonio asks.

"Yes. He told me I will be helping him sand and finish a dining room table. He had promised to have it done by the end of the week, then received a rush job requiring detailed carving work. I'd like him to teach me things when he is slow. I'll ride Jolly into town in the morning, with your permission," Gino notes.

"Yes, by all means, Son. Be safe, and learn well," encourages Antonio.

"Actually, tomorrow is the day your Pop and I are invited to lunch with the king and queen. They've been out of town most of the time since the end of Mayella. Apparently, Prince Rupert is experiencing a medical condition the king and queen are seeking consults for from neighboring kingdoms. It has all been hush, hush. No one in town knows too much, only speculations. Rumors say it's related to Nanny Mary's death, which occurred two days after Marco's. I wish Marco was still with us," Francesca ponders, staring into space for a moment.

Antonio reaches for Francesca's hand giving a gentle squeeze.

"We all do, sweetheart," Sophia empathetically delivers.

"Your mother and I are actually proud of you and Antonio, and you as well, Gino, for the way you are able to compose yourselves, and carry on with life after such a devastating loss. We know it hasn't been easy. You are all very strong. Don't take that lightly," Leonardo discerns.

Gino sets his fork down. "I really miss him."

The family extends their arms, taking and holding the hand of the person sitting on each side of them until they are all joined.

"Lead us, God, when we are in sorrow for the loss of our Marco. Help us to recall the good memories when our hearts begin to ache," Antonio prays.

Squeezing hands, then the family releases their grip, finishing their meal.

Chapter 17

LUNCH WITH THE ROYALS

A ndrew escorts the Mancinis to the royal sitting room.

"I haven't seen you since the funeral. I want to thank you for greeting the people at our home after Marco's service," Antonio shakes Andrew's hand.

"My pleasure, sir. He was an enjoyable young man. Such a tragedy," Andrew comments.

King Theodore and Queen Eloise enter the room greeting their friends.

Antonio and King Theodore give a brief hug, smacking each other's backs.

"I want to thank you for having your kitchen staff bring a ham to our home after the funeral. We deeply appreciate you attending the services, lending your staff and John tethering horses. It really took a load off of us," Antonio confides.

"It's what friends do," expresses the king.

The four friends sit, visiting about light-hearted things. Neither couple discuss the life-changing events occurring almost two full months ago that has forever impacted their lives.

Francesca finds it odd the royals have not mentioned the prince one time. Like most parents, they usually dote on the prince.

"Lunch is ready," Andrew appears in the doorway.

King Theodore stands, "Let's eat." Feeling so at ease with his life-long friends, he lets his proper decorum down.

When Francesca enters the dining area, she instantly senses something is off. She feels something, someone probing her. Inconspicuously sweeping the room with her eyes, she spies nothing out of the ordinary. She recognizes Carol, the new nanny, from the school. Francesca immediately clears her head and refocuses on the queen's words she hears.

"Carol, please bring Rupert to the table to join us," Queen Eloise requests.

Francesca's eyes move back toward Carol bringing the prince to the table. Francesca notices Rupert's eyes appear unusually dark, actually, black in color. Everyone takes a seat. The king leads them in prayer, blessing the food. Servants distribute plates of trout and salmon with salad and sliced hot bread. Francesca once again feels an uncomfortable scrutiny. She glances around the room stopping at Rupert. *That's where it is coming from. I have never felt this sensation in his presence before. My intuition suggests it is not Rupert. I'm putting my guard up. How could it not be Rupert? It's disturbing. I'm going to look him in the eyes and make some type of contact with Rupert. Or whoever it is. I'll have none of this from an unknown intruder, or anyone for that matter.*

Just then Rupert kicks the table hoping to disrupt the place settings.

"Rupert. Rupert, look at me," Francesca persists.

Rupert continues to kick the table violently, hoping to tip glasses. The king and queen are embarrassed. Carol isn't sure what she should do in the presence of company.

"Rupert, honey, look at me now," Francesca demands.

Rupert stops mid-kick, dropping his legs, and stares at Francesca.

"Hello, sweetie," smiles Francesca. "Are you to be three in a couple of months?"

Rupert nods his head several times.

"Rupert, do you know who I am?" Francesca asks.

Rupert nods again, pointing to his mother, "Fend." He attempts to sound out the word.

"Yes, that's correct. I'm your mother's friend. None of the rest of us are kicking the table. I want you to behave. Do you understand?" Francesca requests.

Rupert's tilts his head to the side staring at Francesca as he hears her voice. Francesca notices his eyes lighten while a dark, filmy cloud forms above his head. Francesca is not only puzzled by what she sees, she feels a bit unnerved, making a quick glimpse at the others to see if their expressions indicate they are witnessing the strange phenomenon. From their appearance, they are oblivious.

"Ah, I enjoy you so much, Rupert. You are able to hold your own fork and eat like us. Good job," Francesca smiles.

Carol and Queen Eloise exchange a look of relief at each other. Everyone enjoys conversation and the delicious cuisine Chef Pierre prepared for them.

After dessert, everyone rises departing the dining room. Francesca walks to Rupert while Carol is holding him.

Francesca touches his arm, "It was so nice to have lunch with you today. I look forward to seeing you again. You mind Nanny Carol and your parents," Francesca behests.

Rupert nods his head three times.

The king and queen escort Antonio and Francesca down the hall.

"Well, you certainly made an impact on our son today, Francesca. Thank you." notices the king.

"Yes, thank you, Francesca," Queen Eloise says as she hugs her friend goodbye.

Andrew assists Francesca into the carriage. Antonio takes the reigns from John. The Mancinis wave to their friends as they depart the castle grounds.

"Well, that certainly was an interesting lunch," Antonio voices to Francesca. "Theodore nor Eloise did anything about Rupert's bad behavior at lunch. Thank goodness you stepped in."

Francesca replies, "Oh my, yes. Had that been one of our children, they would have been removed from the table immediately. Neither the king, queen nor Carol behaved as though they knew what to do. Did you notice how dark the prince's eyes were when we saw him? Did you see the black cloud form above his head?"

Antonio glances at his wife, "No. Well, I did notice his eyes appeared black. I thought that was weird. I saw no cloud. You unquestionably seem to have an exceptional ability to detect things the rest of us do not," Antonio reaches his arm around his wife. "Honestly, I'm sure most people may think some of the stuff you state you see and hear is nonsense, but I know you to be truthful and forthcoming."

Francesca leans into his shoulder. "Thank you, for that. You know, I don't want to alarm you, but the cloud above his head resembles in appearance to the ones in my nightmares. The one I experienced near the mine. I also felt an evil presence, as if it was trying to examine me."

"Well, you certainly had a calming effect on Rupert, like you do me," Antonio squeezes Francesca, planting a kiss on her cheek.

Francesca smiles, "You sweet man. I wonder how Gino's day is going."

Chapter 18

THE CHIAWAUKAS INTERACT

Viana stretches, "I sure enjoyed visiting Piper and Pixel yesterday at the castle during the humans' visit and luncheon." Victor, deep in thought mumbles, "Mm hmm."

"Can you believe how the royals reacted to the naughty prince? I'm certainly glad we are not on castle duty! Pixel says they are not allowed to intervene at all," Viana maintains.

"Well, you know it's because we cannot do anything that would cause the Cryptolores to suspect we are here on Soleil," reminds Victor.

"Yes, but they sure seem to sense Francesca is special," Viana worries.

"I agree. Francesca is the prince's only hope. It appears the Cryptolores recognize something in her she may not even be aware of herself yet. We need to find a way to train her." Victor paces.

"Let's be alert for an opportunity to direct her thoughts today. Her mind must be relaxed, which may pose a problem. Timing will be imperative. Why must Francesca be so industrious?" Viana analyzes.

"If we coax her to the river, perhaps we will be able to draw her attention using a technique which allows her to discover her powers. She is familiar to our presence there," Victor scribbles some training notes. "Look!" Victor points toward the ranch's back deck.

"What? Gino is having breakfast on the deck," Viana wrinkles her eyebrows.

"Here's our opportunity. Make a connection with Francesca suggesting she and Gino go to the river for coffee," Victor suggests.

"Okay, but I don't know that she is attune to us just anywhere," Viana implies.

"I think she is, Viana. She clearly recognizes the prince's darkened eye color. She witnessed a filmy, black cloud lingering above him. She distinctly saw the Cryptolores forming above her and Chamberlain Kingdom on the day of the mine accident. She thought they were clouds, but nonetheless, was able to see them. She could hear the Cryptolore's battle, thinking she heard thunder. She was suspicious of our presence when we were on the deck rail. Her powers, and at least her intuition and empathic tendencies, are stronger than what we first speculated. She's instinctively tapped into the unseen world," Victor deduces.

"Well, all humans are able to see Rupert's black eyes. But you're right about the other instances. I will try to communicate with her." Viana places her index and middle fingers to her left temple, "Francesca, go to the river with Gino. A perfect place for a morning coffee and walk."

"We'll listen to their conversations. When Francesca mentions something, lets levitate it toward her. Exposing both of them at the same time may assist our training, and help them know they're not crazy, or seeing things." Victor plans.

Francesca walks out onto the back deck with two tall mugs of fresh homemade hot chocolate. She offers one mug to Gino, "Let's go to the river," invites Francesca, carrying a thermos secure under her armpit.

Gino stands, taking his plate into the kitchen, and returns to the back deck with his mug of hot chocolate where his mother awaits.

"What a wonderful way to begin our day with a hike to the river, hot chocolate and each other." relishes Francesca.

"Yes, thanks for the hot chocolate. I love your recipe," Gino replies.

"Me too. Your great-grandmother gave me this recipe when I was a little girl. I remember helping her make it on my visits to her home," Francesca reminisces.

"Bill Oliver really likes my work, Mother. He says I have a natural knack for carpentry and would like me to develop my skills. He offered me a part-time job." Gino informs. "I really want this. I love carpentry and creating things." Gino has a little laugh like Francesca, "The wood speaks to me like rocks speak to you, Mother," Gino smiles.

"I see no reason for you not to accept the job, Gino. Have you spoken to your Pop?" Francesca asks.

"No. I know he wants me to follow in his shoes, and raise and train horses, among other things. I know I'm only fifteen. But I hope to someday own a carpentry business, maybe even right here on our property. I'm scared to tell Pop." Gino confides.

"Oh, sweetie, your Pop will support you. He may feel a sting of disappointment at first, but he wants you to be happy. He wants you to do what inspires you. And if you are able to earn a living at something you enjoy, well, it's not really work then, is it?" Francesca proposes.

Gino, with a crooked smile relays, "I guess you are right. Okay, I will discuss it at dinner this evening."

"That sounds splendid." Francesca says smiling at her son.

"Hey, you haven't told me, how was your lunch with the Chamberlains?" inquires Gino.

"Oh, well...," Francesca shakes her head. "Let's just say, the prince behaved badly. If he were our son, I would have gotten a twig."

"Yeah, I remember just your threat to us getting 'twigged' shaped our attitudes about obeying." Gino chuckles. "I can't remember once you ever actually swatted us, but we believed you would have if we didn't straighten up."

"Well, nobody in the castle has a bluff on Rupert. I believe he is going to be maniacal and a real challenge for the king and queen," Francesca determines.

Just then, a twig is wisping through the air directly toward Francesca. Startled, she grabs it.

Francesca and Gino exchange a puzzling look. Francesca then turns her attention to the Aspen trees southwest of their location, while Gino thoroughly sweeps the area investigating each leaf, bush, flower, tree, and rock he sees.

Francesca places her hand on Gino's knee. "Do not be afraid. I sense the presence of a supernatural being in the trees across the river. Actually, now that I think of it, I felt a strong urge to come to the river this morning and have you accompany me. I wonder if it lured us here in an attempt to communicate," Francesca ponders.

"I can feel a faint presence, like we're being watched," expresses Gino.

"I actually brought a thermos full of hot chocolate, would you like a refill?" Francesca asks.

Just then the mug Gino had set on a rock becomes airborne along with the thermos. The lid of the thermos unscrews and pours hot chocolate into Gino's mug. The lid, lingering in the air, screws itself back onto the thermos, the thermos returns to the location Francesca had placed it, and Gino's full mug gently breezes to his hand.

Gino jumps up and astonishes, "How did that happen?"

Francesca stands, "It appears the invisible presence we both perceive possesses magical powers," Francesca conjectures.

Gino nods. "I sense there are two life forces. They radiate a peacefulness I am experiencing in gentle waves." Gino pauses for a few moments, "Okay, this is just weird."

"Whoever they are, they seem to desire to communicate with us here. This must remain our secret, Gino, at least for the time being." Francesca conveys. "Maybe they're evaluating us. Testing our ability of discerning their presence."

"Do you think they are from God?" Gino delves.

"I believe all beings, and things on Soleil and in the universe are created by God," Francesca adamantly delivers.

With a little laugh, Gino declares, "Well, this is fascinating, but a little unsettling to say the least."

Francesca exchanges a little laugh, smiling at Gino, "At least we're seeing the same things. And it's not a mirage."

Gino nods at his mother and grins.

"Hello. We are here and are aware of your presence," Francesca loudly says into the air.

Gino begins to walk around keenly scouting different directions. "I don't see anything. I wonder if they just wanted to let us know they are here. Maybe they are testing our response of knowledge of them."

"It's puzzling. As much as I want to stay, you have chores, and I have a full day myself," asserts Francesca.

"Maybe, they are our guardian angels." Gino imagines.

Chapter 19

SEPTEMBRIA 1537

Francesca relishes in the scenic beauty her surroundings behold and the majestic Chianne Mountain range that crosses and runs through her property. Gratefulness fills her spirit as she relaxes in the Chamberlain Park gazebo on the southwest side of town. Fall colors of red, yellow, and orange decorate the trees. The park provides an agreeable location for families to enjoy pleasant fall temperatures and the beauty of the landscape. *What an inspiring spot to plan a festival with Queen Eloise,* Francesca thinks.

Francesca knows that in eight short days the Annual Chamberlain Fall Around Festival will transform this peaceful environment into a bustling mass of busyness. Delicious food, fun and friends from across the kingdom and neighboring kingdoms will come together to renew bonds of friendship and create new ones.

Queen Eloise waves at Francesca as she approaches the gazebo. Nearing the gazebo Prince Rupert breaks free of his mother's grasp running toward Francesca with a menacing glare. He stops in front of Francesca raising his foot to kick her.

Francesca calmly looks Rupert in the eyes shaking her head. His leg stops mid-air. Francesca reaches down shaking his hand, "I'm glad to see you today." Her polite manner momentarily removes all mischief. "Did you bring a toy?" Francesca asks the prince.

Rupert nods, pulling a horse out from behind his back. "Horsey."

Francesca smiles at Rupert, "What a nice horsey."

Queen Eloise bends down in front of Rupert smiling. You may go play with the other children. Nanny Carol will be with you. I will be right here, sweetie."

Rupert nods reaching for Carol's hand.

"Thank you, Francesca, for remembering Rupert's third birthday. He loves the wooden toybox. It certainly showcases Gino's skills. He puts all his toys in it on his own," Queen Eloise shares.

"You're certainly welcome. Gino is quite proud of his exquisite horse design on the lid. We completely understand why you didn't want a party this year, but wanted to drop a gift by," Francesca responds.

"Yes, thank you so much. This is the first time we have come to the park when other children are here. I will try to keep focused on our agenda and not worry too much," Queen Eloise sighs.

"It'll be fine. Shall we begin?" enlists Francesca.

"Yes. Okay, so the Annual Fall Around Festival is so important to me mainly because it is the king's birthday. And what better way to celebrate our great king than with an annual party. I am clueless this year on ideas though, Francesca. The stress of seeking medical treatment for Rupert, among other things, has left me frazzled. I know you will be able to pull it together, making it extraordinary, no matter what kind of year you have," Eloise affirms.

Briefly bowing her head, Francesca addresses, "Thank you for belief in my abilities. Show me your list and I will review what you have."

Carol escorts Rupert over to the playground equipment. Rupert loves climbing and jumping. He gradually distances himself from Carol through the different equipment. He reaches the merry-go-round, then pushes a little girl down. Rupert glances at Francesca, who he sees is looking at him sternly shaking her head no. Rupert just stares at Francesca. A filmy, black cloud forms above the prince's head. Carol helps the little girl to her feet and apologizes to the mother who gathers their things and leaves.

Francesca is side-tracked from the queen's list, *that looks like the same cloud at lunch the other day. Can no one else see it? Why can I see it? I sense it is evil.*

"Eloise, do you see a shadow near Rupert?" Francesca searches.

"What?" Eloise's overprotective nature causes her to jump up to rescue her child; she looks and sees him happily swinging as Carol gently pushes him. "Oh, thank goodness. It must have just been some stirred up dirt, Francesca," the queen sighs with relief.

Francesca normally enjoys event planning strategy sessions with Eloise, but today she finds herself preoccupied with Rupert. As long as Francesca keeps eye

contact with Rupert frequently, the cloud remains above his head, and Rupert plays as a normal three-year-old. However, when Francesca focuses on the festival planning with Eloise, the cloud dims, and Rupert's antisocial behavior escalates as his eyes darken.

"Francesca, you seem preoccupied. Nevertheless, I think we've managed to complete the important items on my list." Eloise folds her notes placing them in her bag. "I'll recruit servants to assist me with these tasks tomorrow. As always, it's been a delight to be with you."

Francesca is almost deaf to Eloise's words. Her attention is on Rupert holding a rock in his hand gripped into a fist. The cloud above his head has vanished. His eyes are dark. A deranged look displays on his face. With a maniacal grin he pulls his arm back ready to hurl the stone at the little boy sitting on the grass. Carol is just to the other side of the sand pile where children are laughing and building sand castles, just out of reach to grab Rupert.

Francesca is scrambling her brain for an idea on how to stop the prince from injuring a child. Francesca's concern takes charge. *Is it possible I can do something to stop him from this distance?* She places her hands on her cheeks, gently shakes her head, then releases her hands into the air.

Instantaneously, a whirlwind filled with fall leaves swiftly descend down from a large tree on the prince. He drops the rock, whimpering.

Francesca stands in astonishment, then repositions her body to a tall, confident stance, letting a breath out. *I did it! I can think about this later.* She quickly refocuses to Eloise and Rupert.

Eloise runs to Rupert. Kneeling down to hug him, "My poor baby! It's only leaves, honey." She takes his hand walking him by Francesca, then hands him to Carol to load into the carriage. Rupert positions his head with each step, not taking his eyes off of Francesca.

Queen Eloise pivots, "Francesca, thank you for your help. Can you meet next Friday to help assemble the children's baskets for the festival?"

Francesca nods.

Chapter 20

RUPERT'S ARSENAL IS GROWING

Francesca gently urges Honor out of the driveway onto the main road. The wagon is full of supplies for the Chamberlain Fall Around baskets the queen will present to the children entering the park during the festival.

Francesca's thoughts wander, What a beautiful autumn day! I should be riding Lady. Marco and I used to ride so often. I miss you, Marco. I'm too busy. I like being at home on our property. Baking, preparing meals. And here I am again, volunteering. Ug. Now I sound selfish. I'm not selfish. I miss being at home more. I miss Marco. This is the first fall without him. I'm not going to schedule any outside activities for an entire week. Is that possible? Yes. Francesca feels peace with the magnificent autumn colors surrounding her. She also feels tired.

As she approaches the castle drive her thoughts shift to Rupert. So, it seems when a filmy, dark cloud appears above Rupert's head, his black eyes lighten in color, and his behavior is that of a normal child his age. When the cloud disappears, his eyes turn black and his behavior is outrageous. What is occurring? Why am I the only one that sees the cloud? Everyone sees Rupert's changing eye color. If I can unravel the logistics of the cloud, perhaps I can help the king and queen understand, and preempt the prince's misbehaviors.

John takes control of Honor, and oversees the unloading of the wagon when Francesca arrives at the castle. Andrew escorts Francesca to the dining room where the staff are organizing items on the table to be distributed into the baskets.

Prince Rupert jumps from behind the door in hopes to startle Francesca. She first feigns his surprise and then steps toward him to give him a hug. The prince side steps her arm, running around the table hooting.

"Carol came down with a cold, so I brought Rupert to help us," explains Queen Eloise. "He's super excited to be among the activity." She watches her son grab a basket and run into the hall circling back into the dining room.

When the prince's black eyes lock on Francesca's eyes, a small cloud begins forming above Rupert's head. Francesca kneels to his level, resulting in the cloud increasing in size. Francesca reaches her hands toward Rupert. The cloud darkens as he walks closer to her.

"Rupert, please sit on my lap. You can help me tie the bows on the baskets," Francesca demonstrates making a half knot. "Place your finger here please, so I can finish the bow."

Rupert obeys.

"Excellent! What a big help you are!" Francesca pats Rupert's pudgy leg. His face shines with a genuine smile looking up sweetly into Francesca's eyes as if he is in love.

"Would you like to hear a story while we tie the rest of the bows?" Francesca asks.

Rupert's eyes dance. Francesca recites her son Marco's favorite childhood tales and the tension in the room subsides. Baskets are soon completed and carried to the royal wagon which will be parked in the barn overnight.

"Rupert, please carry this basket to the wagon for me. I will carry these two," Francesca and the prince pick up the three remaining baskets.

The castle staff spread cloths covering the wagon bed protecting the baskets until the festival.

"Join us in the drawing room for refreshments," Eloise grabs Rupert's hand for the short walk to the castle.

"Thank you for helping. You're very good with Rupert. Will you teach me your secret?" requests the queen.

A number of thoughts quickly soar through Francesca's mind. Today is the first day I truly comprehend that an evil force controls the prince. Just devastating. It astonishes me that in my presence, the sinister formation appears above Rupert when I have his complete attention. Maybe the life forces at the river weren't showing us they have magical powers, maybe they were trying to convey to me that I possess some type of extraordinary, supernatural ability. So much to take in. What is going on? The prince is going to be a real problem I suspect.

"Eloise, lemonade sounds refreshing, but I must be on my way. Just engage Rupert in the activities you do. Enlist the king to do the same," Francesca recommends.

John is standing by the Mancini wagon while the two ladies say their goodbyes. Suddenly, Rupert runs from behind a tree with a branch in his hand. His eyes are black as coal. His face looks frightening. He swings the branch striking Honor while yelling. The startled horse rears twice.

"No!" screams Eloise.

John runs in hopes to protect Rupert from the rearing horse.

Francesca recognizes an evil presence has taken over Rupert.

Francesca hears clear instructions in her head, not knowing the source. Following them, she reacts unemotionally calling, "Rupert. Look at me." She locks her sight on Rupert's eyes, while her hands reach out mimicking holding Honor's reins. She pulls back in her direction, the reins become taut. Even though no one hears her speak, Honor hears her thoughts, "Whoa, Honor. It's okay, boy. I have you."

Honor stomps his right front hoof, shaking his head, then settles waiting for Francesca to mount the wagon.

Queen Eloise swoops her son into her arms hugging him, "Rupert dear, you mustn't swing branches at animals or anyone. It scares them."

Rupert's eyes darken once again. His lips curl in a maleficent grin.

As Francesca instructs Honor to leave, she looks back seeing them standing there. She feels heartbreak for the queen, and fears Rupert's arsenal of defiance and malice is growing.

Chapter 21

MYSTERY ON MANCINI MOUNTAIN

Antonio closes the kitchen cabinet door. He has just set out plates for his family to enjoy a Saturdei breakfast together. The three Mancinis dish up their delicious scrambled eggs, peppered bacon, spicy-seasoned sausage patties, and some toast in the kitchen, then go sit at the dining room table.

"Well, it's nice to dish up in the kitchen sometimes," Gino mentions.

Smiling, Antonio agrees, "Yes, it is."

"Gino and I should be back by around four. I'm looking forward to seeing the horses Sully purchased when he was away," Antonio shares.

"Hey, I'm excited because tonight is game night. What are you going to do today, mom?" asks Gino.

Francesca smiles, "Well, I'm going to clean up, prepare dinner, then ride Lady, maybe up to the lake."

"Our lake?" Antonio quizzes in his deep voice.

"Well, yes. It is so beautiful this time of year. The fall colors, the scent of the pines, yes, I do believe it's calling me," Francesca beams.

"Don't you think it's a bit far by yourself?" Antonio presses.

Gino inquisitively observes his parents.

"Dear," she pauses and is mindful that at times, Antonio's protective nature kicks in because he lost his parents when he was young. "I know it is about an hour away, but it'll be a great ride. It'll help me regroup. I have been feeling tired, and like I have been too busy," Francesca reveals. "If you're really not comfortable, I'll put off my ride until you can join me," she suggests.

"No, no, I know you'll be fine. Enjoy your day, sweetie," Antonio affirms.

Francesca stands, taking her plate and utensils to the kitchen, "Gino, what game would you like to play tonight?"

"Oh, I don't know. I'm sure we will come up with something great!" Gino attests.

Antonio and Gino follow Francesca to the kitchen, assisting with cleanup.

Antonio reaches for Francesca bringing her close to him, chest to chest, wrapping her ever so firmly in an embracing hug, "I love you," he whispers in her ear.

Francesca looks up a bit, kissing him, "I love you, too." She steps back, "Okay now, you two skedaddle, and I will see you and the Carlisles later. Game night! Woohoo!" Francesca exclaims with energy in her voice.

Gino smiles, with his little laugh. His eyes twinkle looking at his mother.

The two Mancini men grab their jackets and head out the back. Francesca tosses the dishtowel on the counter grabbing her jacket, "Hang on, I'll walk with you guys." Gino and Francesca lead their horses out of the stable after saddling them, Gino looks at his mother with inquisitiveness, "The lake, then prepare dinner?"

Francesca looks at her son, "Yes," she lowers her voice to barely audible, "I have been sensing a strong presence again. I'm going to see if I can locate it today. I feel it is near our lake." She pauses, "Then I will prepare dinner. I know I will feel rushed, but I want to take off now."

Gino's eyes widen, his head shakes, "Are you sure about this?"

"Perfectly. All will be well," assures Francesca placing her hand firmly on his arm. "Go enjoy the day with your Pop. I will see you guys soon," Francesca kisses her son on the cheek.

Antonio comes out of the stable with his horse, Chief, "Let's go, Son." Looking at his wife, he nods goodbye, and shoots her a wink.

Antonio and Gino ride off south toward the Carlisles. Francesca sets out west to the trail taking her by the river up the mountain to Mancini Lake. Lady gallops some, then slows to trot, and eventually to a walk once they reach the winding trail.

Francesca can hear the sounds of twigs under hoof, the leaves rustling in the gentle breeze, and the river flowing, even though it is down some at this time of year. She inhales a deep breath, smelling the fall air, exhaling a litany of things she is thankful for. She then begins singing in an upbeat pace, almost with an island beat, *Everywhere I go, I take you with me. Everything I do, I want to share with you. Not a day goes by, when you don't cross my mind, forever in my heart, I love you.* "Now Lady, where are we going, let me see," Francesca talks out loud, stops Lady briefly to remain in touch with her senses. Veering off to the right on a narrow trail, Francesca and Lady continue on. Mancini Lake is on their left. *We have been on this trail a few times through the years,* Francesca recalls.

After walking probably another twenty minutes, what seemed much longer, Francesca brings Lady to a stop. She looks around. "Well, I'll be…. Lady, I think we found it," Francesca says out loud. Dismounting Lady, she takes the reins in her hand leading Lady on a narrow walking path toward where she is sensing a strong presence through the cover of trees.

Francesca ties Lady's reins to a tree.

"Hello, hello, is anyone around?" Francesca calls out walking toward a garden she sees. "Hello?"

Francesca stops and studies her surroundings. And then, she sees it, as if it just magically appeared before her eyes; a cabin, built with tall aspens placed vertically. The roof is a stonecrop roof.

Foliage, shrubs, plants, branches, leaves, and the vertical placement of each log disguise this treasure of a cabin. It is picturesque.

Francesca walks over to the door and raises her arm to knock on the door. From the side of the cabin, a woman, with light brown, hip length, flowing hair appears holding a basket of berries. "May I help you?" she inquires.

A startled Francesca turns and sees her, "Well yes. I…I…I guess I was expecting something, I mean someone else."

"Oh honey," the lady gently laughs, "Come with me." She opens her front door leading Francesca into her home.

"This is quite elegant, and simple," notices Francesca. "And those berries look delicious, but berries at this time of year? I can't get any to grow this late."

Setting her basket of berries down in her kitchen, she invites, "Come on in, we will sit over here. Does your horse need water?"

"Yes, that would be much appreciated," Francesca acknowledges.

"Well, let's take care of your horse first, then we will visit, shall we?" The lady picks up a bucket near her back door, then she fills it with water from the yard hydrant.

"Here, let me help you, a bucket of water can be quite heavy," Francesca insists.

The mysterious woman lets Francesca carry the bucket of water to Lady.

The two women return into the cabin, and sit looking out the view the back of her cabin displays.

"What brings you out here? Are you lost?" the five-foot-three-inch, soft spoken female quizzes.

"Well, no…I'm not lost, I…well you may think this is silly. I sensed you," discloses Francesca.

Laughing ever so gently, the lady questions, "You sensed me? Does my scent carry down this mountain?"

Blushing, Francesca answers, "No, I'm so sorry. I'm embarrassed. I should go," Francesca stands.

"Francesca, please sit down. I have been looking forward to this day," the intriguing lady says. Her words astonish Francesca.

Francesca slowly sits back down searching the eyes of the lady who sits across from her. "You know my name?" queries Francesca.

"I do, honey," the woman tenderly smiles.

"How…how do you know me? Did you lead me here to meet you?" Francesca questions.

"So many questions. So many answers. Francesca, now you may think this sounds silly, but you have a special gift. Like sensing my presence so strongly, it led you here. I was best friends with your great-grandmother and grandfather, and also Antonio's great-grandparents," the lady divulges.

With a little laugh, Francesca states, "That cannot be, why, they…they are all passed from this life, but look at you…"

"Francesca, my name is Genie Arabella A'mato. I was best friends with Antonio's great-grandmother, Aurora Giada Mancini, and his great-grandfather, William Arquette Mancini. I was also best friends with your great-grandparents, Anna Grace Casella, and Dimitri Nicholas Casella. You may call me Arabella. For some reason my parents liked calling me Arabella, so that kind of stuck."

"Okay, so you know the names, you could have known that from history. How…why are you here, on our property? And how can it be possible you are still alive when you say you were best friends with them?" resounds Francesca.

Arabella reaches to Francesca, placing her hand on Francesca's arm, sliding it down to her hand, "I know you have many questions. Your special sense led you here. Your gifted perception, Francesca, has been growing in strength each day of your life. I'm sure you recognize something special, unique about yourself. This is my home. William, Aurora, Dimitri, Anna, and I built it. William said he wanted to build a cabin for us all to enjoy, up here, away from everyone, and that it was to be my cabin, my home, a place they would visit often, until they passed away. Your grandparents came here as well," smiling, reminiscing of memories Arabella continues, "we used to be called the 3 A's. Actually, a couplet was made up,

'Anna, Aurora, and Arabella, a guy with them is the luckiest fella.' My fella, my husband was Gabriel A'mato. Gabe, William and Dimitri were out doing some work in the field, when a horrible storm came up; the winds blew with such force, a limb flew through the air hitting Gabe, ending his life. After that day, William told me they will build me a cabin on their property, and when I pass, it would just be used as a getaway cabin, or retreat. Guess what?" Arabella says in her quirky voice, with her palms up and slightly lifting her shoulders, "I'm still here. So, knowledge of this cabin went to the grave with all of them. I held you for a moment at your great-grandmother's funeral. You nestled right into my shoulder," Arabella recounts.

"I...I...Just don't know what to say. I do believe you. I can feel you. But your age? You appear, well you look not much older than me!" Francesca declares.

"I won't go into it at this time, but what has given you the gift of being able to sense things, is the same thing that gave me the gift of appearing this age forever, I'm guessing. I really don't know," Arabella surmises.

"But you're by yourself up here? All these years? How could no one notice?" questions Francesca. "How do you manage?"

"Well, yes, I am by myself, but then again, I have a very full life. I grow all my own fruits and vegetables. And I am able to hunt when I need meat. I make remedies with natural herbs and berries," Arabella shares, "and now, you finally found me," with an endearing smile, reaches to touch Francesca's knee.

Francesca smiles, "I actually need to be heading back. We're hosting a game night tonight. Come with me."

"Thank you, dear. Not tonight. Maybe...sometime," Arabella considers.

As Francesca walks out, she looks back to the cabin and Arabella, and says, "I still don't get how nobody, anybody, in all these years has not seen you or your cabin."

Arabella stands with her arms outstretched toward the sky, "Sometimes, we don't see things that are visibly there, until we are ready, then they are visible, clear as day," ascertains Arabella in her entrancing, mysterious demeanor. "When we built this, we all agreed not to mention it to anyone, and built it with a design that would be inconspicuous."

"May I share with others about you?" asks Francesca.

"Do what you're led to do, but remember, there will be an aftereffect either way. Whether you share, or whether you don't, maybe for the better, maybe not. There is always an outcome," Arabella concludes.

Francesca turns and walks toward Lady, then turns abruptly to Arabella, dashing to her, and gives Arabella a big hug. "Thank you, Arabella," Francesca smiles, "I will visit you again."

Francesca gets on Lady.

"I'm always a thought away," suggests Arabella.

Francesca curiously smiles, tipping her head to the left at the words Arabella spoke. Urging Lady slowly down the narrow path to the main trail. Arabella's words, 'I'm always a thought a way' replay, resonating in Francesca's mind.

Chapter 22

GAME NIGHT

Francesca arrives home, thinking to herself, *plenty of time to prepare a fabulous dinner and dessert.* "Well, Lady, that was quite an adventure we had," Francesca rubs Lady's face after unsaddling her, then leads her into the paddock.

Francesca walks inside, makes herself something to eat, and gets out the meat and other items for dinner. *I think I will make Pepper & beef soup tonight, hmmm, how about some homemade cinnamon rolls...* Francesca contemplates.

A few hours later Gino and Antonio walk through the door. "Mm, something smells delicious," Gino expresses with his mouth-watering.

Antonio says, "Smells like your mother's pepper soup and homemade cinnamon rolls."

Francesca steps into the kitchen, smiling, "Yes, I thought it would be easy for dinner before we play games."

"Fine idea," Antonio confirms.

The guys go and clean up. About an hour later, Sullivan, Katherine, Ben, and Luke arrive.

"Oh, Francesca, yum, I can't wait to eat!" declares Katherine with a smile.

The Carlisles and Mancinis take their places at the dining room table. It sits perfectly in the dining room for all to enjoy the beautiful view out the large picture window in the family room.

"Well, tell me about the horses," Francesca requests.

"Sully made another great deal," Antonio acknowledges.

"Well, thank you. I thought they would be a great addition," Sully gauges, "Hey, will you pass me some more soup, please."

Katherine smiles, "And I would like another scrumptious cinnamon roll, please. How was your ride today, Francesca? Antonio mentioned you went on a ride to the lake. I don't know how you have time to bake, and ride," chuckles Katherine.

Passing the tray of cinnamon rolls to Katherine, Francesca replies, "Well, I actually had a very nice ride. It was peaceful. The weather was perfect. Probably one of our last beautiful days," assumes Francesca.

"Well, I'm glad you were able to get a ride in, and have time for this incredible dinner," Katherine affirms.

"Thank you," Francesca smiles.

You can hear the spoons in the soup bowls as they empty, the ice hitting the sides of the glasses while they drink, and the scooting of the chairs when everyone gets up to carry their plates to the kitchen.

"I am going to help you with clean-up really quick. The guys can select the game," Katherine directs.

"I appreciate that, thank you," Francesca responds.

The two women can hear the guys in the other room, "How about The Ship Sailed?" Ben suggests.

"No, I like, Mystery in the Mine," Luke contends.

"I think we should play charades. Your mom cracks me up when she plays," Gino claims.

"Francesca, I didn't know your son got such a hoot out of me when I play charades," giggles Katherine.

"Charades it is," Sully takes command, with a brisk wave of his hand, like a handshake in the air. "Let the games begin," leads Sully.

......⚬⟋⟍⚬......

"Another wonderful night with our best friends," Francesca exhales snuggling into the embrace of Antonio watching the Carlisles leave.

"Let's go inside," Antonio suggests, leading Francesca, their arms around each other's waists.

"Mom, how was your ride? Did you see anything?" Gino asks sitting sprawled out on a comfortable chair in the family room.

"See anything? Were you expecting to see something?" inquires Antonio.

Francesca quickly glances to Gino; she lets her arm down from Antonio's waist and sits on the sofa. "I actually did. Have you ever heard of Genie Arabella A'mato?" asks Francesca.

"No, I can't say that name rings a bell," Antonio answers.

"Maybe just Arabella A'mato?" Francesca poses, dropping the first name.

"No, no, can't say the that I have heard of that name either," states Antonio.

"Well, she says, well, never mind what she says. She is living in a cabin your great-grandparents built. It's up past Lake Mancini off Eagle Ridge Trail," Francesca discloses.

"What? You went up to Eagle Ridge Trail? That is a pretty narrow trail. Did I hear you say there is a cabin up there?" exclaims Antonio in his rugged, deep voice.

Smiling, Francesca reasons, "Yeah, I haven't been on Eagle Ridge Trail for years. It actually wasn't too bad. Yes, there is a cabin. Your great-grandparents, Aurora, and William built. Actually, Arabella said my great-grandparents and she also helped."

"Back up, we have somebody living on our property, without permission, and didn't even know there was a cabin there?" Antonio utters disbelief.

"Oh, this is cool. Why did we never see the cabin? We used to hike that trail when we were kids. I remember you two taking Marco and I up there sometimes to see the view," Gino chimes in.

"It actually was cool. A bit unnerving," Francesca shares tilting her head slightly. "When I asked her the same question, how did none of us see this cabin before, she answered, sometimes we don't see things that are visibly there, until we are ready; then they are visible," reveals Francesca.

"Sweet! That's like a real mystery. Forget the game, Mystery in the Mine, we have the real deal, Mystery on the Mountain!" Gino excitedly cheers.

Antonio looks over to his son, "Will you calm down? Are you okay with someone we don't know living on our property?"

"Well, no Pop, but you have to admit, this is intriguing. Tell us more, Mother," Gino pleads.

"Arabella said, if I share, or if I don't share, either way will have an outcome. Good or bad," confides Francesca. "But you are not going to believe this; she says she was best friends with my great grandparents, Anna Grace, and Dimitri Nicholas Casella, as well as yours."

"I don't know how that can be. Our great-grandparents are long passed," Antonio rationalizes.

"Dimitri? I like that name. If I have a son, I will name him that!" Gino declares.

"I found her to be of sound mind, and good natured. She grows her own food. She said she held me when I was a little girl at my great-grandmother's funeral. She told me that I have strong intuition. She said her husband Gabriel was killed by a limb that went airborne during a storm, while working with Dimitri and William. They were trying to get to shelter. The three couples were best friends. William told her he would build her a cabin where the families could all come and visit, but she could live in it until she passes. And that is that," surmises Francesca.

"That is that," Gino says with enthusiasm, "I think this is great! What a terrific story!"

"You aren't concerned in the least bit?" quizzes Antonio.

"I'm not," Francesca smiles.

"I'm not! She's got to be a very old woman. It would be wrong to turn her out. It would be against God, and all we have been taught," Gino addresses.

"Well, you're right there, son. Okay, I won't give it a second thought," surrenders Antonio, "I would like to meet her sometime."

......⚮......

"Viana, did you just hear that?" Victor is in shock.

In her crisp, caring voice, Viana confirms, "I did. We are going to have to inquire about this with the high priests. Possibly, Arabella was nearby when the two females were infused, perhaps at one of their homes?"

"I wonder if she knows about our existence? If she does, I am thankful she did not reveal us to Francesca yet," Victor articulates.

"I know, me too. We already have a full plate. I guess we can handle one more thing, if needed," Viana supposes. "Honestly, she must be a pretty special human to have lived this long on her own," Viana speculates.

"My question is, if she was near when the high priests sent their life force into the two separate bloodlines, and if she was in close proximity of one, why has she not passed away? Humans only live so long, even the original infused females have passed. How is this possible?" Victor queries.

"Another investigation for us to administer," formulates Viana.

......⚮......

Antonio is lying in bed watching Francesca undress. "Hey, you never told me how your day went with the queen and prince yesterday when you took the baskets to the palace."

Francesca sighs reaching for her nightshirt, "I think that is why I so desperately needed a ride and quiet time today," she pauses, slipping her gown on over her head, turning to Antonio. "The king and queen, have a real challenge on their hands. Honestly, you and Gino are correct in saying the prince has got to be the most disobedient child in the kingdom. While Eloise was giving me a hug goodbye, Rupert took a stick and swung it at Honor, striking him. It was a bit chaotic, but we were able to swiftly get the situation under control. Of course, the queen sweeps Rupert into her arms. My heart just aches for our dear friends."

Francesca climbs into their tall bed and lays back on her pillow in her soft pink and white striped flannel night shirt.

Antonio looks at her, "You know, I have to agree with what others have been telling you throughout the years."

"Oh? What's that?" asks Francesca.

"You're tough," Antonio states.

Francesca immediately frowns, "You think I'm tough?"

"My dear, you are the right blend of resilient and feminine," Antonio assures, moving the curls off her forehead, and sweetly kissing her lips.

Francesca reaches her arms around her husband.

"You complete me," Antonio tenderly whispers.

Francesca's spirit calms, "We better get some sleep, tomorrow is the king's birthday, and the Annual Fall Around."

Chapter 23

CAROLS STANDOFF WITH ALCHODOR

Over the next 15 months, some things change, yet some things remain the same.

Rupert's mischievous behaviors increase in frequency and severity.

The queen and Nanny Carol work as a team. Rupert responds well at times, mainly after an encounter with Francesca. Francesca always greets and departs the queen, Carol and Rupert with a hug during her brief visits. For some reason, when Carol receives a hug from Francesca, it's as if she receives an energy transference. A hug from Francesca empowers Carol, enabling her with strength to deal with the prince. One day, Carol even goes so far as to break a toy the prince enjoyed playing with. Rupert breaks his mother's dishes, and anything he can reach while running through the castle. Carol repeatedly tells Rupert if he breaks other people's property, she will break something of his...

"Rupert. Rupert honey, do not touch things that do not belong to you," Carol instructs in her crisp voice.

Rupert is having none of Carol's directions. He picks up a dish off of a table. He stands, glaring directly at Carol, and slams it on the floor causing it to shatter in tiny shards of glass. The queen enters the room. She abruptly stops in disbelief. Carol turns to glance at the queen, then refocuses her attention to Rupert. Carol is a prepared nanny. She pulls one of his favorite toys from her pocket that she totes in case she needs to resort to carrying out the consequence she forewarned Rupert about.

"Do you remember what I told you about touching and breaking other people's things?" Carol interrogates.

Rupert stands staring at Carol. "I think you do remember," Carol insists. She drops the toy to the ground, raises her foot while not breaking eye contact with the prince, then, with a hard stomp of her foot, smashes it.

The queen's mouth flies open, quickly being covered by her hands. Rupert runs to kick Nanny Carol at the moment Andrew brings Francesca in with the lemon-blueberry loafs she had promised the royals next time she came to town. Rupert abruptly ceases his outburst.

An awkward expression overtakes Andrew's face. The queen has a look of horror on her face. Francesca and Carol communicate with their eyes; Carol is saying, 'I've had enough,' and Francesca responds, 'I completely understand;' yet no words are spoken. The prince is beside himself. Infuriated. The prince thinks to himself, *how dare Carol!*

"Francesca, Andrew, will you please take Rupert from the room for a moment? I want to speak to Nanny Carol," Queen Eloise requests.

Francesca takes Rupert's hand escorting him out of the room. Andrew keeps his distance. Queen Eloise privately questions Carol about such a drastic measure. "Do you think your tactics are sound?" Interrogates the queen.

With confidence, Carol assures the queen, "Yes. I do believe extreme measures are necessary regarding your son. I have warned him about the consequences of purposely breaking items that do not belong to him."

Eloise calms down, nodding to Carol.

"I suppose I should have removed all of our keepsake glass knickknacks." offers Eloise.

"Absolutely not!" Carol resounds. "Rupert needs to learn to respect the belongings of others."

Queen Eloise and Carol walk out of the room and approach Francesca and Rupert who have been strolling down the hallway toward the great room.

"Francesca, Carol and I are going to take Rupert to his room. Will you please wait for us? I'd like to try a quick bite of that heavenly loaf you baked for us, if you have a few more minutes to spare." inquires Eloise.

"Yes, I'll wait." Francesca replies.

Eloise and Carol take Rupert to his room. Eloise picks up Rupert and sets him on his bed. "You lay down for a rest. We will be downstairs." Eloise kisses her son's forehead. Carol reaches for a blanket off the shelf to cover Rupert. The queen walks out of the room with Carol, in step behind, when the door mysteriously, instantaneously slams once the queen exits.

Eloise immediately spins back frantically trying to open the door, knocking. Not knowing how it closed she screams, "Let me in! Open this door!" *Is Carol going to spank my son?* She wonders as she continues pounding on the door.

Carol rotates, pressing her back against the door. At first, trembling in fear wondering how the door slammed closed. Then something from deep within her surfaces. She readjusts her stance to a tall, confident posture and stares at the prince who is standing on his bed with his arms outstretched toward the door.

"So, it is *you* that slammed the door." Carol denotes. Not giving the prince a chance to speak, she continues in a composed, stern voice, "Are you going to kill me, too? Fine. I do not fear death. I will then be with my husband. Take your best shot. I do not know who, or what you are, or if you are indeed the prince; but I can assure you if I end up harmed or dead, you will be removed from this kingdom and locked up where they place monstrous, little boys."

Meanwhile, the queen continues to relentlessly pound on the door, shouting. Andrew and Francesca run up the stairs to her aid.

"I thought Carol was right behind me. As soon as I stepped out of Rupert's room, the door slammed. Do you think she is paddling him? He does need a spanking. Oh, if only Theo was here." Eloise bewilders.

Francesca and Andrew's eyes meet with inquisitiveness. The queen is still beating the door.

"Shhh." Francesca reaches to Eloise's fists taking them in her hands. "Sweetie, do you hear Rupert crying? Don't you think if Carol was administering a lashing, he would be bawling?" Francesca calmly rationalizes.

Andrew places his hand on the back of Eloise in hopes to calm her as well.

Eloise stands there as if her entire world is crumbling. "You are right, but what could possibly be going on? Do you think Rupert fell?" the queen carries on.

"No matter what is transpiring, we will soon find out." Francesca adamantly states.

Rupert remains standing on his bed with his arms outstretched toward the door. The words Carol spoke resonate. The Cryptolore warlord that possesses Rupert drops Rupert's arms to his side, fearing imprisonment.

Instantly, the three outside the door hear the handle turn. The door opens, Eloise barges in. Francesca sees Carol posturing. Andrew watches the queen dart toward her son. All appears well.

Eloise swoops Rupert into her arms and hugs him. Francesca fixes her eyes on Rupert's eyes as he peers over his mother's shoulder toward the three adults in the doorway. Francesca does not blink. Rupert's blackened eyes soften to a light brown, then close, falling asleep in his mother's embrace. Francesca sees the eerie, black, filmy cloud lingering near the ceiling.

The four adults leave the room while Rupert naps. You can hear their footsteps swiftly descending the stairs. When the four reach the main level, Francesca turns to them, "I'm so sorry, I am out of time.

I'll be back in town probably next week. I can stop by then, for a few minutes, if you'd like. Give Theodore my best. Where is he?"

Andrew dismisses himself, "Excuse me, ladies, I have a castle to run. Francesca, as always, a pleasure to see you."

"Oh, dear Francesca, I know you must go. I'm so sorry. The king is off fishing, or riding, I don't see him too much these days. As each week passes, it seems I see less and less of him. We are just busy I guess," the queen discloses reaching to give Francesca a goodbye hug.

Carol voices, "If you don't mind, your highness, I will walk Francesca out. I need some fresh air."

The queen nods approval.

Carol and Francesca briskly walk to depart the castle walls.

"Ah, fresh air," inhales Carol.

"Yes," agrees Francesca.

"May I have a hug, Francesca?" Carol asks.

"Of course." Francesca responds wrapping Carol in her mama bear hug.

After a good hug, Carol confides, "For some reason, when you give me a hug, it is as if I feel renewed. I don't know how else to explain it. The strength I need to deal with Rupert. Thank you so much."

Francesca curiously replies, "You're welcome. Is everything okay from earlier? I wasn't there to witness what occurred; however, I sensed some sort of conflict was unfolding."

Carol stands solemnly, "Francesca, I have decided not to let Rupert scare me. If he kills me, he kills me."

Francesca retorts, "He's a child honey, he's not going to kill you."

"Don't be too sure of that, Francesca." Carol resolutely redirects.

"Too sure of what? That he is a child or that he is not going to kill you?" Francesca questions.

"Both." Carol's crisp voice penetrates, "Francesca, I am not sure that Rupert is Rupert. Maybe he is. Maybe he isn't. My speculations are solely based off my first-hand encounters with Rupert. If he is Rupert, he is an evil soul. If he isn't Rupert…well, whatever it is, is evil."

Francesca and Carol exchange another hug, then wave as Francesca climbs on her wagon and signals Honor to go home.

·······ᴄᴚᴏ·······

The king finds himself subconsciously distancing himself from family activities. He has a difficult time accepting that a child from his blood can be so malicious. His relationship with the queen is strained at times. Due to the misbehavior of Rupert, they are both embarrassed to invite friends over or attend an activity when invited. They have only brief encounters with the Mancinis when purchasing baked goods or horses. Mostly, they only see their friends at the quarterly Chamberlain Kingdom Festivals. Queen Eloise invariably looks forward to planning each one. It is an opportunity usually away from Rupert, if only for a bit, to plan festivities with Francesca.

Piper and Pixel continue on castle detail, generally frustrated their orders remain to observe only. Absolutely no interference.

Viana and Victor enjoy their assignment to the Mancinis. Francesca's intuitive ability amazes them. They gently guide her when they deem it necessary, continuing to be inconspicuous, but not confirming any of Francesca's suspicions. Viana and Victor also relish the closeness of the Mancini family.

Zeek and Razel are in the rugged mountain wilderness keeping an eye on the Cryptolores that inhabit a wolf pack.

·······ᴄᴚᴏ·······

"Poor wolves. I feel so sad for them." Razel exhales.

"Yeah. I do too." Zeek empathizes.

Zeek's attention immediately shifts, "Oooo, I love that rock! Look at all the colors!" Zeek excitedly exclaims as he picks up a rock near the river.

"A rock. I swear, now you sound like Francesca. Viana tells me Francesca LOVES her rocks. Viana says she's surprised the river isn't out of rocks because Francesca has carried so many up to their home to decorate gardens and walkways. Viana also tells me Francesca has even named a few! Good Grief. Silly human." Razel professes flinging her hands and arms about.

"Let's make an arc and look!" suggests Zeek.

Razel waves her arm in an arc, making the Mancini property visible. With a pinch and releasing of her index finger and thumb, their view zooms to the yard near the Mancini Ranch home.

"Ah, look at all those beautiful rocks. You can tell Francesca specifically set each one in a certain location for the most enchanting view." Zeek takes a deep breath slowly letting it out, "A human after my own heart," professes Zeek.

Razel immediately points directly to the river with a very firm stance and straight arm, "Look at yourself. You are four feet tall, Zeek! Francesca towers like what, five-feet-nine-inches?"

"Hmmm," Zeek raises his left arm to the sky outreaching with his left hand, stretching to an impressive six-feet-five-inches tall. "You were saying?" Zeek looks down to Razel with a proudly, taller stature.

Razel throws her hand to her forehead, pausing, "Okay, watch this." Razel moves her arm in a circular motion toward a dead tree limb. Then she whisks her hand over a flat area of ground. The limb divides into ten skinny twigs landing onto the ground in a triangle design. Razel then picks up a rock about the size of three grapefruits, moving it between her hands in a very fast movement. She then takes the rock, rolls it toward the sticks standing in a triangle formation, knocking all of them down. "Score!" Razel shines yellow.

Zeek says, "Now what is that? I think my height exhibition is more impressive." Zeek laughs.

Razel shakes her head, "It's called bowling. It's a game. I learned about it when I was doing a research project about Earth. I'm glad the high priest and priestess can't see us." She waves her arm closing the arc to the Mancini Ranch.

"Don't bet on it, Razel. Okay, your bowling game looks somewhat compelling. Let's bowl!" Zeek entreats.

Razel laughs.

......⟳⟲......

Observing through a large sphere, High Priestess Ammerie remarks, "It took longer than I anticipated, but they're at it. I knew those two together would at some point use their powers for entertainment. I'll overlook their silliness for now. Razel has good wit. She also truly feels empathy for every living thing. Zeek just finds it all fascinating. He's easily distracted from one quest to another, yet able to return to the main objective and deliver. They both are independently driven, each with a curious nature."

High Priest Akshai walks closer, taking position next to Ammerie, peering into the sphere. "Yes, they need some fun when they can; because there will be a time the Cryptolores will demand their full attention. Let's not forget the other teams." Almost laughing under his breath, High Priest Akshai continues, "Victor and Viana are a strong team."

"I see why you are laughing. Those two both have received the highest awards a Chiawauka can receive. They show respect for each other. They are very similar in their discipline. They're both extremely knowledgeable. Frankly, I'm surprised they even notify us before they deploy any strategic moves." High Priestess Ammerie surmises.

"I agree, I am sure on occasions during their mission, they disagree. I have no doubt they will each do what they think is right, as long as it doesn't jeopardize their assignment. They both follow the chain of command pretty well, though it won't shock me if they take matters into their own hands at times." High Priest Akshai speculates.

High Priestess Ammerie nods. "Piper and Pixel are quite a team."

"Yes. Now there's a team- I want to laugh out loud again. Piper, also, incredibly knowledgeable and wise regarding nearly everything. And Pixel...well Pixel wings it. She still lacks forbearance, but her passion is definitely an asset. She is completely spooked by the Cryptolores; however, Piper has a remarkable way of remaining patient with her, teaching her, and encouraging her without demeaning or breaking her spirit. I frankly don't believe any other Chiawauka at this time, would be so tolerant of Pixel." reflects High Priest Akshai.

"I agree Akshai. And even though Victor and Viana are both unreservedly confident, I think their personalities would overpower any other Chiawauka we would have paired them with. I believe we made correct decisions when assigning teams to Soleil," assesses High Priestess Ammerie.

High Priestess Ammerie, and High Priest Akshai close the sphere, and leave the observation room.

Chapter 24

A snowstorm mantles the landscape in a mesmerizing panorama of glistening white. Francesca removes her gaze from its beauty, wiping her hands on her seasonal print apron. She surveys her kitchen. The sourdough bread is set to rise. The scrumptious, lemon pound cake has cooled just enough to slice, and a fresh pot of coffee finishes brewing. *Ready for Antonio's mid-morning snack.* Francesca smiles. *Maybe I should make some sandwiches. I'm kind of hungry.*

At the sound of the back door opening, she shouts orders, "Be sure the snow is knocked off your boots. I don't want water puddles on my kitchen floor."

"What do you have to serve two hungry guys?" asks Antonio.

Francesca turns to greet her husband, "Two? Well look who the wind blew in." Francesca envelops Ben Carlisle in a big mama bear hug. "What brings you to the Mancini Ranch?"

Antonio laughs, "Nothing like being interrogated when you arrive. Sit. Enjoy whatever delicious snack my lovely wife has made."

Francesca pours a cup of coffee for Antonio, "It's so nice to see you, Ben." She relays while pouring a cup for Ben as well. Slicing the lemon pound cake, she places a piece on plates for the three of them.

"Ben dropped by this morning at an opportune time. Gino was just leaving for school. I enlisted Ben to help me finish up some chores." Antonio informs.

"I was glad to help you, Papa Mancini. Looks like Gino takes good care of Jolly. He seemed pretty tired heading off to school since he was up overseeing Jolly's foal last night." Ben recognizes.

"Yes. It went well. He named the new life, 'Jewel'." Antonio relays.

"I was at the castle yesterday for the meeting to assess the royal agricultural plans for the new farming year. As you know, my dad is the royal farm and ranch supervisor. He has everything humming along profitably. John's equestrian skills are unmatched, except for the exception of you, Papa Mancini. John has a remarkable love for handsome tack, elegant coaches, plus with his talents, he pleases both the king and queen. The big news is, I've been promoted to agronomy director. Now my dad can focus his attention on ranching." informs Ben.

"Congratulations Ben. The royals have apparently kept an eye on your knowledge placing you in a position that will best serve the kingdom." Francesca smiles, walking around the table to anoint Ben with another hug.

"Great news, Ben." Antonio confirms.

Clasping both hands to the coffee mug, "Thank you both. Okay. I have another reason why I'm here." Ben entrusts.

"An ulterior motive?" Francesca winks.

"You didn't come over to help me, or eat lemon cake?" Antonio jests.

"You guys." Ben laughs. "Since I now have a better job, I'm going to ask Laurie to marry me."

"It's about time, son," approves Antonio.

"A wedding!" Francesca smiles with glee. "Congratulations."

"Well…" Ben adds, "I'd like both of our parents to be present when I ask her, and I'm hoping it will be an unforgettable surprise. I did already ask Mr. Marshall for his permission to marry his daughter. He gave me his blessing."

"Sounds like you have everything under control. How can we help?" inquires Antonio.

"Mama Fran, will you please bake one of your delicious cakes? I thought I would place the engagement ring on top in the frosting as part of the decorations on the cake." Ben submits.

"I love it! How about a chocolate fudge cake, with a raspberry cupcake centered on top? Around the cupcake, on the main cake, I'll write out 'Marry Me' in red or pink frosting. I'll decorate with frosting flowers around the edges, and the top where you can set the ring." Francesca establishes.

"That sounds fantastic! Thank you so much, guys." Ben relaxes.

"Now, how are we going to get everyone together without raising suspicion?" Antonio wonders rubbing his chin.

"I've been giving that some thought as well. It's almost time for your monthly dinner and game night with my family. Can we expand it, inviting Laurie, her parents and sister?" Ben proposes. "And Laurie did join us last month, so she is familiar we have this once a month."

Francesca tilts her head, "Laurie may be suspicious. Let's invite the Gerard's as well. Actually, we could make it a dinner party in honor of your new promotion. Four Carlisles, three Mancinis, four Marshalls, and three Gerards. Laurie won't suspect a thing. I will contact the families and request everyone bring a dish."

"I can see why you've been promoted, Ben. It would appear you touch all bases." Antonio notes.

Chapter 25

L uke Carlisle arrives early to help Antonio and his best friend Gino shovel a walking path from the drive to the front door.

"We're lucky the wind died down last night. I was concerned it was going to turn into a blizzard like it has this time of year in the past." Antonio recalls.

"I love this fresh snow." Luke shares, following the others into the house to set up extra chairs and card game tables in the family room.

"You invited so many people over. Good thing we have a large dining and family room." Gino addresses his mother.

"I have never known Mama Mancini to do anything halfway." Luke hugs Francesca. "It'll be a great day. I'll have new people to conquer at games!"

"You're certainly confident, Mr. Luke" Francesca attests.

"Oh, I'm very confident it'll be a great day, and I will conquer someone at one of the games!" laughs Luke.

"Do you remember on one of our campouts at Mancini Lake, you were set on winning hide and seek?" Francesca asks.

"Yeah. I don't think I will ever forget. I hid in poison ivy. I was so itchy for days." Luke laughs. "But I won. No one found me. Well, no one said they found me because no one else wanted to get poison ivy. I won by default!" Luke boasts.

Francesca removes a hot casserole dish from the oven. "You won by default." laughs Francesca. "Okay, I'll give you that. That's hilarious." smiling as she sets the dish on a pot holder on the dining room table.

"Sully, Katherine and Ben just pulled in," Antonio announces. "Gino and Luke, I see Doctor Gerard and his family pulling in the drive. Will you young men please escort them in? You can help them carry food in," directs Antonio.

Gino hollers to Antonio, "Pop, the Marshalls are also coming up the drive. Luke and I will help Mrs. Marshall and Lila with their dishes for dinner as well."

"I'm sure Ben is going to be mushy with Laurie," Luke teases.

"We'll be inside soon. The men and I are taking the horses to the stables," informs Antonio.

Within minutes, everyone gathers at the handcrafted Mancini dining room table where they fill their plates with food, and sit.

Antonio stands, "I'd like to thank everyone for gathering with us today, gracing us with your presence. After dinner, we will retreat to the family room for stories and games, and a dessert Francesca baked to spoil us with. Let's bow our heads for the blessing."

Everyone is enjoying all the dishes each family brought. Sully stands. "I would like to thank our hosts." Claps and cheers fill the room. "Now if you don't mind, I'd like to begin telling a story. It makes me smile every time I think of it." Pausing, checking for expressions, he sits back down. "Marco and Ben, boy could they create mischief. When our sons were young, our two families would often go to Mancini Lake on Mancini Mountain. It sits next to Chianne Mountain, in the Chianne Mountain range. Anyway, sometimes our wives would join us, sometimes not...." Sully took a breath.

"Oh, let me tell the marshmallow story," Luke chimes in.

Sully smiles and motions outward with a wave from the top-side of his hand for his youngest son to continue.

"Do you remember, Gino? You wanted one of my flawlessly roasted marshmallows. We struggled over the stick my two marshmallows were on, and one went sailing, landing on your Pop's fishing basket."

"Yeah, I believed you should share, since one of mine fell on the ground. Flying through the air fanned the flames on the marshmallows to a full burn by the time they landed." remembers Gino.

Luke laughs, "You grabbed the water bucket we kept near the campfire."

"As I recall," Antonio's deep voice overtakes the story, "My fishing basket was near me. So not only did the bucket of water drench my basket, my leg was also soaked." Antonio shakes his finger at the two teenagers. "Good thing it was a warm evening. After the shock of cold, mountain lake water in my lap, I found it humorous."

Raising his hand, a bit, "Now, to resume with my story." Sully continues. "Ben was thirteen, Marco ten, making Gino and Luke, eight. As we set up camp, Marco and Ben kept hiding behind the trees, leaping out and scaring their younger brothers. When night began to fall, against our better judgement, Antonio and I allowed Ben and Marco to tell spooky stories around the campfire. By the time we all turned in, the younger boys' imagination ruled. Every noise in the forest we heard, even the faintest, they were peering out from their bed rolls. We heard owls hooting, creatures tromping through the woods, and finally a wolf call. Then Ben and Marco slung open our tent yelling 'Boo!' Antonio and I were even startled."

Ben guffaws, "We sure got you guys. Marco and I had been practicing our owl hoots, and wolf calls for weeks before our campout. Stomping on leaves and twigs, we planned every step."

"Well, Ben, from our discussion earlier, I see you were a young age when you began making sure every base is touched, no stone unturned." Antonio recognizes Ben's promotion. "A natural ability at an early age of planning, and executing."

Ben smiles.

Mark Marshall shakes his head. "Raising boys is quite different from girls. I'm sure Doctor George and Laverne will agree. But then, precious Gwen is only four." Mark smiles at George and Laverne. My major worry is paying the bill to keep my daughters in the latest fashions." Mark winks at his youngest daughter, Lila, who playfully wrinkles her nose at him.

Ben pats Laurie's hand when her eyes narrow at her father's teasing. "That's just not so," Laurie protests with an innocent smile.

"Laurie, your dad is just teasing." Ben leans to whisper in Laurie's ear.

Antonio stands after everyone has finished eating. "Let's adjourn to our family room for games and dessert."

Francesca asks Ben, Luke, and Gino to assist her in the kitchen. Everyone else heads to the family room.

Francesca hands Gino a platter of cupcakes. She hands Luke a tray with dessert size plates, forks and napkins. "Please pass these out," she directs both boys. "Ben, I'll have you carry this cake platter with the silver dome into the family room." Francesca winks at Ben.

Gino and Luke take on the role of waiters at an elegant restaurant, transitioning what they were carrying in front of them to atop their shoulders with only one hand underneath for support.

Francesca subtly shakes her head watching Gino and Luke's antics.

Francesca is behind Ben now. She firmly places each of her hands on each of his arms softly speaking, "It'll be okay. Now act like you own this." She gently releases her grip from his arms.

Gino and Luke split, allowing Ben to walk up the center, since he has the main cake. At least, that is what they think.

As Ben passes them by, Luke taps the silver dome lid, "Get with the program, carry it up in the air on one hand, like us."

Ben's attention is momentarily averted, his hands becoming unlevel and the cake platter begins to slip.

Under Francesca's keen observance, she reaches with her hand toward the platter, undetectable to the others, slowing its descent, allowing Ben to secure it in his hands once again.

Ben shoots a look of astonishment at Francesca, followed by a piercing glare toward his younger brother Luke.

Francesca quietly encourages Ben, "Serve your dessert first, please."

Ben turns around from Laurie quickly, examining underneath the dome lid making sure the ring is still intact. A smile of relief and peace comes over him. Circling back toward Laurie, he catches an approving nod from Mr. Marshall and a smile of anticipation from Mrs. Marshall.

Ben kneels in front of Laurie, setting the platter in Laurie's lap. Peering into her eyes, Ben removes the lid.

Laurie gasps, and glances at Ben. She then stares at the exquisite engagement ring set perfectly amongst the words, 'Marry Me'. She gingerly picks it up licking the scrumptious frosting off the ring, "Yes, I'll marry you, Benjamin William Carlisle!" Laurie exclaims.

Chapter 26

GINO MEETS CLAIRE

The next morning you can hear Francesca stirring sugar in her mug of hot tea while she's sitting wrapped in the warmth of a heavy blanket on her porch swing that adorns the back deck.

"I knew I'd find you out here," the depth of Antonio's voice fills the air.

"Yes." Francesca smiles at him. "We have so much on our schedules. Again. The Annual Chamberlain Spring About. Gino graduates from high school. Ben's wedding in Junis. The Annual Chamberlain Summer Fling. Prince Rupert's 5th birthday in Septembria, almost immediately followed by the Annual Chamberlain Fall Around Octobria 1st, which is also the King's birthday!" Francesca pauses, "And that doesn't include Gino's birthday Marleil 11th, your birthday Aprilla 4th, Marco's Birth Mayella 5th, Marco's death, Mayella 25th, my birthday Juliah 19th, the list goes on." Francesca stops with her little laugh. "Plus, the birthdays of my parents."

Antonio shakes his head as he sits beside Francesca on the swing. They look at each other with smiling eyes as their foreheads touch. Antonio reaches his arm around Francesca, giving her a sweet kiss, "I'm going to get busy with my day. I know you'll be busy too."

Taking her hand in his when he stands, they momentarily squeeze each other's hands, both sweetly smiling as he departs, tromping through the snow for his daily work.

Francesca gets ready for the day and loads the winter sleigh to go into town. Gino sees his mother about to leave, "Can I join you?"

Francesca turns her head seeing Gino walking toward her. "Absolutely. I am just heading into town for a bit."

Francesca and Gino enjoy the sleigh ride into Chamberlain Kingdom as they head to her parents' store to unload some fresh baked goods.

Gino carries most of the baked goods in, "Good morning, Grandmother and Grandfather."

Leonardo and Sophia walk toward Gino and Francesca greeting them with big hugs.

Leonardo excuses himself to help a customer in the store. "If you need help finding anything, don't hesitate to ask," Leonardo greets the well-groomed, muscular man accompanied by a lovely teenage girl.

Gino glances over to see the customers his grandfather is waiting on, and beholds the most beautiful girl he has ever laid eyes in his 16 years and 10 months of life. He boldly walks over to position himself next to his grandfather extending his hand to the man, "My name is Gino Mancini. I don't believe we have met."

The man extends his hand, gripping Gino's, "My name is Andre Richards, this is my daughter Claire Louise. Work brings me to Chamberlain Kingdom."

Gino can't take his eyes off of Claire. Reaching for her hand to greet her, "My name is Gino, I'm a senior this year."

Claire and Gino's eyes connect. They both feel as if they are meeting that one person you just know is meant to be your partner. Claire smiles, "I'm a senior as well."

Her long blonde hair and green eyes capture Gino's full attention. "May I show you around my grandparents' store?"

Claire glances at her dad for approval. He nods, redirecting his attention to Leonardo with a list he has brought in.

Gino walks Claire toward his mother and grandmother. Gino is about to introduce them when Claire steps up with her hand and reaches to shake the two women's hands, "Hello, my name is Claire Richards. My family and I just moved here."

"Welcome to our kingdom, Claire. I am Gino's mother, Francesca." Francesca cordially welcomes.

"I'm Gino's grandmother, Sophia." Sophia smiles and greets Claire.

"I'm going to give Claire a tour of the store." Gino announces to his mother.

"Nice to meet you, Claire." Francesca and Sophia both impart.

Gino walks Claire around the store pointing out all the things he thinks she may be interested in, working their way back to the entrance where her dad is waiting after loading the supplies he has just purchased.

"I guess I'll see you at school," Gino expresses.

"Yeah, I guess you will." Claire responds in her crisp, assuring voice.

Gino watches Claire and her father ride away in their wagon. He notices the well-built sleds secured under the wagon wheels, making for easy travel through snowy terrain.

······✑······

Francesca and Gino finish up their business in town and load up to head home.

Well, Claire and her father, Andre, seem nice," Francesca mentions with a smile.

Yes!" Gino happily agrees. "In fact, Mother, I'm going to marry Claire someday."

Francesca, not feeling any sense of surprise or shock, glances at Gino with those blue eyes of hers, "You just know, son? Is that what you're telling me?"

Yes. I just know." Gino confirms.

I hope it all works out the way you foresee, Gino." Francesca affirms.

Chapter 27

You can hear the silverware on dinner plates, and ice hitting the sides of glasses as everyone is enjoying Gino's seventeenth birthday dinner.

"Francesca, you never cease to amaze us with your fabulous meals," Sullivan Carlisle declares.

"Yes, and I thought I knew all your kitchen secrets," Katherine Carlisle laughs.

Francesca beams, "Thank you. I'm grateful we are all able to be together to celebrate Gino."

Gino smiles, peering at everyone gathered around the table; his parents, his grandparents, his best friend Luke Carlisle, along with Ben, Katherine, and Sully. Then a moment of heartache overtakes his expression.

Gino's deep thought is pleasantly interrupted by hearing his grandmother's unique voice. "Marco is celebrating with us in spirit, Gino," Sophia assures, recognizing the look on Gino's face.

"A toast to Gino," Leonardo declares. Everyone raises their glasses, "Seventeen completed years, may you be happy and filled with peace each day of your life," Leonardo honors his grandson.

"Thank you. Every one of you, for making an impact in my life," Gino humbly addresses.

......ஒஜ்ஓ......

Francesca is straightening up a few things. All the guests have left. Gino has gone to bed. She peeks out on the back deck through the large family room window. She walks to the kitchen door, grabs a coat hanging in the side entry way, and sets out for the stables.

She slows her brisk pace to a methodical walk, not wanting to startle Antonio.

She hears him in the room where the tack is kept. She slowly approaches, leaning herself against the frame of the doorway, watching her husband reorganize an already meticulous layout. After a few minutes, she brushes her foot across the floor in a subtle attempt to gain Antonio's attention of her presence. Again, she shuffles her foot against the floor. The bit of sound disrupts the zone Antonio is in. He looks over to the door and lights up, "What brings you out here?"

"I heard there was a good man out here, so I wanted to come and see for myself," Francesca playfully answers.

Antonio takes a few steps towards Francesca, "Is that so?"

Francesca moves closer to Antonio, "Yes, that's so."

Now, within inches of each other, they smile. Antonio reaches to the side of Francesca's face with one hand, tenderly caressing her cheek running his fingers into her hair, reaching with his other arm around her, he then pulls Francesca up into his arms for a passionate kiss and embracing hug.

"Still sweeping me off my feet," Francesca yields, whispering in his ear.

Antonio's deep voice submits, "And you still cast a spell on me no matter what frame of mind I am in."

Their endearing embrace slowly breaks as he runs his hands down her back to her waist. Looking at each other, Francesca quizzes, "Where are your thoughts tonight?"

Antonio, gazes into Francesca's eyes, and drops his head, "I don't want to talk about it."

Francesca takes one step back giving them a bit of spacing for conversation.

Francesca just stares at him. Antonio knows his wife is persistent. His reluctance to divulge his thoughts is outweighed by the fact he knows he should share.

He reaches for her hand, leading her out of the tack room over to where they can comfortably sit on some hay bales.

With his head facing down, "I know it sounds crazy, but part of me is filled with worry that we will lose Gino now. Marco had his seventeenth birthday, graduated high school, began his first real job, then...well you know, we buried him...now Gino is seventeen. In Mayella he graduates and intends to work full time for Bill Oliver. Thoughts race through my head of a carpentry accident, and losing Gino as well," confides Antonio. "I know it sounds farfetched, but that is where my thoughts are." Raising his head, turning his neck to look at Francesca. "I can't help but wonder at times if God even loves me. My parents died when I was eighteen, then our oldest son's life is robbed at a young age." Antonio rests his head in his palms, elbows pressing into his thighs just above his knees. After a few moments of silence, he repositions himself to sit up straight, again turning to peer at Francesca, "Then there is you, Gino, our fabulous friends, our beautiful ranch home, our property, our mine, our horses, our dogs, our livestock, not to mention we live in a magnificent kingdom. I thank God daily for my blessings. But then I feel I cannot truly protect the people I love, and that leaves me feeling... incompetent and bewildered. I know I am truly not bewildered, nor am I incompetent, but these are the thoughts I'm wrestling with."

Francesca, running her hand over Antonio's back, lays her head on his shoulder. "I don't think we have taken time to visit like this since Marco's accident, two years ago, come Mayella."

"I think you're right. The loss of Marco took me back to being eighteen years old, a few months before my nineteenth birthday, when I received word of the avalanche that caused the sleigh accident resulting in the death of my parents, along with King Theodore's parents and little sister. Our friendship deepened. He immediately inherited the throne. I walked into your parents' store to purchase supplies, and there you were. A gift from God," Antonio reaches his arm positioning it around Francesca. "I am thankful for all I have. But I do not like feeling vulnerable. The thought of losing another son is unbearable. The fear of it grips me at times."

Francesca sits in silence for minutes beside her husband. She soon softly smiles. "Well, that makes two of us. To keep me going, I have just been thankful in my spirit that I had Marco for seventeen years to enjoy, and one day I will see him again."

Antonio nods, "That is a good way to look at it, sweetie. I will work on being thankful that I had the privilege of being with Marco for the years we had. Maybe that same concept will help me when I think of my parents and am overtaken with the emotion of tremendous loss."

......⁀♊︎⁀......

"I can't say it enough, Victor. I am so thankful we were assigned to the Mancinis instead of the castle and royals. Or the wolf pack for that matter." Viana's crisp voice confirms.

"I agree. I actually think our high priest and priestess were wise in their assignments," Victor concurs.

Victor and Viana exchange a confident smile, both experiencing the peace and love that exist in the Mancini family.

Chapter 28

ANNUAL SPRING ABOUT

The Annual Chamberlain Kingdom Spring About is tomorrow. Most all the people in the kingdom, along with people from neighboring kingdoms join in the activities.

"Pixel, we have really got to watch Rupert at the festival. I know he is only four-and-a-half, but his demeanor is menacing. Not to mention our protecting of others must appear as luck." Piper paces.

"I would say menacing is an understatement." Pixel voices. "Nevertheless, I will do my best, Piper. Honestly, the only thing I cling to sometimes is knowing we are part of The Ancient Writings. The prince's behavior is so atrocious that I just want to send him off this planet." Pixel crosses her arms matter of fact, tapping one foot.

A grin overtakes Piper, "I get a kick out of some of the things you say, Pixel."

"You do? Thanks." Pixel conveys still sporting her red hue with tiny white dots.

Piper again smiles, tossing his head.

"I have the wagon loaded, honey, is there anything else?" Antonio asks Francesca.

Francesca walks out carrying a basket, "That covers it, I believe we're ready."

"I'll ride Jolly there." Gino says as he turns Jolly away from the wagon. Waving, he rides off.

"At least this year it is a beautiful day for the 'Annual Spring About'." Francesca notes.

Antonio nods, "Yes," driving them down their long scenic driveway.

......ᖆᖇᴏ......

Francesca and Antonio are unloading baked goods and other items to sell. Gino joins them unloading some wooden items he made to sell at the Spring About.

Andre and Emma Richards, along with their family approach the Mancinis for a formal introduction. It has been a few months since Andre and Claire were in Francesca's parents' store.

Extending his hand to Antonio, "Hello, my name is Andre Richards. This is my lovely wife, Emma, our daughters, Claire and Charlotte, and this is our son Chandler."

"Well nice to meet you. I am Antonio Mancini, this is my beautiful wife, Francesca, and our son, Gino."

"Yes, Claire and I met your wife and your son a few months back at the store."

"Sir, may I show Claire around the Spring About?" Gino seeks permission from Andre.

Emma and Andre Richards glance at each other, then Claire, "Yes, if Claire wants to accompany you, she may."

Gino smiles, "Well, Miss Claire, would you like to enjoy the Spring About with me?"

"Yeah, I think that sounds like a fine idea." Claire replies with her clear, somewhat concise voice.

Gino and Claire stroll around glancing at all the food carts, homemade items, and games that lay out before them across a few acres of the Chamberlain Park.

"Oh, there is the king and queen, and that must be their precious little one. Will you introduce me?" Claire requests.

Gino looks at Claire. He is filled with reservation from the things he has heard about the prince, but will fulfill the request of Claire. "Yes." Smiling at Claire, he reaches for her hand. They walk over to where the king and queen are with the prince.

"Hello, Gino," greets King Theodore.

"Hello. I'd like to introduce you to Claire Richards. This is King Theodore, Queen Eloise, and their son, Prince Rupert," Gino announces.

"So nice to meet you, my dear," Queen Eloise nods and smiles.

"Yes, nice to meet you, Claire," acknowledges King Theodore.

The prince has a mischievous look on his face, swinging his arm in an attempt to hit Claire.

"Hey, we'll be having none of that," Gino places his arm between the prince and Claire. "That's no way to greet people," Gino instructs.

The embarrassed king and queen look at each other. Queen Eloise immediately spies for Francesca in the vicinity, hoping she will have some effect on her unruly child.

King Theodore embarks, "Miss Claire, forgive the queen and I for our son's inappropriate behavior. Welcome to our kingdom. It is a pleasure meeting you."

"Oh, sir, it is a pleasure meeting the both of you," Claire cordially offers.

Gino and Claire begin to walk away when Gino clearly hears in a ghoulish deep voice, "I want you to make me more toys. You'll have no time if you're with her." Gino abruptly stops. Looking at Claire, "Did you hear that?"

"Hear what, Gino?" Claire inquires.

Gino turns and peers over to Prince Rupert feeling disgusted. He glares at the prince. The prince is holding a toy horse Gino carved for him. The prince is manipulating it from one hand to the other with a contemptuous grin, staring at Gino.

Gino shakes his head and returns his attention to Claire. "Let's get as far away from that kid as we can."

"Ah, he's just a little boy." Claire comforts.

Not wanting to alarm Claire, "Yes, you're right." Gino agrees.

The two stroll away enjoying the rest of the festivities the annual Spring About hosts.

......⟳ℓ⟲......

That evening at the palace, King Theodore paces in their chambers, "Eloise, Rupert is an embarrassment. I was looking forward to having a son, someone to leave my throne to. But as he ages, his behavior is becoming worse. It is very clear to me, you nor I have any control over him at all. If he behaves, I deduce it is solely on his own accord because he wants to impress someone. It has absolutely nothing to do with respect for authority! He has none!" the king gruffs.

Queen Eloise sits perplexed in silence as she watches her husband pace with agitation.

"I predict, if Rupert remains on this self-indulgent, destructive path, someone could be seriously harmed. What then? We will be liable to the victim's family. He could drain everything we have built in one ill deed. I absolutely do not know what to do, Eloise." The king stresses as he paces to the window staring out over their kingdom to the east.

"Seeing you so devastated, I would suggest we take him to another kingdom, far from here and leave him at an orphanage. That would leave us free of him, but forever haunted, wondering what chaos he is causing for innocent lives in that kingdom." Queen Eloise hypothesizes.

The king turns from viewing out their window, and rests his eyes on his wife. Shaking his head, slowly walking toward her, "You are correct. This is our burden. I can't think of a more lovely and wise woman to bear this agonizing cross with. I have been so wrapped up in my anger that I have neglected you, and the devastation you no doubt also feel." The king sits on the bed beside Eloise leaning his head into her. "I would say, it is easier to lose a son by death, than to have lost one the way we did. Still alive, but distinctly lost." King Theodore speculates.

Chapter 29

A FEW WEDDING DETAILS

The Mancinis arrive at the Carlisle Ranch. An early morning shower has passed, leaving water droplets glistening from the sun, now brightly shining.

"We are so glad you are here!" Katherine dashes out the door, followed by Sully, addressing the three Mancinis.

"Well, just a few more weeks until Ben's wedding. We are glad you asked us to help." Francesca says hugging Katherine.

Antonio and Sully greet with handshakes. Sully looks at Gino, "Luke and Ben are out in the field. They'll be up shortly."

"Okay, I'll just head out to where they are," Gino replies.

"I can't believe the king and queen insisted Ben and Laurie have their wedding on the palace grounds!" Katherine exclaims.

"Well, I suppose that is a way they can take care of their people. Sully has worked for the royals for years, and now, Ben has received a promotion," Francesca proposes. "Plus, Eloise and Sully *are* cousins," winks Francesca.

"Yes, Laurie's family was definitely concerned about the finances, but Queen Eloise assured them not to worry. So gracious of her," Katherine recognizes.

"It is very exciting indeed! What can we do to help?" asks Francesca.

"I think just help us at the tables," Katherine surmises.

"I'm pretty sure the queen will have her staff at all the tables," Sully laughs.

Katherine nods, "You are probably right. I just can't believe our son is going to be married on the castle grounds! Of course, Ben and Laurie are going to have Prince Rupert be the ring bearer."

Antonio and Francesca both reserve from making eye contact, being respectful, by not displaying concerns they have of Rupert.

"Luke will of course be Ben's best man, and Gino will be his groomsman." Katherine excitedly lays out details.

"Yes, thank you. Gino is very honored Ben asked him to be his groomsman," Antonio confides.

"Ben wouldn't have it any other way," Sully confirms, "we raised them like brothers."

Chapter 30

The sun is just coming up, casting light on the stunning castle grounds. Workers are placing exquisite bouquets of white roses throughout the area selected for the wedding. Hand crafted, vibrant, red bows line the rows of chairs, and beautiful flowers that represent spring and summer in Chamberlain Kingdom adorn the arch where the couple will be united. The king and queen made sure their palace grounds are simply elegant for Ben and Laurie's wedding.

Queen Eloise is next to the king in their bed. Her head is on his shoulder, with his arm around her. He kisses her head, "I'm glad we are doing this for Ben and Laurie."

"Me too. It gives my heart joy," smiles the queen. A look of concern overtakes her face, "I do hope Rupert behaves."

The king shakes his head a bit, "As do I. I wonder if they may have felt obligated to have Rupert be their ring bearer," postulates King Theodore.

"Is that why you hired Sully and Ben? Because Sully and I are cousins?" quizzes the queen.

"Not at all!" the king assuredly smiles at Eloise, "I hired Sully, and then Ben, because of their expertise in their fields, which best serves our kingdom."

Queen Eloise smiles at her husband, "I love you. A sound man with good judgement." She kisses his cheek.

......ᘒᕽᓏ......

"Razel, look at the wolf pack we have been tracking. Does it appear that lone wolf is behaving peculiarly?" Zeek asks, pointing to a wolf about fifty-feet from the pack.

Razel looks, "I see a cloud coming out of his mouth!"

Zeek and Razel watch in silence as what appears to be a filmy, black cloud exit from the wolf's mouth with a grotesque, elongated head elevating high into the sky. Out of the mouth of the unusually shaped head comes a deafening, shrill, ear-piercing scream that seems to last for a full minute if not longer.

Zeek and Razel stand with their hands covering their ears looking at each other and the ghoulie sight. Zeek communicates, "We have to let the others know!"

Zeek and Razel keep hidden from the wolves, running a jaunt down the mountain top. When they stop, they scan back and see the ghastly head lowering, returning into the wolf from which it emerged.

Razel places two fingers to her left temple, "Victor, Viana, Piper, Pixel, it appears one of the Cryptolores that is inhabiting a wolf just sent some type of communication. Be watchful."

Zeek places his hand on Razel's arm, "Good job. I wonder what is going to happen now."

"I don't know. Let's remain calm and alert," Razel asserts.

Zeek and Razel look at each other, then make way into their position, observing the wolf pack once again.

......ᘒᕽᓏ......

Francesca almost chokes on her mug of hot chocolate. She sets it on the counter and dashes out the kitchen door. She looks intently to the west, scrutinizing the landscape and sky, as far as her eyes can see. Antonio approaches from the stables.

"What are you looking for, dear?" Antonio asks.

Francesca frowns, "I see nothing, but a few minutes ago, I heard a bizarre, spine-chilling howl. I am just sure I heard it from the west. I see nothing.

"Well, let's go get ready for the day," Antonio suggests after squeezing both of Francesca's arms with tenderness.

She pats his hand, "You're right."

They walk inside of their home.

......⁊ℒℴ......

At the castle, Prince Rupert lies asleep. Suddenly, his eyes open wide. His mouth then opens and a filmy, black cloud emerges. The Cryptolore warlord, Alchodor, departs the prince's body. The prince lies undisturbed.

Piper and Pixel see the filmy cloud jet out of the nursery window.

Piper immediately places two fingers on his left temple, "Zeek, Razel, Victor, Viana, we just witnessed a filmy cloud dart out of the prince's room. We believe it to be the Cryptolore warlord, Alchodor."

Pixel's red and white polka dot body begins to change colors. Piper glances at Pixel, and calmly places his hands on her shoulders. "Remember, we are a part of the Ancient Writings," Piper assures.

Pixel smiles and settles back into her red, with tiny white polka dot color.

"Pixel, we have other issues today. The wedding is a few short hours away. We still have duties, and must ensure the well-being of everyone," Piper ascertains.

"Roger that," Pixel says with glee.

......⌒♄⌒......

"What are you thinking, Victor?" quizzes Viana.

"Well, I believe Zeek and Razel are excellent at tracking, and will be able to handle anything, but we must be ready to transport to them at a moment's notice. In fact, if Scaleon and Alchodor are about to have a meeting, which is what I suspect, this is huge. They have not had one on this scale since they went separate ways two years ago." Victor theorizes. "In fact, I'm going to make a decision," Victor places his index and middle finger to his left temple, "Zeek, Razel, I believe Alchodor is on his way to have a meeting with Scaleon. We have a wedding at the castle today. However, when you see Alchodor approaching, let us know. We will transport to your coordinates immediately," instructs Victor.

Viana agrees, "Good call, Victor."

"Thank you. If Alchodor is out of the prince for a while, well, I suspect things will run smoothly and peacefully for a change, in the life of the royals, and the wedding today," Victor predicts.

"You're absolutely right," Viana concurs.

......⌒♄⌒......

"I'm surprised Rupert isn't awake yet," Queen Eloise conveys.

"After we finish dressing, we'll go up and check on him," assures the king.

Opening Rupert's door, they see him peacefully sleeping. Stepping closer they notice the beautiful pinkish color on his cheeks. King Theodore places his hand on his son. Rupert stirs, opens his eyes, and gives his parents the sweetest, most innocent smile, they have rarely seen in a long time now.

Queen Eloise sits on the bed beside Rupert. He sits up and crawls into her lap hugging her ever so tightly. "Well, good morning, my sweet Prince," Queen Eloise gently speaks.

Rupert molds to his mother's embrace resting his head on her shoulder. She feels she has her child back for the first time in two years.

"Rupert, do you know what today is?" asks the king.

Rupert nods, "I'm going to carry rings."

"That's correct, Son." Theodore states.

Rupert raises his head off of his mother's shoulder and lifts his arms to his dad. The king, a bit astonished, glances at his wife. She nods. The king reaches for Rupert and lifts him into his arms. Rupert wraps his arms around his father's neck, and his legs around his father's waist, laying his head onto the king's shoulder. King Theodore places one of his hands on Rupert's head while the other is wrapped around Rupert. It's as if they are exchanging years of love and affection.

Queen Eloise stands after enjoying moments of tenderness. "It's time for breakfast, then we need to get ready for the wedding."

"Carry me," Rupert says to the king.

"I believe I will," replies Theodore.

The three saunter down the stairs and enter the dining area where Chef Pierre and staff are awaiting with a nutritional breakfast.

The staff is mesmerized at Rupert's skin coloring, his brown eyes, and loving behavior.

Nanny Carol enters the room, a bit taken back when she sees the royals and Rupert sitting at the table. Rupert reaches for Nanny Carol. She glances to the queen. Eloise nods. Carol walks with reserve over to Rupert who has his arms out waiting for her. Carol steps close to Rupert. Rupert takes his outstretched arms wrapping them around Carol, "I love you, Nanny Carol."

Puzzled, but with relief, Carol accepts Rupert's hug, "I love you too, honey."

Carol looks to the king and queen inquisitively, then sits to enjoy her breakfast with them.

......⚶......

Razel points, "I see Alchodor approaching!"

Placing two fingers on his temple, Zeek communicates, "Chiawaukas, Alchodor is approaching."

Razel is shaking Zeek's arm to notice something. She points to the wolves. Zeek adds, "It appears Scaleon is leaving the wolf he inhabits."

Piper, Pixel, Victor and Viana all transport to the coordinates Zeek sent.

Covering her ears, Pixel complains, "Ug, their chattering of clicks and shrieks. So noisy!"

"Well, I wish we knew what they were saying," Victor gruffs.

Pixel imitates the clicking and screeching sounds. Victor leers at Pixel. Razel, Zeek, Viana and Piper all stand looking at Pixel as well. Zeek and Razel are fighting off grins.

"What?" asks Pixel.

"We are in a serious situation, Pixel, and you want to play games. We must know what they are saying," Victor scorns.

"Pixel, really, you need to remain focused," Razel asserts reaching her hand to Pixel.

The two VeNoma leaders are a hideous sight. Their faces are ghoulishly long. Their mouths have sharp pointed teeth. They have long noses reaching up on their forehead with meeting eyebrows that arch with some definition above their beady eyes.

Victor paces, tossing his hands in the air, "Does anyone speak VeNoma?!" Quickly turning, pointing at Pixel, "No more clicking and screeching."

"Aye, aye, Captain," Pixel salutes.

Victor, about to come unglued, "Piper, how do you put up with her nonsense! Pixel, you are wasting our time. We need to be translating what they are discussing."

Viana and Razel cast their hands, making an arc so they can have a closer view of the two Cryptolores' meeting. Zeek applies some snaps of his fingers for translation...coming into a conversation the Chiawaukas hear...

"...I would like to know why you did not enter the body of an adult. I demand you enter the king, and take over these humans! My minions and I are stuck in wolves!" Scaleon addresses Alchodor in a slithering, cryptic voice.

"Always quick to a rash decision! I have a methodical plan. Due to the life span of humans, it made more sense to enter the two-and-a-half-year-old toddler than an adult. My powers will be able to grow. My skills of master manipulation will become highly enhanced, so by the time the prince reaches maturity he will be a cunning manipulator, my powers manifested in full, and I will rule the land, the humans and dominate all that exist. And you, Scaleon, shall bite your tongue when challenging my decisions. I do not take that lightly," Alchodor discloses in a slow, eerie, deep-pitched voice. "You have potential, Scaleon, but your impatience could be your ruin. You and your myrmidons will have a place. The time is for me to know. Then I will let you know. For now, continue living in the pack of wolves. Plus, have you forgotten that body hopping weakens us?"

Scaleon quivers. After a few minutes of silence, he conforms, "As you wish, Alchodor. And no, I have not forgotten." The sound of freakish, abnormal rattles fills the air.

Razel and Viana close the arc.

"So, that's it! Alchodor chose the prince because of his age, and has plans to take over when the prince reaches maturity," Zeek attests.

"Yes. It's a wicked plan. We will not let that happen though. Hopefully by then, the two Chords of Chiawauka families will have been united by a marriage, resulting in their powers igniting. Not that we need them. But they are an intricate part of the Ancient Writings," Piper postulates.

"You are correct. The two families play an important role of the fulfilment of the Ancient Writings. They may not be pure, full-blooded Chiawaukas, but they were infused with the DNA of the high priest and high priestess centuries ago, as a backup protection in case the Cryptolores escaped their captivity or something happened to the Chiawaukas," Victor concludes.

Chapter 31

THE WEDDING

The Carlisles and Mancinis arrive at the castle about the same time. Laurie Kay Marshall and her family also arrive. Everyone breaks off, going to their designated areas. Laurie Kay, her mother; Linda, her sister; Lila, and dear friend, Angela Thomas, are in a room dressing. Ben, Luke, Gino, Sully, and Antonio are together. Francesca, Katherine, and Queen Eloise enjoy sitting at a patio table while everyone else is getting dressed. The King is dressing Rupert and himself. The king instructs Rupert on how to behave while walking down the aisle and present the rings to the priests.

Standing next to his father, in front of the full-length mirror, Prince Rupert gazes up to his dad and reaches for his hand, "I love you."

The King is moved with a loving spirit, and kneels down to look at Rupert in his eyes; "I love you, son. Let's be on our way. We don't want to be late."

The two leave the King's chambers and walk to the patio.

Rupert lets go of his dad's hand, runs to his mother, and gives her a hug. Quickly turning, he walks to Francesca, giving her a hug, then he walks to Katherine to give her a hug. The three women smile with wonder of the prince's sweet demeanor.

Katherine addresses the prince, "You have such a big job today, carrying the rings for my son Ben and his bride Laurie."

"Yes," Rupert says as he nods, beaming.

"Let's make our way over to where we will be for the run through," recommends the king.

King Theodore and Prince Rupert depart the company of the ladies.

Katherine and Francesca are smiling at the queen who clearly is about to burst into all kinds of happy. "We went up to Rupert's room this morning to wake him. His pinkish, youthful skin color has reappeared, his eyes are brown, his sweet, loving personality has returned. It's as if a miracle has happened!" exclaims Queen Eloise.

"That is certainly a blessing!" states Katherine.

"Yes, I'm so happy for you," says Francesca.

The queen sighs, "Theodore and I do realize, this may be just temporary. It is a fear that plagues us both. But for today, for the moments we have, we are cherishing our son's behavior, and going to enjoy this splendid wedding of Ben and Laurie."

"Yes," smiles Katherine.

"Absolutely," assures Francesca.

......⁊⧓......

The guests are arriving, filling the rows of chairs. The wedding tables for the reception are being prepared by the castle staff while the wedding commences.

Father Romano and Father Lanzreth take their place under the arch alter.

Ben is escorted to the alter by his mother Katherine and father Sully.

Katherine and Sullivan then seat themselves on the first row.

Ben's younger brother and best man Luke, escorts Laurie's maid of honor which is her younger sister, Lila. They are quickly followed by Gino escorting Angela, Laurie's bridesmaid and good friend. The wedding party takes their designated places.

The bridal music begins, signaling the bridal party is about to enter. Those gathered stand to watch as Laurie Kay is escorted down the aisle by her dad, Mark Marshall. Once they reach the alter, Mark places Laurie's hand into Ben's, and then joins his wife, Linda, in the first row.

Father Romano and Father Lanzreth take turns reading the scripture readings.

An unusual breeze comes up during the ceremony that momentarily captures the attention of Francesca. She looks and spies a filmy, black cloud zooming toward the castle grounds from the northwest. *Can anyone else see this?* Francesca wonders as she quickly looks around. *Hmmm, no one appears to be aware of it. Oh, no! I wonder if it is coming for Rupert! It appears to be the same filmy cloud that I see leave him when in my presence.* Francesca redirects her attention to Rupert as he is about to walk down the aisle. She notices the cloud forming above the guests, just hovering. Rupert walks down the aisle without a glitch, handing the rings to the priests. Both priests bless the rings. Rupert turns to go sit by his parents, but Francesca motions to the prince inviting him to come sit by her. The prince complies.

Piper, Pixel, Viana, and Victor arrive, remaining invisible to the Cryptolore Warlord. Francesca senses the presence of the supernatural beings as she has felt them before. She inconspicuously ganders around, but with everything going on; the exchanging of vows, Rupert sitting on her lap, the hovering, filmy cloud, she has trouble discerning the direction of the supernatural presence she senses.

"We now pronounce you Mr. and Mrs. Benjamin William Carlisle." Father Lanzreth and Father Romano announce in synchrony.

Francesca's full attention is on the bride and groom, along with Rupert. Mass is over. As the closing music plays, the priests, bride and groom, along with their wedding party, proceed down the aisle exiting the area, closely followed by their families and friends.

Everyone makes way to where the cake, punch, champagne, and refreshments are being served. The castle musicians are playing soft, romantic music, in preparation of the first dance for Ben and Laurie as Mr. & Mrs. Carlisle.

Francesca has a hold of Rupert's hand in line for cake and punch. Antonio whispers to her, "Shouldn't you let him enjoy this time with his parents, my sweet?"

Francesca's blue eyes just gaze into her husband's eyes. She quietly replies, "Yes, I suppose you are right. I am trying to protect him, but you are correct. The king and queen need to enjoy these precious moments as I fear they will soon be gone."

Antonio stands behind Francesca, gently placing his large hands on each of her arms, and softly kisses the back of her head.

Queen Eloise and King Theodore approach the Mancinis and their son. They reach for him, and help him with a plate of cake and glass of punch, "Thank you so much, our dear friends, for watching Rupert. We will take it from here." Queen Eloise smiles and kisses Francesca on the cheek, while the king helps Rupert to a table to enjoy the refreshments.

Carol also approaches the Mancinis, "Wow, it must be a miracle! I have never seen Rupert look so healthy, and behave so happily."

Francesca agrees smiling, but does not give away her suspicions, "Yes. Enjoy the reception, Carol."

"I will, my friend. Thank you." Carol cordially says.

Francesca and Antonio make way to a table that no one else is sitting at. "I just don't know how long it will last," Francesca confides to Antonio.

"How long what will last?" inquires Antonio.

"Rupert's normal, healthy behavior," Francesca sighs.

Just then, Gino slides into a chair. "Question. It is a celebration; may I please have some champagne to celebrate? Sully is allowing Luke to have some with Ben."

Antonio and Francesca make eye contact for what Gino feels is the longest sixteen seconds he has ever endured. Antonio looks at his son, "We do not do things because other people are allowed to do them. However, your mother and I are in agreement, that yes, Gino, you may have some champagne."

"Just be careful, son. You've never had any alcohol, it may make you dizzy or sick," Francesca warns.

"Mother, I am right here in the same location as you and Pop. If I am not fine, I will find you, or someone will find you," Gino assures. "Then I can say, well, you warned me," laughing with his little laugh.

Antonio and Francesca smile at Gino. "Just be careful, son," Antonio expresses.

"I will, Pop," Gino stands, placing his hand on his Pop's shoulder and walks around to kiss his mother on her cheek. "Thank you, guys."

Music fills the air. Ben and Laurie step onto the dance floor for their first dance as husband and wife. Next, Laurie dances with her dad, Mark, while Ben dances with his mother, Katherine. After those dances, the dance floor opens to everyone.

The king and queen take the prince onto the dance floor. The three of them dance together, smiling ever so joyfully.

Antonio stands, reaching for Francesca's hand, "Dance with me."

Not breaking her eye contact with Antonio, Francesca stands, smiling at him.

"At least our first dance is a slow dance," Antonio rubs his cheek against Francesca's cheek, pulling her close in a romantic embrace of his arms. They enjoy their slow dance cheek to cheek. "We don't do this often enough," Antonio ponders.

"Well, we could dance in the kitchen, the family room, or out on our deck." Francesca suggests.

"I believe we will add that to our activities, Mrs. Mancini," Antonio softly says as he snuggles into Francesca's neck with his face.

Gino steps in beside Luke as he reaches for a glass of champagne. Luke expresses amazement, "Your parents said 'yes'?"

"Yes!" Gino pats Luke's back. "They of course want me to be careful."

Ben says to the young men, "Well then, let's have a toast." The three raise their glasses of champagne. "To the best brothers a guy could have. And Marco, in heaven, we miss you. Brothers forever."

You could hear the clink of the champagne glasses as the three young men complete their toast.

"Wow! That tastes pretty good! I think I'll have another glass." Gino decides. "Then I am going to go ask Miss Claire to dance with me. I'm going to marry that beautiful girl."

Ben and Luke smile. Luke walks over to Camille, asking her to dance. Ben whisps Laurie away from her girlfriends for a dance. Gino nears Claire. "May I have this dance, Claire Louise Richards?"

She looks at Gino with her captivating green eyes, "Yes, I'd like that," and extends her hand for Gino to take; he leads her to the dance floor.

"Now let my moves sweep you away," Gino laughs his little laugh.

Claire smiles. The two enjoy the entire evening together, dancing, talking, and eating. From time to time, Gino helps himself to another glass of champagne.

"You seem pretty fond of that champagne, Gino," Claire notices.

"Well, all this dancing keeps me thirsty. It does taste delicious. I've never had any before in my life, and I am dancing with the most beautiful girl in the kingdom. Yeah, I'm pretty happy." Gino raises another glass of champagne toward Claire, before swallowing it.

"Just be careful, Gino. Since you have never drank alcohol before, it may sneak up on you." Claire advises.

The evening turns to dark; the palace grounds are illuminated by Krystyleen lights. Some guests begin to leave. Others remain visiting with friends. The musicians continue to play. Some continue to dance.

Francesca keeps close watch on Rupert while she and Antonio sit at a table with the king, queen, Sully, and Katherine Carlisle. She knows the black, filmy cloud is lingering, though she can no longer see it.

The Chiawaukas enjoy their time together while remaining ever so observant at the festivities.

Gino and Claire go for a walk. Gino grabs one more glass of champagne as the two leave the reception area, their hands locked together ever so tightly.

They distance themselves from the wedding area, and arrive close to the Chamberlain River that runs through the property.

"Do you love the sound of the river?" Gino asks Claire.

"I do." Claire smiles.

"One of these years, those are two words I want to hear from you." Gino flirts.

Claire is blushing, though the night prohibits visibility.

Gino plops down on the ground reaching up to Claire's hand, "Sit by me."

Claire looks at Gino, and positions herself next to Gino, resting her head on his shoulder. The two sit quietly star gazing.

"May I lay my head in your lap?" Gino asks Claire.

"Yes." Claire replies.

Gino spins his body, and lays his head in Claire's lap. "I'm pretty tired, Claire," Gino says as he closes his eyes, and passes out.

"Maybe we should head back," Claire suggests.

No response from Gino.

"Gino, Gino," Claire quietly says while rubbing his face.

Gino's body was out. Claire felt scared. *Is he alive? Is this normal if he drinks? He did have several glasses.* Claire gingerly slides herself out from under Gino's head, and carefully places his head on the ground. She gets up, and runs back to the reception area to find his parents.

Reaching the well-lit reception area, Claire sees Gino's parents sitting with the Chamberlains, and the Carlisles. Claire feels apprehensive about approaching Gino's parents in the midst of others. She also doesn't want to have the attention of her parents sitting at a nearby table with other guests. She remains calm, walking to Mrs. Mancini. "Hi, you guys." Claire says.

"Well, hello, sweetie." Francesca responds.

The other adults at the table smile, acknowledging Claire's presence as well.

"Um, can I pull you away for a minute?" Claire reservedly asks Francesca.

"Well, of course, dear," Francesca stands taking Claire's hand to escort her to a more private area.

Francesca stops and turns to Claire, "What is it, honey?"

"It's Gino, I think he's alive, but he is just lying there. I think he drank too much champagne. I don't know, we were having so much fun eating, dancing, then star gazing, but then he was out." Claire explains.

"You are right to get me. I'll get Antonio. You stay here." Francesca orders.

Returning to the table, Francesca delivers in her composed manner to Antonio, "Hey, sweetie, join me."

Antonio looks up at Francesca and sees in her eyes he needs to get up without delay.

"If you all leave before we get back, it was a splendid wedding." Francesca acknowledges.

The others watch Francesca and Antonio head over to where Claire is waiting. The three of them head toward the river.

"What's going on?" Antonio quizzes.

"It appears Gino enjoyed the champagne a bit too much," Francesca assesses.

Antonio picks up his pace. Claire begins to run. Francesca and Antonio follow.

Claire drops to Gino's side and look to Antonio and Francesca. Antonio has a haunting memory, remembering how he dropped to Marco's side.

Antonio and Francesca both kneel down at the side of Gino.

"Gino, Gino," Antonio gently shakes his son.

"Hey, Pop, what are you guys doing out here?" Gino looks around, dazed.

"It's time to go home, son," Antonio asserts.

"Cool. Hey wait, I've got to tell Claire bye," Gino slurs.

"I'm right here, Gino," Claire quietly speaks.

"I'm glad. Goodnight, Claire. I had a great day with you," Gino professes.

"I enjoyed my time with you. Sleep well," Claire peacefully says.

"Let's get you up, Son," Antonio directs.

"Is Mom here?" Gino asks.

"Yes, sweetie. We are all here," Francesca says.

Antonio stares at Francesca, "You know, I don't want everyone to know what's happened."

"I know," replies Francesca. "I will make sure Claire gets to her parents; you take Gino straight to the wagon, and I will tell everyone goodnight."

Antonio nods at Francesca, "I'll see you at the wagon. Be safe.

Chapter 32

CELESTIAL AND BLAZER MAKE CONTACT

Francesca and Claire reach the reception area. Francesca gives Claire a hug. "He'll be okay. Don't worry," Francesca assures Claire.

"I know. Thank you," Claire nods with a concerned look.

"Goodness, what a fabulous day it was," Francesca ponders.

"It was a great day," Claire agrees. "I had a lot of fun with your son."

The two depart and make their separate ways through the remaining guests. Claire heads to the table her parents are sitting at. Francesca walks to the Carlisles and Chamberlains. "Goodnight. The wedding and reception were splendid," Francesca recaps. Looking at Rupert, "Take care. Remember what a wonderful time you had today. You did such a good job being the ring bearer." She gives them all hugs.

Rupert gets up out of his chair, and gives Francesca a big hug goodbye.

Francesca walks away, departing her close friends, worried about Gino, and concerned about the filmy, black cloud she knows is waiting for an opportune time to re-enter the prince. *Why am I the only one to see the cloud? And why does it leave Rupert in my presence? But today, the royals did say Rupert woke up fine. Hmmm, I wonder what is going on.*

"That's our cue," Victor says to his Chiawauka comrades. "We'll be leaving with the Mancinis, and you two, well, Piper and Pixel, the Warlord Alchodor is here. He will no doubt return to the prince when he feels there is an opening. Be vigilant."

Francesca climbs onto the wagon and sits next to Antonio, then glances back at Gino.

"Ready?" Antonio asks.

"Yes," Francesca replies.

Antonio signals Honor. Honor pulls the wagon down the long castle driveway.

Francesca expects to hear a shrill scream any moment from Rupert before they depart the palace grounds.

She begins to relax as they make way through town not once hearing what she had dreaded the most all evening.

Ben and Laurie retreat to a cabin on the palace grounds that is private for honeymoons and special occasions. The other guests leave. The musicians pack up. The staff clean. The king carries Rupert with the queen by his side to their castle home. Rupert has fallen asleep, molding to his father's body. Upon entering the door, the filmy, black cloud swoops down entering Rupert through his ears, his eyes, his nose, and his mouth. Rupert raises his head coughing, and screams a terrifying wail. The king and queen's eyes meet. What they were fearful of just transpired.

They carry Rupert to his room; Rupert begins to kick the king nearing the top of the stairs. The king and queen enter Rupert's room and lay him in his bed. Rupert is still kicking and being defiant as they undress him, changing him into pajamas.

The king looks sternly, yet with a gentle spirit, "Good night, Son. Sleep well. I enjoyed our time together," admits the king, kissing his son's forehead.

Queen Eloise hesitantly reaches to kiss Rupert goodnight, not knowing if he is going to hit or kick at her. He lies still, but stares at the queen, as she too, kisses his forehead.

Theodore and Eloise peer at Rupert lying there. They wonder if they should leave the room, not knowing what is going to happen next. They both feel bewildered. Rupert stares blankly at the ceiling for some time, but finally closes his eyes. His parents leave his room, quietly closing his door.

......⚮......

The Chiawauka team Celestial (Celest) and Blazer are in charge of Marco.

"The protective shield Victor and Viana reactively placed over Marco is indeed preserving what life was left in him. I anticipate he will have a full recovery. His brain waves have been active, and it was so unexpected when he communicated to his mother the day of the funeral. That really surprised me and was unprecedented," Blazer recaps to Celest. "We need to contact Victor and Viana immediately. I believe his brain activity is at full capacity and actually has been for most of this time. He may even be able to penetrate the restrictive barrier guard we placed over him to prevent communication."

"Yes, I agree. In addition, we need to introduce ourselves to Marco, and explain the situation," Celestial adds.

Celestial places her left index and middle finger to her left temple, "Victor, Viana, this is Celest. Blazer and I need you to come to the mausoleum, tonight if possible."

Victor and Viana receive Blazer and Celestial's request. "We should ask Piper or Pixel to stand guard over the Mancinis while we go to the mausoleum," recommends Viana.

Shaking his head, "I absolutely do not feel comfortable splitting them up with Alchodor hovering around the castle," Victor deliberates.

"What else are we to do? Would you like to enlist Zeek or Razel to teleport to us?" Viana inquires.

Victor pauses then looks at Viana, "I do believe so. Yes."

Viana places her left index finger and middle finger to her left temple, "Zeek, Razel, we need one of you to transport to the Mancini Ranch for a bit to stand watch."

Razel says to Zeek, "I will go."

"Wait a minute, do you mind if I step in? You told me Francesca loves rocks. Maybe this evening while guarding the Mancinis, I will have an opportunity to guide her to some beautiful specimens I have found out there," conveys Zeek. "Actually, it is too dark, but I would like the opportunity to see what she has collected, and maybe I can send her a message as to where to find some exceptional rocks for her collection."

Razel smiles, "You and your rocks. Alright, I understand. I'm sure Francesca will appreciate your assistance, even though I'm sure she is unaware we send her messages."

"Well, alright. I'm out," Zeek says as he is about to transport, "Be safe. Contact me if you need assistance."

Razel smiles, "Of course."

Chapter 33

THE CHIAWAUKAS CONSULT THE HIGH PRIESTS

Zeek arrives at the coordinates Viana sent. Looking around, Zeek acknowledges, "This treehouse is an excellent place to surveille the property!"

"We thought so as well. When we selected this location, we were not even aware that it was on the property of one of the Chords of Chiawaukas families," Victor discloses.

"So, what's going on?" Zeek asks.

"Celest and Blazer summoned us to arrive at the mausoleum as soon as possible. No doubt it has something to do with Marco Mancini," Viana assumes.

"The Mancinis arrived home a short time ago. They assisted Gino to his room since he was still wabbly from the effects of alcohol. Antonio and Francesca are unwinding on the main level. We use the arc to view. Sometimes Francesca sits on their back deck star gazing. You shouldn't have any trouble. Alchodor is at the castle," Victor briefs, "Oh, and be careful if you go near Francesca. She appears to be able to sense our presence."

"Yes, she refers to us as 'invisible beings'," Viana shares in her crisp voice making quotation gestures with her fingers.

"Alright. I'll stand guard, you two take off," Zeek states waving his hands in an outward motion.

......⚬〰⚬......

Victor and Viana transport to the Mancini mausoleum.

"Good to see you two," Blazer welcomes.

"Yes, we want to discuss some action plans regarding Marco," Celest informs.

"That is what we suspected," Victor shares.

The four Chiawaukas stand on a long, marble tile step viewing Marco. Blazer motions for them to step away for some privacy. "You may or may not be aware of this. On the day of Marco's funeral, Marco communicated with his mother through the Flower of Virtue," Blazer briefs. "Such a communication is unprecedented, and caught us off guard."

"We actually were aware of it, but didn't worry since Francesca was so distraught. We assessed she processed it as wishful thinking, or accredited it to the overwhelming stress she was experiencing," Victor surmises, "We're frankly surprised he never tried to communicate again over these last two years."

Blazer and Celest look at each other, then to their comrades, "Well, we speculate he has attempted communication; however, after the unanticipated contact the day of the funeral, we instinctively placed a barrier guard over his area, not allowing any thoughts of his to penetrate the outside world. He is only able to view through the flower, which he perceives as dreams."

The four Chiawaukas acknowledge each other. "Well, that brings us to now. It's been a little over two years since you two placed Marco in the protective shield to prevent deterioration. His brain activity is extremely strong; I infer fully functioning. It is now necessary we communicate with him, and bring him up to speed on his current condition and situation. We also believe his body has experienced a full recovery. However, we have not yet been given authority by our high priest and priestess to remove the protective shield from Marco so he can enjoy his life once again," Celest instructs.

"Celest and I believe we need to introduce the four of us to Marco, and encourage him to speak to his mother, with of course, strict instructions. Do you believe Francesca is ready to receive communication from Marco?" Blazer questions.

Looking at each other, then to Celest and Blazer, Victor and Viana stand in silence. Glancing at each other again, Viana says, "I believe she will welcome the opportunity to visit with Marco. We have not confirmed her suspicions of our existence. She does sense our presence. She also sees the Cryptolore Warlord in the form of a filmy, black cloud when he leaves the child's body. We believe Alchodor recognizes Francesca's supernatural powers, since he leaves the prince when she is near, and also because of the behavior he displayed when he escaped imprisonment and encountered her."

"Francesca also heard the deafening thunderous sounds of the Cryptolores. She thought it was a storm in a neighboring kingdom. We have not yet received orders to make ourselves known to her, though," Victor relays.

"I think communication from Marco will be one more peculiar phenomenon that she will file as a mystery along with sensing our presence, seeing a filmy, black cloud, and unexplained supernatural happenings," Viana ascertains.

"Well, we will proceed interacting with Marco," Blazer formulates.

"I don't believe we can tell him who we are as he might tell Francesca. In fact, he mustn't know about the Cryptolores either," Victor says adamantly.

Celest and Viana are exchanging looks. "Okay, this is becoming complicated. Let's ask our high priest and priestess what we *can* tell Francesca, and what we can tell Marco," Viana recommends.

"I agree," Celest concurs. "Divulging to Marco some of what is going on, without enlightening Francesca, may be more difficult than we think."

The four Chiawaukas gather in a circle. Viana places her left index finger and middle finger on her left temple, communicating to their command center.

"We need to speak to High Priest Akshai, and High Priestess Ammerie," Viana requests. Pausing, "Yes, it is urgent," Viana confirms. Viana nods and relays to the others, "They will see us."

The four Chiawaukas make fists, then releasing with their palms up, a snow globe shape object appears, levitating into the air between the four Chiawaukas.

High Priest Akshai and High Priestess Ammerie appear adorned in beautiful priestly robes. "Greetings, Viana, Victor, Celestial and Blazer," addresses High Priestess Ammerie.

"How may we guide you?" inquires High Priest Akshai.

"Marco's brain activity is at full-capacity. Celest and I believe he will attempt communication with his mother, who has not been informed yet of our presence, the Cryptolores, The Ancient Writings, well the list goes on. We deem it necessary to seek your counsel on this circumstance," Blazer engages.

"Francesca senses our presence. She sees the Warlord Alchodor in the form of a filmy substance when he leaves the prince. She was able to hear the sounds of the Cryptolores, thinking it was thunder. She is also experiencing her abilities of magical powers in small ways. Not to mention, she is able to perceive messages Viana sends to her through telepathy. She is truly tapped into the supernatural world without verification," adds Victor in his deliberate voice.

"We clearly need some direction on how to proceed with Francesca and the communication between Marco and his mother," Celestial petitions.

"We were discussing the complexities when we decided it was time to enlist your guidance," Viana implores.

An unexpected grin consumes the face of High Priest Akshai. High Priestess Ammerie notices him with a double take. An overwhelming smile also appears on her face, winking at Akshai.

The four Chiawaukas quietly observe their leaders, curious as to 'what on Soleil' they find amusing.

High Priestess Ammerie sweeps her arm whimsically through the air, with a gentle twist of her hand. "Dear guardians, we are enjoying a memory of a private conversation from some time back. It pleases us you follow directives and seek our advice in this perplexing situation."

"We have decided it is time to let Marco communicate with Francesca. We agree with your strict guideline policy. Introduce yourselves tonight to Marco. Plan for his contacting Francesca tomorrow night.

Victor and Viana, in timing with Marco's contacting Francesca through the Flower, reveal yourselves visibly to her, making your presence known," High Priest Akshai instructs. "How much you reveal in one evening is at your discretion. It will take some time for her to process the information. It may take as long as a month, or even more, to fully disclose the mission of the Chiawaukas."

Victor, Viana, Blazer and Celestial each thank the High Priests.

The snow globe shape object and the High Priest and Priestess vanish.

The four Chiawaukas relax from the attentive posture they were in. "I believe I speak for us all when I say, 'that is a relief.' They granted us the authority to apprise Marco of his situation and reveal ourselves to Francesca," Victor recounts.

"Well, let's get to work," signals Blazer.

Chapter 34

AN EVENING WITH FRANCESCA

Zeek sweeps the property making sure no Cryptolores are in sight. He then places himself on the deck rail near Francesca. *Just like Victor and Viana stated, Francesca is sitting out back.*
I think I am going to explore the rocks she has placed in her yard. Zeek lifts off the rail flying low to the ground to inspect the rocks Francesca has collected. Zeek sees out of the corner of his eye Francesca giving a quick turn to the rail as he took off. *Man, were my comrades accurate! She must sense my presence! I should be able to view these rocks without raising her attention.* Zeek reaches for a rock; upon touching it, his energy lights up the rock, making it visible to his sight. *Oh my, what a beautiful specimen of listwanite!* He reaches for another; *blue slate, what an exquisite array of blue colors, and quite a large specimen. Oh my...*Zeek glances at the porch; Francesca is not there. He moves into an upright position not realizing Francesca is standing near him. Zeek darts straight up, and peers down to watch Francesca.

Francesca touches each rock that Zeek had just inspected. Francesca searches around, puzzled... curious. Zeek begins to calm down when he hears Francesca's voice declare out loud, "I can't explain it, I believe someone, something, is out here with me, admiring my rock collection."

Zeek is just not sure how to engage…if he should engage. He remembers that Victor and Viana have not yet confirmed their existence to Francesca. *What to do? I so want to visit with her about rocks.* Zeek relocates about six feet away from Francesca. Then, he stretches himself so he his standing an impressive six-foot-three-inches tall. If a smile could light the night sky, Zeek's smile just illuminated the back area of the Mancini property.

Francesca turns, scanning in Zeek's direction, then up a bit, as if making direct eye contact, "I know you are here. I just know it! I don't know who you are, but I trust my senses."

Francesca pauses, looks around and sighs. *I don't know, maybe no one is here. Maybe it is my imagination.* She takes a deep breath, *no, too many things have occurred. Something is definitely coexisting on Soliel with us. At least in our kingdom.*

Zeek so wants to speak to Francesca; he reaches out toward her long curls blowing in the gentle breeze. His fingers touch the ends of some strands of her hair which momentarily appears luminescent at his touch. He quickly pulls his hand back as if not meaning to actually make contact. He watches as the strands of her hair light up the split second he gently brushed the tips. Each strand he lightly touched illuminates to her scalp, then dissipates, as if a bit of his energy ran the length of her hair.

Zeek, now hovering within a few feet, thinks, *oh my, I wonder if she felt that. How will I explain this to Victor and Viana?*

Francesca reaches to the top of her head, and runs her hands and fingers throughout her hair. *I don't feel anything in my hair. Now that is weird. It felt like something touched my hair.* Then she smiles, turns around, assuredly communicating aloud, "I like rocks, too."

Zeek lets out a sigh of relief, *if that's all she received from me, good. Boy was that close! I didn't realize she had such abilities! I believe I should wait for another time before I send her locations of some cool rocks. I think she would be extremely suspicious if she isn't already.*

Zeek watches Francesca step up onto the deck, turn, and search the area. After some time, Francesca retreats inside.

Chapter 35

"Man, do I have a headache," Gino complains pulling out a chair at the dining table. He leans his head into his hands. "Where's Pop?"

"Well, he's doing his morning chores, sweetie. Would you like something to eat?" Francesca asks.

"I hope Pop didn't mind doing my chores. Yes, I would like something to eat. Nothing sounds good though," Gino says still holding his head in his hands while resting his elbows on the table top.

Francesca brings Gino a glass of water, a cup of coffee, and a toasted bacon and egg sandwich with cheese. "Oh no, son, you'll do your own chores."

Gino glances up to his mother in astonishment, "What? I figured since you guys knew I am sick, Pop would do my chores."

Francesca has her little laugh, "Oh sweetie, you're not sick with an illness. You're not feeling well from self-indulgence. That will not get you out of your chores, or your responsibilities, or work at Bill Oliver's Woodworking Shop. You'll be expected to show up to your job tomorrow after your chores. And today, when you down that water, and what I served, you'll go do your Sundei chores as usual," Francesca strictly instructs.

Gino's shoulders lower, his elbows spread out, and he drops his head to the table. Turning his head sideways, he looks to his mother, "Are you sure I am not sick? Because I feel pretty sick."

"Just stop, Gino. Set your mind right. You drank. Apparently more than you should have. Now, your body is not happy," Francesca pauses, "You still have responsibilities. I'm telling you straight, set your brain to dictate your body. Drink the water, eat your food. Drink the coffee. Go get your chores done. The sooner you mentally pull yourself together, the quicker you will feel back to normal. Now quit whining."

Gino reluctantly follows his mother's directions. Scooting his chair back, he stands, taking his plate to the kitchen, "Well, I see there is no mercy at the Mancinis," Gino grumbles with a little chuckle in his voice as well.

Francesca is standing, resting her body against the counter with her arms folded, looking at Gino, as he sets his plate and utensils in the sink.

She reaches out to give him a hug, "See, not so bad. You'll be fine. How about I make an apple pie for dessert after this evening dinner?" Francesca smiles.

Gino still wants to be fussy, but he is softened by his mother's persistence on engaging with him, "I think that would be pretty awesome of you, Mom," Gino says.

"Alright then. I'll get busy with preparations. You set your mind right, and get on your chores. Hey, you only have to feed the horses, then it is a day of rest," Francesca reminds Gino.

Gino nods, "Thanks, Mom." *Okay, body, you are just going to have to be still. I need to feed the horses, and the dogs for that matter.* Gino heads out to the stables. Pepper, Snowy, and Abby always run to greet Gino when they see him outside. Bending down to pet them, "You guys are the best friends a guy could have." Gino addresses them while giving each of them hugs and rubs.

Gino reaches the stables. Antonio is just walking out of the barn across from the stables. Gino is expecting a lecture from his Pop. "I'll see you up at the house," Antonio waves as his long strides lead him back to their ranch home.

Gino stands perplexed, then refocuses his attention to Pepper, Abby and Snowy at his side. He enters the stables to complete his Sundei tasks, then returns to their ranch home.

"Some wedding, wasn't it?" Antonio speaks to Gino.

"It sure was, Pop." Gino acknowledges.

"Your mother and I had a good time. We hope you did too," Antonio hints.

Gino can't keep back his smile, "I sure did enjoy being one of the groomsmen, and spending the entire evening with Claire. Don't you think she's great?" Gino seeks approval.

Antonio nods, "What little I have been around her, yes, Son, I would say she's great."

Francesca enters the family room, "Gino, I think Claire is a real delight, and I think I will take her up on her offer of helping me with baked goods."

"She'll be working here?" inquires Gino.

"Well, yes. She seems like a determined young woman. Unless you have a reason, you do not want me to hire her," Francesca yields.

Gino gently shakes his head, "No, no, that'll be quite alright. Honestly, I am telling you both now, I hope to marry Claire someday, and build our home on this property, as you two have often discussed with Marco and me. I hope you both approve."

Antonio and Francesca smile at each other, Francesca slides from the arm of the chair onto Antonio's lap, "Son, we approve," assures Antonio.

Gino feels a peace within, but a headache at the same time. "Do you guys mind if I go lay down?"

"Not feeling so hot?" guesses Antonio.

"Yeah, you could say that," answers Gino.

Francesca stands, "Follow me, Gino."

Francesca leads Gino to the kitchen. "Here, I want you to drink this glass of water. Then I want you to walk outside, and make sure the dogs have plenty of water. Then you may go lay down."

Gino casts his eyes upon his mother in amazement, "I don't remember this treatment when any of us have been sick before."

Francesca looks at her son while he drinks the glass of water she gave him. "You haven't been sick from this source before."

Gino sets the glass down with his eyes fixed on his mother. He heads out the back door obeying her instructions. Then he heads to his room to lie down.

......⁊ℰ......

"Simply another amazing dinner, dear," Antonio compliments Francesca.

"Thank you," Francesca renders as she sets the pie on the table. "I made some homemade ice-cream while you were sleeping, Gino, to go with that apple pie."

A big grin overtakes Gino's face. "I am truly blessed to have such great parents, and a good brother. I bet he would approve of Claire, don't you think?"

His parents are both smiling. "Well, of course he would, dear," Francesca winks at Gino.

Antonio nods, "Gino, your brother would approve."

"Thanks. Hey, do you guys mind if I turn in after dessert? I have work tomorrow, and I need some rest. You were right about the champagne. Boy did that kick me," Gino admits.

"Absolutely, son," Antonio states.

"Why of course, sweetie," Francesca adds.

"I know we usually visit or play games on Sundei evenings, thanks for understanding," Gino adds.

"We've all had a busy weekend. After I help your mother with dishes, I'm going to turn in myself," Antonio shares, winking at his wife.

"Goodnight, sweet Gino. I love you," Francesca gives her son a big mama bear hug.

"Goodnight, Mom. Goodnight, Pop," Gino departs.

"As for you, young lady," Antonio pulls Francesca into his arms and begins to dance with her, "Will you be joining me soon?" Antonio asks as he spins Francesca out, then she twirls back into his arms.

"I will be there soon," Francesca gently kisses Antonio's cheek.

Antonio gives Francesca an embracing hug, "See you soon," he kisses her lips, then walks to their bedroom.

Francesca walks out onto their back deck. She admires the evening sun slowly setting behind the mountains. For a summer evening, they all feel like retiring to bed early. She then steps back into their family room, and walks over to the fireplace to gaze at the mysterious flower they found on Marco. *It's been two years, not one petal has wilted. Puzzling.* She then walks to the master bedroom to see Antonio is already sound asleep. Francesca decides to return to the family room. She sits down in her most comfortable rocker. She rocks back and forth ever so slowly, closing her eyes to unwind. Several moments later she hears, "Mom, are you awake?" Francesca opens her eyes expecting to see Gino. No one is standing there. Again, she hears, "Mom."

Francesca stands on full alert. She knows now it is Marco's voice she recognizes. She steps closer to the fireplace curiously peering at the unusual flower on the mantel.

"Yes, Mother, it is me, Marco. I know…this must be completely strange to you. I did not die, Mother," Marco reveals.

Francesca places one hand on the mantel, the other covering her mouth. She is in awe and disbelief.

"Mother, the suspicions you have of another life form on Soleil, in our kingdom, well, it's accurate," Marco conveys.

Francesca takes her hand from over her mouth to rub her forehead, and then runs it through her hair. She turns her neck from side to side beginning to feel some anxiety.

"Mother, I did not die. The Supreme Guardian beings assigned to Soleil saw my aura, detected I still had life in me, and immediately placed me in a protective shield," Marco continues.

"The what? Guardian beings? Did you say your aura?" Francesca quizzes trying to make sense of it all.

Just then, Victor and Viana appear standing on each side of Francesca in their three to four-feet tall stature. She looks down with astonishment, and then returns her focus on the flower. She glances back down to each side of her, studies the two blue, small beings, and hears Marco's voice, "Mother, meet Victor and Viana. They are Chiawaukas. Supreme Guardian Beings," Marco introduces.

Victor and Vianna both smile as Francesca reaches to touch Viana. Viana gently slides her hand into Francesca's hand. Victor places Francesca's other hand between his two hands. Francesca begins to laugh and cry at the same time. She pulls her hands from the little beings to wipes tears from her eyes. She dabs her drippy nose with the tail of her shirt.

Francesca smiles at Victor and Viana while she continues to dab her nose and wipe her eyes. "I…I don't know what to say. Am I dreaming?" Francesca wonders.

Viana and Victor leap to sit on the mantel to make better eye contact with Francesca. "You're not dreaming, dear Francesca," Viana assures in her crisp, loving voice.

"We are Chiawaukas, Supreme Guardian beings, just as Marco described. We have so wanted to introduce ourselves to you, but have been waiting for approval from our high priest and priestess. It's all about timing. We have a lot to bring you up to speed," Victor divulges.

Francesca is shaking her head, trying to wrap her mind around all she has been told.

"Yes, Mom, there are other Chiawaukas. One was with you last night out back. His name is Zeek. And, I guess you can say, although he is a Chiawauka, his passion is archeology and geology. He also keeps journals of all the missions he is assigned to. Zeek greatly enjoyed seeing a few of the rocks you've collected," Marco communicates.

"When can I see you, Marco? Where are you?" Francesca inquires.

"I have been in a protective shield, in our mausoleum. Celestial and Blazer have been monitoring my recovery. In fact, I will be staying with them until further notice," Marco discloses.

Francesca is fidgety, placing her hands on her hips, running her hands through her hair, lifting and tossing her long, thick, brunette, curly hair, and finally places her hands on the mantel. Viana reaches to Francesca, touching her shoulders. Francesca is almost mesmerized, as she accepts the hug Viana is giving, and then wraps her arms around Viana. Francesca calms.

"Mother, I don't know when I can see you, but I can tell you I have seen things that have gone on. You handled Gino incredibly this morning in regards to him not feeling well. And, I realize now, when I said you looked beautiful, you were in one of my favorite outfits, going to my funeral," Marco details.

Francesca begins fidgeting again. Viana places her hands on Francesca hands.

"Mother, Victor and Viana saw that I had an aura. Their quick action prevented my death. You have an aura as well. Our entire family does, Mother. YOU are the primary source," Marco enlightens.

Francesca begins to laugh nervously, then cry. "I don't understand."

"You will. Victor and Viana have been assigned to our family. They will educate you, on all you need to know. On all your suspicions. They are here to protect, and to train our family," Marco instructs.

Francesca tosses her hands about, "Protect us? Train us? You didn't die? We saw you. The doctor said you were...gone." Francesca drops her head with a sigh.

"Mother, I know you have so many questions. I have to go for now. I did not die. The two Chiawaukas with you protected me. I love you," Marco pauses, "and Mom, you absolutely cannot convey any of this to Gino, Pop, or anyone at this time. Not even a hint." Marco instructs, "I love you."

Francesca looks at Victor and Viana, reaches out to the flower, and as her fingertips touches it, she whispers, "I love you, Marco."

Chapter 36

A ntonio wakes up to see Francesca still sleeping. He gets dressed, makes coffee, and does some early morning chores. Gino, too, has gotten himself around and left for work at Bill Oliver's Woodworking Shop. Antonio returns to the house, still seeing no sign of Francesca, he prepares a mug of hot chocolate for her.

Antonio enters their bedroom, and pauses; he admires her beauty as she appears to be in a deep sleep. He sets the mug on the table near their bed and seats himself next to her. He massages her right arm as she lays on her left side. Antonio gently runs his fingers across her hair trying to not get caught in tangles of her curls. Francesca rolls onto her back opening her eyes; she smiles up at Antonio. She then glances around the room and curiously thinks, *How did I get here? I don't even remember coming to bed last night.* Then, in a panic, sits up, "What time is it?" she questions.

With tenderness in his rugged voice, Antonio replies, "It's around 8:30." He reaches for the mug of one of her favorite drinks and slowly hands it to her, "I made you some hot chocolate."

"Thank you. Why did you let me sleep so late? I have so much to do," Francesca presses.

Antonio stands, "I let you sleep because apparently your body needed the rest."

Francesca quickly gets out of bed, "I feel so rushed now."

Antonio gets out of her way, "I'm going out to the stables, then I'm going to ride the fence line today to check posts."

"Alright, babe…and thank you for the hot chocolate," Francesca twinkles.

She walks to her closet to select clothes for the day with thoughts racing, *Key-a what? Auras? Marco's alive? How did I get to bed?"* She quickly selects the perfect outfit for the day, dresses, brushes her teeth, washes her face, and sets out.

"Good morning, Lady," Francesca greets her horse while saddling her.

She gets on Lady and rides off to town to her parents' store, and to pay a visit to Claire.

Was I dreaming last night? I do remember falling asleep in the rocker. Were there two little life forms on my mantel? So many thoughts fill her head while she rides towards town. She ties Lady up when she arrives at her parents' store.

She enters the store, "Good morning, Mother, good morning, Father," Francesca says in a loud voice to make sure her parents hear her. She runs into Claire, "Well, Claire, what a nice surprise to see you in here. I was coming to see you after I stopped in here," announces Francesca.

"Good morning. You were coming to see me?" inquires Claire.

"Yes, I was wondering, now that you have graduated high school, if you do not have a job yet, I would certainly like to hire you to help me with baked goods. My orders have increased tremendously, plus with gardening, ranching, helping the Queen…well I can get pretty busy," Francesca conveys.

"I'd be honored to work at your side. When may I start?" Claire asks.

"Tomorrow, 8 AM," Francesca states.

Claire smiles, "Thank you, Mrs. Mancini."

"Claire, you may call me by my first name," insists Francesca.

"Alright then," Claire notes as she departs the store with sacks of purchased items.

......෴......

"How are you doing today?" Sophia asks her daughter walking out from behind the register to give Francesca a hug.

"Well, I overslept," admits Francesca.

Leonardo briskly walks to his daughter placing his hand on her forehead, "Are you feeling, alright?"

Francesca laughs her little laugh, "Yeah, I actually do feel fine. Antonio thought my body required the sleep, so he didn't wake me."

Smiling, Leonardo declares, "I always liked that boy."

"Well, Dad, I would hardly consider a 40-year man a boy," Francesca winks.

Motioning with his hand, "I know, I know, he's quite the fine man. And he takes excellent care of my sweet daughter. And that my dear, has excelled him to top notch in my books," Leonardo proclaims.

"Well, thank you, Daddy," Francesca kisses her dad on his cheek.

"I think it's wonderful you decided to hire some help, Francie dear," Sophia affirms, "and Claire, well, that one," Sophia points with her index finger motioning like a hand shake, "I can tell she is going to mesh with you very well."

"Thank you, Mother. I better head back; I have a full day. I love you guys," expresses Francesca.

"Love you too, Honey," Sophia squeezes Francesca.

"Bye, Dear," Leonardo holds open the door.

Francesca rides Lady back to her home, enjoying the summer day as thoughts run through her head: *I wonder where the key-a, key-a, I don't know. I wonder when I will see them again. Will I see Marco? Did I dream this? I don't even remember going to bed. How* *did I get to bed? Ug, I need some answers! Maybe it was their presence I have been sensing, but then my intuition led me to Arabella. Well, there was definitely a different feeling when I sensed Arabella. Maybe, they **ARE** our guardian angels. That would explain things!*

Francesca sees her herding dogs, Pepper and Snowy, and, her guardian dog, Abby, running toward her and Lady on approach. "Hello, my sweet babies," Francesca greets her beloved dogs, while they circle, wagging their tails, "I think I'm going to ride out to find Antonio," she voices to them as if they understand every word she says. Francesca turns Lady heading her out toward the fence line to search for Antonio, feeling somewhat perplexed about what she thinks was real and not a dream, *where are you two? Are you going to show up to...*

"We are going to show up right now," answers Viana interrupting Francesca's thoughts, as she and Victor appear hovering to each side of Francesca.

"Whoa...Lady," commands Francesca, pulling the reins. You can hear Lady's hooves circle a bit, coming to a stop.

Viana reaches to Lady's face stroking from her nose to her eyes, up and down. "Beautiful horse you have."

"Yes, thank you," Francesca offers with a questioning voice.

"We just wanted to assure you; we are not a dream. You have been sensing our presence for some time now. We are Supreme Guardian Beings, the Chiawaukas (Key-a-wau-kas). We were sent to Soleil for our mission, to find you," Viana briefs.

"Me?" Francesca gazes at both, Viana and Victor.

"Yes, you, your family, and actually another family. We just haven't located them, yet," Victor reveals.

"I don't understand. How can I be of help to guardian angels?" questions Francesca.

"Honey, we are guardian beings," Viana corrects.

"Is there a difference?" Francesca inquires.

Victor and Viana stare at each other, then look to Francesca, "Yes, Francesca, there is a difference," Victor states matter-of-fact in his direct voice.

"I'm sorry, I didn't mean to offend you," Francesca submits.

"No offense taken. I will briefly give you a definition. Guardian Angels are spiritual beings. They are protectors and shepherds. They are servants, and messengers of God. To our knowledge, one Guardian Angel is assigned to one human. We are Chiawaukas, Supreme Guardian Beings. We are given assignments, which may be one person, but usually it involves many, and our missions vary," educates Victor.

Viana adds, "Francesca, there is a lot of information to give you. For now, just know, we are here if you need us. We can communicate telepathically. There are two families we refer to as The Chords of Chiawaukas. Your family is one. We are still seeking to discover the location of the other one. We will tell you at another time what that actually means. Though you and your family are a top priority of our mission to Soleil, we also have another mission. That too, will be disclosed at a later encounter with you. For now, go about your life, and know, we are here to guard and keep the peacefulness your people have enjoyed for centuries," Viana assures.

Victor's expression is more of a business exchange, "Remember, you must not share knowledge of us, or Marco, to anyone."

Francesca sighs, "I understand."

Viana and Victor reach out to Francesca, Victor placing his hands on her right arm, Viana placing her hands on her left arm, "Close your eyes, feel our presence," instructs Viana.

Several moments pass, before Francesca opens her eyes. "I do feel your presence."

Viana smiles at Francesca, and slides her hands down Francesca's arm onto her hand. She squeezes it firmly for a few moments, then the two Chiawaukas vanish leaving Francesca sitting on Lady in a peaceful silence. *That's another déjà vu experience,*

Francesca recalls, *the moment when Viana placed her hands on my arm, then ran her hands down my arm into my hand. Genie Arabella made the same gesture.* Francesca signals Lady to move out. She continues on her gallop of the fence line until she catches up with Antonio.

⋯⋯⸱❦⸱⋯⋯

"By requesting Francesca not even hint that Marco is alive or of our existence and presence to Antonio and Gino, well…you realize we have placed her in a difficult situation," Viana renders.

"I have considered that. If she tells Antonio and Gino before we introduce ourselves, we could possibly conclude we can't trust her with sensitive information, and of course if she doesn't tell, then Antonio's trust in her will waver, at least for a bit. If she tells, when Marco also made it clear not to tell, it may appear we can't confide in her, but if she doesn't tell Antonio and Gino, they will no doubt feel she isn't loyal to them. Either way, we did place her in a situation that will challenge the reputation she values," Victor frowns.

⋯⋯⸱❦⸱⋯⋯

Antonio hears a horse approaching. He stops to look up. A smile decorates his face, "Nice to see you." His deep voice is music to Francesca's ears. "You look...well, you look at peace," Antonio notices, "a good morning I take it?"

"Yes, a good morning," Francesca conveys getting down off Lady.

Antonio sets his tools aside and reaches for Francesca, embracing her tightly.

"Mm, I should come visit you more often, cowboy," Francesca twinkles.

"I always enjoy you by my side," shares Antonio.

Antonio gets back to the fence while they visit.

"Have you ever wondered if we will see Marco again?" Francesca asks.

"Well, that's an odd question. Of course, when we join him in heaven," Antonio answers.

"Do you ever wonder if we have a higher purpose than ranching, mining, baking...our daily lives? Do you ever wonder what we are designed to actually do, what purpose to fulfill?" quizzes Francesca.

"What's with the questions? I don't know. I guess I believe I am fulfilling my purpose. I work hard, I believe in God, and try to be a just and noble man. I don't know," Antonio replies. "Where are these questions coming from?"

Francesca looks around as far as her eyes can see of their 21,000-acre mountain, valley ranch. She rests her eyes back on Antonio placing her hands in her front pockets, "I don't know, maybe it was all the sleep you let me have this morning," winks Francesca flexing onto her tiptoes.

A little chuckle comes from Antonio. He glances at her with a smile and nod, "Maybe so."

Chapter 37

CLAIRES FIRST DAY OF WORK

Gino heads out on his horse Jolly to go to work at Bill Oliver's. He sees Claire entering their driveway. Once near, he smiles, "Well, hello...to the most beautiful girl in all the land." He places two fingers and his thumb on the side brim of his cowboy hat, and makes a gesture like a salute.

Claire smiles, her dimples show, and her brilliant green eyes shine, "Thank you, Gino. Have a good day at work."

"I will. You have a good day with my mother," Gino exchanges.

"I'm sure it is going to work out just fine," Claire submits.

"I'm pretty sure you are correct," acknowledges Gino with a big smile. "Maybe I'll be home before you're gone."

"Maybe so," Claire agrees, as her face blushes a bit.

After exchanging smiles and nods, Claire continues up to the Mancini Ranch home, and Gino down the driveway toward work.

Francesca steps out onto the front deck, "Good morning, Claire."

Claire dismounts and ties up her horse. She conveys, "Good morning to you!" Stepping up onto the deck, Claire walks in while Francesca holds open the door.

"I have a huge order this week, so it's a perfect day for you to begin," Francesca encourages Claire.

"Well, I'm ready. Show me what you need," Claire responds with eagerness.

"Here is the list of orders we need to fill," Francesca points to a piece of paper. "This is my pantry, our work area, the ovens. If you have any questions, feel free to ask. Oh, the bathroom is in the hallway on the right. And actually, let's take your horse to the paddock for the day," Francesca details.

After the two unsaddle Claire's horse, Cocoa Bean, and place her in the paddock, Claire and Francesca head back. Upon their journey from the paddock to the side door which enters the kitchen, Francesca points out her gardens, and briefly highlights her goals for her backyard.

Claire, ever intently listens to Francesca's passionate outline of her design plans and smiles ever so peacefully. "Wow! That will look incredible when you complete it. Thank you for sharing your ideas with me."

Francesca wraps her left arm around Claire, "Well, thank you for letting me share how I envision these areas."

The two ladies return to the kitchen and begin prepping the items on the order list. They connect so well they are able to work in quiet peace without feeling awkward or the need to be constantly talking, which suits them both.

Hours pass by, Antonio enters the kitchen from outside. After hanging his hat, he greets Claire, "Nice to see my wife has a helper. I hope you are enjoying working here."

"I am. I think this will be a good fit," Claire maintains.

"I'm glad to hear that," offers Antonio as he steps next to Francesca, giving her a kiss on her cheek.

Francesca smiles at Antonio, "Go wash up, I'll set your lunch on the table."

Francesca sets plates and sandwiches for the three of them. Antonio leads them in prayer.

"Claire, what do you think of being Francesca's assistant so far?" asks Antonio.

Claire nods while she's chewing a bite. After swallowing she discloses, "I am enjoying the recipes, and the energy baking seems to give."

Francesca gently smiles.

"Well, is that the secret to my wife's energy?" Antonio chuckles, "baking?"

Francesca laughs.

Claire gazes at the two Mancinis and smiles, recognizing Gino has the same little laugh his mother does.

......⁓ℰ❧......

The day presses on. Francesca and Claire complete the orders. Claire is on Cocoa Bean, ready to depart to town. Francesca secures the baked items in the specially designed bags Antonio made.

"I really appreciate your help. I'm glad you said 'yes'. I can tell you are going to be an asset to my business," Francesca conveys.

"I'm glad, too. Do you want me to return tomorrow or the next day?" Claire inquires.

"Let's plan three days a week for now. This week...today, tomorrow and Fridei. Next week we will begin Mondei, Wednesdei, Fridei," Francesca relays. "Also, when you drop those off at my parents' store, they will probably have a new list. You can pick up the list Wednesdei before you come out," instructs Francesca.

"Will do, thank you," Claire motions Cocoa Bean to head out.

Upon Claire's journey down the Mancini drive way, Gino is approaching on Jolly.

Stopping Jolly next to Cocoa Bean and Claire, Gino declares, "Well, I'm liking this pattern."

Smiling, Claire curiously asks in her deliberate, slightly, crisp voice, "What pattern might that be?"

"Seeing you when I head off for work, and seeing you when I return home," Gino discloses with a confident smile.

Claire blushes, "I'm enjoying that as well. I have to go; I need to get these items to your grandparents' store before they close."

"How about if I accompany you?" asks Gino.

"Aren't you tired from work? You really don't have to," Claire replies.

"I am never too tired to accompany you, let's go," Gino signals Jolly to take off.

Claire motions Cocoa Bean. They ride along next to each other, visiting, enjoying the summer day.

"Hey, after we drop off the items at my grandparents' store, how about we go to the fork of the Chianne River and Chamberlain River?" Gino proposes.

Claire looks over to him with a playful grin, "Are you sure your name isn't Trouble?"

Gino flings his arms out, and upward into the sky, "Trouble? I am a mere cowboy, suggesting to the most beautiful girl in the kingdom to accompany me to a cool place."

"Well, alright then. Your persuasion tactics are effective. I think it'll be fun. Plus, it is pretty hot out," Claire submits with a flirty smile.

Gino and Claire arrive at Montanelli's Mercantile. They unload the baked goods and carry them in.

"Hello, grandparents!" exclaims Gino.

Sophia and Leonardo walk toward their grandson Gino, and Claire. Sophia gives Gino a big hug, "This is an added bonus getting to see you and Claire!" Sophia then pats her grandson on the center of his chest.

"Yes, I hope you enjoyed your first day of work with Francesca," Leonardo offers while reaching for the baked items.

"I did, thank you," Claire respectfully answers.

Gino kisses his grandmother's cheek, "We best be going. We're going to the Double C-Fork."

"Yeah, well, it's a beautiful day for it. Be safe," Leonardo states patting his grandson on his upper arm.

"We will. Love you guys," Gino expresses affection towards his grandparents.

"It was so good to see you both," Sophia imparts as she touches both Claire and Gino on their arms, and slides her hands down to their hands, squeezing them.

"It was nice to see you as well. Oh, and I will stop by tomorrow morning for the new order list," Claire responds.

Gino and Claire turn and walk out the door. They get on their horses and head north through town. "So, the nickname for the fork of the Chianne and Chamberlain Rivers is called the Double C-Fork?"

"Yes. The Chianne River then runs through our property. The Chamberlain River runs along the east side of Chamberlain Kingdom and the base of Chamberlain Mountain Range. I will show you all the wonderful places here, that is, if you would like me to," offers Gino.

Claire tips her head ever so slightly, and glances at Gino. She smiles, "I'd like that. Maybe we can find some new places you've never seen."

"Well, I doubt that's possible since I grew up here," Gino says with a little laugh, "but I'm up for the adventure," Gino confirms.

Claire smiles.

After about thirty minutes they reach the C-Fork.

"Oh, Gino, this is absolutely breathtaking!" Claire exclaims.

"Yeah, it's pretty amazing. Here, let's get off our horses. There's a pretty good spot right over there where we can tie off the horses, they can drink, and there is a calm pool," Gino points.

The two walk Jolly and Cocoa Bean down the trail, to the sandy shore. Both horses' drink. Gino ties the horses to a nearby Aspen Tree. He turns looking at Claire. "So, what do those pretty green eyes of yours see?" asks Gino.

Claire turns, glances at Gino, then turns back gazing out upon the spectacular view of the magnificent Chianne River and the fork, where the river splits. "So much energy, and beauty, Gino. Thank you, for bringing me here."

Gino walks to position himself next to Claire. "You're welcome." Gino reaches to pull off his boots.

"What are you doing?" Claire quizzes.

"Well, I'm taking my boots off, rolling up my pants and getting my feet wet. Join me." Gino reaches out to Claire after he gets his boots off and rolls up his pants.

"Well, I don't know," Claire behaves timidly.

"Suit yourself, but my hand is here for your hand; have a little fun," coaxes Gino as he steps into the crystal-clear, river water.

"Oh, what the heck," Claire declares. She takes her socks and shoes off and rolls up her pants, as well. Claire steps to the river's edge and reaches for Gino's hand.

Gino steps closer to the shore and reaches to hold Claire's hand, securing her, while she steps in. "Brr, the water is still chilly!" shrieks Claire.

"Well, it's Junis. Snows are still melting. We don't need to stay in long," Gino empathizes.

Claire begins to laugh as she tries to step across some rocks while holding onto Gino's hand. "Be careful there," cautions Gino.

Laughing more, Claire reaches to Gino hastily with her other hand, "Oh! I don't want to fall, yikes!" Claire slips and plunges herself into Gino.

Gino's feet are well placed, so he is able to catch her without them both falling completely into the river. They are both laughing so hard. Claire stands on her two feet, still holding onto Gino's shirt. "Oh, my gosh, this is so much fun!" Claire establishes.

Gino smiles and reaches for Claire's long slender hand with his hand. He places her hand on his chest, with his large hand laying over her hand. She looks at him with her eyes sparkling. "Gino, this is really remarkable." Claire admits.

"You're remarkable, Claire," Gino submits.

Claire lays her head on Gino's shoulder, and Gino wraps his arms around her. They melt in the moment and experience a tenderness with each other. Claire then bends down and splashes Gino.

"Hey!" Gino expresses as the cold-water lands on his arms.

Laughing, Claire splashes him again as she makes way for the shore.

"Really? Is that how you want to play?" Gino laughs, reaching to splash some water on Claire as she nears the edge of the river.

They both step onto the shore that's decorated with red sand and pebbles. Laughing, they both sit down on some logs that were placed there ages ago for people to rest on.

"I don't even remember what day this is," Claire laughs.

"It's Tuesdei, only three work days left," informs Gino.

"Oh, yeah. Well, if every day is as relaxing as this, how wonderful life is!" reflects Claire.

"Every day may not be as relaxing, but life is wonderful," assures Gino.

There is a long, peaceful silence as the two view the scenery and smell the mountain air, while they listen to the sounds that surround them.

"We better head back," Gino supposes.

"Yeah, thank you, Gino. Maybe you're right. Maybe, life is wonderful," considers Claire.

Gino stands after he puts his socks and boots on, and rolls down his jean cuffs. He extends his hand to help Claire stand after she too puts her socks and shoes on and rolls down her pant legs.

They stand, studying the magnificent view one last time before they leave.

Gino helps Claire onto Cocoa Bean, then gets on Jolly. Gino escorts Claire to her home.

"Thank you for the afterwork fun," Claire says to Gino.

"Anytime." He places his index, middle finger, and thumb on the side brim of his hat, sliding them forward as if in a salute motion.

Claire gazes upon Gino as he rides off, thinking, *I sure like that cowboy.*

Chapter 38

"It sure was delightful watching the Mancinis celebrate Francesca's thirty-seventh birthday," Viana states.

"Again...," Victor clears his throat, with a smirky smile. "It's been a few years since her actual thirty-seventh, but I do like her attitude."

"Oh, Victor," Viana begins in her crisp voice, "I am so thankful we are the team assigned to the Mancinis! I know...I'm sure I have mentioned that before, but watching a Chord of Chiawauka family interact and grow, well, it's just rewarding."

"I have to agree with you, Viana," Victor concurs.

"Now what about Genie Arabella? I know we discussed we are going to investigate, though we just haven't made time for it yet," Viana recounts.

"Let's do that tomorrow. It's late, time for our nightly property rounds, and we need to check in with the other teams," directs Victor.

"Agreed," Viana confirms.

.......⚬⧉⚬.......

"The Mancinis are off to another good start of their day, let's head up the mountain," Viana nudges.

"Alright," Victor stretches.

The two Chiawaukas leisurely fly to the cabin Francesca discovered.

"I am still puzzled how Arabella could still be alive. What is her role in the Ancient Writings? Do the high priests know she was present, let alone affected?" Viana ponders.

"All good queries, Viana. Hey, isn't that Mancini Lake? We need to veer off to the right if I heard Francesca correctly," Victor advances.

Viana follows Victor's lead. "This scenery is captivating," Viana states as she inhales the scent of the pines. "Just heavenly," she exclaims.

"What is just heavenly?" Victor wonders.

"The scent of the pines," Viana beams.

"We are on a mission, the path should be visible soon," Victor reiterates.

"Yes, we are on a mission; I was merely enjoying the scent and the mesmerizing landscape," Viana utters.

Victor peers over to his Chiawauka teammate as they slowly fly, keeping an eye out for their destination, and gives her a nod of acknowledgement.

"Victor, there it is!" states Viana, pointing. "Are we going to make contact, or just observe?"

"Viana, we're going to wing it," Victor delivers.

Laughing, Viana almost chokes, "Wing it? I don't believe I have ever known you to 'wing' anything."

Victor shakes his head, "I know, I'm as perplexed about it as you are," he chuckles. "Let's just observe, and then decide."

"Good idea," smiles Viana.

Circling the perimeter of the cabin, they spy Genie Arabella in her garden.

Arabella stands. She looks around. She surveys the area she calls home then raises her face toward the sky, followed by, "I know you are here. I can feel you. Please identify yourselves," Arabella's sweet voice casts into the air.

Astounded, Victor and Viana stare at each other. "Shall we?" Victor questions.

Viana nods.

"I'm waiting," Arabella softly speaks into the air again.

Victor and Viana gently touch down, and walk toward Arabella.

Arabella turns and sees the two, blue, just under four-foot-tall beings approach her.

"It is so nice of you two to visit me," Arabella greets the duo.

Viana and Victor both extend their arms to offer Arabella a handshake.

"My name is Victor, this is Viana," Victor introduces.

"We are Chiawaukas, Supreme Guardian Beings," Viana imparts.

Arabella gives the sweetest smile to her two visitors, then conveys in her soft-spoken manner, "I am glad you finally found me. My name is Genie Arabella. But you probably know that already."

Viana smiles at Genie Arabella.

"I'm curious, Arabella, how you know of us? You speak like you have been awaiting our arrival," Victor surmises.

"I've known of the Chiawaukas ever since I was a young girl. They visited my friend, Anna Grace," recalls Arabella. "I remember that night. I was spending the night and for some reason, I couldn't sleep, and was lying in bed staring at the stars when I saw a snow globe shaped object descend from the night sky. I hid. The snow globe shaped object came right through the glass of the window without breaking it. You would think I would have been trembling in fear, but I was frozen in awe and wonder."

"Do you remember what happened?" Viana questions.

"I do," Arabella, says as she sweetly smiles. "Two people, well, they were not people, they actually looked like the both of you, just taller; anyway, two beings adorned in beautiful, priestly garments placed their hands above Anna Grace while she peacefully slept. They moved their hands above her, over her, in a figure eight motion. A beam of golden light left their hands. It appeared as though droplets of gold entered Anna Grace, without disturbing her. It seemed like it lasted for many minutes; but now, thinking back, it probably was only moments."

"Do you recall anything else?" Victor asks.

"I remember the two of them chanting something. I will have to think about it," recounts Arabella.

"Do you have any idea how it has come to be that you have outlived Anna Grace, by three generations?" Viana wonders.

"No, I have no idea. I do remember before they returned to the snow globe shaped object, or maybe as they were returning to it, the entire room filled with a golden, luminescent light. I remember holding my arms out from my hiding place in hopes that some of the golden droplets would fall on me. Silly things kids do," Arabella gently laughs.

"Fascinating. Did you ever tell Anna Grace what you witnessed? Did you notice anything peculiar in Anna's behavior, or yours, for that matter, after the incident?" Victor queries.

Arabella answers in her collected voice, "No, I never did disclose to Anna what I witnessed. With each passing day, I was scared to. But at the same time, I felt like everything was going to be okay. Plus, I did feel a strong sense not to say anything. The only thing I did notice was that Anna and myself had heightened intuition abilities. Nowadays, I would identify it as our empathic awareness being magnified. As little girls, we just thought it was normal to have the keen intuition and senses that we did. In the back of my mind, I often wondered if it was a gift to Anna for some reason, and because I was there, I received the gifts as well. Why I outlived her, and Aurora, I have no idea. But here I am."

Viana smiles, "Here you are," Viana affirms in her crisp voice, "just a beautiful story."

Arabella sits on a stump near her garden, "Well, I am glad you are finally here. My intuition tells me there is a lot going on."

"Your intuition serves you well," recognizes Victor.

Viana takes Arabella's hand in hers, and gazes at Arabella in wonder, with her big, beautiful eyes.

Chapter 39

PLANET CHIARAS

"Marco, open your eyes. Wake up," Blazer says with his serious, calm voice.

Marco opens his eyes and sees the two Chiawaukas, Blazer and Celestial, staring at him. Sitting up, he looks around, "Where are we?"

"We are at the Chiawauka headquarters, on the planet Chiaras," Celest reveals.

Hopping down off of the comfortable, queen size bed, he stands looking at them. Marco walks over to the windows. "I knew there are other planets in our galaxy; I just had no idea they had life on them," admits Marco, turning to glance back at the two Chiawaukas.

Celestial walks over to Marco's side, "Chiaras will be your home for now. We will introduce you to the Chiarians later. They resemble humans, just taller, and they are very kind people."

"I guess. I do miss being at home...with my family," discloses Marco, as he views out the large, glass windows with handcrafted woodwork framing each one.

Blazer steps to Marco's other side, "Anytime you want to check in on your family, or contact your mother, we will set it up, Marco."

Marco hangs his head and turns to walk back toward the bed, "I think I'm just going to lie down awhile."

Celestial and Blazer watch as Marco crawls up into the tall, queen size bed, and rolls over to his side. They glance at each other. Blazer motions, suggesting they leave the room.

"Clearly, Marco clearly seems bummed out," Blazer states, once they are in the hallway.

"I know. I feel so bad for him. Bringing him to Chiaras is a solid idea and a good plan.

He will gather his strength. He can learn about the Ancient Writings, and befriend families here until it is time for us to reunite him with his," Celest contends.

"Yes. Just be prepared if he seems resistant or upset in the beginning, that you don't take it personally," recommends Blazer.

Celestial smiles at her assigned Chiawauka teammate, "Always thinking of your partner."

"Well, I just know how I would feel if I were Marco. And I know you get heartfully attached to our assignments," Blazer states matter-of-factly, in his medium-bass voice.

"I will be mindful of your words if Marco should display any negativity toward us," assures Celestial in her raspy voice and soft smile.

Meanwhile, Marco pulls the covers up over him, overloaded with thoughts racing in his head. *Maybe when I wake up, I will be at home. No, this seems pretty real. It'll be okay. I don't know. I was set to show Mom and Pop how strong I am, what a good worker I am, now here I am. I'm sure I wasn't very patient at times to Mother. I gave Pop a reason to think I wasn't listening to him. I sure hope they know how much I love them. And Gino, I can only imagine how he feels. It's been over TWO years. I did have a good visit with Mother though,* Marco reflects. Knowing he had a meaningful conversation with his mother, gives him a sense of peace. He drifts into sleep with tears in his eyes.

Chapter 40

AUGUSTIEL 30TH

Gino is helping his mother set the table for dinner.

"Mom, I just don't know about that kid," asserts Gino.

"What kid are you referring to?" questions Francesca.

"The prince!" Gino declares setting the plates on the hand-crafted, wooden dining room table. "That kid has got to be the absolute worst behaved kid in the entire kingdom! He's creepy, too!"

Francesca looks at her son inquisitively while carrying in the main course. "I know he can be a bit of a challenge at times," Francesca admits.

"Mother, he is a menace. No reason to dance around with me or Pop. At the Annual Spring About, he basically threatened me, stating I couldn't make toys for him if I am dating Claire," Gino discloses.

"He actually said that?" Francesca is in disbelief.

"Yeah, not those exact words, but yeah, he actually said, 'I want you to make me more toys, you'll have no time if you're with her.' Now, I find that to be disturbing, also because I heard him loud and clear, and Claire, who was right next to me did not hear anything. I think he got into my head. I know that sounds weird, but honestly, nothing sounds too far-fetched to me anymore," Gino asserts.

Antonio enters the room, he pats Gino on the back as he walks by on his way to pull out his chair, and take his place at the table. "Did I miss something?" Antonio asks.

Gino and Francesca both take their seats. Antonio prays the blessing.

Glancing at his mother and then at his pop, Gino reveals, "I was just telling mother how creepy I think the prince is. I bet he is also the most disobedient child in the entire kingdom."

Antonio discloses in his rugged voice and a bit of a light hearted laugh, "Well son, I think you're probably correct." He peers at Francesca, then back to Gino, "I know I want to give the prince the benefit of the doubt, since he is the only child of our friends, but I agree with Gino, he is disobedient, and even a little creepy," Antonio grins a bit, reaching to pat Gino's arm.

"Did you have any trouble with him at the Summer Fling?" questions Antonio.

"No, not really. I guess I'm still haunted by his words at the Spring About," admits Gino.

"Well, the prince is coming to our home for his fifth birthday," Francesca discloses.

"Oh, Mom, no," Gino requests, setting both his hands on the table.

Antonio eyes focus to his son and wife, "Do you really think that's a good idea, honey?"

Francesca looks at her two men, "Here's the deal, he has so many material things, and he always shows interest in the baked goods I bring to the queen, I just thought it would be a nice opportunity to bring him out here. He can help me make and bake his cake and the dinner for his birthday. But if you two are dead set against it, well then, I won't press the issue."

Gino laughs, "Okay, Mother, I have never known you not to press an issue."

Antonio glances to his son and then to Francesca, "I have to agree," Antonio says with a big grin and a bit of humor; "I have never known you not to press an issue. I suppose we can handle him for one day. Gino and I will be here if you need our assistance. How soon is this dinner?" Antonio asks in his deep, rugged voice.

"In about three weeks. His birthday is Septembria 21st. I'll ask the queen if they can bring him out around noon," Francesca shares.

"Hey, I actually have a question about our property," Gino discloses.

"What would that be, Son?" asks Antonio.

"If I recollect correctly, I remember you two always saying how you hope Marco and I would build our homes on the family property. Do you still feel that way?" inquires Gino.

"Absolutely!" Francesca says without hesitation.

"Yes. What are you thinking, Son?" quizzes Antonio.

"Well, Bill has been saying how he wants to focus more on iron works and phase out of carpentry. It would mean the world to me if you would allow me to build onto our woodworking shop here, so I could work from home. And of course, I would like to build my home on our ranch as well," Gino reveals.

Antonio glances at his wife, then to Gino, "I am fine with both of your ideas. I believe your mother is as well."

Francesca nods in agreement.

"I'd like to get started on building my shop as soon as possible. Bill said he will direct his clientele to me. And, as for my home, well, we can wait a bit on that. I have a site I think you'll approve of. I don't want it too far away from your home. I want my wife and kids to be able to get to your home quickly if needed," Gino states his thought-out plans.

"Wife and kids?" Antonio inquisitively chuckles.

"Do you have someone in mind?" Francesca questions.

"Well, you guys know that I do. I hope Claire will say 'yes'. I hope you two approve of her. And yes, I want to marry her…have my own family," Gino admits.

"Claire is lovely. I hope she will accept," Francesca confirms.

"I approve. Do you know when you're going to propose?" Antonio asks.

"I'm not sure. I still need to save up some money and buy a ring. First, I would like to have my carpentry shop completed," Gino discloses.

"Well, let's take the wagon to town tomorrow, get the supplies we need and get this project built," recommends Antonio.

Standing to take his empty plate to the kitchen, Gino contends, "You guys are the best."

Antonio smiles at his wife, "You hear that? We're the best."

"We are indeed," winks Francesca.

Chapter 41

RUPERT'S 5TH BIRTHDAY

"Rupert, let's get you dressed. Today we are going to the Mancinis. Mrs. Mancini has a birthday surprise for you," the queen says to her son in her sweet voice.

"Do you have plans for your day off, Carol?" asks the queen.

"I actually do. I'm going to fill my day with pleasant things, then have dinner with some friends," Carol replies in her crisp voice.

"Well, I hope you have a very enjoyable day off," assures the queen.

"Thank you. Rupert, happy birthday. I hope you have a wonderful day at the Mancinis," expresses Nanny Carol.

John has the team ready for the journey. The queen and Rupert climb into the carriage. Guards, Steve Carrington, and David Williams, will escort the queen and Rupert to the Mancinis.

"Rupert, I want you to behave. This is your first visit to someone else's home. I expect you to follow the Mancini rules," instructs his father. "I will be joining you and your mother later," he lovingly delivers.

Rupert just stares at his dad. The king pats the queen on her knee, exchanging a look of tenderness. The king then signals his guards and John to set off.

"Rupert, I do believe you are going to love your fifth birthday surprise." Queen Eloise pats her son's leg.

Rupert is taking in the surroundings. He hears the sound of the horses' hooves and the wheels of the carriage. He sees the countryside adorned in beautiful fall colors. The queen is at peace that her son is quiet and seems to be enjoying the ride. Their carriage nears the Mancini property.

"Oh, look sweetie, we are about to their property," the queen softly says to her son.

Rupert peers at the scenery. Instantly, a long, excruciatingly loud, shrill, blood-curdling scream comes out of Rupert's mouth causing John to stop the carriage. The guards, Steve and David, abruptly stop their horses. David directs his horse to the left side of the carriage, while Steve to the right.

To their dismay, they see the prince laying unresponsive on his back, in his mother's lap.

"Rupert, Rupert honey," the queen gently shakes Rupert, though her heart is racing.

John gets down, quickly stepping toward the carriage door, "What happened?"

The queen rubs Rupert's face. "Rupert, honey," she stresses. Rupert opens his eyes, and gazes up at his mother. He smiles.

"Oh, sweetie, are you okay?" the queen asks her son.

Rupert sits up quickly, exclaiming, "Yes! Are we about there? Why are we stopped?"

With curiosity lurking in their thoughts, the queen, Steve, David, and John all exchange eye contact with each other.

"We are about there," says the queen. "Shall we go?" she addresses the men.

The three men nod, and resume their travels.

......⚬⅊⚬......

"Is everything, alright?" Gino asks his mother as he bends down to help her pick up some cloth napkins she has just dropped.

"Yes, something just startled me," Francesca answers.

"What? Second thoughts of having the prince out today?" Gino inquires with a little laugh.

Francesca smiles at her son, "No, actually they should be pulling in. I don't know, something just unsettled me. Let's go out on the front deck and see if we see them."

Gino and Francesca walk out onto the front deck. To Francesca's surprise, she sees a filmy, black cloud lingering to the east of their property. "Gino, do you see that? What do you make of it?"

"What do I make of what?" Gino curiously questions his mother, "What am I looking at?"

Francesca turns to face her son expressing a puzzled look, "Really?"

"Seriously, Mom, what am I supposed to see? Oh wait, I do see two guards and the royal carriage approaching," Gino states.

Francesca puts her hand on Gino's arm, "Well, let's make this a good day. I love you, sweetie," she softly says.

"Yeah, having a good day with the most menacing kid in the kingdom will require constant mental determination," Gino presumes.

Francesca smiles at her son, followed with a sigh, "We can deal with it for one day; his family, and the palace staff, deal with it daily."

Gino glances at his mother, then returns his sight to the approaching guards and carriage.

······◦◦······

Francesca and Gino step off the front deck and walk over to welcome their guests. "I hope Pop gets home soon," whispers Gino.

Francesca and Gino exchange eye contact.

John holds the door open, assisting the queen and prince down. David and Steve step down from their horses, remove their hats, and shake Gino's hand. Both Steve and David nod to Francesca, "Nice to see you," states David.

Steve also expresses to Francesca, "Nice to see you."

Francesca smiles at both guards, "It is so good to see you two! Will you be staying today?"

Steve and David glance at the queen, "Oh Francesca, no, I'm sending the men on their way to enjoy their day. Theo will join Rupert and I later."

Francesca searches into the eyes of Steve and David, "You two be safe. Enjoy your day!"

Steve and David both acknowledge Francesca's kind words with a nod and smile.

Steve, David, and John mount up, returning to the castle.

Francesca extends her hand to Rupert's hand, "Shall we go in, Rupert?"

Gino and Francesca escort the queen and Rupert inside their home.

Francesca stops, turns to Rupert, "Happy Birthday! For your birthday gift, we are going to bake a birthday cake and prepare a fabulous dinner for your family and mine. How does that sound to you?"

An enormous smile overtakes Rupert's face, "Oh boy! What a great present!" Rupert wraps his arms around Francesca's legs.

Gino, not sold on what appears to be genuinely kind behavior, keeps a speculative expression on his face.

Queen Eloise basks in the peace she is experiencing.

······૭ℛ◟······

"Rupert, let's go to the kitchen and begin, shall we?" Francesca looks at Rupert.

"Yes!" exclaims Rupert.

"Eloise, you are welcome to join us, or go out back, or whatever you would like to do," Francesca offers.

"Thank you. I will take you up on that. Actually, Gino, do you mind showing me around?" the queen turns to Gino.

"Yes, that is fine. Let's start out back," suggests Gino.

Gino leads Queen Eloise out the back through the family room, where he begins showing her the garden his mother is working on, then takes her over to where they have been expanding the woodshop, and then escorts her to the stables.

Francesca and Rupert work diligently in the kitchen preparing Rupert's birthday cake, and spaghetti bake for dinner. Earlier, before breakfast, Francesca prepared the dough for hot rolls they will be eating at the meal.

······ ⚬ℛ⚬ ······

As Gino escorts the queen around their property he explains their plans, showing off their finished projects, telling her the name of each dog that eagerly walks by their side, and each horse once they reach the stables.

Francesca hears a loud crash, like an explosion. She runs to the front door peering out. She is puzzled by a dark cloud she sees east of their property. It appears to be the same filmy cloud she saw when Eloise and Rupert were approaching their home. Now, the cloud formation is rising high into the sky. Lightning bolts shoot throughout the ominous dark cloud causing a loud, thunderous noise followed by what sounds like a whip striking the air with echoes of eerie rattles, like the sound of a rattlesnake's nest.

Francesca is momentarily frozen staring at the bizarre sight. *I cannot believe I am the only one that sees this. I wonder if the Chiawaukas know about this.* She returns into her home, to the kitchen, where Rupert is methodically stirring frosting.

Smiling, "I see you have stirred the frosting to a perfect consistency," Francesca affirms.

"I have. Thank you. I love being five!" Rupert exclaims.

Francesca laughs, "Well, that is good to hear. Let's move on to our next task, shall we?"

Rupert nods, as he views around the kitchen and the ingredients Francesca is laying out to prepare the main course.

......⊙ℛ......

"Oh, Gino, quite impressive. Your parents, and you have certainly created a beautiful landscape with your home, gardens, carpentry shop, barn, and stable. The rock paths your mother has designed, so much work! I had no idea how busy you all are out here. I guess I am preoccupied with our life at the palace, that I just didn't even realize how full and busy your lives were. Forgive me, for that, will you?" the queen appeals.

"There is nothing to forgive. I'm glad I was able to give you a tour," assures Gino, "my parents have worked very hard and I'm thankful I am a part of it."

Queen Eloise smiles at Gino taking his arm as he leads her up the stairs of the deck.

"Oh, something smells delicious," Queen Eloise notices.

Rupert smiles with glee at his mother, "You smell dinner baking! I think I am going to be a chef when I grow up!"

"I think that sounds fabulous, son," Queen Eloise expresses.

"Gino, join me for a moment. Excuse us, please," Francesca addresses Eloise and Rupert.

Gino follows his mother. She leads them out the front door some distance from their home. Pointing to the east, "Do you not see that billowing cloud?" Francesca questions.

Gino looks at his mom, then in the direction she's pointing, "I see nothing."

"A while ago, did you hear what sounded like an explosion?" quizzes Francesca with frustration in her voice.

"No, I'm sorry, I didn't hear anything," Gino states.

Francesca stands next to her son, surveying the cloud, thinking, *how can he not see, nor hear that? He is blood of my blood. I have an idea.*

"Gino, I am going to place my hands on your head. I don't know if that will help, but you have to see this. You are of my blood. I know you have a very keen, empathic sense. I just don't understand why I am the only one to see it," Francesca communicates.

Francesca places one hand on each side of Gino's head, hoping he will hear or see the chilling cloud that's looming east of their property. After standing there for a few minutes Francesca lowers her hands.

"Well?" asks Francesca.

"Nothing. Mom, I believe you. Pop always taught me, if you see it, or hear it, it's there, but I don't see or hear anything. I'm sorry," Gino submits.

Frowning, Francesca offers, "It's okay, and I'm glad you and your Pop believe in me. I just wish you two could also see and hear what I do. Then maybe we could solve the mystery. It appears to be the same black, filmy cloud I see hovering on the ceiling above Rupert when I am in his presence. Frustrating," Francesca shrugs.

"So, this phenomenon occurs when you are in the presence of Rupert?" Gino asks.

"Yes, every single time, since, well…since Marco's accident, and since his Nanny Mary was found dead," Francesca reveals.

Gino continues scanning to the east with his mother. "That is unusual. Creepy even," Gino acknowledges, placing his arm around his mother.

"Yes," Francesca sighs.

Chapter 42

There's Pop! I'm glad he made it home in time for dinner," Gino conveys.

"Yes, I'm sure Sully and he had quite an adventure," Francesca assumes.

"Well, you go out and help your Pop with anything he needs, I'll go tend to our guests. Theodore should be arriving anytime now," Francesca directs.

Gino heads off for the stables. Francesca begins to retreat into their home when she hears what sounds like a whip lashing through the air then landing on concrete. She sharply turns to glance back only to see the same ominous cloud that has been lingering since the royals arrived. *Very peculiar.*

Antonio is unsaddling Chief when Gino approaches, "Hey, Pop. Have a good day?"

"I did. How is it going with the prince?" inquires Antonio.

"Well, I think he is behaving. I gave the queen a tour of our property. She said she didn't realize all the hard work we do. She loves the place though," Gino answers.

"How's your mother?" asks Antonio.

"You know, she's always chipper. However, she is witnessing a shuddering cloud. She confided that it resembles the same cloud that hovers above Rupert when she is near him. I guess it is making some deafening sounds as well. She was hoping I could see it, or hear it for that matter. But I did not," Gino informs.

"Well, your mother has always been able to sense things the rest of us do not. I never doubt what she tells me," Antonio confides while brushing Chief.

"Maybe the cloud Mother sees has something to do with Rupert's menacing behavior," suggests Gino.

"Yeah, maybe so. Your mother thinks the same thing. It's a mystery, alright," Antonio exchanges eye contact with Gino placing the brush back on the shelf. "I'm hungry, let's go in," Antonio states.

······⚬⧖⚬······

"Well, that is one of the most delicious meals I have eaten," asserts King Theodore. He smiles at his son Rupert, "I can tell you had a wonderful birthday."

"I did!" exclaims Rupert making silly faces.

Everyone stands, carrying their dishes and utensils to the kitchen. Eloise helps Francesca clean up. The guys walk out to the front. Rupert reaches out and places his little hand in Gino's. Gino looks down and isn't sure he is going to let his guard down. "Swing me!" Rupert shouts.

"Swing you?" questions Gino.

"Yes! Swing me!" insists Rupert.

"I don't think I can swing you, but I'll give you a piggyback ride," offers Gino.

Gino picks Rupert up in a motion that swoops Rupert to his back. Gino carries Rupert piggyback to the carriage the king rode out. Queen Eloise and Francesca join the guys outside.

Hugging Francesca, Queen Eloise says, "Thank you, so much, for giving up your day. It was splendid. I appreciate it!"

"You're quite welcome," Francesca replies.

The royals load up, and wave to their friends as they depart down the drive.

The Mancinis stand there. Antonio wraps his arm around Francesca. She rests her head on his shoulder, and reaches her arms around him.

"Is the cloud still there, Mom? I wonder when or if it will disappear," Gino speculates.

"It is still there. Let's go in, I'm spent," Francesca shares.

......⁓🙢⁓......

"I have to say, Pixel, I'm impressed that you remained silent and invisible when the Cryptolores left the prince before crossing onto the Mancini property," Piper acknowledges.

Viana and Victor both nod, "What a challenge that must have been," Viana concurs.

Pixel smiles, "Well, thanks, guys. I am trying to be an effective Chiawauka."

"You're doing a good job," Victor validates.

Pixel blushes with a proud smile.

"Now, aside from us all being aware of Pixel's growth as a Chiawauka, what do you make of the Cryptolores leaving Rupert every single time Francesca is near, and today, even their property?" Victor questions.

"Very puzzling," Piper notes.

"They seem to detect something about Francesca that causes them fear," Viana theorizes.

"They flee. They fear, then flee," Pixel formulates.

"I would agree," Victor voices, "We remain invisible and the Cryptolores seem unable to detect us, but something about Francesca keeps them at bay."

"I think we have done a good job being vigilant; I will update Razel and Zeek on our way back to the castle," informs Piper.

"Good idea," Victor agrees. "Keep us posted, no doubt the Cryptolores will return to Rupert before arriving at the castle.

"You know, Francesca heard and saw the Cryptolores in cloud formation. When are you going to interact with her?" questions Pixel. "You need to tell Antonio and Gino as well, of our presence. They are part of the family, but that's just my opinion."

Viana's crisp, assertive voice fills the air, "You're exactly right, sweetie, we do need to meet with Francesca, Antonio, and Gino."

"Well, I'm not going to tell you what to do, but I think it needs to happen soon," Pixel reiterates.

"Your advice is noted," Victor assures.

......⊙ℜ☉......

The king is driving the carriage with his wife and son inside.

"This was sure a great day," exclaims Rupert, leaning his head into his mother's lap with sleepy eyes and a yawn.

"Happy birthday, Son," Queen Eloise softly says stroking her son's cheek.

Nearing the castle, Pixel and Piper are astonished there are no signs of the Cryptolores.

John meets the king at the stables, "Welcome back, Sir," greets John.

"Thank you," acknowledges the king.

King Theodore then opens the carriage for his wife and son. "Here, I will carry Rupert," the king says reaching for his son.

The king and queen walk inside and carry Rupert to his room, help him undress and assist him into his night clothes.

"Goodnight, my son," the king kisses his son's forehead.

"Goodnight, my sweet," Queen Eloise whispers kissing Rupert's cheek.

They leave his room, and retire to their chambers for the night.

"I can't believe there hasn't been any..." the king is gently interrupted by the queen.

"Don't even say it. It's coming. Whatever takes over our son, just don't say it," requests the queen.

"You're right," Theodore says and kisses his wife goodnight. The king and queen lay back onto their pillows and wonder when will they hear that shrill, terrifying, scream that correlates with their son's behavior change.

Chapter 43

CHALLENGES ON CHIARAS

Marco begins to feel anxious. He never spied on anyone before. He sees the high priests leave the communications room. Marco quietly inches closer, hoping to be undetected, and enters the communications room. He dashes to the transmission board. He thinks he knows how to contact his mother. Marco begins to push a button, then hesitates. *Which one was it? Think!* Taking a deep breath in, he selects another button and presses it.

"Mother, can you hear me? Mother, this is Marco," Marco exhales with an urgency in his voice. "Mother, it's Marco."

Francesca is out in the back planting some bulbs. She sets her shovel down, thinking she hears Marco calling her. *Do I hear Marco?* She stands, and listens carefully. She pulls her gloves off, and dashes to the stairs of the deck and into their home to the mantel where the mysterious flower is kept.

"Marco, I'm here," Francesca says panicked believing she missed an opportunity to talk with him.

"Good, it's me, how are things?" questions Marco.

"Well, interesting and busy to say the least, but what about you? How are you feeling? I hope fully recovered," Francesca empathizes.

"No, I'm not good…" Marco says bluntly.

Hearing his words cause Francesca instant worry, "What do you mean you're not good? I thought the Chiawaukas were going to take care of you? Protect and train you? Why are you not good?" Francesca interrogates.

"I don't know. I guess I am good. I just miss being there with you and Pop and Gino. Can't I just come home?" Marco pleads.

Francesca stands straight, flexing her shoulder blade muscles, "Marco, I will discuss this with Victor and Viana, however; I haven't seen or heard from them for three months. I do trust the Chiawaukas know things we do not. At this time, I believe the best thing you can do is learn from them. You are blessed to have this extraordinary experience none of the rest of us will have. Like it or not, this is the situation we are all in. Gino would love to have you here. Part of his life. We all would. For whatever reason, things happened. I am thankful you are alive, and not dead. We miss you, too, Marco. What can I do to help, besides speak to Victor and Viana? What can you do?" Francesca asks her son.

Pausing, and sighing, Marco reluctantly admits, "I guess, I jumped the gun. Sometimes, I get so overwhelmed with missing you guys, it consumes me. Then I can't focus on any task at hand. Then I get angry. The truth is, the Chiawaukas are great. The Chiarians, for that matter, have been nothing but very kind to me. When I really think about it, you're right. I need to focus on where I am at knowing that I can at least communicate with you at any time. I want to make my family proud, so I should be a good representative," Marco submits.

Francesca smiles, "I knew once you settled, you would realize the rare and unique opportunity you have been given."

"Yeah, I am ashamed to say, I get in the way of myself at times. Especially when I think, poor me, I am missing out on my life there with you guys," Marco humbly offers.

Francesca just smiles at her son, "I know. But your life, for whatever reason, took a different course. You are alive. You are healthy. You know your roots. Let them know who Marco Mancini is. We all love you, Son."

"I love you, too, Mother," Marco yields.

"Any other concerns, babe?" Francesca asks.

"Other than wanting Pop and Gino to know, no, I better go. I snuck in here to talk to you," confesses Marco.

"Oh, Marco," Francesca shakes her head.

"I know, I know. Talk to you soon," Marco conveys.

Francesca nods, smiling, "Yes, soon."

......⚬⅋⚬......

Marco turns, and sees Celestial, Blazer, and both high priests standing just inside the door next to the wall.

"I know, I know," Marco motions with his hands waving up and down, "I took it upon myself to speak to my mother without your permission," Marco grumbles.

Blazer and Celestial are both shaking their heads, "It's not that, Marco," Blazer expresses, "It's the fact..."

Blazer's sentence is taken over by High Priest Akshai, who grows to six-feet-five-inches in height, as he approaches Marco, "It's the fact that your communication was not protected by our security realm. Without transmitting through our protective security realm, well, who knows who intercepted that communication! We are aware you miss your family, Marco, and we are doing everything in our power to keep you, your family, and the people of your planet, safe. However, careless actions, even though they may seem minor to you, could lead to disaster and potentially place others in harm! Plus, not to mention, entering our communications room without permission. Are you okay with other people entering your private area without permission?" High Priest Akshai scolds.

Anxiety fills Marco's mind. Hearing the words of the high priest resonate, causing Marco to reflect on the well-being of others and not just himself. "Clearly, saying I'm sorry sounds pretty lame compared to possibly putting everyone in jeopardy," Marco acknowledges. "I'll give you no more trouble or reason not to trust me."

High Priest Akshai reaches his right hand to Marco's right shoulder.

Marco cringes, expecting to hear more from the high priest; but High Priest Akshai just firmly places his hand on Marco's shoulder, resting it there for a few moments with a firm grip. High Priest Akshai then turns, leaving the room with High Priestess Ammerie.

Blazer and Celestial remain silent, studying Marco.

......⟡⟡......

Francesca steps back from the Flower of Virtue. She then folds her arms, and tries to process that Marco is not only alive, but the Chiawaukas have taken him to the planet Chiaras. *I wish Victor and Viana would allow me to share with Antonio and Gino. I haven't heard a word from them since Junis.*

Unaware to Francesca, Antonio and Gino had arrived home and overheard the ending of her conversation with Marco.

"Who is that you are talking to? It sounds like Marco's voice!" Antonio quizzes with astonishment as he moves quickly toward Francesca.

Francesca jumps. Startled, she turns to see both her husband and son.

"Was that Marco?" Antonio presses.

"Wow! Is Marco alive, Mom? I recognize his voice. What's going on?" Gino questions with excitement.

Francesca peers at Antonio and Gino while words from Marco and the Chiawaukas race through her mind of keeping this matter private for now, "Yes, Marco is alive…" she reluctantly voices.

"Marco is alive? Where is he?" Antonio places each of his hands on Francesca's arms, kissing her cheek with an urgency, "That's incredible!" Antonio then takes a step back, "Wait… how long have you known this? Have you been keeping this from me?" Antonio scoffs.

Francesca, standing almost frozen, confirms, "I recently found out, and..."

Antonio interrupts and motions for Francesca to go to their bedroom, "Let's go to our room to discuss this, Gino you stay out here," Antonio orders.

Francesca reaches out to Gino, stroking his arm with her hand, giving him a loving smile.

She follows Antonio and closes their bedroom door.

Antonio turns to face Francesca, "I...I am in shock. I can't believe you didn't tell me. What else have you kept from me?" scowls Antonio.

"When I heard the thunder a few years ago, I asked if you heard it. You replied no, but acknowledged that I have a keen sense. When I saw a filmy cloud appear above Rupert, I asked if you saw it. Again, you told me you did not see it, but you trusted I did. When I discovered a cabin on our property, and met Genie Arabella, I could have kept that a secret, but I told you," Francesca begins to snap with shortness in her tone, "Your accusation is stirring a fire in me, but I recognize you are in disbelief, as I was when I found out, and hurt I didn't tell you."

"Why didn't you tell me? How could you not tell me!" barks Antonio.

Gino, wanting to hear what's being said, quietly positions himself outside of their bedroom door. Hearing the cross words of his Pop fill him with anxiety, he knows his mother always has an earnest reason on why she does things. *I think I will go in.*

Just then he feels something in each of his hands and looks down. It is Victor and Viana. Gino is astonished. "Who are you two?" exclaims Gino.

"Shhh, we are the Chiawaukas (key-a-wau-kas)," Victor whispers, revealing their presence, "Marco is alive and safe. My name is Victor and this is Viana."

"Gino, when your Pop calms down, we will fill you both in," affirms Viana.

Meanwhile, the three quietly listen.

"Why didn't you tell me? Wouldn't you want me to tell you?" interrogates Antonio in an elevated tone.

Francesca, standing her ground conveys with a stern voice, "Of course, I would want you to tell me. Antonio, I was instructed not to."

"Instructed not to? I cannot believe you kept this from me!" shouts Antonio with anger.

Gino and the Chiawaukas quietly stare at each other. Victor opens their door. Antonio and Francesca both turn to see Gino, Victor and Viana enter their bedroom.

Antonio postures himself, "Who are you two? What is going on?" yells Antonio, flinging his arms about.

Francesca and Gino both fix their eyes at Antonio.

"Antonio, my name is Victor, and this is Viana. We are Chiawaukas, Supreme Guardian Beings. We have been watching Francesca and your family for years. We were at the mine when you were kneeling over Marco. It was then we first saw Marco's aura, and knew we had to protect him. So yes, Marco is alive, and well, for that matter."

An expression of heartbreak overtakes Antonio's face. Feeling betrayed, angry, hurt, and left out, he drops his head and storms out of the room. Francesca and Gino stand in silence with Victor and Viana.

They hear the back door close.

"Francesca, I am aware we put you in a compromising situation. Please accept our apology." Victor then addresses Gino, "We asked your mother not to disclose the knowledge that your brother is alive. Hindsight, well, we should have implemented another plan which would not have caused an altercation between your parents. It bothers me that we clearly got off to a bad start with your Pop," Victor yields.

"Oh, Francesca, honey," Viana says with empathy, "We are so sorry. We are Supreme Guardian Beings, but clearly, not infallible."

Francesca hugs Viana, trying to discreetly dab the tears sitting in the corners of her eyes. With a little laugh, Francesca says, "Gino, meet Victor and Viana. They protected Marco at the mine. Marco is now on the planet Chiaras with other Chiawaukas and the Chiarians," Francesca smiles with an anxious little laugh, still dabbing her eyes.

Gino is feeling exuberance, "Man, that's great! Can I talk to him? Can I see him? When will he be back home? Wait! He's where? So, there *IS* life on other planets?"

Viana smiles, "Well, yes, first things first. We will make arrangements for you to communicate. But let's first tend to your Pop and try to soothe his broken spirit."

Gino, Francesca, Victor, and Viana stand quietly exchanging eye contact.

Chapter 44

YIELDING

Antonio organizes his already pristine office in the stables. Feeling deeply left out, he thinks to himself while he piddles with things, *how could she not tell me? Why didn't the blue critters tell me instead of her? Or both of us at the same time? I'd like to know what is going on!* He walks over to the window and peers out; *maybe I should go up to the house and initiate an interrogation. It is MY family. Who are these blue ones? What gives them the right to be watching my family? Are they holding Marco?* Antonio takes a deep breath attempting to calm himself; *Now, don't get yourself all worked up. I'm sure there are reasonable explanations. So many triggers, though, that remind me I am not in control of anything, nor can I really protect anyone. Well, that's not true either. I can't prevent accidents, but immediate threats and danger I fair well. This is ridiculous. I'm out here stewing, perpetuating something in my mind, when I can go directly to the source that is inside my home, and find resolution to these racing thoughts. Wow, my wife must think I'm some kind of man to storm out, behaving like a boy.* Antonio walks to his office door, turns off the light and shakes his head. *What a bad example of adult behavior I displayed to Gino. He* walks over and strokes Chief's head before he leaves the stables. "You've always been a good horse, Chief," Antonio expresses affection to his beloved horse, resting his head against Chief's.

"Shouldn't we go out and get Pop?" Gino questions.

"Actually, I was going to go visit with him," states Victor. "However, your Pop is on his way back here."

"Wow! That's incredible you know things!" exclaims Gino.

"Well, we know some things," renders Viana is her crisp voice.

Francesca takes her hand placing it on Gino's arm, and slides it down to his strong hand, "Let's go out to the dining room and greet him, shall we?" Francesca softly offers.

The four of them leave the master bedroom and go into the dining room. Francesca sets the round dish of chocolate meringue pie she had made earlier in the day, on the dining room table.

Antonio prays as he walks toward his home, knowing his wife and son are inside with blue creatures whom he has no idea what they are, or where they came from. "God, help me understand what is going on. Help me live up to the man you created me to be. I know I should also ask you to bless me with an open spirit and listening ears. Thank you. Amen."

Antonio reaches the stairs. You can hear the soles of his boots sound against each wooden stair he climbs. Reaching the door, he casts his eyes up into the sky, as if searching for heaven. He enters through the back door, then into the kitchen. He walks into the dining room and evaluates the scene before him; two blue beings along with his wife and son sit at the beautiful wooden table he handcrafted with Francesca decades ago. A vase of exquisite seasonal flowers sits in the center, with a perfectly placed homemade pie near the vase.

Francesca studies Antonio with anticipation of his next course of action. Antonio stands with his tall stature, humbly before them, just staring at his wife. Gino, Victor and Viana are all anxiously awaiting Antonio's next move. Antonio then winks at Francesca, and submits, "Well, I guess it's time you all catch me up on what is going on here." He leans over to kiss Francesca's cheek, then pulls up his chair to join them.

"First let me offer an apology to you, Antonio," Victor addresses, "We should have devised a better plan of first contact with the knowledge of Marco being alive without placing Francesca in an awkward position, and requesting that she not tell you or Gino. That was our error. It placed Francesca in a situation that if she told, we may not have trusted her, and if she didn't tell you, then, well, you would feel…well, here we are."

"I'm trying to understand, can you go to the beginning, please?" requests Antonio. "I do understand what you just said though, about placing my wife in a compromising position."

"We are Chiawaukas (Key-a-wau-kas), Supreme Guardian Beings. Our headquarters is stationed on the planet Chiaras with the Chiarians. Generations ago, a planet named VeNoma was destroyed. Some of the life on that planet unexplainably evolved into a black, filmy cloud form, and roamed through the galaxy to wreak havoc with the ability to possess or destroy life on planets. They are the Cryptolores. The Chiawaukas banished them to the planet Soleil deep into a cavern with an anesthetizing gas that would keep them indefinitely in a comatose state. As a back-up plan, and to actually fulfill The Ancient Writings, the Chiawauka High Priest and High Priestess came to the planet Soleil, and infused two unrelated females with their DNA. This unique transfer meant that these two females would have a blood line unique to them. It would only pass to the oldest daughter through families. She must be the oldest child of the family as well. That is how the bloodline is passed. These two families are called the Chords of Chiawaukas. According to The Ancient Writings, at some point in time, the two unrelated families of this unique bloodline will join by a marriage. It is at that time we will ordain the families as Keepers of the Universe," Viana pauses, taking a breath.

Victor continues, "The females have a red and white aura that are only visible to the Chiawaukas. How strong the aura is entirely depends on if the female is tapped into her inner sense that she has unique gifts. The more in tune she is to her inner self, the stronger her aura is."

"What about her kids? Do boys receive these gifts if the bloodline is only given to the eldest girl?" Gino curiously wonders.

"They do, Gino. You and Marco both have a blue and purple aura. It is passed to the eldest girl if she is the oldest child as well. Then of course her children, male or female will have her bloodline, and grandchildren and so on. However, to have both the red and white auras, you must be the oldest daughter and the oldest child," Viana then sets her eyes on Antonio and enlightens, "Antonio, you have a green aura. That is the color spouses can get depending on the strength of awareness the female is to her inner gifts, and how close the husband and wife are. The thing is, the females with red and white auras are able to use their powers by themselves. The rest of you must be in proximity of each other in order to implement your powers."

"We have powers?" exclaims Gino.

Victor's face breaks with a smile, "Yes, Gino. At this point, you nor your Pop are tapped into them yet, but you will be."

"Well, this is a lot to take in," Antonio states in his deep voice as he shakes his head in amazement and looks at Francesca. "Tell me about the mine, and our son, Marco. What are you supposed to protect us from? Chamberlain Kingdom has never encountered an enemy."

"We were sent to Soleil to find both families of the Chords of Chiawaukas, verify the coordinates the Cryptolores were imprisoned, protect the families from the Cryptolores, and should they escape, train the two families to prepare them for their calling," Viana educates.

"We were stationed outside of the mine on the day of Marco's incident. He had broken through the wall where the Cryptolores were imprisoned. The chasm filled with air which compromised the anesthetizing gas causing the effect to wear off. The Cryptolores escaped. On his way out, Alchodor, their leader, attempted to suck the life force from Marco. That is when Curtis found him. We entered the area and saw Marco's faint aura, and then yours, Antonio. We knew we had to place a protective shield over Marco immediately to preserve what life was in him. That is why he remained alive and now on the planet Chiaras," informs Victor.

"And the filmy, black cloud I see hover above Prince Rupert? Tell us about that, please," Francesca requests.

"Ah, yes," Victor clears his throat, "That is Alchodor. He and his minions took over the castle and sucked the life out of Nanny Mary. Alchodor then entered the child prince, possessing him. For some reason, Alchodor detects in you, Francesca, something he fears. That is why Alchodor leaves Rupert's body when in your presence. In fact, Alchodor hovered above you the day of the mine incident then fled."

Viana divulges, "Francesca, honey, you are keenly tapped into the unseen world. You may not be able to identify what is going on, but you are very perceptive. When you believed you heard thunder, it actually was the Cryptolores battling amongst themselves. Scaleon leads the other group of Cryptolores. They are residing in a neighboring kingdom, living in a pack of wolves."

"There are more of those things?" Antonio vocalizes.

Victor directly asserts, "Oh, yes. And they will possess any living creature, human or animal they deem will be safe for their survival."

An eerie chill rushes through the three Mancinis as they listen.

Francesca's left elbow is on the table while her left hand supports her head. She suddenly sits straight up dropping her forearm to the table with her hand spread out, "Wait, I thought I heard you say it passes through generations to the oldest daughter, if she is also the oldest child, is that correct?"

"Yes," Viana answers.

Antonio and Gino both suspect where this is going.

"So, my mother, Sophia, has these special gifts? These magical powers you speak of?" Francesca quizzes.

"She does, Francesca. However, for some reason, your mother did not nurture her empathic abilities and grow the gifts within her," Victor remarks.

"But does she still have the ability if she so chooses? Does she even know about you or these gifts?" inquires Francesca.

"No, she does not know of our existence. We have not revealed ourselves to any generation until now. Yes, if she were to begin her journey of self-awareness, she would be able to develop the gifts within her, and her aura would become visible to us," discloses Victor.

"Does she know I have a keen sense?" Francesca wonders.

"Your mother always encouraged you when you were a child, so yes, we assume she is aware that you at least have empathic gifts," Viana answers.

"I have a question," conveys Gino.

"Yes, go ahead, what is it?" Victor asks.

"There was a flower on Marco's body at the mine. Mother brought it home, and it still looks as new today as it did almost two-and-a-half years ago. What gives?" Gino queries. "Also, what are our powers for?"

"The Flower of Virtue is a sacred flower that allows communication between Marco and your family. Once Viana and I saw the faint aura above Marco, we instantly placed a protective shield around him, then chanted the Guardian Chant over him, and the glorious Flower of Virtue appeared. While Marco was still sleeping, he was able to hear interactions going on inside of your home. Not every word necessarily, but enough to bring him peace while he slept as he was recovering," Victor reveals.

"The powers that lie dormant within you are for protection against the Cryptolores." Viana sheds light.

"So, Marco is on the planet Chiaras now? Ha, we have always speculated there is life on other planets, but nothing to sustain that concept," Antonio shares.

"Most of the planets in the Estellas Galaxy have life," Viana unfolds.

"Was it you two at the river my mother and I sensed?" questions Gino, "because I was thinking it was our guardian angels. Did God create you?"

Antonio raises an eyebrow peering at Francesca, "I don't believe I heard about you two at the river," Antonio states.

"You knew about our hikes, it was a couple of times we hiked to the river, Pop. I wondered if they were our guardian angels," Gino says with excitement in his voice.

Francesca softly smiles at Antonio, "Yes, we perceived an unknown presence on a couple of our hikes together. I chose to not mention it to you, because it was only a feeling, and at the time I didn't want to alarm you with it since I had no tangible evidence."

"I know...you were protecting me," Antonio nods, "It's alright," he says tossing his hand.

"To answer your question, yes, God created us. He created all living things. All universes, and galaxies. Everything is created by God," Viana boldly states.

"When can we speak to Marco? How soon can he come home?" inquires Antonio.

"Well, we will facilitate communication with Marco when we are done with this briefing. As for him returning home, at this time, it is just not possible. It will disrupt the community of Chamberlain Kingdom, causing countless questions, and suspicions. No one can know Marco is alive. No one. This is a secret the three of you must keep. Our identity and that of the Cryptolores is also to be kept secret. Our Chiawauka team that is assigned to Marco will train him. He will live in freedom on the planet Chiaras. The Chiarians are similar to humans, just taller. Celestial and Blazer will train Marco on his powers and responsibilities of being part of the Chords of Chiawaukas Family. You will continue to live out your normal lives, and interact naturally. We will continue to monitor the Cryptolores, and of course, we are here for you. In addition, we'll commence training the three of you," Victor affirms.

A somber look overtakes Francesca's face momentarily, "Now we know why Rupert behaves so badly. He is possessed by those hideous beings, and we can do nothing to help our friends."

"This is true, Francesca, but don't lose heart. The Cryptolores fear you. We are thankful they do not detect our presence, but they are able to sense something about you. Maybe, because we are Guardian Beings and have mastered being undetected," contemplates Victor.

Francesca extends her arms to each side of her reaching her left hand to Gino and Viana her right. They take her hand in theirs, and extend each of their arms to grasp hands with Victor and Antonio. They bow their heads for a moment of silence.

Chapter 45

KEEPING THE BEST NEWS PRIVATE

Francesca lays her head on Antonio, snuggling next to him in their bed. He wraps his arm around her holding her close.

"I can't believe my mother hasn't given me any information of our special gifts," Francesca ponders.

"Well, if I heard them correctly, your mother isn't really aware of her abilities, and has not known to tap into her inner gifts," Antonio recaps.

Francesca readjusts her head a bit on Antonio's shoulder to get more comfortable, "You're right. Plus, the Chiawaukas never revealed themselves to any generation until now," Francesca settles.

Antonio is stroking Francesca's head of hair while they lie visiting, "Well, you must have done something right. It's mind-boggling to think we are a part of their Ancient Writings they speak of."

"I know. There is so much to take in," Francesca concurs while her thoughts race.

"I want to tell you, I'm sorry for storming off. I was behaving like a boy. I hope you will forgive me," submits Antonio.

Francesca rolls up to kiss Antonio's lips, "Of course. I hope you forgive me for not telling you our son is alive."

"Well, that's a pretty big one," Antonio acts stern, but then he smiles at his wife, "You were being true to keeping your word, regardless of the outcome. How can I be upset with you for doing what is right?" Antonio yields, giving Francesca a big hug.

They exchange a passionate kiss, Antonio pauses, "And Marco is alive!" he smiles then resumes lovingly kissing his wife.

Just then, Gino barges in their room, "I'm sorry to just walk in, I'm just so excited to hear Marco is alive! Do you think I can tell Ben and Luke? We are all like brothers," Gino requests. "Oh, and Grandmother and Grandfather?"

"Son, the Chiawaukas made it very clear we are to tell no one," Antonio's voice resonates the room.

Gino walks over and sits on the end of their bed, "I know, I was just wishing we could."

"We cannot even hint as to make others suspicious either," Antonio infers.

Gino frowns, "I know."

"Keeping this private is extremely important, Gino," Francesca adds.

"I know. Wow! This is just the best news!" Gino stands. "Okay, goodnight." Gino turns to leave his parents' bedroom.

"Goodnight, sweetie, love you," Francesca says.

"Goodnight, son. Sleep well," Antonio expresses.

Chapter 46

RAZEL AND ZEEK

Razel is standing in a plié, then completes a pirouette, extending her hands toward a small herd of deer.

"Razel, what are you doing?" questions Zeek.

"Do you see those crazed wolves stalking those beautiful, defenseless deer?" Razel replies.

"I do, but that doesn't answer my question," Zeek presses.

"Watch. Just be patient," Razel directs.

The wolves inch closer to the deer, getting ready to attack. The Alpha wolf, who is possessed by the Cryptolore, Scaleon, leaps toward one of the deer, and falls to the ground in mid-air, as if hitting an invisible pane of shatterproof glass.

Zeek quickly turns to his partner, Razel, and sees a proud and smirky smile on her face. "Ah, I know what you did, you placed a forcefield around the deer," assesses Zeek.

"I did! I am not going to let those Cryptolores rob the innocent deer of their lives," Razel adamantly states.

"Well, if the wolves weren't inhabited by the Cryptolores, would you interfere with the nature of things?" Zeek inquires in his proper stance with one arm behind him and his other arm outstretched.

Razel, feeling like Zeek is popping her bubble, "No, I wouldn't. Nature must take its course. Those Cryptolores just infuriate me so! I can't believe our ancestors chose to imprison them instead of completely obliterating them!" Razel answers.

"Well, I can see your passion," Zeek affirms.

"Don't you feel the same, Zeek?" Razel expresses annoyance.

"I actually am enjoying every day of our mission. It is an exciting adventure to be part of The Ancient Writings, and to not know really what we are going to encounter next. Not to mention all the beautiful, exquisite rocks I get to spy along the way," Zeek conveys.

Razel gently swats at Zeek's arm, "You are hopeless!"

Zeek smiles at Razel, "As hopeless as you are. We are both passionate about things. You about all life, from deer to humans. Me, about adventures, rocks and fossils."

Razel relaxes her posture and smiles at her teammate, "I suppose you're correct, if I interfere too often with the wolves' hunting, they may become suspicious."

"Yes, and that would be detrimental to our mission," reminds Zeek.

Razel shoots Zeek a look of frustration, "You are correct."

Zeek sees another expression overtake Razel's face, "I can see you formulating a different plan."

A huge smile beams across the face of Razel, "I am," she assuredly winks at her partner.

Chapter 47

ARRANGEMENTS ARE MADE

Queen Eloise and Andrew finish hanging some family portraits Eloise had restored. Andrew and Eloise stand back admiring the portraits perfectly placed on the wall.

"Well, you two did a fine job," King Theodore approaches, standing behind his wife, lovingly, squeezing her arms. "Thank you for helping, Andrew."

"My pleasure, Sir," Andrew replies, "If you'll excuse me, I have a castle to run," Andrew bows and smiles, dismissing himself.

The king steps next to Eloise, wrapping his arm around her as they stand gazing at the portraits. Eloise drops her head into his chest while they stand there.

"She's just beautiful, isn't she?" inquires Queen Eloise.

"She is, indeed," acknowledges Theo. "I guess, she will remain a mystery."

Eloise smiles and glances up to her husband, "I was thinking, since we offered Ben to have his wedding here at our palace, well, it would only be right to host Luke's wedding when he gets married. Wouldn't you agree?"

"I do, of course. They are both your cousin's sons. We will let Katherine and Sully know next time we see them," affirms Theodore.

Eloise smiles with delight, giving Theodore a huge hug. "Let's have the Mancinis over for dinner next weekend," Eloise proposes.

"I like that idea," agrees Theo.

⁓⁓⁓

"Viana, we need to have a meeting with the Chiawaukas. Will you organize it, please?" Victor requests. "I will contact headquarters and discuss when we can have the Mancinis talk to Marco."

Viana nods, placing her left index and middle finger to her left temple, she notifies the other Chiawauka teams.

Victor returns to Viana. "We will have communication with Marco tonight in the Mancini family room," informs Victor.

"The Mancinis will appreciate the timely manner of some interaction with Marco. Let's go tell them," Viana suggests.

Antonio, Gino, and Francesca are at the dining room table eating lunch when they hear a knock at the back door. The three exchange an inquisitive look at each other. Antonio stands, walks to the door, and opens it. He sees two blue Chiawaukas hovering at his height. "Well, knowing the powers you have, thank you for knocking. Come on in," greets Antonio.

Victor and Viana descend to their feet and walk into the dining room. They each hop onto a chair.

Francesca smiles, "It's nice to see you two again."

Gino is beaming, "Seeing you two in the daylight just put away any notion I was dreaming! This is so great!"

Viana smiles, "Ah, thank you. I speak for us both when I say, we are very thankful to be assigned to your family for the duration of this mission."

Victor clears his throat, then in his deliberate, stern, yet kind voice, informs the Mancinis, "We have spoken with the high priest and priestess. You will be able to communicate with Marco this evening in your family room."

"Well, that is terrific news," Antonio stands, and extends his hand to shake Victor and Viana's hands.

"My heart is full of joy! Thank you both so much!" exclaims Francesca.

"That's awesome! Will we be able to see him? Or will it be audio only?" inquires Gino.

"You'll be pleased to know, yes, you will be able to see each other," answers Victor.

Francesca places her hand on her heart.

Antonio nods, smiles and winks at his wife and son.

"May I be excused? I want to get all my chores done early, so I have time to clean up," Gino asks.

"Certainly," Antonio replies.

Viana and Victor shoot a smile at each other seeing the Mancinis so happy.

Francesca addresses the Chiawaukas as she stands, and begins stacking lunch dishes in her hands, "We will see you this evening. We all have things to do."

Antonio scoots his chair out from under the dining room table, grabs the rest of the dishes and follows Francesca to the kitchen, "I will see you in a bit," Antonio kisses Francesca on the cheek and heads out to the stables.

Francesca smiles.

Victor and Viana are very satisfied with the disclosure of their identity, and the Mancini's reactions.

Chapter 48

CONTACT WITH MARCO

Francesca prepares sandwiches and soup for dinner, knowing they are too anxious to eat a big meal.

"Thanks, Mom," I always love potato soup and sandwiches," attests Gino.

Francesca smiles, "Thank you. I knew we would all be too wound up to eat a heavy meal."

"You're correct, as usual, I might add," winks Antonio.

The three Mancinis finish their evening meal and clean up, eager to meet in the family room.

Victor and Viana are already there. Gino, Antonio, and Francesca join them.

"Should we sit or stand?" asks Antonio.

"You can all relax. When the high priest and priestess appear with Marco, you are welcome to stand," conveys Victor.

Blazer and Celest walk outside and see Marco in the garden, "Are you busy, Marco? High Priest Akshai and High Priestess Ammerie would like to see you," announces Blazer.

"I'm not busy with anything I can't set aside," Marco pleasantly conveys.

"Well, let's go," Blazer motions.

While Blazer, Celest, and Marco walk inside of the Chiawaukas' Headquarters to their destination, Marco shares, "I'm sure glad you guys introduced me to Paul, the consul's son. You were correct, I do have a lot in common with him. We hung out earlier today."

"Oh, yes, we thought you would enjoy Paul. He is the son of the Chiarian consul, Augustus," smiles Celestial.

Stopping outside of the communications room, Blazer opens the door, "Well, let's go in."

Celest and Marco enter the large room, followed by Blazer. They walk to the front of the room where the high priest and high priestess are waiting.

"Come join us, Marco," High Priestess Ammerie communicates, reaching her arm out.

Marco walks with purpose. Both high priests are standing at around six-foot-three inches in height. High Priest Akshai puts his arm around Marco, drawing him close.

"We have something special for you this evening," reveals High Priest Akshai.

High Priestess Ammerie caringly smiles at Marco as he is guided to stand between them, "We are going to visit your family. You will not be able to touch them, but you will be able to see them and visit."

"Oh, wow! Thank you for this! All of you!" Marco makes eye contact with each high priest and then Celestial and Blazer.

"Have a good visit," relays Blazer in his bass, country like accent.

"We are so happy for you, Marco," Celest offers in her sweet, tender voice.

Marco looks at the high priests. Before he can get his next question out, both High Priest Akshai and High Priestess Ammerie bow their heads. Marco follows suit and lowers his head. The exquisite, golden star hanging above them releases a droplet of what appears to be water. The droplet descends and encases the three of them. High Priest Akshai takes ahold of Marcos' right hand, and High Priestess Ammerie holds firmly to Marco's left hand with her right hand. Instantaneously, they transport.

Viana has been standing in the family room with her hand closed tightly in a fist, she releases her fist so the palm of her hand is facing upward. A snow globe shaped object appears before them which enlarges to six-feet-five inches tall. High Priest Akshai, High Priestess Ammerie, and Marco are now clearly visible in the Mancini family room.

Gino, Francesca and Antonio jump to their feet. Victor and Viana stand at attention.

Marco steps toward his family, forgetting he cannot get out of the sphere he is in.

"Wow! This is great to see you all!" Marco proclaims.

"Son, it is so good to see you," Antonio chokes up a bit.

"Oh, man, I have got so much to tell you!" Gino conveys.

Francesca is beaming.

"How are Grandmother and Grandfather?" Marco asks. "Do they know I am alive?"

"They're doing fine, son. No, I believe at this time, they do not know," answers Francesca. "How are you doing on Chiaras?"

"I heeded your advice to be thankful for my life no matter my location. I met a Chiarian named Paul. He is a few years older than I am, but we have a lot in common. He is knowledgeable about The Ancient Writings, and of the Estellas Galaxy we live in, so I have enjoyed learning from him. You guys would really like him," Marco describes.

"Marco, I just can't tell you enough how happy I am you are alive," surrenders Antonio.

"Me too, Marco! I have my brother back!" Gino elates.

"I know! I don't even recall what all happened! I remember chiseling on a wall in the mine, then I broke through the Krystyleen rock wall. I remember a surge of bitter, cold air blasting me off my feet backwards. Then I woke up. The Chiawaukas relocated me to Chiaras. The cool thing is, while I was recovering, it's like I had visions of what was going on in your lives, so, that was pretty cool. And Gino, stay away from the champagne!" laughs Marco.

"Oh, you saw Ben and Laurie's wedding?" asks Gino.

"No, I heard you the morning after whine to mom; there is no mercy at the Mancinis," Marco says laughing.

Gino laughs and shakes his head, "Yeah, looking back, that was pretty funny."

"Oh, where are my manners? I'd like to introduce you to High Priest Akshai, and High Priestess Ammerie," Marco presents.

"Welcome to our home," Antonio honors.

"It is so nice to meet you. Being in your presence, I feel I've known you my entire life," reveals Francesca.

"My name is Gino, it's very nice to meet you both. Thank you for taking care of my brother!" Gino conveys.

"My dear Mancinis, it is very nice to meet you as well. Having Marco with us on Chiaras may not be an ideal situation for your family, but necessary due to circumstances," High Priestess Ammerie expresses in her whimsical, endearing manner.

"Our Chiawaukas, Blazer and Celestial, have been in charge of Marco's well-being ever since that day at the mine, after Victor and Viana instinctively placed the protective shield over him. They will continue to be assigned to him, teaching and training him. It is our hope, that someday, he will be able to rejoin you here on Soleil," earnestly discloses High Priest Akshai.

"Well, we certainly understand it would cause alarm and panic among the people of the kingdom if Marco showed up after two years, when everyone believes he has died. We aren't jumping for joy about the situation; however, we are rational people and realize the gravity of the circumstances," Antonio deduces.

"You are a wise man," High Priest Akshai acknowledges.

"Victor and Viana will begin to teach and train your family, preparing you for the day you will be ordained Keepers of the Universe. That day will happen when the two Chords of Chiawaukas Families are joined by a marriage," High Priestess Ammerie unveils.

"We will do our best to be ready," confirms Francesca.

Antonio and Gino both nod in agreement. Victor and Viana subtly nod their heads, both display pleased looks on their faces.

"And know, I will do my part, learning my role as a Keeper of the Universe," Marco asserts.

High Priest Akshai places his right hand on Marco's shoulder, "We trust you will. It is time for us to depart. Anytime you want to visit with each other, please let Victor and Viana know, and Marco will inform us," High Priest Akshai maintains.

"I love you guys!" Marco exclaims, "and Gino, I miss being here, doing things together, but now, we are on a new adventure."

"I know," Gino replies, "I love you, brother," reaching his hands to the sphere.

Francesca smiles, placing her right hand on her heart, then extends it to Marco. She then blows him a kiss, "I love you always."

Antonio nods, "Know we think of you, Son. Our love is always with you," Antonio internally restrains from being emotional.

High Priest Akshai takes Marco's right hand, and High Priestess Ammerie holds Marco's left hand. The snow globe shaped object holding Marco and the high priests vanishes before their eyes.

The three Mancinis, along with Victor and Viana, stand momentarily in stillness.

Chapter 49

GINO'S PLANS

"Well, it seems we certainly go from one thing to another," Antonio says as he twirls Francesca's curls with his fingers while they lie in bed.

"I know. I think I mentioned that a while back, like a year ago," Francesca chuckles. "Fridei we have dinner with the king and queen, Saturdei is the Annual Chamberlain Fall Around, and Sundei my parents are coming out for family dinner," Francesca details.

Antonio gives Francesca a squeeze.

"Come in, Gino," Francesca says.

Antonio expresses a curious look on his face.

Gino enters their bedroom and sits at the end of their bed, "There is so much going on!" He lies back on their bed, turning on his side to see his parents, "This is phenomenal Marco is alive! Also, there's Claire. I intend to marry her, as I have already discussed with you two. I am going to ask permission from her parents, of course."

"We completely support you, Son," Antonio expresses.

"When do you plan to do this?" inquires Francesca.

"I'm not sure. I'm hoping for a wedding next fall, maybe the night of the Autumn Moon, when it is full and a brilliant orange,"

Gino discloses. "I intend to ask her parents for permission next week, maybe on a lunch break, when I know Claire is out here working."

"Sounds like you have formulated your strategy," Antonio affirms his son.

Francesca smiles, "We are very happy for you. We both enjoy Claire. She is a conscientious worker, which makes it very enjoyable to work with her."

"Yes, she is a hard worker. I'm excited as we should be done with the remodeling of our woodworking shop in a few weeks," Gino lays out.

"It has come together quite well," Antonio nods.

"Have you thought about if Claire wants your wedding in a different season? Are you open to another time of the year?" Francesca poses possibilities.

"Well, I guess I am. I can't imagine her not wanting it on the evening that has the most spectacular phase of the fall moon though," Gino surmises.

Francesca and Antonio both smile at their son.

Gino hops up from their bed, "Goodnight, we have so much going on."

"Goodnight, Son," Antonio conveys.

"Night, sweet Gino. Love you," Francesca expresses.

"Love you guys," Gino declares exiting his parents' bedroom.

Chapter 50

PORTRAIT ON THE WALL

"I've got to say, Claire, you have done a splendid job on learning the recipes and helping me with my business," Francesca compliments.

"You're certainly welcome. I enjoy this. In the spring, if you need my help with gardening, I am happy to learn that as well," Claire offers.

Francesca laughs, "I will take you up on that."

They each carry items to place in the saddlebags designed to carry food items.

"Have a good weekend. I'm sure we will see you tomorrow at the Annual Chamberlain Fall Around," Francesca smiles and reaches to give Claire a hug.

"I'm sure you will. I will drop off these items at your parents' store as usual, and then I'm going to help my mother with dinner. Gino is coming to dinner tonight," Claire excitedly states.

"You guys have a lovely evening. We are actually going to have dinner at the castle with the king and queen," shares Francesca.

"You both have a great night as well." Claire mounts on her horse and departs.

Gino walks in the back door about the same time Antonio does.

"Two of my favorite men. I hope you both had a good day," Francesca smiles with a towel draped around her wet hair.

"I did. Bill has so many orders. He is basically referring them all to me as he fires up his welding shop. Now I need to go clean up, and get to Claire's for dinner. I don't want to be late," Gino sets his lunch tote on a shelf in the entryway of the kitchen.

Antonio smiles, and reaches out to hug Francesca. "I did have a good day," he whispers in her ear with his passionate, deep voice.

"I'm glad. I have a snack in case you need one before we eat dinner," Francesca offers.

"I'll just grab an apple, take a shower and be ready to leave soon," states Antonio, "join me?" Antonio gives Francesca a wink.

"Rain check? I think I am going to dress up a bit for tonight. I just feel like it," Francesca voices.

The three Mancinis depart their home at the same time. Their dogs circle around them until Francesca kneels down to show them affection, "We will just be gone awhile, then we will return. I love you girls so much!" She pets and snuggles each one.

Antonio helps Francesca into their wagon. Gino rides alongside them on Jolly.

"Have a good dinner, Son," Antonio gestures as they head different directions once they arrive near the town.

"Thanks, Pop. Love you guys," Gino replies.

"Love you. Be safe," Francesca lovingly expresses.

Antonio lifts Francesca as he helps her down from the wagon. "Always the romantic," smiles Francesca.

"Forever, my beauty, inside and out," Antonio tenderly indicates. Wrapping his arm around his wife, they walk up the stairs to the front door of the castle.

Andrew greets them at the door, "Welcome, Mr. and Mrs. Mancini."

"Hello, Andrew. No need to be so formal," Antonio shakes Andrew's hand.

"Hello, Andrew. I agree with my husband, no formalities necessary," Francesca insists.

"Well, I must say, that sometimes as the chief of staff, I enjoy greeting guests with proper decorum," smiles Andrew.

Antonio nods with a smile, "I guess it's in the air; we even dressed up a bit."

"Indeed, you did, Sir," Andrew comments.

King Theodore and Queen Eloise appear in the hallway. They walk toward their guests.

"It is good to see you two," King Theodore extends his hand to Antonio's, firmly shaking it.

Queen Eloise wraps her arms around Francesca, "You look just as beautiful as ever! I love your dress!"

"Thank you. It is so good to see you!" greets Francesca.

"Come with us. We want to show you our remodel," the queen takes Francesca's hand leading her.

Antonio and Theodore follow. They go down the hall and turn into a room on the right.

"Oh, it's delightful!" admires Francesca. "The soft pastel yellow paint is soothing, yet inviting."

Francesca and Antonio enter the room and walk to the newly-installed, large, picture window with a beautiful view out the palace toward the Chamberlain River and stables, Antonio nods his head several times in approval.

"I so enjoyed my time at your home and Gino giving me a tour, well, it inspired me to enlarge a couple of rooms we have and make it into our family room," describes the queen.

Turning from the window, Francesca commends, "You've done a marvelous job! I'm sure you all will enjoy this room."

Francesca spies something on one of the walls she hadn't seen when she entered the room, as the new, large, picture window had captured her full attention on arrival. But now, something else does. Gently squeezing Antonio's muscular arm, he too, turns from gazing out the window and glances at his wife. She motions with a look to see what she has set her eyes on.

"Are you okay, Francesca?" questions the queen, "You appear as though you have seen a ghost."

Francesca draws nearer to the riveting portrait she is studying, "She is lovely, where did you get this? Who is she?"

Antonio and the king both take several deliberate steps to be next to Francesca and Eloise. They all converge in front of the unnamed portrait.

"That is a painting of Eloise's great aunt. Well, I'll let her tell the story," Theodore says.

Francesca glances at Eloise, then back to the portrait.

"I found that in storage while going through some things. I took it to have it restored, and I am just so pleased with the way it turned out. Yes, she is very beautiful. She is, well, was, my Great Aunt, Genie Arabella A'mato."

"We have just never heard Sully mention her, or you for that matter," mulls Francesca.

"Well, you know, sometimes, we just forget. And she was a great aunt. She just disappeared according to her sisters Vanessa and Victoria, who are twins. At least, that is what has been passed down through the years. I was told Genie Arabella and her husband, Gabe, were quite close to both of your great-grandparents. I was told she even attended your great-grandmother's funeral. To my recollection of what the twins said, Genie Arabella even held you, Francesca. You were probably one or two months old. I don't recall all the details," the queen clarifies, peering at Antonio and Francesca.

They all stand in silence for a few moments, noticing the faint scent of the freshly painted room, the decor, and the unforgettable portrait.

"Let's go eat, shall we?" King Theodore leads, patting Antonio on the back.

Andrew pulls out the chairs for the ladies, slightly bowing his head at each of them. Chef Pierre and his kitchen staff appear. The aroma of the food has everyone's mouths watering.

"Oh my, it smells so delicious. What have you prepared?" asks Francesca.

Chef Pierre tips his head, and with his arms outstretched, he lifts off the beautifully designed stainless-steel cover, "Chicken Scallopini with Saffron Crème Sauce."

"It smells heavenly," Eloise breathes in, then exhales.

Chef Pierre serves the four. His kitchen staff fill the wine and water glasses and serves the vegetables and bread. The two couples partake in another fabulous meal.

"Tell me, where are Carol and Rupert this evening?" Francesca inquires.

"Theodore and I decided we wanted the two of you all to ourselves," the queen says with gest.

The king has an austere expression on his face, "We asked Carol if she would take Rupert for a few hours." He looks at his wife, "Honestly, sometimes, I feel bad to even ask Carol for additional help. I know Rupert can be a real drain on her as well...probably anyone he is with for any extended amount of time," the king dabs his mouth with his napkin.

Eloise is subtly shaking her head, "Our friends don't need to hear the sordid details of our struggles with Rupert."

"I'm sure they are well aware of what a handful he can be," the king respectfully implies.

Antonio observes, "You know, he is an only child, and he receives your full attention and love. He will grow out of these troublesome years. Don't feel ashamed to share with other parents, especially us. We're friends."

Francesca adds, "Yes, family. Don't feel ashamed or embarrassed."

"Thank you for that. I'm sorry if I embarrassed you, Eloise. I seem to easily lose my composure when it comes to Rupert," reveals Theodore.

"It's alright, we can't always be as composed as we'd like to be. I don't know who I'd rather let our guard down in front of, other than the two of you," the queen addresses as her eyes meet the Mancinis.

Antonio raises his glass of wine, "A toast, to one of my best friends. May God bless you with another wonderful birthday."

"To friendship and birthdays," Theodore raises his wine glass clinking it to Antonio's.

"To friendships and birthdays," the four of them say together in unison with their wine glasses raised gently tapping each one.

Chapter 51

ALL KINDS OF NEWS

The aroma of scrambled eggs with peppers and onions, sausage, gravy, hash browns, and biscuits fill the Mancini home.

Francesca is setting the breakfast feast on the table before they head out to the Annual Chamberlain Fall Around.

"Breakfast sure smells good, Mom," Gino compliments.

"Thank you. I thought we could all use a good meal before leaving," Francesca contends.

After Antonio leads them in a blessing, he looks at Gino, "How was your dinner at the Richards'?"

"It was great! We had a baked apple dessert and pork and potatoes were the main course," Gino describes.

"That sounds delicious," Francesca comments.

"Then we sat and visited, and played cards afterwards. Claire's parents are pretty cool," Gino adds, "I'll stop by her parents this coming week and seek their permission to ask Claire to marry me."

Antonio smiles and winks at Gino.

Francesca gently reminds, "Be sure to ask God to prepare the way before you."

"Definitely," assures Gino. "How was your night with the royals? Was Rupert a menace?" Gino laughs.

Francesca and Antonio both shoot Gino a quick look. "Actually, Carol was watching Rupert, so we were able to enjoy an adult-only dinner," Francesca shares. "But you know what? We did find out something interesting," Francesca discloses.

"What?" inquires Gino.

"Do you remember 'Mystery on Mancini Mountain', as you coined it?" Francesca smiles.

Antonio, too, is exhibiting his full attention even though he was there.

"I do remember! We have a lady living in a cabin you have yet to take us to," announces Gino.

"Well, a portrait of her is hanging in the new family room of the palace," informs Francesca.

"Wow! No way! How do they know her? Did you tell them you met her?" quizzes Gino.

"Settle down, Son," Antonio chuckles, "It is not our place to divulge her whereabouts. It just so happens she is the great-aunt of Sully and Queen Eloise," reveals Antonio.

"Hmmm, well, *that* is cool. More pieces of the mysterious puzzle right here in our humble kingdom," Gino ascertains.

Francesca lets out her little laugh, "That is a great way to look at it."

......◦⦿◦......

Chamberlain Kingdom is decorated with beautiful flags representing the kingdom and the Annual Fall Around. People travel from neighboring kingdoms to join in the festivities, sell their foods and goods, and to see their friends.

The Mancinis arrive and walk toward the large, colorful banner that proudly states, "Welcome to our Annual Chamberlain Kingdom Fall Around". The Mancinis see their lifelong friends, the Carlisles, about thirty feet in front of them.

"Hey," Gino hollers, waving his arm.

The Carlisles look. Seeing their friends, they wave.

Gino and Luke approach each other, "I have been waiting for you to get here," declares Luke.

"Really? Well, I have been wanting to visit with you," Gino asserts. "Let's go walk around."

"Great idea!" Luke agrees. Then says to his parents, Sully and Katherine, "See you guys later."

"We'll catch up to you later," Sully waves.

"Have fun," Katherine offers in her sweet, high-pitched voice.

Gino gives his mom a quick hug, and glances at both his parents, "I hope you guys don't mind. Luke and I have a lot we need to catch up on!"

"We don't mind at all," Antonio nods.

"Love you," Francesca softly says.

"Well, those two haven't seen much of each other this past summer since they are both working," recognizes Sully.

Katherine reaches to Francesca and gives her a hug, "I am looking forward to next Saturdei's game night. It seems so much has happened since the last time we saw you."

Francesca and Antonio smile at their friends. The four of them stroll amongst the booths that are set up, and see faces, both familiar and unfamiliar.

Francesca leans into Antonio while they're holding hands, "I'm so glad I sent all the baked goods into town yesterday."

Antonio nods and smiles, "Me too. It was nice to not be so rushed this morning."

"Okay, I can't wait until next weekend to tell you," Katherine proclaims as she comes to a stop.

Sully and the Mancinis stop and stand in a circle.

"Ben and Laurie are expecting a baby!" announces Katherine.

Antonio shakes Sully's hand. Francesca and Katherine exchange another hug.

"That is fabulous news!" Francesca expresses, reaching to give Sully a hug as well.

Antonio hugs Katherine as well, "That is pretty exciting. It's hard to think we are even old enough to be grandparents."

Sully laughs a bit, and nods.

······⚮······

"Man, I have some news for you," Luke tells Gino.

Gino smiles, "Well, I have news for you!"

"Alright, you first," Luke says.

"No, you first," laughs Gino.

Gino blurts out, "I'm going to ask Claire to marry me!" At the exact same time Luke declares, "I'm going to ask Camille to marry me!"

Both young men stare at each other and laugh. After a few minutes, Luke suggests, "Double wedding?"

"My thoughts exactly!" Gino agrees. "I was actually hoping for a wedding next fall, on the night of the Autumn Moon."

"I like that idea. Of course, we will have to discuss it with our fiancés, that is, if they say 'yes'," Luke submits.

"Have you asked Camille's parents yet?" Gino inquires.

"No, I plan to this week. What about you?" Luke questions.

"Me too, I'm planning on asking her parents this week," informs Gino.

"How can either set of parents say no to the most eligible bachelors in the kingdom?" Luke assuredly states as he tosses the back of his hand across Ginos' chest.

"Yeah, that's right!" agrees Gino.

The two young men walk around together discussing their jobs and their goals.

Francesca's parents had asked Camille to help at their booth, along with Claire. The two young ladies were talking, laughing, and dutifully making the Montanelli Mercantile booth quite an eye-catching display.

"You girls sure know how to make an inviting exhibit," Sophia comments.

"Well, thank you," Claire proudly smiles.

"Thank you, Mrs. Montanelli," Camille politely replies.

"You girls, so formal," Leonardo notices. "Just call us by our first names."

Both young ladies smile and continue to work and wait on the customers now arriving.

Chapter 52

MARCO AND PAUL

"I really appreciate you teaching me about the Ancient Writings," Marco expresses to Paul.

"It is good for you to learn the history, especially since you are a family member to one of the Chords of Chiawauka families," Paul emphasizes in his distinct Northern Chiaras accent.

"Yeah, I still don't understand it all. It's a lot to comprehend," admits Marco.

"If you're up for a hike, I will take you to a pretty cool cave. There is some history there as well," Paul offers.

"Lead the way," Marco extends his left arm with his hand outstretched.

The two young men set forth on the journey.

"It'll take us a couple of hours each way," Paul informs.

"That's okay," Marco assures.

"This is really some good-looking scenery; the fields, the mountains, it reminds me of Soleil," observes Marco. "Except, of course, some of your trees are incredibly tall," Marco laughs, "probably to support the Chiarians' tall stature."

Paul chuckles, "Possibly, and yes, I have been told that Chiaras is similar to Soleil. I personally have never traveled to Soleil," Paul indicates.

"I wasn't aware life even existed on other planets. My family always speculated there was, but no factual evidence," Marco reflects.

As the two hike up a winding trail through some tall trees leaving the fields behind, Paul shares, "Well, centuries ago, the Cryptolores fled to our planet after the planet they inhabited was destroyed. That is when the Estellas Galaxy High Court and the Chiawauka High Priests and council convened. They deliberated at great length and decided to banish them to a cavern deep within Soleil. It was either that or completely annihilate them."

"Wow, they must be pretty bad for the Chiawaukas to go to such extreme measures," recognizes Marco.

"They are pure evil, which is why the Chiawaukas formulated a back-up plan they implemented on each planet in the galaxy. At one time, the Cryptolore leaders were actually Chiawaukas. However, they were extremely envious, ruthless, and demanded power. They rejected the notion of serving others and decided to break ranks, fleeing Chiaras. They were stripped of their supernatural powers the Chiawaukas possess. They fled to the planet VeNoma. They overthrew the beings on VeNoma. The protectors of the galaxy pursued the Cryptolores to offer them repeated opportunities to repent and live noble. The Cryptolores refused. The protectors unleashed their weapon on the planet VeNoma hoping to obliviate the Cryptolores. As a result, from what I remember reading, whatever peculiar forces of the universe there are, the ones who rebelled, also lost their physical blue shape, and the rebels form became that of a filmy, black cloud substance. For some reason, they are able to inhabit bodies of other life, animal or human, even though the supernatural powers they possessed as Chiawaukas were taken from them. Shortly after, they were given the name 'Cryptolores'." Paul explains.

"Like a possession?" asks Marco.

"Yes," answers Paul.

"Well, that's creepy," Marco states.

"It is. Can you imagine having a demonic Cryptolore inhabit you? Control your thoughts, your actions, even your feelings?" Paul poses.

"Well," Marco gives a little laugh, and motions with his hand, "I actually did have an encounter with a Cryptolore."

"That's right, I apologize for discussing them," Paul offers.

"It's alright. I guess you could say I actually had a first-hand experience with them," reflects Marco.

"You don't need to share if it's uncomfortable," empathizes Paul.

"It's fine. I never have really discussed the matter with anyone. Ha, my mother often encouraged my brother and me to share our feelings. She would tell us we would feel better, like bouncing a ball," Marco recalls. "Maybe, I will share. That is, if you want to hear."

Paul humbly and eagerly lets Marco know he is interested, "I would, indeed."

"I remember it was my first day working at the Krystyleen Mine that has been in my family for years. Curtis, the foreman, explained techniques to me. My Pop had given me so many safety instructions that I definitely felt I knew what I was doing," Marco pauses with a little laugh. "Then, after a while, Curtis went to get us some water. I remember I felt I was ready to return to work, so I picked up my tool and began swinging away at the rock wall. The next thing I remember is a blast of chilling air knocking me backward. I lost my balance and fell…"

"Oh, wow!" exclaims Paul, "Then what happened?"

"I remember lying there. Unable to move. A filmy vortex was hovering over me, and I felt as if it were consuming the life out of me. That's the last thing I remember. I do recall I had some weird dreams. I saw my mother in one of my personal, favorite dresses that she would wear. I could see her, and I tried to communicate to her.

Another time, I saw my brother and Pop, but then, I woke up," Marco recollects.

"Where? What happened?" Paul queries.

"Get this, I woke up in our family mausoleum," Marco answers.

Paul rolls his head, "Oh no, the worst! Did you panic?"

"No, actually, it went pretty smoothly. The Chiawaukas, Blazer and Celestial were at my side. Victor and Viana were there as well. They all explained to me what happened. Now, here I am," Marco avers.

"Well, I'm sorry you experienced such a devastating event. I am glad you are here though. I'll take you in as my younger brother," Paul voices.

"I am used to being the older brother, but I know, you are older, and most definitely wiser in these matters," Marco admits.

Paul laughs, "It's only because the Chiawaukas made their home on Chiaras centuries ago. So, the Chiarians are familiar with them. It's really kind of cool to have Supreme Guardian Beings stationed on our planet. Plus, I have studied a lot of their history so I would be knowledgeable."

"That's impressive," acknowledges Marco.

"I guess, thanks. Hey, have you met any other Chiawaukas?" inquires Paul.

"No, just High Priest Akshai and High Priestess Ammerie, and the four I mentioned," conveys Marco.

"Well, enjoy each one. They are so different. When I was a kid, I thought it was cool I was as tall as them. I just wanted to squeeze them," Paul laughs, "Victor would let me know without hesitation he is not a blue toy. I remember frequently asking my parents if I could take one home," Paul laughs hard, "Viana had a much better disposition about the matter. Victor was not having any of my childish nonsense. They're just cute with their variances in shades of blue, and different heights. Although, I think only a few grow to reach four-feet tall, the rest are somewhere between three-feet and three-feet-eleven inches," Paul describes.

"Yeah, they seem pretty awesome," agrees Marco.

"Did you know they can extend themselves in height?" asks Paul.

"Yes," Marco chuckles, "High Priest Akshai gave me a demonstration when he wasn't too pleased with a stunt of mine," discloses Marco.

"Yeah, well, the Chiawaukas, being created as Supreme Guardian Beings, are incredible," attests Paul. "They can change colors, and have innumerable powers beyond belief. Oh, cool, we're here." Paul pushes through some bushes revealing an opening in a cave.

Marco follows Paul, pushing back the bushes as he enters into the cave.

"Hey, where did you get the light?" asks Marco.

"The bushes that cover the entrance. When you squish the leaves in your hand and then open your hand, they create this light," informs Paul. "It's called a Pepperlyte."

"Fascinating," Marco states. He returns to the opening to grab a few leaves.

The two journey into the cave.

"Why the name Pepperlyte?" inquires Marco.

Paul smiles, "Good question. The leaves taste like pepper, so the animals don't eat them, and the leaves create light once squished."

Marco smiles and nods, "Ah, I see."

"Creation, it is indeed a masterpiece," declares Paul.

"Yes, I do agree," Marco confirms.

Paul continues to give Marco a history lesson of Chiaras, the Chiawaukas, and the Estellas Galaxy they live in while they explore the history in the cave.

After some time exploring, Paul stops in his tracks and curiously investigates a chilling image he does not recall seeing before.

Marco stops as well, noticing Paul's intense studying of the cave wall. Marco's eyes follow to where Paul's eyes are keenly focused, but remains silent. Paul then turns to Marco. "I have not seen this before. We need to see the Chiawaukas as soon as we return so I can relay this image."

Chapter 53

SUNDEI AT THE MANCINIS

"Your grandparents will be here soon, Gino; help me set the table, please," enlists Francesca.

"What are we having?" asks Gino, standing behind his mother, peeking over her shoulder.

"We are having a dish your Pop and I ate at dinner the other night with the king and queen. It was so delicious, I wanted to try it," shares Francesca. "It is called Chicken Scallopini with Saffron Crème Sauce."

Gino takes a spoon and sweeps around his mother's side to dish up a bite. Francesca turns; they bump into each other. Gino almost drops the scoop out of the spoon, but is able to maneuver his body, save the spoonful, take a bite and exclaim, "Wow! That is good! I'm glad you made it!"

Francesca smiles, "Well, I'm glad you approve Mr. Mancini."

"I do, indeed, Mother Mancini," bows Gino in a playful, endearing manner.

"Now scoot, and let's get everything ready," Francesca focuses.

Antonio greets Sophia and Leonardo as he reaches for the sacks they brought, to carry them inside, "How are you two, today?"

"I'm doing just fine, thank you," Sophia gently touches Antonio's arm.

Covering his mouth, coughing a bit, Leonardo mumbles, "I am good. Glad we are here."

"You don't sound too well," Antonio utters.

Sophia has a stern look on her face, which softens when she sees her grandson and daughter, "Well, there's my handsome grandson and beautiful daughter! I love family dinner days."

Gino gives his grandmother a hug, then walks to his grandfather who is still coughing. Gino begins to approach his grandfather when he decides, "I'm going to get you a glass of water."

"Thank you," replies Leonardo.

Gino returns with a glass of water. Leonardo takes his seat at the table.

"Well, let's all sit down, I will bring in the rest of the food," announces Francesca.

Sophia sits next to Leonardo and across from Gino. Francesca and Antonio are at each end. Antonio leads them in prayer.

"Oh, everything smells delicious, honey," compliments Sophia.

"Thank you. It is a new recipe. I think you will all enjoy it," submits Francesca.

Everyone is intently eating, savoring each bite.

"How did your booth do at the Annual Fall Around?" inquires Francesca.

"We had a very good day. The king and queen from Monterei purchased quite a few of the pastries you baked," Leonardo states, "they complimented your skills many times before leaving."

"How sweet of them. Yes, Antonio and I actually had the pleasure of visiting with them. They seem like humble and grounded people," Francesca comments.

Leonardo begins coughing some, and covers his mouth with his napkin as he turns away.

"Are you sick, Grandfather?" asks Gino.

Leonardo shakes his head, "No," while he is trying to hold in his cough.

Francesca and Antonio glance at each other. Sophia has a stern and concerned expression on her face.

Leonardo rotates back to the table once his coughing subsides. "Gino, I am as healthy as an ox. You don't need to worry."

"Why don't you tell them?" Sophia presses.

"Tell them what? That I have a cough? Poppycock," Leonardo states with his confident smile.

"Poppycock?" Sophia glances at Francesca, Antonio, and then to Gino. "He coughs like that because he still smokes the pipe. Oh, its black cherry tobacco, it has a good taste he says, but listen to you," Sophia glares at Leonardo, "It is hurting your lungs, Leonardo!" Sophia lashes out momentarily losing her composure.

"Dad, you did promise you would stop," Francesca gently reminds.

"If that's why you're coughing, maybe you should quit. After all, I want you alive so you can be at my wedding and when I have children," expresses Gino.

"Oh, honey, are you engaged?" asks Sophia.

"Well, not yet. I plan to ask her parents for permission this week, then, if approved, I will come up with the perfect time to ask Claire," explains Gino. "Grandfather, I want you healthy."

"I am just fine," asserts Leonardo, winking at his grandson. "Don't you worry about a thing."

Sophia composes herself as she always does. The family finishes off the dessert Francesca made.

Gino peers at everyone and smiles, "I love our family." His words soften everyone's spirit.

After everyone clears the table, Francesca invites her mother onto the back deck, "Let's go out back, I want to show you the new garden I planted."

"Well, I'd like to see, too, Honey," Leonardo chimes in.

"Of course, Daddy," Francesca smiles.

The three walk out back and down the steps to Francesca's new garden area.

"Your landscape is just breathtaking," exclaims Sophia.

"You have put in a lot of hard work. I hope you take care of yourself as good as this landscaping," states Leonardo.

Sophia cannot help herself, "Like you take care of yourself?" she says glaring at Leonardo.

"Alright, enough. Stop, you two. What is going on?" Francesca demands.

In her sweet, loving voice, Sophia adamantly spells it out, "Look, I love your father. I do not want him to die on me. I know we are all going to die. But I fear if he continues to smoke his pipe, it will be sooner than later. I don't want him to miss out on Gino's wedding, or our grandbabies. So honestly, I'm hurt, and I'm angry," confesses Sophia.

Leonardo stands there with a crooked smile, "Come over here, Francie," he reaches ahold of Francesca's hand and twirls her out and then back to him. "Do you remember all the times I danced with you and your mother when you were young?"

"I do," Francesca nods.

"I will be fine. I am fine, and poppycock to this mumbo jumbo. No disrespect to your mother intended, of course, but I am fine," Leonardo twirls Francesca once more.

Sophia throws up her hands, "Well, there you have it, your dad is fine," in a direct, mildly sarcastic, but softly spoken voice.

Leonardo steps next to Sophia, "I'm sorry if I hurt and anger you. It is not my intention. You are my love."

Sophia reluctantly smiles, "Well, alright then, I guess that makes everything better, huh?" with seemingly more sarcasm in her voice.

Leonardo now tosses his hands about, "What can I do to please you?"

"You know the answer to that," implies Sophia.

"I wish you would just let me live each day in peace with you," Leonardo requests.

"Well, I do try; but sometimes I get so angry and hurt when I hear you coughing…knowing it is robbing you, robbing us," Sophia defends.

Leonardo drops his head, then glances at Sophia, "Look, let's enjoy today with our family. And then tomorrow, let's enjoy that day, and each day after that."

Sophia wants to be mad, and wants to list out her reasons, but she understands what her husband is suggesting. "You're right," smiles Sophia. "Let's enjoy this day with our family. I will try to enjoy each day I have with you. I love you. You are the hardest working man; you give the shirt off your back for anyone. I know you love me and our family," Sophia pauses, "I guess that is why I get so infuriated though, because you won't take care of yourself!" Sophia stops and realizes she is getting testy again, "Alright...I'll stop. I just can't think about it!" motioning with her hands she is done with the subject.

Leonardo kisses Sophia's cheek, "If you two don't mind, now, I will go have a look at that new fly-fishing rod Antonio's been boasting about."

Sophia smiles at Leonardo.

"That's fine, Dad, Antonio and Gino have been wanting to show you the addition to the woodworking shop as well," Francesca informs.

"I have been looking forward to that," Leonardo says as he walks away.

"Let's sit on the deck," Francesca suggests.

"Alright, then I would like to see the updates to the shop as well," Sophia conveys.

"Certainly, of course." Francesca pauses, then gazes at Sophia, "Mother, when you were a little girl, did you have special senses?" inquires Francesca.

"Special senses?" Sophia questions.

"Yes. I can't explain it, but like maybe a heightened intuition," relays Francesca.

"I don't know. I guess I felt I did sense things before they would happen. I know you have that ability. I recognized it when you were a little girl and always encouraged you to trust your instincts. I don't recognize that I had anything special. Why are you asking?" inquires Sophia.

"I just want you to think back when you were a little girl and if you remember anything special, that's all. And what do you remember about your grandmother Anna Grace Casella?" asks Francesca.

"Ah, your great-grandmother was an amazing woman. She was gentle, yet fierce. Now," Sophia pauses, "I always thought *she* had remarkable insight, actually. Come to think of it, you remind me a lot of her."

"Really?" Francesca feels humble and honored.

"Absolutely, honey," Sophia confirms.

"But you never felt like you had a keen insight or special, unique gifts?" presses Francesca.

"Well, I guess maybe I did. But I must say, living with your dad, and running our business, I think somewhere along the way, I have suppressed anything I personally deemed as unusual, or special to me," reveals Sophia.

"Yet, you always encouraged me," Francesca adamantly states.

"Well, yes. That's what parents do when they see special gifts in their children, they encourage them," claims Sophia in her tender voice.

"Will you do me a favor?" Francesca asks Sophia.

"If I can, certainly," responds Sophia.

"Will you please open yourself up to your potential? Nurture your God-given gifts. I'm curious to see if we will both sense the same things, and be connected in some mysterious, supernatural way," Francesca pleads.

"Oh, honey," Sophia pats Francesca's knee, we will always be connected as mother and daughter.

"I know. I sense there is more for us to unfold, though. Deep within me I feel there is something unexplained, something we can be sharing...on a spiritual realm," Francesca directs.

"Well, yes, of course, we share in our faith and belief in God," adds Sophia, appearing a bit puzzled.

Francesca stands, takes a few steps and searches out over their property and to the river, experiencing a bit of frustration, "Yes, but I must have gotten my powers from you...I mean my intuitive ability."

Sophia laughs in her sweet voice, "Powers? I am glad you clarified that," still laughing softly, "I do not know what it is you want of me, but I will set aside some time each day to reflect on my childhood, and what my *gifts* are, and *'nurture'* them as you request," smiles Sophia. "I know I so admired my grandmother Anna Grace."

"Maybe, sometime, you can tell me stories that you remember. I would like to know who she was," discloses Francesca.

"I can do that," Sophia confirms as she smiles lovingly at her daughter.

Francesca regroups herself, "Shall we join the guys and you can see the work they've done on the shop?"

"Absolutely," Sophia affirms.

Chapter 54

THE PROPOSAL

G ino is ecstatic about the approval from Claires' parents of his marriage proposal to Claire. *I cannot wait to ask her,* he thinks, as he grabs his jacket and rushes out of his room.

Francesca and Antonio walk into the dining room and greet Gino as he dashes down the stairs from his bedroom.

"We'd like you to sit down a minute, Gino," Antonio says.

"Well, okay, but can it be quick? I am off to purchase an engagement ring and then to meet Claire," asserts Gino.

"We don't need to sit. We have something for you," Francesca discloses. She swings her left arm out from behind her back which holds a small box in her hand.

"What's this?" quizzes Gino.

"Well, take it and open it," Antonio says. Both he and Francesca are smiling at their son.

Gino takes the small box out of his mother's palm inquisitively making eye contact with her. He opens it and sees an exquisite engagement ring with delicate flowers sculpted around an elegant stone. "Wow! This is incredible! Where did this come from?" inquires Gino.

"Well, it has been in my family and passed down for generations. It first belonged to your great-great Grandmother, Anna Grace Casella. It was her engagement ring. Your Pop and I thought you might want to offer it to Claire," suggests Francesca.

"Wow! I certainly do! Thank you!" exclaims Gino.

"You're quite welcome." Francesca smiles and gives her son a hug and kiss on the cheek.

Antonio shakes his son's hand. "Now, get on your way, and we hope all the best for you."

"Thanks Pop! Thank you, Mom," Gino voices. He begins to walk away but stops and turns back, "Are you sure? I know how nostalgic you are about things passed down."

"Yes." lovingly nods Francesca. "Your Pop and I discussed it and it is our joy to offer it to you and Claire."

Gino's face lights up. "Thank you!" He kisses his mother on the cheek and pats his Pop on his arm. Gino then dashes out the door to the stables to saddle Jolly. His dogs are running with him by his side. He bends down and pets them, "I love you guys! I am going to take Claire on a trail ride today and ask her to marry me!" Gino gives each of his beloved dogs a big hug.

Claire is coming up the drive on her horse Cocoa Bean. Gino rides Jolly to meet her.

"Hey, nice to see you," greets Gino.

"I know, I'm early. I know you said you had an errand to go on. Would it be alright if I go with you, then we would have more of the day together? If that's okay." wonders Claire.

"Well, actually, I no longer need to go on that errand, so it's perfect. Let's go up to Mancini Lake, shall we?" Gino poses.

"I like that idea," Claire states.

Fall colors surround them. The sun warms their day.

"You know, I'm glad we are able to ride today, it's probably one of the last days of the year we will be able to get up to the lake," Gino conveys.

"Yes, the weather is perfect today," Claire relishes.

"You know, I will be moving all my work to the new woodshop on our property, so I will be able to work from home. Bill is referring all of his customers to me so he can focus on his passions, which is welding and cattle. He bought a small spread on the other side of Chamberlain River," Gino conveys.

"That's good, Gino," Claire smiles.

"Yeah, I hope to be completely set up by the end of next week," shares Gino.

"That's terrific!" confirms Claire.

They finally near the lake, "Man, the water looks inviting!" Gino expresses.

Claire views out over the majestic landscape, "It sure does, not a ripple on it."

The two of them lead their horses to a picnic area, let their horses drink from the crystal-clear mountain lake, and then tie them up.

"Let's go on a walk. There are some cool trails around here," Gino suggests.

"Sounds good. Lead the way," Claire insists.

Gino takes Claire's hand in his and they walk on a trail that goes completely around the lake. "We won't go all the way around, there is just a really cool place up here I want to show you," Gino informs.

"Sure, whatever you'd like," Claire expresses.

Aspens and Pines line the elevating trail. They come to an opening that has a spectacular view. Red dirt and red granite rock, along with trees, a crystal-clear lake full of colorful rock, and mountain peaks all around, create the perfect setting that Gino had hoped for. He twirls Claire into his arms.

"Wow, that was unexpected. I must say, I like your moves," Claire admits, her big, green eyes staring into Gino's eyes.

Gino smiles with confidence, "I do have a few more moves."

Claire laughs, "I'm sure you do. Hey, look at that! Isn't that a bull elk?" pointing to the far side of the lake.

Gino confirms, "I think so, we should stay here for safety."

Gino is in the motion of kneeling precisely at the same time Claire steps forward. They collide in such an unusual manner that Claire trips over Gino, and flies forward.

Gino instantly jumps over to Claire, "Oh no! Are you okay?" Gino asks, kneeling next to her.

Claire is lying flat on her stomach, "I think so."

"Let me help you sit up. Take it easy there," Gino places his arms around Claire as he helps her roll over. "Your jeans are torn, let me take a peek."

Claire nods.

"Babe, your knee is bleeding. Are you in pain? Can you bend it?" asks Gino.

"It hurts a little. I think I can bend my knee and my arm," answers Claire.

"We need to go back and get this cleaned up," recommends Gino. "Hold on," Gino says standing. He takes off his jacket and flannel shirt, then pulls off his T-shirt. I'll be right back.

Gino runs down to the lake and gets his t-shirt wet, wrings it out, and runs back up to Claire. He then rips open the hole in her jeans, making it large enough for him to see better and cleans her wound.

"Here, let me clean the blood off your arm as well," Gino says gingerly securing Claire's arm in his hand while he cleans it. He laughs, "What were you doing?" Gino says smiling at Claire.

"Well, I was going to take a few steps closer to get a better view of that elk," Claire laughs and kind of cries at the same time, "I can't believe I tripped and fell, what a klutz. What were *you* doing?" Claire quizzes.

While Gino dabs her wounds with the water off his shirt, he playfully smiles at her, "Well, I **was** kneeling down to ask you to marry me."

"What?" Claire laughs and cries.

Gino repositions himself so he is genuflecting, "Claire, I would like to spend every day, of every year, loving you. Will you marry me?" Gino reaches into his pocket, opens the ring box, and holds it before Claire.

"Oh, Gino! This ring is beautiful! I've never seen anything like it!" Claire is momentarily taken back by the unique design of the ring, then refocuses on Gino. "I would be honored to be Mrs. Gino Mancini!" Claire smiles so big, that her dimples seem to light up.

Gino takes the ring from the box and places it on Claire's ring finger. Claire extends her other arm around Gino, and with her hand now sporting the exquisite engagement ring she wipes the tears from her face. Claire laughs and cries at the same time, as all the emotions flood in. She snuggles into Gino's neck.

Gino kisses Claire's cheek, "I can't believe you tripped right over me," he says with a bit of laughter in his voice.

"I know. I'm sorry," Claire replies, still a bit shaky.

"Babe, it's all good. There is nothing for you to be sorry for. You, nor I did anything wrong. It's a great story, and it's ours," Gino cheerfully communicates. "But we do need to get you back so we can clean these wounds better."

"Well, I don't disagree. I'm sorry, Gino, I was looking forward to spending more time with you here," Claire sighs.

"Hey, we *are* spending time together. Maybe not what either of us had planned or hoped for, but I cannot think of anywhere I'd rather be, or anyone I'd rather be with, than right here with you," Gino lovingly smiles at Claire.

"You always have my back," Claire softly says.

"And I always will. Now let's get back to our horses and get you to the ranch," directs Gino.

Claire wraps her arm around Gino as he helps her to her feet. They work their way down the trail to their horses.

"Here, let me lift you up on Cocoa Bean," Gino offers.

The two journey back to the ranch.

Antonio and Francesca are out on the back deck. "I'm surprised they're returning already; do you suppose she said 'no'?" asks Antonio.

Francesca inquisitively studies the two riding in, "I think something else must have happened.

Antonio and Francesca walk down the stairs of the back deck and meet Gino and Claire. "Mom, Pop, help me get Claire inside please," Gino anxiously requests. She fell and needs these wounds cleaned up.

"Of course," Antonio says. He and Francesca help assist Claire down from Cocoa Bean. "You two take Claire inside, I'll unsaddle the horses," Antonio offers.

Gino and Francesca help set Claire in a comfortable chair in the family room. Francesca orders, "Gino, please go get my scissors."

Gino goes to the kitchen to get the shears.

Francesca is kneeling in front of Claire, "Well, I hope you two at least enjoyed your day."

"Funny you should say that. I was apologizing to Gino for wrecking my knee and my arm, and he said he couldn't think of anywhere else he'd rather be. So, yeah, I guess we have had a good day together, although it didn't go as planned," sighs Claire.

"Well, sometimes, days do not go as we hope, but knowing we are with people who love us, well, that can make all the difference in the world," shares Francesca.

Gino hands his mother the scissors. "I'm going to cut your jeans off from the knee down, if that's alright with you," Francesca calmly says.

"Certainly, these jeans are ruined anyway," Claire replies.

"Well, cut the other leg off and you'll have a new pair of shorts," Gino maintains.

Claire laughs, "Always the optimist."

"Is there any other way to be?" wonders Gino.

"Oh, honey, it appears you have some small pebbles embedded in your open wound. Parts of this look pretty deep," Francesca informs.

"Well, can you get it out, Mother?" Gino asks.

Claire is intently examining Francesca's expression. Antonio is now standing behind Gino and Francesca.

"Honey, I can attempt to get these smalls pieces of gravel out. It may be as simple as getting in a bath and washing them out. Are you up for that?" asks Francesca.

"I am. Lead the way," confirms Claire.

"Well, hang on, let me take a look at your arm," Francesca gently inspects the scrape on Claire's arm. "Okay, this seems well cleaned out. Nice job. Your arm and knee will probably bruise, swell, and be sore, though."

Francesca helps Claire to the guest bathroom, and fills the tub. "Are you good now? I will be right outside if you need me. I have a flannel shirt and robe you can wear. Just holler if you need anything," Francesca conveys closing the door.

"Yes, I am fine, thank you," Claire replies.

Gino is waiting for his mother. He motions her to him.

"What is it?" Francesca asks.

Just then, Claire comes out of the bathroom wrapped in a towel, limping. "Well, I think there may be a piece in there still, it may require some sort of tool to remove it," Claire speculates.

Francesca hands Claire a long flannel shirt and warm bathrobe. "Here, put these on. If you need help to the family room, let me know," Francesca gently says.

Claire gets dressed and appreciates how soft Francesca's flannel shirt and bathrobe are.

"Alrighty, I'm coming out," announces Claire.

Seeing Claire hobble, Gino goes to assist Claire instantly.

He helps her back to the most comfortable chair in the family room.

"I will go and get you some water, Claire," Francesca says. Antonio leaves the room with Francesca.

Gino kneels in front of Claire, "I know the day I had planned did not go as expected," Gino submits.

"I know, me either, I can't believe we had that awkward accident," laughs Claire. "I can't believe I tripped over you, splat on my belly!" sighs Claire.

"Yeah, if we could see it replay, I'm sure we would both laugh," Gino lightheartedly shares.

"I suppose you're right," Claire smiles.

Francesca and Antonio walk in with water and a snack for everyone.

"We should probably have Doctor Gerard look at that wound," recommends Antonio.

"I can take her in the wagon," Gino says.

"Why don't we all go?" Francesca suggests.

"That's fine," answers Claire, "It is beginning to hurt. It appears swollen."

"It does," Francesca says, "it is a fresh wound, and bound to be swollen and painful."

"I agree," concurs Claire.

Gino steps back inside, "The wagon is ready to go. Let's get you up."

"Well, some memorable proposal," Claire comments.

"Congratulations! Our first daughter in the family!" Francesca rejoices.

Antonio walks in, "I asked Claire to marry me, and she said yes!" exclaims Gino while he is helping Claire walk to the door.

"That is some excellent news," states Antonio.

Claire and the Mancinis load up in the wagon. Honor and the team lead them away. Gino rides Cocoa Bean.

······⚮······

After coming out of the exam room, Doctor Gerard smiles at the Mancinis and then at Claire, "I think she is going to live. There was only one stubborn pebble that didn't want to come out, but I was able to flush it out."

"Well, that's great news," Antonio shakes Doctor Gerard's hand.

Gino also shakes Doctor Gerard's hand, "Thank you so much."

Francesca thanks Doctor Gerard and reaches for Claire, "Let's get you home. Are your parents back in town, yet?"

"They are supposed to be this evening," Claire notes.

"Thank you, Doctor Gerard," Claire acknowledges.

"You're welcome. Dress it as I directed. If you have any issues, don't hesitate to come back," Doctor Gerard encourages.

The Mancinis take Claire and Cocoa Bean to Claire's home.

"Take care, honey. Sounds like there is a wedding to plan!" Francesca sings out.

Claire smiles and gives Francesca a big hug.

Gino escorts Claire to the door and takes her hands in his, "I know you'll recover quickly; I just look forward to the day I no longer have to drop you off." He leans in and kisses her cheek.

"Yes, me too. I'd like to just go lie down and snuggle," Claire mentions.

"Yeah, me too. Well, get some rest. Sweet dreams," Gino departs.

"Bye, Claire. Take care of your wounds and get some rest," Antonio gestures.

"I will, thank you," Claire turns and goes inside.

Chapter 55

A PICNIC AT THE CARLISLES

Luke was also given the blessing from Camille's parents to marry her. Luke had spent hours early in the morning to set up a captivating picnic area to which he would bring Camille to.

Okay, I've cleared the area. I have the table cloth on the picnic table. I'll grab the picnic basket of food when Camille arrives. Luke mentally goes over his checklist.

He rides back to his home and waits for Camille to arrive.

"I'm so excited for you," Katherine dotes.

"We couldn't be happier for you, Son," Sully pats Luke on the back.

"I know. Thank you, both. And thank you for making us lunch, Mom," Luke says extending his gratitude. "I don't know if you guys know this, you'll probably find out at game night this weekend, but Gino is asking Claire to marry him. And, well, the two of us would like a double wedding," Luke informs.

"Oh, my," Katherine says, "I think that is just splendid!"

"Well, alright, hopefully the girls won't oppose your ideas." Sully communicates.

"Yeah, well, they are friends, so Gino and I are hoping they both say yes to us, and yes to the double wedding," Luke informs.

"Sounds like a good plan. You and Gino are like brothers," conveys Sully.

"And how could the girls say no to the most eligible bachelors in the kingdom?" laughs Luke.

"Oh, my, you are so confident. I like it," Katherine says with a giggle and claps her hands.

Sully laughs and does the eye roll he is notorious for.

Camille arrives on her horse. Sully and Katherine step outside to greet her.

Luke carries the picnic basket outside, "This is great that you were free today!"

Camille sweetly smiles, "I know, my parents said they didn't need me, and to go have some fun."

"Well, let's be on our way, unless you want to visit with my parents for a while," Luke extends.

Sully and Katherine both smile. "Son, thank you for that, but you two go enjoy your ride. Be safe," Sully replies with appreciation.

Luke assists Camille up on her horse. "I was thinking we could ride over to the west and work our way down to the river."

"I think that's a fine idea," Camille agrees.

The two, young adults head out from the Carlisle Ranch home.

"Mom made us a picnic lunch," Luke says.

"Aw, that's so sweet of her. Your parents are the best!" Camille praises.

"I think so, thank you. Hey, did I tell you I'm going to be an uncle?" Luke asks.

"You are? Wow! When?" questions Camille.

"I think Ben said their baby is due in Mayella," informs Luke.

"Oh, wow, that's exciting! Congrats, Uncle Luke," Camille playfully teases.

"Thanks. It's been weird not having Ben live at home anymore. But I have gotten used to it," Luke states.

"I bet," giggles Camille. "My older sister is still at home, and then of course my younger brother.

"Yeah, every family has different dynamics," Luke says.

"They do," Camille softly confirms. "My older sister, Angela, is such a sweetie. Sometimes I really feel sad for her. She never got to know her mother since she died giving birth to her. Then of course, my dad took care of her and raised her until he met my mother. I can't imagine never knowing my mother. But I guess that is all she has ever known. I'm glad my mother loves Angela as her own."

"Yeah, that must be tough at times for Angela," Luke empathizes.

Luke and Camille continue on their way enjoying the scenery, and seeing nature's display of its brilliant fall colors.

"This is a perfect day as far as the weather goes!" Luke exclaims.

"I know. Last year I think the leaves were already off the trees by now," recalls Camille.

Luke laughs a bit, "I honestly don't remember."

On approach to the cleared area where the Carlisle picnic table sits, Camille jumps off her horse, "Luke, a tablecloth? And a bouquet of flowers in the center? Luke Carlisle, you are quite the decorator!"

"Well, I'm glad there isn't any wind today, or I would have had to come up with an alternate plan," Luke attests.

Camille laughs surveying the area, "I have no doubt." She walks the pathway lined with boulders to the picnic table area. The hand laid rock edge circles around to the other side of the picnic table. Camille walks around and is taken with the splendor of the river before her. She peers down and notices more rocks spelling out 'Marry Me' followed by pebbles designed in the shape of a heart. Camille turns to Luke, but he is now kneeling. She smiles, gazing down at him, "You are quite creative!"

"I guess you bring that out in me," Luke admits as he continues to kneel while holding before her a delicate ring embossed with crystal clear stones circling a large center gem.

Camille says, "Oh, Luke!" She peers closer, "That looks like my grandmother's ring!"

"It is. Your parents offered it to me when I asked for their permission," Luke explains.

Camille reaches to take it from Luke's fingers, but he keeps the ring in his grasp, smiles and says, "Ah, ah." Luke then takes Camille's hand in his, and tenderly slides the ring onto her finger.

Luke stands facing Camille. "Have I ever told you how I love your cute freckles?"

Camille blushes, "No, I haven't heard you say that."

"Well, I do. I love your shiny brunette hair, your freckles, and your smile. I love the fact you have the kindest, most genuine heart. Are you going to answer my question?" Luke's hands are on Camille's waist as they sway back and forth talking.

"Oh, that question?" Camille points to the rocks. She breaks their embrace and takes a couple of steps, and bends down to write in the dirt. "No peeking, Luke Carlisle!"

Camille positions herself to block Luke's view.

"Are you going to keep me in suspense?" Luke asks.

"I may," Camille gests, then stands and brushes off her jeans. "Alright, you can look."

Luke inches next to Camille and is pleased to read she has written, 'Yes, my Luke', with a drawing of two hearts intertwined.

Luke turns, smiles at Camille, and takes both of her hands in his hands, "I am the luckiest guy around."

"I think I am pretty lucky, too," Camille adds, glowing.

Luke pulls Camille close to him and tenderly kisses her lips. After a loving embrace, they hold hands and return to the picnic table to unpack the lunch Katherine prepared for them.

"Hey, tomorrow is game night at the Mancinis. Let's announce our engagement," Luke suggests.

"I like that idea!" Camille agrees.

Chapter 56

RAZEL'S ROAR

"I enjoy being on Soleil, even when winter is around the corner," conveys Razel.

"I do as well. And, I am still delighted at the unique rocks I am finding," Zeek conveys as he carries another rock to their campsite.

Razel leaps up into a tree to view the perimeter, "I can't believe how many rocks you have collected."

"Well, some are fossils. It's all fascinating," Zeek states as he walks with his back straight making him a tall stature of four feet. "What a great adventure we are on, … I mean assignment," Zeek laughs, peering up as if the high priests may be watching.

Razel is content sitting on a branch until she spies a couple of deer. As she examines their surroundings, she sees some wolves. "I know they are going to try and take down that doe, I just know it!"

"Whoa, settle down there. We have had this discussion before. Your interference could cause Scaleon and his minions to be suspicious," reminds Zeek.

Razel briefly glances at Zeek while shaking her head with an expression of frustration. She then casts her full attention on the wolves' well-orchestrated tactics.

"I can see you're thinking; I can almost feel it!" outlines Zeek. Razel motions with her arm for Zeek to stop. She hops up on her feet, now standing with her three-feet-ten-inch-tall body on the branch while her left hand holds onto the branch above her. *I can see the buck not too far from the doe,* she thinks to herself.

Zeek stands tall, while he quietly watches his teammate. He can see the intensity in her posture and eyes, and wonders what mischief is about to unfold. He chimes out, "Razel, our mission is to remain undetected."

The wolves are strategically maneuvering toward the doe. Razel's blood is boiling, she feels a surge of intense emotion and struggles to contain it. She can hear Zeek's voice, which normally keeps her grounded, but suddenly a lightbulb comes on with a brilliant idea! Razel leaps from the tree, sails through the air, and lands near the buck. Instantly she extends her arms with her hands spread open toward the buck. The buck launches toward the pack of wolves, and stands firmly between them and the doe just in time. Razel opens her mouth like she's screaming, and the buck **ROARS** like a lion! The startled wolves jump back and run. The doe lifts her head and gazes, but doesn't run. The buck scans all around, confused, seeming as though he was wondering what just occurred.

Razel lets out a breath and slightly relaxes her posture. Zeek jumps and lands next to her, "Okay, well...that was ingenious!" Zeek announces with amazement, "Even though you are still interfering. What gives?" Zeek turns and stares at Razel directly in her eyes, "It is unlike you to be insubordinate."

Instantly, Razel's confident posture and beaming with victory, disappear. Her face is downcast as she sinks into a dark memory. Tears swell up in her eyes.

Zeek places his right hand atop her left shoulder, "I'm so sorry, Razel. I am a good listener."

Razel dabs the tears from her eyes with the back of her hands. She laughs a bit, "I can't believe I am still haunted. And that it still affects my decisions!" A now green Razel stomps her feet in exasperation.

271

"What is it? Maybe sharing will help," offers Zeek.

Razel raises her head and rests her eyes on Zeek, "I was off at the academy; my parents were stationed on Tertammi for their mission. Of course, my younger sister was with them. VeNoma had recently been blown to bits, oh, but not the Cryptolores. They managed to escape in full wrath. Tertammi was one of the first planets they sought out. You know that is the home-base planet for the protectors of our Galaxy. Anyway, my parents and sister were asleep when the Cryptolores ambushed them entering into their throats, blocking their airways, killing them. After several deaths that evening, the Cryptolores then fled Tertammi, and went to Acheeas, and finally ended up on Chiaras with the Protectors in pursuit. Our high priests believed imprisoning them was the most noble, upright thing to do. However, the protectors wanted a back-up plan. So, the Chiawauka High Priests, leaders, and the protectors met, formulated a plan, which is now in the Ancient Writings. Word came to me about my family. I was infuriated and wanted to kill every last Cryptolore. I swore I would. I hate them," Razel adamantly describes.

"I don't know what to say. I had no idea. I'm so sorry," Zeek pauses and gazes upon Razel, "I do know though, when you speak of this hate, the shine you normally have in your blue eyes, dims, as does the color of your blueish-green body, Razel. Hate is poisonous to your spirit and soul. Somehow, you need to get the hate for them out of you," Zeek tenderly expresses.

"Do you know what you're asking? They robbed me of my family! I can never let that go!" Razel rages.

"You can. The Razel I know can do anything she sets her mind to. This may be the greatest task you have encountered, but I have confidence in your tenacity," Zeek passionately offers. "And respectfully, though I never met your parents, I am pretty sure they would not want you to live with hate, or being haunted. They would want to see that shine in your eyes. They are in Heaven. Watching. Isn't that what you believe?" Zeek inquires.

Razel begins to soften, lifting and tilting her head a bit, "Yeah, I guess you are right. Oooo, the Cryptolores just infuriate me so!" Razel folds her arms.

"Understandably. Did anyone help you at the academy?" questions Zeek.

Razel drops her folded arms, and smiles, "Yes, Ollie and Omar. Oh my gosh, I love them so much! They took me in as their daughter, and taught me so much. I know I was a mess for a while, and a handful," Razel recalls with a big grin.

"No doubt, I can see that," laughs Zeek.

Razel reaches out to Zeek, and slightly pushes his shoulder with a laugh, "Oh, so you can see that?"

"Calm down," Zeek steps his four-foot-tall body back a step, "Have you spoken with them lately?"

"No, but that is actually a good idea. I wish they were stationed on Soleil with us for this mission. Have you met them?" asks Razel.

"I have not. I know they have served on many missions with Victor and Viana, and if they helped raised you, well, I look forward to working with them," attests Zeek.

Razel agrees, "You are right. Being filled with hate will only poison my spirit, then I will be of no use to help others."

"Now, that's the Razel I have come to know. So passionate about every life, full of balance and compassion," affirms Zeek.

Razel smiles, "Thank you," Razel kicks a rock as they walk down the hill.

"Hey, no kicking rocks," Zeek hollers and runs after it shouting back at Razel as his voice trails off with distance, "It may be one I have not seen!"

Razel and Zeek both laugh.

Chapter 57

ANNOUNCEMENTS AT GAME NIGHT

"**M**om, did you invite the entire kingdom to game night?" Gino gests as he is standing at the front window watching Ben and Laurie pull in, followed by the Carlisles.

"No, just the usual Carlisle family. You may not be used to Ben and Laurie always being able to attend though. I also invited your grandparents." Francesca conveys. "Oh, I did extend an invitation to the king and queen, and Claire's parents."

"Oh, no, does that mean Rupert will be here?" Gino scoffs.

"Son, that is no way to speak of another person, but, 'no', is the answer to your question. The royals agreed they needed a fun night, just the two of them with friends and family. And remember, the queen and Sully *are* cousins," Francesca reminds.

"Yeah, I know. That kid still creeps me out," Gino shares.

"Rightly so. Now, greet our guests, please, and let's have a fabulous evening full of laughter," Francesca expresses.

Antonio walks in the back door and kisses Francesca, "Now, I am ready for the night."

Francesca smiles at her husband, "I'm thankful for all our opportunities to experience fun and fellowship with our family and friends." She hugs Antonio.

You can hear the many footsteps coming up the stairs of the front deck and across into their home.

"Welcome! Oh, Laurie, you are glowing, congratulations on the little one!" Francesca hugs Laurie and Ben.

"Katherine, I am so glad you could come over tonight!" Francesca hugs Katherine.

"Well, you know we wouldn't miss game night, plus I needed my hug fix from my best friend," Katherine says with her sweet voice, hugging Francesca.

"Hello Sully," Francesca smiles and nods, squeezing his arm as he passes by.

Sully nods and smiles at Francesca. He heads directly for Antonio, "How about a fishing trip next weekend?"

"That sounds like a fine idea," Antonio concurs.

King Theodore and Queen Eloise enter next. "Welcome to our home. So glad you two could come," cordially greets Francesca.

Queen Eloise gives Francesca a big hug.

Camille and Luke walk in, followed by Claire, with the assistance of Gino, to get up the stairs.

"Hey, what gives? You're limping," inquires Luke.

"Long story," Claire retorts.

"I have all night," Luke proclaims gleefully smiling as he places one hand across his chest.

The four friends just laugh.

Antonio holds the door open while Sophia and Leonardo enter the home of their loved ones.

Everyone has a seat at the familiar Mancini dining room table.

"Well, let the games begin," Sully announces as he situates himself in a large arm chair built to accommodate his tall frame at the end of the Mancini table.

Antonio motions, offering the king his seat at the other end of the table. "No, no. Thank you, though. You sit there, Tony. I will sit right here," asserts Theodore in a very kind voice.

Francesca and Katherine pass out drinks to everyone, then sit down as well.

"Will your parents be joining us, Claire?" Francesca asks.

"I don't think so. They just got back last night and are pretty tired, plus they wanted to keep Charlotte and Chandler at home since they have runny noses," Claire states.

"Oh, yes. Completely understandable," relays Francesca.

"So, Laurie, Luke tells me you are expecting a baby! Congratulations!" exclaims Camille.

"Oh, yes, in Mayella, seven months away," Laurie happily announces.

"I guess that will make the baby my third cousin," Queen Eloise calculates.

Ben laughs, "I guess so. I have always wanted to call you aunt, but I know you are my dad's cousin."

"Well, honey, you may call me 'aunt' anytime. I will not take offense. Speaking of aunts...Sully, I found a portrait of our great-aunt Genie Arabella A'mato and had it restored. It's just breathtaking! Theo and I hung it in our family room," Eloise discloses.

Sully nods, "Yeah, I remember stories of her. Very peculiar how she just vanished."

"Yes," agrees Queen Eloise.

"I love a good mystery," smiles Gino as he winks to his parents.

"I remember hearing stories of my grandmother and your great-aunt being best friends." Sophia shares glancing at Sully and Eloise.

Everyone at the table is laughing and enjoying their time together.

"Are we going to begin the game?" Sully motions with a wave of his hand.

Everyone laughs.

"Wait, wait. I have an announcement to make, or I should say…we do," Luke stands and is beaming at Camille.

Gino immediately stands, "*We* also have an announcement to make!" taking Claire's hand, helping her to stand.

All eyes are upon the two couples. Claire and Camille are inquisitively smiling at each other. Claire points at her ring finger signing to Camille. Camille smiles and nonchalantly does the same thing. The two girls quietly giggle.

Luke proudly announces, "Yesterday, I asked Camille to marry me, and she said 'yes'!"

Everyone begins clapping and saying 'congratulations' when they hear Gino's elevated, elated voice, "I asked Claire yesterday to marry me, and she said 'yes'!"

Katherine peeks at Francesca, and the two friends smile with complete joy.

Sully and Antonio glance at each other, nod and raise their glasses.

"Look at you two! Grown up and now engaged! Congratulations!" exclaims Ben.

"Do you have date set, yet?" asks Laurie.

Gino and Luke smile at each other with very confident smiles, "Well, I was hoping for a double wedding. I can't think of anything more fitting than marrying the girl of my dreams, alongside my life-long best friend while he marries his soulmate," acclaims Gino.

Claire and Camille are both beaming and jump up and down across the table from each other, "I would LOVE to have a double wedding!" Camille exclaims.

"I would like that," Claire speaks in her composed, yet very happy voice.

"Alright!" Luke shouts.

"I was hoping to wed next fall, the day of the Autumn Moon," declares Gino.

The king and queen smile and look at each other and nod. King Theodore stands, "Luke, since you are family, and we did host Ben and Laurie's wedding, we only see it fitting to host the wedding of

Camille and you, and that offer extents to Gino and Claire. Afterall, we are all family, if not by blood, by bond," the king assures.

Claire and Camille excitedly reach across the table and hold each other's hands, then turn to their fiancés and give them a huge hug. Ben and Laurie smile. Laurie lays her head on Ben's shoulder as if reminiscing. Sully and Antonio again look at each other from the ends of the table, and acceptingly nod. Katherine smiles and claps her hands. Francesca is beaming with thankfulness for the treasures and blessings in her life. She then glances at the Flower of Virtue lying on the mantel, and thinks, *so many blessings every day to be thankful for.*

"Hey, wait. I want to hear the story of why Claire is limping a bit," declares Luke with laughter in his voice.

"Well, that *IS* a funny story," Gino claims.

Claire looks at him with a playful stare.

"Do you want to tell the story, babe?" Gino asks Claire.

"No, I'd like to hear you tell it," Claire says shaking her head in a playful way.

Gino has the full attention of everyone at the table.

"Okay, man, it was crazy! Claire sees an elk on the other side of Mancini Lake, and decides to take a few steps closer to get a better view at the **exact** same moment I decide to kneel down to propose. And man, she trips right over me. Splat!" explains Gino with a chuckle in his voice. "I am so sorry, babe. How on Soleil did that happen?" Gino describes while looking at Claire and placing his hand on her shoulder to rub it.

"Oh, no, sweet Claire! Are you okay?" exclaims the queen.

"I am. Thank you," Claire amiably smiles.

Everyone around the table turns toward Claire and Gino with tender smiles.

"Well, Luke took me to the Carlisle picnic area by the river where he had spelled out with rocks 'Marry Me'," describes Camille. "Quite the romantic," Camile reminisces.

"I think you both have wonderful stories," sweetly affirms Katherine.

Sophia places one hand on Leonardo and her other hand across her heart, "This all is just the best news. Congratulations, to each of you."

"A toast," Sully announces.

Everyone raises their glass.

"To wonderful stories and a lifetime of memories," salutes Sully.

"Cheers," King Theodore adds.

Everyone clinks their glasses. Smiles and laughter fill the atmosphere.

Games commence.

……⚬⧡⚬……

"More weddings! Yet, we have not discovered the other Chords of Chiawaukas Family. I see no auras in Claire's family, or Camille's, so these weddings will not be the wedding The Ancient Writings speak of," speculates Victor.

"It's okay. You never know what's going to unfold," Viana articulates.

"You are most certainly correct, Viana," states Victor in his matter-of-fact, deliberate voice.

"One thing, you will never complain again about this being a boring assignment," Viana contends in her loving, crackly voice.

A slight grin overtakes Victor's face, "No…no I will not."

Viana and Victor smile at each other then scan their surroundings, making sure all is as it should be.

"I am going to say this again. I am so thankful we are assigned to the Mancinis," Viana reiterates.

"As am I, Viana. As am I." Victor concurs and nods.

Chapter 58

ALCHODORS SCHEME

"While your parents are visiting the Mancinis, why don't we go play ball outside before dinner?" Carol suggests to Rupert.

Rupert takes Carol's hand and walks with her to the door. On the way outside, Carol grabs for the blue ball from the shelves near the door to the patio.

They walk onto the patio area away from furniture.

"You stand here, and I will stand over in this patio square. Let's bounce the ball back and forth to each other," proposes Carol.

Rupert nods. Carol and the Prince bounce the ball back and forth to each other.

"You're doing a good job, Rupert," notices Carol.

After a while Rupert decides to kick the ball. "Well, you've got quite a leg there. You'll need to go get the ball; I'm not going to chase it," Carol states.

Rupert stares at Carol, then complies and runs out onto the grass to get the ball. Rupert walks back up to the patio carrying the ball then launches it at Carol. Surprisingly, she catches it!

"Are you done playing?" quizzes Nanny Carol.

Rupert just stands there glaring at Carol.

"Let's bounce the ball back and forth again," offers Carol.

Rupert agrees to play her way.

"You're very good at this, Rupert," reaffirms Carol.

Rupert smiles, "I'm five years old now, so I should be."

"You most certainly are," acknowledges Carol with a smile while she remains on guard for more mischief.

Andrew steps onto the patio, "Carol, Chef Pierre wants you to know dinner is ready."

"Thank you, Andrew," Carol responds.

"Rupert, we will play ball another day if you would like. Let's go eat our dinner," directs Carol.

Rupert takes the ball and begins to run around.

"If you don't want dinner that's fine. I can just give you a bath and read a book to you before you go to bed," Carol renders in a loving, yet stern voice.

Rupert stops in disbelief hearing Carol suggest he skip dinner. Rupert again glares at Carol for a few minutes, then stomps to the door.

"Aren't you forgetting something?" asks Carol.

Rupert looks at her, and then at the ball in his hands. She nods. Rupert places the ball on the shelf by the door. The two approach the table and take their seats.

Chef Pierre serves them a fabulously baked, macaroni casserole with ham, and broccoli as a side, with lightly-toasted, buttery, seasoned bread.

"We will pray first, Rupert," Carol maintains.

They bow their heads while Carol says the blessing.

"Oh, Chef, this tastes as incredible as it looks! Thank you, for this delicious meal," esteems Carol.

Chef Pierre slightly bows, "You are quite welcome, Nanny Carol. Excuse me, now, I will bring the dessert back in a few minutes."

Rupert is eating everything he was served. Carol relaxes a bit. They both enjoy a second helping. Chef Pierre enters the dining area carrying a silver platter with dessert atop.

"Nanny, Rupert," Chef serves each of them a plate of scrumptious, lemon-zest blueberry pound cake with a glaze. Then he sets a small glass of milk beside each plate. "I hope you both enjoy this dessert," Chef Pierre slightly bows awaiting their response.

Carol gingerly brings a forkful to her mouth and savors the bite. "Mmm...you do not cease to amaze my taste buds," relishes Carol.

Rupert is kicking his legs under the table in excitement. "I like this, Chef!"

"Very good," the Chef cordially declares.

After dinner, Carol and Rupert proceed upstairs. To her surprise, he agrees to a bath without a fuss. Carol helps him dress for bed. Rupert crawls into bed as Carol sits beside him and begins to read him a book. Prince Rupert lays his head on the pillow. "I like playing ball," Rupert asserts.

"Well, I'm glad you do," Nanny Carol replies, then continues read.

Rupert falls asleep. Nanny Carol quietly leaves the room. She retires to her room, takes a shower, and goes to bed.

Rupert's mouth opens and a black, filmy form comes out, slithering down to the floor, and continues out of the room, through the hall, and into Nanny Carol's room. An elongated, grotesque head forms and rises above Carol. Long, spindly formed fingers ever so slightly stroke Carol's hair. Carol begins to swat at her head as if she feels something, although her eyes remain closed.

"You are a strong one, I believe I will have great use for you," Alchodor quietly articulates in an eerie, sinister voice, continuing to stroke Carol's head with his gruesome fingers while he lurks above her.

Carol is startled. She abruptly opens her eyes, yet remains in a frozen stillness. She feels unnerved thinking that she heard a ghastly voice, yet sees nothing. She sweeps the area visible to her eyes without moving a muscle. Feeling terror, she prays for protection as she lies there in the warmth and comfort of her bed.

......⚬�֍⚬......

"Piper! Did you just hear that diabolical plot from Alchodor?" Pixel exclaims.

"I did. Simmer down, there is nothing we can do about it right now," Piper calmly whispers.

"Well, boy, oh boy, that just isn't right. I am going to do everything I can to protect Nanny Carol." Pixel folds her arms.

Piper glimpses over at her. He has a pair of reading glassing on his nose. He focuses above them at Pixel, "Pixel…"

"I know," Pixel motions with her hand and arm, "No interference. Doesn't that just take the cake! No interference!" mumbles Pixel. *I am not going to let anything happen to that strong, lovely woman,* Pixel thinks to herself.

"Pixel," Piper warns.

"Yeah?" Pixel answers.

"I can hear you. I can hear your thoughts, too. Remember?" Piper asserts in his calm manner, with a slightly humorous smile.

"Oh…yeah…my bad," with a bit of a laugh Pixel concedes in her quirky voice. "You have to remember we are not to intervene. And if we do, to make it appear natural." Piper reminds.

"That is a pretty big request!" Pixel claims.

Piper smiles, "That it is," and then continues reading.

Chapter 59

THE HUNT

"Okay, I have enough food packed for several days. Please be safe," Francesca steps next to Antonio, snuggles and kisses him. They exchange a loving embrace in their large kitchen.

"Sully should be here soon," Antonio says between kisses. "I will be safe. I do wish Gino and Luke were going with us this year."

"I know, me too. I would feel better knowing my young buck is out there to protect my old buck," Francesca jests.

"Who are you calling old?" Antonio playfully asks.

"No one. I am just playing; I do wish Gino and Luke could hunt with you this year. It'll be the first year they haven't since they were old enough," recollects Francesca.

"There will be next year. Hopefully, they will be able to plan the date with their employers," Antonio surmises. "Wait, next year, he will be his own employer." Antonio chuckles.

"Yes. Good luck and please be safe," reiterates Francesca.

"I will, besides, I want to get back home to you," Antonio whispers in Francesca's ear.

"I anticipate your return," Francesca softly replies, kissing Antonio's cheek.

Their long, enduring embrace ceases when they hear a knock at their door.

"Alright, time for you to go. Sully's here." Francesca takes charge in her typical manner and directs.

Antonio nods and smiles at his wife. They carry supplies out the side door from the kitchen to load the pack horses.

"Good morning, Sully," Francesca welcomes.

"Good morning. Katherine wanted me to tell you she is looking forward to coming over tomorrow evening," Sully greets.

"It's always my pleasure," notes Francesca. "I may just ask her to stay over, and I'll make us a delicious homemade breakfast."

"I'm sure she'll love that!" acknowledges Sully.

The three of them finish loading. Francesca gives Antonio and Sully a hug, "Good luck you two. Be safe."

Sully nods to Francesca.

Antonio winks at his wife and in his deep voice reassures, "We will."

The two friends mount their horses with the pack mules in tow and ride off to Mancini Lake for their annual hunting trip.

"Sully," Antonio nods and touches the brim of his hat, "Here's to a successful and safe hunt."

"Agreed," Sully nods, and reaches his fingers to his hat as well.

Francesca's furry companions accompany her back to the house. She sits on the deck and talks to each one, Pepper, Snowy, and Abby while she pets them.

……⦿⦿……

"Today may be a good day for some training. What do you think?" Viana questions Victor.

"I suppose we could work that in," Victor formulates.

"Oh, you suppose," Viana laughs in her distinct voice.

"Let's visit Francesca and see if she is ready," Victor suggests.

"I like that idea," Viana grins, knowing it was her idea.

Francesca is busy out back, making sure everything is in its place before Katherine comes over tomorrow, but mainly before winter sets in. Her beloved fur companions are with her.

Viana and Victor appear on Francesca's yard swing. Francesca turns, "Hello you two. What's the occasion that I am receiving a visit?" asks Francesca.

"We thought we would ask if you would like some training today," answers Viana.

"We can see you sense our presence. That is extremely good," notices Victor.

"Sure. I'm up for whatever you have," Francesca assuredly answers.

"The fact that you are highly intuitive is an excellent foundation," Viana confirms.

"Yes, and your willingness to learn," adds Victor.

"Honestly, the powers you can possess will be almost equal to that of the Chiawaukas," informs Viana.

"And remember, only you and the other females who have a red and white aura have the ability to use powers by themselves. Children or spouses must be in proximity of another with an aura, and be working together," reminds Victor.

"I understand," expresses Francesca.

"Our mission is to contain or eliminate the Cryptolores, while protecting others. The Cryptolores are here on Soleil with a perilous plot. We do not know what time or year it will unfold, but we must be ever vigilant and ready," Victor adamantly addresses.

"I'm ready. I will do my part. Teach me what you want me to know," Francesca submits.

Victor and Viana hop down from the swing and walk over to Francesca, each takes ahold of one of her hands between both of theirs.

"I always enjoy the ride up here. Let's make camp over there," points Antonio.

"Ah, yes. We have camped there many of times through the years," Sully nods.

The two friends unpack and make camp before nightfall. The scent of the pine trees is inviting. Hearing the few leaves that are still on the Aspen trees rustle in the gentle wind is music to their ears. The crackling fire they now have going completes the scenery, along with the view of the snow atop Mancini Mountain and nearby peaks.

"It's been a long time since we have enjoyed the company of our wives up here," Sully reflects.

"You're right. I know Francesca has come up for a ride. We all have come up for picnics, but they haven't joined us for an overnight for several years," Antonio recollects.

"Why don't we plan on that next summer?" Sully suggests.

"I think that is a good idea," agrees Antonio. "Although, you may have a hard time pulling Katherine away from your grandbaby due in Mayella," chuckles Antonio.

"You're right, there. I'll convince her," Sully confidently smiles then adds, "Francesca can work her magic, if necessary."

Baffled, Antonio inquisitively blurts, "What magic are you referring to?"

"Oh, I don't mean anything by it, you know, Francesca just has a way with people. Moving them. It seems magical or mystifying," Sully relays. "You very well know your wife is enchanting."

"Oh, yeah, I can see what you're saying. She sure does have a way with me," Antonio relaxes and laughs.

"Yeah. Our wives should have that effect on us," nods Sully.

"So, you're going to be a grandparent. Does that make you feel old?" questions Antonio.

"No, I didn't need a grandchild to feel that," laughs Sully, "but in all fairness, now I feel alive again, ready for new adventures. Katherine wants to travel. Ben and Laurie will be having children.

Knowing Camille, she and Luke will be having children. I feel like I have a new zest for life. I can't explain it," Sully shares.

In his deep, rugged voice Antonio assures, "I think you did a fine job explaining it, Sully."

The men sip their hot coffee, and enjoy the spectacular night sky unveil a sparkling canopy.

Antonio stands, "Let's get some rest. Our hunt begins early. Night, Sully."

Sully also stands, "Good night, Tony. See you in the morning."

The men duck into their tents and turn in.

The sounds of the night soothe their excited thoughts of the hunt. They are lulled, yet aware of their surroundings as they drift to sleep, hearing an owl in the distance, howls of remote wolves, and the sound of the water splashing at the edge of the lake.

……⋅⋅⋅∞⋅⋅⋅……

"Good morning, Antonio. How did you sleep?" Sully greets Antonio as he hands him a cup of coffee.

"For the few hours we slept, I have to admit, I slept like a baby. Next best place to Francesca," Antonio stretches.

"I hear ya," Sully concurs. "I slept like a log, myself. Why don't I hunt up near Eagle Ridge Trail, and you go over to the east side of the lake this year?" suggests Sully.

Antonio nods, "Fine idea. And Sully, be safe."

"I will, my friend. Good luck and you be safe," extends Sully.

The two men take their rifles and trek their separate directions for the early morning hunt.

Antonio makes his way to the east side of Mancini Lake following a game trail that leads to a small valley. He is dressed in his flannel shirt, denim pants, and a short leather trench coat. Though he is trying to quietly make his way to a clearing, branches brush across him and twigs break under foot… just then he spies the elk. He kneels on one knee to position himself for the shot. He takes in a deep breath, and pulls the trigger. "I got him!" whispers Antonio to himself while nodding with the satisfaction of success. He makes his way to the elk to gut the bull. It takes Antonio a couple of hours to quarter the nearly 700-pound elk, followed by additional time to cut out the tenderloins and backstraps. He prepares himself for the grueling task of carrying everything back to camp. *I must admit, I do wish Gino and Luke were with us.* Antonio thinks to himself. *Their young, strong bodies wouldn't even cringe at lifting this. I am glad we brought the pack mules. I wonder if Sully had success.*

Sully has made his way up Eagle Ridge Trail, traversing through the trees also following a game trail. *I'm going to be a grandfather. I want to teach my grandchild so much.* Sully's thoughts wander far from the hunt as he makes his way to a clearing where another herd of elk reside. *There is so much I want to give and do for my family and others.* Again, Sully's thoughts drift from the hunt, and he stumbles over a tree root, but is able to remain on his feet. He gathers his bearings and approaches the clearing. He sees his target. Sully positions himself and takes a breath, firing his gun. He misses. He quickly stays on task, aims again, and squeezes the trigger. Success. His target goes down. Sully stands and realizes a bear is standing near him maybe twelve feet away. Sully is frozen with racing thoughts; *how could I have not seen this bear? Evidently, the bear, also, was not paying attention. Now here we both are, having a meeting. Remain calm. Dear Lord, I pray it is not my time to depart. But if it is, thank you for the life you gave me.*

Just then, a much larger bear appears from the left, seemingly the mama bear, and charges Sully. She strikes Sully with the weight of her front claw. The impact from her sheer weight causes Sully to fall striking his head on a rock as he hits the ground. The mama bear stands on her hind legs, gives out a load roar, then drops and retreats with her cub. Sully does not move and blood gushes from the wounds of the bear claw and the impact from the rock.

Load after load, Antonio finishes hauling the meat and is now back to their base camp. *I wonder why Sully isn't back yet. His hunt site is much closer. I'll secure this meat, then Chief and I will go look for him.* Antonio secures camp, mounts Chief, and rides out to the west side of Mancini Lake where Eagle Ridge Trail is. He makes his way up the trail with mulling over things, *I cannot believe my wife came up here on a ride without anyone else. Wait, it's Francesca, of course I can believe it! Where is Sully?*

"Sully?" Antonio yells out for his best friend. "Suullllyyyy..." Antonio shouts again.

He slows Chief down seeing the game trail that veers off Eagle Ridge Trail, "Okay, boy, here we go," Antonio says to Chief as he slowly walks him up the winding game trail. Bending over to avoid branches, Antonio begins to fill with worry. Around a curve on the game trail Antonio sees a clearing. He slowly approaches. His fears are confirmed when he sees Sully lying on the ground with a pool of blood surrounding his head. Antonio jumps off Chief and runs to Sully. Antonio drops to his knees and cries out, "NOOOOOO!" Ever so gently he places his arm under Sully's head. "I'm here. Stay with me. Sully, I am going to have to ride to get help. Can you hear me? Don't leave us."

"Do you hate me, God?" Antonio cries out, "first my parents, then my son, now my best friend? Well, my son is with us, but please, dear God, do not take this good man, yet. He has so much he wants to do. This man is like my brother. Please, protect his life!" pleads Antonio, sobbing.

"Sully, Sully, can you hear me, buddy?" anguishes Antonio. Antonio grabs Sully's canteen and gingerly tips the canteen just enough to allow some drops of water onto Sully's lips and into his mouth. Antonio gently lays Sully's head back down and goes to get the first aid kit. *Well, let me see, what does Francesca have in here?* Antonio thinks to himself. *Well, what have we here? She has packed a needle with stitching string already threaded.* Antonio lets out a short, loud laugh shaking his head in amazement. Antonio grabs the kit and returns to Sully. "Sully, I am going to stitch your head wound. I'm going to dab it first with this numbing solution." Antonio talks to Sully, hoping Sully can hear him. Antonio methodically tends to Sully's head wound, pulling out his knife to cut the thread; then Antonio sits holding his best friend when he realizes there is blood on Sully's coat as well. Antonio sees a rip and anxiously opens Sully's coat. "Oh no, look at that! It appears to be a bear wound," Antonio speaks out loud. He goes to get more dressings from the first aid kit to tend to the four-inch-long gashes. "I...I have to go get help. I don't think you'll make it down the mountain if I put you over Chief. I'm not leaving you, my friend. Please don't leave me." Antonio cries holding Sully in his arms, rocking him back and forth in his lap.

Sully struggles but manages to reach for Antonio's arm, squeezes it and whispers, "I won't leave. Go get help. I'll be right here."

Antonio casts his eyes down at his friend, wipes the snot from his nose with the sleeve of his shirt, and pulls Sully to him, hugging him, "I love you."

"I love you, too. Now, go get help. I have a grandbaby on the way," reminds Sully as he coughs and grapples with pain to speak.

Antonio kisses Sully's head, "God, keep this good man." He gently sets Sully's head down on a roll, then covers him with a blanket.

Antonio dashes to Chief and rides like he is in a race for life.

Sully lies there in and out of consciousness. He thinks he is hallucinating when he sees a silhouette of a petite woman with extremely long hair standing before him.

"Are you my guardian angel?" Sully asks.

"No, Sully. I am your great-aunt, Genie Arabella A'mato," the slight-framed woman introduces herself.

"I must be dreaming," murmurs Sully. "I'm glad I am having a good dream, with family," insists Sully as he smiles trying to stay awake, yet nodding off.

"My sweet, great nephew, I have watched you from afar. I am here to help," Genie Arabella claims.

Sully peacefully smiles and closes his eyes.

Genie Arabella lays her hands over Sully and appears to be praying and meditating. She begins moving her hands, hovering over his wounds repeatedly in a figure eight movement, just as she remembered seeing the high priests of the Chiawaukas do over her friend, Anna Grace. She relentlessly continues until tiny droplets of what appears like golden rain drip from her hands onto his wounds. She then lifts his head and offers him a cup of juice that she has prepared from the special berries she grows. "Take a sip of this, my dear," encourages Genie Arabella in her sweet, soft-spoken voice.

"What is it?" Sully, barely audible, asks as he slowly opens his eyes.

"Oh, it's a healing berry juice I make," Genie Arabella discloses.

"Thank you, my dear, great aunt. When will I see you again?" Sully manages to ask before he lays his head back and passes out.

Genie Arabella kisses his forehead, "You'll see me in your dreams, nephew."

·······ତ୬ତ·······

Antonio is riding Chief hard to reach his home.

Viana, Victor and Francesca have just finished a successful training session when Francesca can sense Antonio's anxiousness. She can hear Chief's hoofs pounding against the ground, riding hard.

"Do you hear that? It's Antonio and Chief!" Francesca exclaims.

Viana and Victor meet eyes in astonishment as Francesca can already hear the sounds of Chief galloping across the property, yet no rider or horse are visible.

Francesca dashes in a panic toward the stables. Antonio and Chief approach. Antonio jumps off of Chief and runs to Francesca. He places each of his hands on each of her arms, "It's Sully. I think a bear must have attacked him! We need to get Doctor Gerard up there! And I'll need the wagon! Oh, and, we need to get Katherine!"

Francesca directs, "Wait! Gino's in the shop- send him to get the doctor. I will get Katherine, and have her pack some clothes and keep her here. You get the wagon ready with the supplies you may need!"

"Good idea!" Antonio sprints over to the woodshop where Gino is working. "Son, I need you to go get Doctor Gerard, now! There's been an accident!"

"What? Who? Okay!" Gino turns things off and follows his pop out of his shop, and rushes to the stables.

While they hurriedly make their way across the property, Antonio conveys to Gino, "It's Sully! I think he was attacked by a bear, and must have hit his head against a rock when he fell."

Gino saddles and mounts his horse, then turns to look at his Pop, "Should I bring Father Lanzreth as well?"

"Wouldn't hurt. Yes! Good idea!" Antonio confirms.

Gino swiftly rides to town to gather Doctor Gerard and Father Lanzreth.

The three men ride hard back to the Mancinis where Antonio is awaiting their arrival.

"Where's Francesca?" asks Doctor Gerard.

Antonio motions. "She went to get Katherine. I think a bear attacked Sully. He was too weak, and I felt he had too much blood loss for me to safely transport him by horseback down the mountain!"

"Oh, no!" Doctor Gerard nudges the sides of his horse to gallop at a faster pace.

Father Lanzreth is riding with Antonio in the wagon.

Gino swiftly hurries to notify Luke and Ben.

Francesca rides Lady like her life depends on it, and reaches the Carlisle Ranch in record time. Francesca dismounts Lady and runs to the door and knocks.

Katherine casually comes to the door, "What an unexpected surprise!"

Francesca takes Katherine's hands in hers, "Honey, there's been an accident, I need you to get some clothes and come with me."

Katherine turns white as a ghost, "Oh, my! Is it Sully? Is he alive?"

"Yes! To my knowledge he is alive. Antonio tended to his wounds and rode back for the wagon to transport Sully home. He is taking Doctor Gerard with him." answers Francesca.

"Okay, okay, that's good. Let me grab some clothes," Katherine fumbles around.

"Here, let me help," insists Francesca.

The two women pack a few things for both Sully and Katherine, then return to the Mancini Ranch.

Katherine is pacing in the family room, viewing out the picture window.

"Honey, have some tea. It'll be another hour before they get back. Don't expend all your energy. Sit with me a minute and let's pray," suggests Francesca.

Katherine stops long enough for Francesca's words to resonate. "You're right. I should be praying, not pacing," Katherine states.

The two friends sit on a sofa, join hands and pray together for a bit.

"You know, Sully was disappointed that Ben, Luke nor Gino could join them this year on their annual elk hunt," shares Katherine.

"Yes, Antonio was as well. But he enjoys his time with Sully, and he wasn't about to postpone the hunt," discloses Francesca.

Katherine laughs, "Nor would Sully. Only a blizzard would keep him from his time with Antonio and the hunt!"

The two best friends laugh. Katherine dabs a tear, "Sully is so excited about becoming a grandparent and teaching that child things. I do pray he will be alright."

"All we can do is trust. Worrying is not going to do anything for us except make us sick," reminds Francesca.

"You're right," confirms Katherine. "That, of course, is easier said than done."

"Come with me into the kitchen. They are going to be hungry. We will be hungry. Let's prepare food. In fact, let's take your things into the guest room in case you and Sully stay here this evening," Francesca orders.

"You're right. I'll go get the bed turned down and put our clothes in there. Then I will help you bake," Katherine regroups.

The two women embark on their tasks. Katherine soon joins Francesca in the kitchen.

"I almost forgot how much fun it is to cook together!" exclaims Katherine.

"Open spirits, loving hearts, keep a family strong when apart," Francesca is being creative making up lyrics.

Katherine laughs, "I had a silly thought and was going to say a word that starts with an 'f' and ends with a 't' and fills the room with stink!" Katherine is laughing out loud at her silly thoughts. She is now laughing hard, "You know, having a house full of males, I'm sorry. I couldn't help myself." Katherine is now laughing and crying and the same time.

Francesca smiles, "It's quite alright. That is pretty funny what you thought, and has more humor."

Katherine dabs her eyes. "Oh, my, my brain is just being goofy right now."

"Completely understandable. No need to feel bad. It's normal, considering the stress you're experiencing," Francesca reassures as she rolls out pie dough.

"I do hope Sully will be okay. I don't know what I would do without him," confides Katherine as she stirs together a fruit mixture for the pie filling.

Francesca pauses and appears as though she is deep in thought, "Katherine, I believe all will be well."

Katherine remarks, "I hope you're right. I am going to trust your instinct," smiles Katherine.

The two move from making a pie, to preparing and baking bread, and then the main course.

......⎯⎯⎯......

The men reach Mancini Lake. Antonio drives the wagon as far as he can, then he and Father Lanzreth ride horseback. They accompany

Doctor Gerard up the trails to the area where he left Sully. Antonio's thoughts are racing but he diligently remains on task leading the way.

When Antonio sees Sully, he rushes to him. Father Lanzreth and Doctor Gerard follow. Antonio drops to his knees and tells Sully, "I am back. I brought Father, and the Doc."

"Sully...Sully, can you hear me?" asks Doctor Gerard.

As if struggling to wake up from a deep, deep sleep, Sully opens his eyes and sees his friends surrounding him. Sully smiles a relaxed smile. "You know, I knew you would be back for me, Tony," Sully smiles and closes his eyes.

Father Lanzreth begins the prayer of the Anointing of the Sick while Doctor Gerard takes off the bandages that Antonio had dressed Sully's wounds with.

After carefully inspecting his head wound and stitch work, the doctor turns to Antonio and says in astonishment, "You must have done some miraculous dressing, his wound is no longer bleeding, and almost looks as if it beginning to scab over. That's unheard of." The physician gently lays Sully's head back down and then inspects Sully's arm and chest area where the other dressings are. Doctor Gerard questions Antonio, "Did you put some ointment or something on these wounds? They appear clean, and seem to have already began healing."

Antonio focuses on the wounds the doctor is describing. "No, no ointment. I did clean the wounds, then dressed them, and prayed for him," recounts Antonio.

"Well, God certainly heard your prayers. I would say Sully is going to be back to 100 percent in no time. Absolutely miraculous!" accesses Doctor Gerard.

Father Lanzreth smiles and gratefully says, "Thanks be to God."

Sully opens his eyes and turns to his side to push off the ground to sit up.

"Here, let me help you," Antonio insists.

Sully rests on his Sitz Bones, "The elk I shot is over there. Did you get the meat?" points Sully.

"I don't know if it'll still be good, Sully. It's been several hours," Antonio informs.

"Nonsense. It'll be fine," assures Sully in a calm voice.

Antonio pats Sully's back, "Alright, I'll take care of it."

Sully voices, "Well, let's get back to camp. We'll load up the meat and go home."

The three friends are amazed at Sully's seemingly rapid recovery, and oblige his requests.

Antonio tends to the elk, while Father and Doctor Gerard assist Sully to the campsite where they wait for Antonio.

To Antonio's surprise, the meat is still in immaculate condition. Once prepared, Antonio returns to camp with the meat from Sully's elk.

Father Lanzreth addresses Antonio, "It is so peaceful up here. The sounds of nature are inspiring."

"You are certainly correct, Father," Antonio concurs.

"Sully is peacefully resting in the back of the wagon," Father Lanzreth informs.

"Good. I'll finish loading, and we will head out," directs Antonio.

Father Lanzreth and Doctor Gerard help Antonio with task completion. Father Lanzreth and Antonio climb into the wagon, with Sully comfortable in the flatbed.

Doc accompanies on his horse with the pack mules in tow. The men journey back to the Mancini Ranch.

After some time, Sully pulls himself up and says, "Well, I hope the entire town isn't there."

Antonio assures, "No, I'm sure it'll just be our families."

"I really don't even need that. I am just fine," declares Sullivan.

In his kind, soft-spoken, mild-mannered voice, Father Lanzreth responds, "Sully, the people waiting for you, love you. Part of processing this incident is for them to welcome you home and make sure, with their own eyes that you are safe. You are very blessed to be so loved."

"Katherine probably won't let me out of her sight," sighs Sully. "You are correct, though, Father. Thank you," adds Sully.

With a slight chuckle, Father replies, "Well, you're quite welcome, my brother."

Antonio laughs and says, "You are probably right, Sully. Katherine is not going to let you out of her sight for a long time."

Sully reclines back down, folds his arms across his chest and reminisces, "It is good to be loved."

As the men approach the Mancini stables, they see Katherine, Ben, Laurie, Luke, Camille, Gino, Claire and Francesca waiting. Gino, Luke, and Ben assist Sullivan out of the wagon, and into the Mancini Ranch home.

"I am going to check Sully one more time before I take off," Dr Gerard states to Antonio and Father.

"Absolutely," agrees Antonio.

The three men follow the family into the house.

"Father and Doc, we have enough dinner here for you to join us if you would like to stay," offers Francesca.

"No, not tonight, Francesca. Thank you, though," affirms the doctor.

"I thank you, too, Francesca, but I need to get back," Father states.

"Alright, thank you so much for being here, and helping," Francesca conveys.

Sully has made himself comfortable in a chair in the family room. Doctor Gerard checks Sully over before he leaves.

The rest of the family stand around.

"Well, Sully, God has certainly blessed you today. Your wounds seem to be healing incredibly fast. You're alive. Your blood pressure is good, your heart sounds good. I frankly have never seen anything like it. Antonio, you did good work with your triage," commends Doctor Gerard.

Antonio nods with appreciation and an expression with love and concern at his friend.

Sully motions his hand, "Alright, thank you. May I eat now? I have quite an appetite."

"Yes, absolutely. Just take it easy for a few days, Sully," recommends Doctor Gerard.

Sully nods.

Doctor Gerard and Father Lanzreth shake Sully and Antonio's hands and depart saying their goodbyes to everyone on their way out.

The rest of the family get in line and serve a feast in the kitchen. Katherine carries Sully a plate full of delicious food and a drink.

The family sit around quietly talking while they eat.

Ben, in his clear, deep voice suggests to his parents, "Maybe you two should move in with us for a while."

Katherine immediately begins shaking her head. Sully calmly nods his head and replies, "I know you mean well, Son, but neither your mother nor I need to live with anyone right now. This was just one of those things that happens sometimes. I do appreciate your concern, but we are nowhere near ready to live with anyone."

"Laurie and I are always nearby if you need us," conveys Ben in his inviting, baritone voice.

Sully peacefully smiles, "Thank you, Son."

Everyone enjoys conversation and hearing about Sully and Antonio's adventures at the lake.

Claire stands and conveys good wishes to Sully then lets everyone know, "I have to go."

"I'll walk you out," Gino stands to escort Claire the entire way.

Francesca stands and gives Claire a hug.

Gino gives Claire a hug outside and a kiss. "I should have been there with Pop and Sully."

"You couldn't have prevented what happened," Claire reassures.

"No, maybe not, but I'm not going to miss next year's hunt," claims Gino.

"It's a year away and after our wedding. I'm sure things will work out," Claire encourages as she turns and gets on her horse.

"You're right. Be safe. See you tomorrow," Gino genuinely expresses.

Claire rides away. Gino starts for the house, but remembers the meat. He goes and tends to it, placing it in all in their freezers. Ben and Laurie also say their goodbyes for the night. Luke and Camille follow suit, hugging Luke's dad and mom.

"See you all back at our ranch?" Luke questions.

"No, we are actually going to stay here tonight," Katherine tells her sons.

"I like that idea," Ben says.

Sully nods and motions 'bye' to them all.

Gino arrives just in time to accompany Luke, Ben, Laurie, and Camille out.

"I'm not going to miss the hunt next year!" exclaims Gino.

"Me neither," agrees Luke.

"I'm sure I will be able to get off work as well," Ben relays.

Laurie and Camille smile and say their goodbyes.

Gino returns to the house to say his goodnights, and then goes upstairs to his room.

Katherine plops on a chair in the family room. Antonio sits in his favorite chair, and Francesca lays across a sofa. The four friends just relax in the presence of each other.

"Well, I think it is a miracle you're alive, my dear," Katherine imparts to Sully.

After some silence, Sully lifts his head and conveys, "Honestly, I really think I saw my guardian angel today, and she came to take care of me."

"Oh, that's wonderful!" sweetly exclaims Katherine.

"What makes you say that? Will you share with us?" Francesca asks.

"I remember Antonio leaving, closing my eyes, and thinking I could possibly die. The next thing I know, I hear a voice and open my eyes to see a petite woman with extremely long hair standing before me. She told me she is my Great Aunt Genie Arabella," recalls Sully.

"Oh, my! That's exciting! So apparently your guardian angel is your great aunt!" accesses Katherine.

Antonio quickly glances to Francesca. Neither Mancini give a hint of the knowledge they have.

"That's fascinating, Sully. Did she say anything?" inquires Francesca.

"Honestly, I don't remember. But I did ask if I would see her again, and she said 'in my dreams'," recounts Sully. "It's all kind of a blur."

"Of course, it is. You apparently hit your head hard, and thanks to Antonio's medical skills, you are still with us," exclaims Katherine very concisely.

"I can't take any credit for Sully's recovery," Antonio humbly submits.

"Whatever happened, I am blessed to have a wonderful family and friends," shares Sully before shutting his eyes.

"Oh, don't you want to go to the bed?" Katherine asks.

Sully is sleeping peaceful, and does not respond to his wife's question.

Francesca stands and reaches for a blanket and drapes it over Sully. "He will be fine here. You go on to bed and get some rest," Francesca urges.

Antonio and Katherine both stand.

"Goodnight. Thank you for offering your food, and home to us…and your love," Katherine hugs Antonio and Francesca.

"Good night," Antonio expresses.

"Good night, sleep well," extends Francesca.

Francesca and Antonio collapse into their king size bed.

Francesca snuggles into her husband's arms. Antonio gently caresses her thick head of curls.

"Hmmm, I wonder what Genie Arabella did," ponders Francesca.

"I don't know. But I do know I didn't think the meat from the elk he shot would be any good, but Sully insisted I go get it," Antonio discloses.

"Well, was it any good?" asks Francesca.

"Yes, like it had just been shot and no time had elapsed," Antonio answers in a curious tone.

"Interesting," Francesca surmises.

Antonio hugs Francesca a little tighter and kisses her head, "I love you."

"I love you, too," Francesca nestles into his arms.

The two close their eyes and fall asleep.

Chapter 60

A TURN FOR THE WORSE

Claire enters Montanelli Mercantile to deliver fresh baked goods. "Hello," she chimes out. Claire only hears coughing. She abruptly sets down the basket of items she is carrying, and runs to where she hears the distressing sounds. She sees Leonardo in the back room bent over, choking and struggling for air. Claire leans in beside him, "How can I help?" Claire asks.

Leonardo motions to hang on. "I'm fine," he proclaims wheezing and gasping for air.

"Well, I haven't heard that kind of *fine* before. I'm going to go get the doctor!" states Claire.

"No, no. Just give me a minute," insists Leonardo.

"I'm going to get you a glass of water," Claire quickly makes her way to the sink and fills a glass.

She rushes back to Leonardo, "Here, take a sip," directs Claire.

Leonardo reaches for the glass and drinks half of it. "I appreciate the water. Thank you," Leonardo says.

"Well, you're welcome. Where is Sophia?" Claire asks.

"She had some errands to run. Look, I am fine, no reason to upset her," Leonardo states.

"I'm sure she hears you cough like that. How often does this happen?" Claire inquires.

"I appreciate the water and your interest, but really, I'm fine, I must have inhaled something and it just choked me up," justifies Leonardo.

"Well, if you're sure you're alright, I'll go. I set the baked goods on the counter," informs Claire.

"Yes, I'm am feeling much better. Thank you, again," Leonardo expresses.

"Alright. Tell Sophia hello for me, and I will see you two tomorrow," Claire departs.

"I will. Take care," Leonardo gestures.

"Thank you. Remember, we have a wedding in the fall and then hopefully grandbabies, so *YOU* take care!" Claire lovingly and directly reminds.

"I'll be fine. Thank you, again," reaffirms Leonardo.

Claire leaves the mercantile thinking to herself, *how can I not at least share with Gino, or Francesca? Did I tell Leonardo I wouldn't say anything? If I don't let Gino know, and something happens to Leonardo, the family may blame me for not telling them how serious his cough is. However, they must already realize how severe his ongoing condition is. Nothing they have said or done has moved Leonardo to change his ways. If I do tell, Leonardo may not trust me...what to do?* Claire feels perplexed on the course of action she should take, if any.

Sophia returns to their store about thirty minutes later and sees Leonardo stocking shelves.

"How have things been?" Sophia inquires.

"Perfect. We have had a busy day," informs Leonardo.

Sophia walks closer to her husband, "Is that dry blood on the left side of your mouth? Did you cut yourself?"

Leonardo pulls out a handkerchief and rubs the crusty corners of his lips. Flakes of dried blood drop onto his hanky.

"Hmmm, I don't know," answers Leonardo.

Sophia just shakes her head, "I've told you to lay off that pipe."

"You're being kind of judgy and presuming," states Leonardo.

"If I am incorrect, then I apologize for my assumptions," declares Sophia as she turns to begin work around their store.

Leonardo continues to stock shelves. He walks into the back room to get another cart full of merchandise when he begins coughing again. Sophia stops what she is doing and darts to his side. "I am going to go get Doctor Gerard right now! Just sit down, please!" instructs Sophia assisting Leonardo to one of the chairs in the stock room.

Leonardo sits down, still gasping for air. Sophia leaves and goes directly to Doctor Gerard's office.

Doctor Gerard and Sophia return to find Leonardo resting in a chair.

"How long have you been experiencing this?" Doctor Gerard inquires.

"Today," Leonardo answers.

"Today? You have had coughing spells before today," Sophia scoffs.

"The good doctor asked me how long I have been coughing like *this*. The answer is today," Leonardo calmly says in his endearing voice.

"Let me have a listen," winks Doctor Gerard.

After thoroughly listening to Leonardo's lungs, through his chest and back, then checking for a fever, Doctor Gerard pulls up a chair and sits across from Leonardo.

"Considering who I am dealing with, I mean this in a most respectful way, Leo. I know you have never missed a day of work in your entire life except for funerals or the birth of Francesca. I am prescribing that for every minute you cough, double the time, that is how long I want you to lie down for bed rest. I'm also giving you some cough syrup, to suppress your episodes," recommends Doctor Gerard.

"What about the pipe he smokes? Shouldn't you tell him to stop!" Sophia quickly jumps in.

"Pipe, schmipe," Leonardo shakes his head making up words.

"Sophia, I understand your concern. Leo, cutting back or quitting the pipe entirely *IS* in your best interest, which I strongly suggest you do. Give your lungs some fresh air and time to heal. You have a lot of upcoming events we all want you around for," Doctor Gerard continues, "and I'd like you to take it easy the rest of today."

Leonardo shakes Doctor Gerard's hand, "Thank you, for coming. I'll consider what you said."

Doctor Gerard smiles, "Just remember to rest, Leo. Take care of the only body God gave you. Sophia, I will have the bottle of the cough syrup ready at my office if you will come by and pick it up."

"Absolutely, I will be there shortly," confirms Sophia.

Doctor Gerard leaves the Montanelli Mercantile.

Sophia stands and stares at her husband.

"What?" questions Leonardo in his calm, pleasant voice.

Sophia slightly shakes her head, a bit irritated from concern, "What? You know what. Okay. Well, I am going to purchase the medicine Doc wants you to take."

"Thank you," smiles Leonardo.

Sophia leaves the store that she and Leonardo built.

Chapter 61

APRILLA BIRTHDAY DINNER

"**H**appy Birthday to you, happy birthday to you, happy birthday Dear Antonio, happy birthday to you," leads Francesca. The guests join in as she carries out Antonio's birthday cake.

"Here's to you Antonio, a good friend, a great father, a loving husband, and a good man. Happy Birthday, my friend," Sully toasts while standing at the end of the Mancini dining room table.

"Happy Birthday," the rest cheer in unison as they gather around the table, both sitting and standing.

"Thank you, everyone. We have certainly had our excitement this year with engagements, Sully's encounter with the bear, Leonardo's health scare, Ben and Laurie's baby being due next month, and the approaching weddings," recalls Antonio making eye contact with each guest. "May God be with us."

Sheriff Ryan Patrick and his wife Darlene, the Richards family (Claire's family), the Gerards, the king and queen, the Carlisles, the Thomas's (Camille's family), Father Romano and Father Lanzreth, and of course, Sophia and Leonardo are all in attendance to celebrate Antonio's forty-second birthday.

Nanny Carol has remained back at the castle with Rupert, the palace staff, and guards.

The Mancini dining room and family room are filled with conversation and laughter.

Sully sits in the family room, in one of his favorite chairs, recapping his encounter with the bears, "...I aimed, took my second shot, got my target. I then stood and there it was, a cub, not a year old, then out of nowhere appeared a protective mother..."

Those listening were awestruck with his story.

"I honestly do not recollect much after that. But I am thankful my life was spared," Sully attests.

"Yes, that was quite an experience!" Doctor George Gerard nods.

"My brother, we are all thankful your life was spared," Father Lanzreth articulates in his mild, gentle manner.

"I believe I would like to join you next year when you hunt. I'm usually too busy taking care of things throughout the kingdom that I seldom have time for any outings with Darlene or for myself," implies Sheriff Patrick.

"You are more than welcome to join us," Antonio confirms.

Queen Eloise, Katherine, Darlene Patrick, Laverne Gerard, Emma Richards, Caroline Thomas, Camille, Sophia, Claire and Francesca gather in the dining area while the men fill the family room.

Claire's younger brother Chandler is with the men, and her younger sister Charlotte is enjoying time with the women of the kingdom.

"Francesca, this cake is simply scrumptious!" announces Katherine.

"Mm, yes," Darlene compliments, "I would like to serve this when Ryan has his birthday."

Francesca smiles, "Claire helped me create the cake this year."

"I think my daughter has a gift with making cakes and meals," Emma proudly states.

"I agree," Francesca concurs, giving Claire a wink.

"So, Emma, tell me. Do you and Andre enjoy living in Chamberlain Kingdom?" inquires Queen Eloise. "I'm always curious, and like to ask the people of our kingdom. It's very important to Theo and I, that everyone thrives and feels safe."

In her crisp, North-Eastern region accent Emma answers, "Oh, Andre and I love this kingdom. It has just been wonderful working here and meeting everyone. We are, however, considering a move just over to Martinelli Kingdom."

Claire almost chokes on the water she was swallowing, then stands in fury, "You what? You and Dad are moving and taking my brother and sister away from me? When were you going to tell me this? How could you!"

"Claire, your dad and I just haven't had time to visit with you...well, with planning your wedding and everything," Emma avers.

"Don't blame this on my wedding plans! I live at home! There have been opportunities! And then you reveal this huge news here, before telling me first? How could you?!" Claire stands and storms off in a rage.

The remaining women sit silent, each completely understanding the feelings Emma and Claire are experiencing. Charlotte studies the females and slides off her chair to follow her older sister out the door.

"Claire, wait. Wait for me," Charlotte shouts while running after her sister down the back deck stairs.

Claire stops and waits for Charlotte. The two briskly trek through the picturesque landscape in the backyard.

Charlotte has to walk fast to keep up with her older sister, "You'll still have me in your wedding, won't you?" innocently asks the thirteen-year-old Charlotte.

In her sharp, Northern accent, Claire snaps, "Of course, Charlotte!" Claire sighs, "I'm sorry. I don't mean to snap. I'm just furious our parents didn't tell me they were planning on relocating...again! And before my wedding!"

Charlotte reaches for her older sister's hand and slows the pace of their walk, "I'm sorry, Claire. I thought we were going to live here forever."

Holding hands, the sisters continue to venture around at a leisurely stride, and end up on the trail that leads to the river.

"This is the most beautiful kingdom we have ever lived in!" exclaims Charlotte in her young, sweet voice.

Claire, still stewing, "It is! So why would they want to pack up and leave me here?"

Claire and Charlotte reach the river's edge.

Charlotte lets go of Claire's hand. "This is perfect! You'll be living on this property with Gino! Can I come and visit?" questions Charlotte.

"Yes. Of course! Anytime you want!" Claire states, and begins to relax.

"You're right. Gino has *NO* plans to move from here. I will finally have a secure life with a man who loves me and that I love. We will raise our children here," formulates Claire.

"I will be Aunt Charlotte and can come and visit," Charlotte smiles with satisfaction.

Claire stops. Staring out over the river and concentrates on her younger sister then smiles, "Yes. You will be Aunt Charlotte and can visit anytime you like," Claire gives Charlotte a big hug.

"Maybe we should go back to enjoy the party?" Charlotte suggests with her thirteen-year-old wisdom.

"Yes, maybe we should, but I am still not happy with Mother! Or Dad for that matter!" declares Claire.

"That's okay. The party is to celebrate Mr. Mancini," reminds Charlotte.

Claire rubs the top of Charlotte's head and laughs, "When did you get so insightful?"

"It just comes naturally," grins Charlotte peering up at her older sister.

......⚭......

"Does anyone need a refill on anything?" Francesca inquires, trying to break the tension in the room, and the embarrassment Emma may feel.

"I'm good for now. Thank you, though," Emma states. "I apologize for my daughter's outburst."

"Well, Emma, honey, that was such big news to spring on her in front of us all," Queen Eloise bravely says.

"Yes, sometimes it is better to deal with things in private, depending on the subject and the person," Caroline adds.

"You ladies are correct. I handled the situation wrong," Emma acknowledges. "I apologize."

"Apology accepted. We all have said or done things at inappropriate times," Katherine recognizes.

"Well, thank you for that, Katherine. I don't know. When it concerns Claire, it seems I always put my foot in my mouth, and the two of us butt heads," Emma conveys.

Caroline assures, "I raised Camille's older sister, Angela, as my own. Her mother died during Angela's birth. A few years later I met Brian, and we married. We added Camille and Kenneth. It hasn't always been easy, but I always wanted Angela to know I love her as if she is my blood. Overall, I feel we have raised them all with love and respect for each other, as one family."

"Oh, my, I didn't realize that. Thank you for sharing," Emma relaxes some.

"Well, how could you know? You haven't lived here long enough to get to know everyone. But I want to let you in on a secret. Butting of heads is not uncommon. We all experience something difficult with each child," discloses Caroline.

"I appreciate your openness," Emma expresses.

"Just hang in there, and your relationship will smooth out," adds Darlene.

Katherine smiles, "I just love it when we are all together, even when things get a bit heavy."

Francesca laughs. The other females laugh as well.

311

Chapter 62

IT'S OFF!

Gino joins Claire outside. Claire spouts, "Did you hear my mother say they may move to Martinelli Kingdom?"

"No, babe. I did not hear that, nor did your dad mention it," reveals Gino with a concerned, loving voice.

"Yes, she announced it in front of everyone!" Claire lashes out swinging her arms about. "I am so furious at my parents. Taking my brother and sister away from me. Abandoning me! And doing this before my wedding! It's supposed to be a happy time in my life, planning my wedding! And now, I have the weight of this! My mother! Why didn't she and dad just tell me what they are considering! Why are they thinking of moving again? I don't know, Gino. Maybe, with your grandfather's breathing trouble, Sully's bear accident, and now this, maybe, it's all signs we shouldn't get married! Maybe we should call it off!" Claire miffs.

"Hold on there, my firecracker. First of all, yeah, your mother definitely doesn't always have the best delivery method for information. But you *know* this about her, so you shouldn't be surprised. Second, it is *OUR* wedding. As for my grandfather and Sully, life happens. There will *always* be things that happen," Gino assures. He puts his hands on Claire's arms and gazes directly into her captivating green eyes, "Don't let illnesses or events keep you from living life. Don't let anything keep you from saying 'yes' to good things, Claire. You are strong. Don't let the unexpected things in life rob you of your dreams and goals. I am your family. My family is your family. If your family relocates, we can visit them, or they can visit. You're a woman, and will be my wife. We will create our own family. And I promise you, I have no intention of moving. This is our home." Gino lovingly says outstretching his arms. Then he tenderly takes her hand and places it on his heart while he places his hand on her heart, "This is our home, where we each are," he affirmingly comforts.

Claire looks at Gino and rests her head, leaning into Gino's chest. After a long embrace in silence, Claire whispers, "You're right. I do look forward to being Mrs. Gino Mancini."

Chapter 63

THE BAPTISM

JULIAH 18ᵀᴴ

Everyone in the Kingdom is at church. Ben and Laurie are sitting in the front with their healthy, beautiful bundle of joy Matthew Kent. They are surrounded by their family and friends.

Father Lanzreth and Father Romano celebrate Mass and baptize Matthew Kent Carlisle.

After Mass, many join in the reception in the festival hall.

Laurie and Ben are enjoying the family and friends who come forward to meet their new, little darling.

King Theodore and Queen Eloise approach with a rambunctious Prince Rupert.

Francesca glances to see the royals next in line to meet the newest, little one in the kingdom. Francesca manages to work her way closer through the crowd of people.

"What a beautiful little boy he is!" exclaims the queen.

"He is certainly a handsome fellow," nods the king, "Congratulations!"

"I want to see! Let me see!" Rupert is trying to break his hand free from his father's hand to reach for the baby.

Francesca appears out of nowhere and simply requests, "Ben and Laurie, may I hold Matthew?"

"Well, certainly," Laurie smiles and gently releases Matthew into Francesca's protective arms.

Francesca sits down, smiles, and looks at Rupert, staring into his dark eyes. "You may see the baby now if you'd like."

A black, filmy cloud formation instantly leaves Rupert's body like clockwork when in the presence of Francesca. Rupert becomes calm and congenial. He curiously steps closer and gazes upon the two-month-old baby.

"Was I this small?" Rupert glances up to his parents.

The queen squats to Rupert's eye level and softly, lovingly shares, "Oh, yes, sweetie. And everyone came to meet you as well, just like we are doing today for Matthew."

Rupert timidly reaches to touch Matthew. Matthew coos. Rupert pats Matthew, then reaches for his father's hand.

"Thank you, Francesca," relays the king.

Francesca nods and smiles, "You all have a good day."

Francesca stands and gently passes Matthew back to Laurie. "He's quite a cutie," expresses Francesca. She gives Laurie and Ben a quick hug, then mingles before leaving with Antonio.

......⚬𝓵⚬......

Antonio and Francesca are in their carriage riding home.

"What was all that about?" inquires Antonio.

"What was what about?" Francesca asks.

"You know. You swooped in like a hawk and cradled Matthew before the king and queen had a chance," recaps Antonio.

"Oh, that. It stands to reason, if the Cryptolore is living in Prince Rupert and possesses him, who's to say the warlord won't try to enter into Matthew? I don't know. It's just a fear I felt creeping over me, and I had to take some immediate course of action," discloses Francesca.

"I understand, but I also don't want you to burden yourself with the sole responsibility of protecting everyone. That is just too big of a feat. I know you are magical and want the best for everyone, but being filled with worry and anxiety over things we cannot control will consume you," Antonio speaks his heart, "and, I can't be having my beautiful wife preoccupied with worry when she has so much life and energy to offer," Antonio flirtingly leans into Francesca, brushing arms.

Francesca relaxes her head upon Antonio's shoulder the remainder of the journey home.

Chapter 64

THE DOUBLE WEDDING
SEPTEMBRIA 26TH

"Gino, Gino." Gino hears his name being called. He swiftly moves to the family room fireplace mantel.

"I'm here," Gino states.

"Hey, Brother, I wanted to wish you all the best on your wedding today!" Marco delivers.

"Man, it is so good to hear your voice. You know I wish you were here, as my best man!" expresses Gino.

"I am your best man, always!" Marco laughs. "I will be watching along with Celestial and Blazer. Paul, and the high priests are all going to be watching your wedding today," informs Marco.

"Wow! That's terrific! Speaking of, I hate to cut it short, but…" Gino relays.

"I know, I know, you have a lot to do. Hey, by the way, I saw the home you have been building for Claire and you. Great skills you have! I wish I could be there helping you," extends Marco.

"Thanks. Pop and I have been working on it as time permits, since last year. We will be able to live in it now, but I will continue to finish up a few things after moving in," shares Gino.

"That's terrific! Okay, I'll talk to you later! Remember, I will be there watching!" Marco communicates.

"That's great! Talk later," Gino concludes.

Marco drops his head in disappointment and turns from the communications screen. Blazer and Celestial are standing there.

"We can't remove the hurt and pain you experience from not being able to be with your family. You just have to remain focused on the future, Marco." Celestial gently says in her raspy voice, touching Marco's arm as she hovers in the air.

"I know. Sometimes, it's like experiencing a death and being gripped with tremendous grief, but I know it was just a shift in my life plan and I need to be thankful and embrace it. I do struggle at times, but I am trying," reveals Marco.

"We recognize that, Marco. That's all you can do," Blazer adds.

......ⱷ৹......

Francesca comes out of the bedroom with her elegant, long, burgundy lace dress folded in her arms. "I will change at the palace. I am so looking forward to this!" Francesca smiles at her son.

"Thanks, Mom," Gino says.

"You seem a bit gloomy for your wedding day, what gives?" pries Francesca.

"Nothing. I briefly spoke with Marco a few minutes ago. I just wish he was here," shares Gino.

"That's wonderful you were able to speak with Marco. Remember, if he were not alive, you would not have spoken to him at all. It is tough for each of us," proclaims Francesca.

"You're right," Gino nods, pauses, and refocuses, "Well, we have a wedding!"

"We do indeed!" Antonio chimes in his deep, rugged voice, sporting his dashing suit which conceals his muscular body.

"Ah, look at you!" Francesca melts.

Gino smiles big, "Wow, Pop! I haven't seen you dressed up this sharp in a long time!"

Antonio stands tall, "I guess, I'd better go take it off until later."

"Yeah, that's a good idea. The rest of us will be dressing at the castle," voices Francesca.

"I just wanted to show you two. And you," gazing now at his wife, Antonio asserts, "I'll be dancing with you."

"You know how to make my heart pitter-pat," laughs Francesca.

Gino lovingly grins at the frolicking interactions of his parents.

······᪥᪥······

The trees are displaying brilliant, fall foliage. The weather is simply perfect. The sun is shining. The temperature is pleasant. The staff at the castle have been working the past few days setting up and preparing everything for today's festivities.

The flowers are exquisite, autumn colors that adorn the arch and outside wedding alter. The band is rehearsing. The entire kingdom, along with families from neighboring kingdoms are arriving to witness the union of these two couples. The king and queen of Martinelli are attending as well.

Camille is dressed now in her delicate gown, a soft pink satin is revealed underneath white lace, with a medium length train. The dress features a sweetheart neckline with gathered, short, puffy sleeves of white lace. The front of her dress is adorned with a small, soft pink satin bow. Her shoes are white lace and she is crowned with a wreath of white, and soft pink petals woven into her reddish-brunette hair.

Claire's dress has a one-inch row of floral lace that wraps over her shoulders and drops to the mid-part of her back. In the front the neckline forms a heart shape, with lace for the bodice that extends to the train with a soft beige satin fabric beneath the white lace. The train is a medium length and displays a beautiful, floral artistry design.

Both grooms are in navy jackets, denim jeans, with dark pink and white gingham shirts. The groomsmen all sport the same dark pink and white gingham long-sleeved shirts with a navy-blue vest and denim jeans. All the males in the wedding party are wearing boots. The maids of honors both wear a beautiful rich, plum-colored satin and lace, short-sleeved dress. The bridesmaids' dresses are a burnt orange satin fabric with burnt-orange lace for the sleeves and bodices.

The families hear the musicians playing traditional wedding selections.

Katherine declares, "It is time!" She knocks at the door of the room where her son, Luke, and all the young men are.

Luke opens the door.

"It's time, Son," Katherine is glowing with pride seeing her handsome youngest son.

The groomsmen make their way onto the castle grounds and move into their assigned places.

Francesca, Antonio, Sully, Katherine, Emma, Andre, and Camille's parents, Caroline and Brian, proudly cast their eyes upon their children. Andre and Brian step away and retreat to the back awaiting their daughters.

"I am so excited!" exclaims Camille.

"Me too!" proclaims Claire.

"This is like a fairy-tale wedding!" maintains Camille.

"Yes. It's our story, Camille. Let's make it a good one!" Claire smiles glancing at Camille.

"Yes! Promise me we will always stay close! Like Gino and Luke's parents," Camille requests.

"I promise," Claire adamantly vows.

The young women take their places at the arms of their fathers. The ceremony begins. Father John Lanzreth and Father Steve Romano celebrate the ceremonial Mass.

"I now introduce to you, Mr. and Mrs. Gino Mancini, and Mr. and Mrs. Luke Carlisle," Father Lanzreth and Father Romano each announce a couple.

Music plays while the couples walk down the aisle, followed by family, then guests.

At the reception area the two couples each hold a glass of champagne, while Sullivan leads a toast, "To my son, Luke, and his bride Camille, and Gino, who is like my son, and his bride, Claire. May God watch over you all and lead you in your lives. Amen."

The guests raise their glasses and toast the couples. The reception music begins.

The first dance is for newlywed couples, then, after Luke, Camille, Gino and Claire dance with their parents the king announces, "The dance floor is now open to you all. Enjoy the evening."

Antonio winks at Francesca and in his very inviting voice delivers, "You know what that means?" and extends his hand to her.

"A dance?" Francesca giggles.

"Yes, ma'am," Antonio pursues.

He tenderly pulls the love of his life close to him, and embraces her as they dance across the floor.

......⌒ℛ⌒......

Gino takes his arms from around Claire and reaches to hold her hands, "I'm going to go see my grandparents. Look at them on the dance floor. Would you like to come with me?"

"Yes, I'd like that," answers Claire. Holding hands, the newlyweds walk over to where Sophia and Leonardo are enjoying a slow dance.

Gino steps in close and wraps his arms around them both. He leans his head in and places it on his grandmother's head for a moment, and then switches to lean his head gently onto his grandfather's head while keeping the slow dance in motion. "I love you guys! I am so thankful you are both still alive to celebrate this day with me! Family...what life is all about!" Gino squeezes them both.

"Aw, sweet, Gino, we wouldn't miss it for the world!" smiles Sophia.

Leonardo stops the dancing moves and takes Ginos' hand into both of his, smiles and says, "I am glad I am alive to be here with you." Then Leo places one hand to Gino's cheek and pats it.

......⚬⧈⚬......

"Oh, I so love watching humans dance!" exclaims Pixel.

"I do too, Pixel!" chimes Razel.

"I have to say…" Viana begins to speak and is interrupted by her fellow Chiawaukas as if choreographed.

"You are so thankful you are assigned to the Mancinis," the comrades giggle teasing Viana.

"You guys," Viana laughs in her crisp, somewhat low voice. "Well, okay, you got me. I was going to say that," Viana laughs as well. "I do enjoy watching them dance, too."

......⚬⧈⚬......

The king and queen finish their dance and return to their seats. "Rupert, will you dance with me?" asks his mother in an engaging manner.

Rupert seems a bit distant; his eyes are darkening.

"Rupert, your mother would like you to dance with her," King Theodore lovingly says as he places his hand on his son's shoulder.

The prince glares at his father with ominous, dark eyes. Rupert places his hand on top of his fathers. The king soon begins to appear grey, and peaked. He drops his hand from Rupert's shoulder. Francesca hears the king coughing and excuses herself from Antonio, darting to aid the king.

Francesca glares at Rupert. A dark, filmy cloud quickly exits Rupert's body. Francesca firmly places her hands on the king's shoulders and whispers, "You will be fine, drink some water." Francesca gently rubs the king's shoulders.

The king reaches for a glass of water and drinks. His color returns and he slowly regains his strength.

"I don't know what just happened, but thank you, Francesca," conveys King Theodore.

The queen appears puzzled and unnerved.

"Everything will be fine. This is such a beautiful wedding you two are hosting. Thank you so much for creating an incredible environment. The moon will be coming out soon. Just a glorious day!" Francesca declares with hopes it will take their mind off of what just happened.

Francesca stands tall studying Rupert, "Go have a fun dance with your mother. You just turned six. I bet you're a mighty fine dancer."

Rupert jumps up with energy and extends his little hand to his mother. The queen smiles from ear to ear. The two dance across the floor laughing, and doing twirls. The queen winks at Francesca with satisfaction and a happy heart.

Antonio discreetly leans toward Francesca like he is kissing her cheek and whispers in her ear, "What was that all about?"

"I think Rupert just discovered another weapon," Francesca divulges.

"Oh, that's not good," replies Antonio. "Should we be concerned?"

"Very," Francesca whispers in return.

……⚬⚭⚬……

Gino and Claire walk out away from the dance floor toward the river. Gino unfolds the blanket he is carrying, and the two sit on it.

"Look at that, Claire!" points Gino.

"Oh, Gino! Our full moon!" declares Claire.

Gino takes Claire into his arms and kisses her. "Well, Mrs. Mancini, I will love you forever."

Claire laughs and retorts, "For a minute I was concerned we were going to have a repeat of what happened at Ben and Laurie's wedding when you drank too much and passed out!"

Gino laughs, "No, not tonight, babe! I'm all yours," then he drops to her lap.

Claire scoffs, "Oh, no!" and shakes Gino vigorously.

"Hey, you don't have to be so rough, I was only pretending," laughs Gino.

Claire gently smacks Gino's arm, "Well, I didn't think it was funny," she sternly says.

Gino laughs. The two exchange a passionate kiss and gaze back upon the mesmerizing Autumn Moon, snuggled in each other's arms.

·······ণ৫ৄ৹·······

Antonio and Francesca stand next to each other waiting for the next dance to begin. Katherine and Sully join them.

"Such a wonderful wedding!" exclaims Katherine.

"Yes, it is," smiles Francesca.

The four are enjoying the sounds of the music and watching their guests dance.

While Francesca and Katherine are deep in conversation and awe of so many beautiful dress designs, Sully motions Antonio to step aside with him.

In a quiet voice Sully conveys, "Hey, I've been meaning to mention something to you."

"What's that, my friend?" inquires Antonio.

"I've been meaning to mention this on several occasions throughout the past year, but always got distracted. When I was lying there, injured, I could have sworn I heard you say Marco isn't really dead while you were praying," Sully discloses.

Just then, Katherine grabs Sully's hand, "This is our song, dance with me."

Sully glances back at Antonio, "We'll talk later."

Antonio nods.

Antonio reaches for Francesca's hand leading her onto the dance floor and twirls her into his arms. He whispers, "We may have another conundrum."

......⚬⚬......

The Chiawaukas are enjoying the celebration and are sitting on a high ledge.

"You know, thinking of my time here on Soleil, I have to say, when I saw Francesca's collection of rocks, my heart instantly felt fondness for her," Zeek smiles and nods, "And for the best laugh...well, you guys should have seen it! I don't think we've shared this story. Razel was determined to interfere with the nature of things, and not let the Cryptolore-inhabited wolves feast on a nearby doe. She swooped down landing close to a buck, and used her powers to make the buck roar like a lion. It was quite the performance!" recalls Zeek.

Razel giggles and smiles, "Yeah, I have to say I liked it when Zeek stretched himself to over six-feet tall. Plus, being assigned to this particular mission with all of you has made every moment count." Razel makes eye contact with each teammate.

"You guys did what?" Victor displays disbelief at the playfulness and nonsense of his fellow Chiawaukas.

Viana shakes her head a bit, peering at Victor. Then she glances at all of her Chiawauka friends and describes, "Well, I have said many times I am so thankful Victor and I are assigned to the Mancinis. Francesca is remarkable and the steadfast love the family share, well, it's empowering."

Piper confesses, "It's been a real challenge at the palace making sure no one is in harm's way from Rupert. We are protecting, yet making it appear like it's natural or a coincidence. I still remember when Pixel, turned red with white dots, outside the castle the day Nanny Mary was killed by the Cryptolores. Pixel was furious and full of emotion, yet through these few years she hasn't ceased to amaze me with her candor and insight."

Victor speaks next. "Well, I have to admit, Viana knows this, but I actually felt this assignment was boring and not worth my service. I was almost going to question the high priests. However, I have been reminded many times and by many things, this assignment is far from humdrum. I am looking forward to seeing how our mission unfolds, and discovering who the other Chords of Chiawaukas family is, and what sinister plots the evil Cryptolores have in mind for Soleil," Victor reveals.

The Chiawaukas sit quietly meditating on all the stories and testimonies they just heard while listening to the dynamic music. They enjoy seeing people dance. The Chiawaukas cherish the spectacular surroundings, the breathtaking Autumn Moon that lights the night sky, and breathing in the aroma of the food and the scent of the mountain air.

The peaceful vibes they are all enjoying come to an abrupt halt when Pixel's voice breaks the glorious silence, "Guys," Pixel states practically and sensibly, with her arms outstretched and palms up.

"What, Pixel?" interrogates Victor.

"What's up, Pixel?" questions Piper.

"We're forgetting one very crucial detail," Pixel matter-of-factly says.

"What's that, honey?" inquires Viana.

Pixel has the full attention of all the Chiawaukas.

"Didn't you all say that Alchodor sucked the lifeforce from Marco?" Pixel continues.

The Chiawaukas peer at each other and each nod in agreement.

"Well, with that being said, I think it stands to reason that in doing so, Alchodor acquired the powers the Chords of Chiawaukas family members were given," Pixel deduces.

Victor and Viana sharply turn their heads to glance at each other and exchange a look of alarm.

Zeek and Razel also make eye contact with an expression of grave concern.

Piper has his hands on his knees, and shakes his head as he views out over the top of his reading glasses across the castle grounds and murmurs, "Oh boy!"

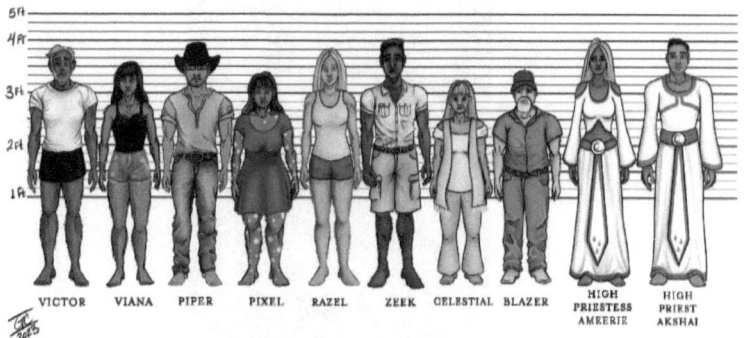

About the Author

Alexandria Chiaro spent her childhood and adolescent summers traveling through beautiful mountain states with her parents. During this time, she began writing poems, songs, and lyrics, which later transitioned into writing short stories.

Many years later, an idea for a title came to her while attending church with her mother. However, it wasn't until an additional three years later that someone asked about the characters in her story, unlocking the treasure chest that is in this trilogy. The particulars of the cast of characters came quickly thereafter, and some in somewhat prophetic places. The dark of a winter night brought evil beings, and the supreme guardian beings came to her in her dining room, where she gathers and strengthens her own family. The story itself takes many twists and turns, foreshadowing events which unfold as the reader progresses through the trilogy journey.

Sharing her story with you has brought Alexandria great joy.

Alexandria fills her time with church, family, friends, fur babies, work, writing, and projects. She greatly enjoys the outdoors and mountains, just as she did those summers long ago.

Enjoy!